WAY
BEYOND
A LIE

HARRY FISHER

For Chris

with my best wishes

Harry Fisher

🐦 @iamselfpub
www.iamselfpublishing.com

For Shiona.
My wonderful, fabulous wife.
With you, all things are possible.

WINTER

1

A Friday evening in February

The mobile phone trilled just once before the deeply tanned man plucked it off the desk. He had craggy features, recently softened by the addition of a beard. His fingertips brushed against the bristles as he held the phone to his ear, a sensation he was still getting used to. He realised his face now felt much like his grandfather's face had felt to him as a small boy. *God rest his soul.*

He'd been expecting the call so he skipped any pleasantries and asked the simple question: 'It is done?' The form of words suggested English was not his native tongue.

'Yes.'

He marvelled at the clear reception, given the distance between them. 'Everything is tidy?'

'Yes, tidy.'

'There is nothing I should be concerned about?'

'Nothing.' Then, the caveat. 'Just that one small matter. It needs to wait till morning.'

The man nodded. 'Good. I expected nothing different. Now, return to the safe house until it is time for you to resume your normal activities.'

'Understood. I will hear from you again soon?'

'Just as soon,' he said deliberately, 'as we have something else for you.'

He hit the red button on the phone with his left thumb and at the same time jiggled his mouse with his other hand, disturbing his PC from its slumber. He opened a file, made two changes to the data, saved it and emailed it to one of his contacts. He had fewer than a dozen names on his address list, and all were aliases. The email required no text as the recipient knew to expect it. Furthermore, she knew exactly what to do with it.

One by one, he closed down all the open applications on his PC and strolled over to the window. Two floors below, a

1

red and cream tram of eighties' vintage clanked and sparked as it crossed a complicated junction. He watched as it bent round a corner two blocks down and disappeared in the direction of Letňany.

Once the sound of the PC's fan had died away he reached down to the wall by the side of his chair, clicked the socket switch to off, and pulled out the power cord.

He took one final look over his desk, completely unnecessary as it was clear of all paperwork. He slotted his chair neatly underneath, flipped his jacket off its hook and walked out the door.

Twenty minutes later, the lights in the room switched off automatically.

2

The girl looked up at him through the grey steel mesh that formed the cage. It was about two feet square by six high.

She was three weeks shy of her nineteenth birthday, with the build of a high-jumper and a mop of curly red hair she'd given up trying to control. She knelt on the hard tiles, her feet tucked underneath her, flat against the floor. It was not a comfortable position. The bottle in her right hand contained a pale amber liquid.

She judged he was probably in his fifties, about five eleven and carrying a few extra kilos. He had short hair going grey, and was dressed in an odd mix of colour and style: polished black shoes, bottle green chinos and a dark brown overcoat. His glasses had slipped down his nose and he poked them back into place.

Everything about the man's demeanour as he approached the cage indicated he required something from her. Perhaps she would have to perform a task for him. Or maybe he wanted some information.

Automatically, before he reached her, she stood up. It would have been disrespectful to remain on the floor while he spoke to her.

He was familiar. He'd been in a few times before but this would be the first time they'd ever spoken. She was used to the idea that she was more or less invisible unless her services were required.

As she rose, she placed the bottle of olive oil temporarily on a shelf. She stepped round the almost empty cage and wheeled it closer to the racking.

'Can I help you?' she asked him.

Ross McKinlay flapped a hand in the general direction of the next aisle. 'My wife sent me over here to pick up some cashew nuts but I can't find them.'

The young store assistant had a scattering of freckles across the bridge of her nose, and a naturally cheerful expression. Which meant he could easily see the stud that pierced her gum just above her two front teeth.

Ross's eyes widened. *Ouch! That must have hurt.*

'Cashew nuts?' Her brow furrowed for a second, then her face split into one of those ear-to-ear grins that brighten up the place. She zipped up and down the aisle, searching the shelves. 'I thought they were here but hang on a minute and I'll ask someone. Back in a mo.'

Ross loitered in the aisle, moving from one side to the other to allow shoppers to pass or pick an item from the shelves. He was studying the cavernous ceiling with all its giant Meccano architecture, wiring conduits and the regularly spaced pods he knew to be security cameras, when the girl reappeared. She had a triumphant air about her.

'I've found them. Come with me, please, I'll show you.' And there they were, stacked with all the other nuts at the end of the aisle.

Ross smiled. 'What a dummy. I really should have figured that out by myself.'

'No bother,' she chirped. 'Happy to help.'

She was turning back to her shelf stacking when Ross spoke again. 'I should have asked, where do you keep fruit juice, smoothies, stuff like that? My wife said I was to meet her there.'

The girl laughed but this time she knew the answer. 'Top of aisle eighteen, on the left, just past the cheeses.'

At the rendezvous point, a few minutes later, the same girl breezed by with another bemused shopper, plus grumpy child in tow. 'No luck?'

Ross signalled his impatience with an exaggerated shrug. 'I think she's got lost somewhere. Probably blethering to someone.'

He stepped back to allow an elderly couple to squeeze through the gap. The woman was chattering away but her husband didn't look like he was paying the slightest attention. The man leaned towards Ross as he passed. 'Wish mine was lost too, pal.'

After a few minutes of fruitless standing around, Ross moved to an intersection where he could see in four directions.

He stood there for a while too, then gave up. On the move again, he rolled his trolley along the centre aisle, glancing left and right. He crossed paths with the elderly couple once more. She was still rabbiting away and he still wore his long-suffering expression like a hard earned campaign medal.

Ross about-turned, looking more deliberately this time. He checked every aisle, every side section. Up, down, back and forth. Nothing. Now he was becoming flustered, showing little consideration to his fellow-shoppers, some of whom muttered or glared at him for what they perceived to be his rude behaviour.

Back at the same intersection he stopped right in the centre. Had he been driving a car there would have been squealing tyres and honking horns. A young mother clipped the front of her trolley into the heels of a be-suited businessman, who thought about giving her an earful until he saw she was at least a nine.

Apparently oblivious to the commotion he had caused, Ross ferreted about for his phone, which his wife had pushed him into buying. 'Ross. Everybody has a smartphone now.' But his call diverted immediately to her voicemail.

He spoke far too stridently for his surroundings. 'Carla, I've no idea where you're hiding but please come out. I'm at the fruit juices, as instructed.' Now realising he'd become a one-man blockade, he parked his trolley off to the side, next to a large display of discounted cranberry juice.

He stalked the intersection with increasing impatience. The young assistant walked past again. She offered him an encouraging smile but he blanked her completely. A hurt look instantly replaced the smile.

He called again with the same result. He left a similar message then sent a text. Ross was a bit of a grammar Nazi so he used proper words with proper punctuation, including the occasional semi-colon.

As he turned to look in the opposite direction, he almost jumped out of his shirt. A small, rotund, gimlet-eyed woman was standing so close they'd have been toe to toe were it not for her shape.

It was Joan, his neighbour from two doors down. She of the twitchy blinds and wife of Joe, the henpecked husband. *Joe and Joan Jones. I ask you.*

Ross was flustered. 'Oh, sorry. I'm, em, looking for Carla. Have you seen her, Mrs Jones?'

He detested having to address her so formally but he was equally buggered if he would call her by her first name. She'd been friendly, albeit a little aloof, when he first moved in. But a few months back for some reason she stopped taking him on. If he started up a conversation with Joe, Mrs J would materialise from nowhere with some urgent task the poor bugger had apparently forgotten to do, and her husband usually trailed away after her, wearing his best sad spaniel expression.

So clearly she didn't like him, and he was perfectly happy for the feeling to be entirely mutual.

Ross kept his serious face on but inwardly he was laughing so hard he could have startled a statue. *Boy, does this have potential. There's no way she would ever help me but she'll be fucking desperate to find out what's going on, so she'll have to. What a hoot!*

Ross upped the ante with the worried expression. 'I've lost her, you see, somewhere in the store.'

Joan could do haughty with the best of them. 'Are you sure Mrs McKinlay is actually *in* the supermarket?'

He answered a little too quickly. 'What do you mean? Of course she is. Why wouldn't she be?'

The woman took a small step back and studied him over the rim of her glasses. 'Well, she could be outside at the car, or the cash machine, or something.'

'No, I don't think she'll have gone outside. It's pouring down.' He turned away, as if he was still searching, so he missed Joan giving the sleeve of her coat a pointed look. It was a light-coloured raincoat, and bone dry.

Ross thought this conversation could well go round in circles. It was time to make his escape so he tried to lighten the mood. He wasn't to know the attempt would bomb.

'Anyway, I'm sorry to rush off but I'd better go and look for her. I'll be in trouble otherwise.' He winked at his neighbour. 'She'll probably bash me if I don't.'

Spinning the trolley round again he walked briskly away, completely oblivious to the acidic glare that Joan Jones lasered at the back of his retreating skull.

* * *

'This is a staff announcement. All till-trained staff report to checkouts. Till-trained staff to checkouts, please.'

Having trailed all the way round the store for a third time, Ross decided it was time to seek help. At the Customer Services desk he waited relatively patiently while a woman complained that a pack of courgettes she'd bought should have lasted longer than eight days before going soft. Eventually the assistant agreed she *could* have a refund, which then took a similar time to process.

He was practically dancing a jig by the time she eventually turned her attention to him. The woman looked to be well into her sixties but had jet-black hair, dyed to within an inch of its life. She tapped a leg of her glasses on the counter in a manner that only accentuated her already highly irritated state.

She used the words: 'Yes sir, how may I help you?' but her expression and her tone screamed she was clean out of help for that day.

'My wife's gone missing in the store.' He pointed at the microphone on the counter. 'Could you make an announcement for her, please?'

'I'm not sure if I'm allowed to do that without the manager's permission, sir. And he's not here just now. Can it wait?' Her gaze wandered to the three or four customers standing behind him.

'Wait?' He glared at her. 'No, it can't wait. I've told you I can't find my wife, and I need you to make a Tannoy announcement for her. Now!'

She reached out for the microphone, then hesitated. 'Have you looked for her?'

Ross wasn't normally a sarcastic person but several smart-arse comments clambered about on the tip of his tongue. He reckoned most of the queue was listening in so he answered her calmly. 'Yes, I have. I've been all over the store. Several times, in fact.'

'And have you checked the Ladies?'

He was annoyed. She'd made a good point. But the tilt of his head and the blank stare told her no, he hadn't checked the Ladies.

'I've been looking for her for about . . .' he checked his watch, 'fifteen minutes. So I doubt she'll be in there. But just in case, could you take a look?'

'I can't leave the desk unattended, sir.' She pointed past Ross. 'And I have other customers waiting.'

The man next in line then spoke up. Half the store would have heard him. 'Jesus, dear. Make the effin' announcement then you can serve the rest of us while *His Lordship* here waits for his missus. Yeah?'

Clearly she wasn't happy being told what to do but she picked up the mike. Without looking at Ross, she asked, 'What's your wife's name?' The *sir* was conspicuous by its absence.

'It's Carla McKinlay.'

She made the call. But any smile, no matter how disingenuous, had long been discarded like an empty fag packet. Now she looked straight past Ross, switching her attention to the man with the hard hat. 'How may I help you, sir?'

Help? thought Ross. *Good luck with that!*

Ross stood off to the side and scanned the shoppers walking in his direction. But none of them were Carla. He checked his phone, again. Made yet another call.

Nothing. No answer. No Carla.

'Where the hell is she?' he said out loud.

3

Miroslav was relaxing in his study, reading a historical novel and scratching distractedly at his beard. The new growth hadn't yet passed the itching phase.

He closed the book immediately his mobile phone rang. The ringtone told him it was his business partner, Danijela, so there had to be something wrong. She would never call him at home on a Sunday without very good reason.

'I'm guessing we have a problem, Dani. So just give me the punch line.'

'Jean-Luc Dornier has been skimming.'

He didn't even consider asking her if she was certain. Miroslav trusted his long-time friend implicitly. He knew she would have triple-checked all her facts before approaching him.

He didn't waste words. 'How much? For how long? And, when did you find out?'

'As of yesterday, just over 106,000 euros. I first began to suspect the figures weren't adding up at the end of last month so I started digging. I can't be sure precisely when he began diverting money to his own account but I do know it's been at least three months.'

'Pica!' Miroslav spoke almost in a whisper but there was no doubting the violence in his tone. Danijela flinched. She could swear like any navvy but she rarely used this word. Someone had once told her that Bulgarian woman used it, or their translations of it at any rate, as a term of endearment to their closest girlfriends but Danijela thought the story was probably apocryphal. But in most languages, especially English in which both were fluent, its hard sound and vulgar connotations meant most women rarely said the word, and detested hearing it.

Miroslav suffered no such sensitivity and repeated himself, louder and with more intensity this time. 'Pica!' With a hard slap on the arm of his chair for emphasis.

Danijela already had a good idea what he was likely to say next but she waited for Miroslav to make his decision. That's how things worked. He decided, she arranged.

He placed his novel on the coffee table, there would be no more light reading for him today. 'You've already contacted Zelenka, I presume?'

'A few minutes ago. He is waiting for our call.'

'Good. Then meet me at the office.' He checked his watch. 'In thirty minutes.'

4

Recalling these events later, Ross would readily admit they began to blur. First, he walked out to the car park to check the car. It was still there. A black Golf GTi in serious need of a good clean, parked out in the open although there were covered spaces in front of the store.

There was no note on the windscreen nor any sign Carla had been back in the meantime.

Back inside, he rescued their trolley and took another turn round the aisles, walking much more quickly and determinedly this time. With precisely the same result.

Then he asked Smiler at Customer Services to make a second announcement. She started to object, didn't, and made the call. There was a real edge to her voice this time. So much so that a tall man in a suit hurried up to the desk with a *what on earth?* air about him. His badge identified him as the Store Manager.

A hurried confab ensued between them with Smiler doing a lot of thumb-jerking in Ross's direction. The manager turned to Ross, buttoning his suit jacket as if he were about to stand up in court. He was a couple of inches taller, and in his late twenties. His suit hung on his rangy frame like it was on a wire coat hanger. He had space for two or three fingers between his company tie and his throat.

'Mr McKinlay? I'm Steve Carroll, the Store Manager. I understand you're having some difficulty locating your wife.'

Just then, Joan sailed past on her way out. Quite how she didn't collide either with another customer or the floral display was beyond Ross, so fixed was her stare at the two men talking.

'That's right. I don't know where she's gone but I can't find her anywhere, and now I'm getting worried. We've made two announcements but there's no sign of her.'

'Has anyone checked the rest rooms? Perhaps she's been taken ill.'

'I did ask your colleague but she couldn't, or wouldn't, leave the desk.'

'No. We try not to leave the desk unattended but she should have asked someone else to go. Wait there a minute, please.'

Steve despatched Smiler off to the Ladies, taking her place behind the desk. It seemed like only seconds later and she was back, shaking her head.

Steve walked over to Ross, the manager had his game face on. He grasped the rim of Ross's trolley and spoke gently, but firmly. 'I'm sorry, Mr McKinlay, your wife's not in the Ladies. Where else have you looked?'

Over the course of the next half an hour or so, the manager and his security staff helped Ross to check the store, inside and out.

Ross explained what Carla had been wearing. 'A black padded winter coat. Not quite down to her knees.'

Steve insisted they look in the café despite Ross telling him she wouldn't be there because they were planning to make dinner as soon as they got home.

They checked all the internal areas that Carla could possibly have accessed, even inadvertently: the warehouse, staff rooms and two small changing cubicles in the clothing department. Steve confirmed that none of the external door alarms had triggered.

They drew a blank in all the external locations too. She hadn't returned to the car, wasn't at the ATM or anywhere in the car park. They even checked the landscaping that bordered the road.

Ross's missing wife wasn't *anywhere* on the supermarket's premises.

With seemingly every possibility exhausted, Steve said, 'Daft question I know, but is it possible she's gone home?'

Ross looked at him. 'Why would she do that and leave the car here?'

'Like I said, daft question.'

Steve knew he had to call a halt. 'I'm sorry, Ross, but there's nothing more we can do here.'

Ross looked down at the floor. He'd hadn't ever noticed the colour: pale blue. 'Could you please make just one more announcement?'

'I'm sorry, Ross. I can't. If your wife was in the store I'm sure she would have responded. And I need to be careful not to alarm the other customers.'

Steve pointed to the items in the shopping trolley but Ross explained he'd have to leave them. He hadn't brought his wallet because: 'Carla was going to pay.' So Steve offered to lay it aside for the moment.

Ross didn't have car keys because Carla had driven to the store but he declined a lift home. 'I don't live far away. But thanks anyway.'

Steve hesitated before asking one final question: 'Would you like me to call the police?'

Ross didn't take any time to think. 'No. No, please don't. I'm sure it's not necessary.'

So now, here he was, standing below the Perspex canopy outside with no choice but to walk home. He stayed below the canopy for another few minutes, reluctant to move. Dreading going home because of what he might find there. And that dread was now constricting his breathing like a waistcoat several sizes too small.

But he couldn't stand there all night. Decision made, he jammed his hands in his pockets, looked back one final time and muttered, 'This wasn't part of the plan, Carla. Not part of the plan at all.'

Then he hunched his shoulders and walked out into the night.

* * *

Ross's problems were fourfold. No keys to the car, no money for a bus or a cab, no keys to his house. And no wife. Black humour always surfaces at some point, he thought, although he didn't find it remotely funny.

He scrounged a piece of paper and a pen from a guy sitting smoking in his car, and left a note under the Golf's windscreen wiper saying he was going home to collect his car keys. Belt and braces, he sent a text saying the same thing. Then he glared at the phone for several seconds, challenging it to respond.

He set off to walk home, about a mile and a half. After a few minutes hunching his shoulders against the rain all he had to show for it was a sharp pain at the top of his spine, and he wasn't one iota drier. So he relaxed, straightened up and let the weather do its worst. After all, he didn't have that much

13

hair for the rain to ruin. But he took off his glasses and stuck them in his pocket. He couldn't see out of them anyway.

By the time he turned the final corner into his street he was so anxious he was scared he might throw up. Their house was at the end of a curved cul-de-sac in a new development in the Newhaven area of Leith, Edinburgh's cheeky co-habitee. Where Edinburgh was all high and mighty upmarket everything, tall sandstone tenements and New Town immodesty, neighbouring Leith had attitude and loads of it. Brash and multicultural with a sprinkling of latent-ghetto thrown in.

He knew exactly at which point on the curve his house would come into view and, as it did, he immediately spotted lights shining in the vestibule and the living room. He didn't mean to cry out but he did. He stopped dead in the middle of the pavement. Then, as if he'd been kick-started, and ignoring the driving rain and the surface water beneath his feet, he ran across the road and up to the house.

Ross slithered to a stop at the front door, his right knee on the verge of buckling under him as his foot hit the step. He jammed his thumb on the doorbell, and from the inside echoed that damned annoying eight-note jingle, reminiscent of an old-fashioned ice cream van. He could just make out the layout of their hall through the small pane of heavily frosted glass set at eye level in the door, and he waited, hopping from foot to foot on the step, mainly through impatience but also because he was desperate to pee.

'Come on, Carla. *Hurry up!*'

He expected her either to come down the stairs from the left or out of the living room to the right.

He was just raising his left arm to thumb the doorbell one more time when the truth hit him like a logging truck. The lights were on a timer. Carla wasn't in the house.

Ross collapsed forward, his hands leaning on the door frame and his forehead flat against the glass. He was frustrated, disappointed and downright bewildered. He couldn't stop the tears from falling.

'Where are you, Carla? Where the bloody hell *are* you?'

5

Ross had retrieved the spare key from its hiding place in the back garden, inside one of those fake rocks he'd spotted in a gadget magazine. Naff, but it did the job.

Then he worked his way round the house, checking all the rooms and looking for any signs Carla had been there since they'd left for the store. Everything was just as it should be, as far as he could tell at any rate.

He changed out of his wet clothes, grabbed a coat and his golf umbrella and walked back to the supermarket. As he climbed back into the car he snagged the now soggy and illegible note he'd written from under the windscreen wiper, scrunched it up and threw it on the ground. He instantly felt bad. *No need let standards slip, Ross. Just no need.*

Back home again, he was sitting at the kitchen table drinking a decaf, trying to figure out what to do next. He moved the mug in a series of widening and decreasing circles like tracing the track on a vinyl LP.

His previous messages to Carla's voicemail remained unanswered but he decided to try one more time. He stared at his phone for a good minute before activating the call. 'Carla. It's me, again. Listen, I don't know where you are but I'm really, really worried. I don't know if there's something wrong, pet, but I know we can sort it out… whatever it is. Please call me, would you? I'm at home now and… well, I'm at home. Okay? Call me. Please.'

Ross realised that was really garbled. He knew what he wanted to say but he hadn't given any thought about how to end the call, so he babbled on till he eventually ran out of steam like a balloon exhaling air. He plugged the phone into the charger and turned it round to face him, as if *that* would make any difference.

He rested his forearms on the table, hands clasped together on the white melamine surface. What was the next step? He considered his options, there appeared to be three.

The first was to call the police and report Carla missing. *No, it's only been an hour and a half so I'd be surprised if they took it seriously. It's way too early. They'll probably think we've had some sort of domestic, or that Carla is having an affair.*

Then he recalled something his best buddy, Martin, had said when he discovered his *slag of a wife* had been cheating on him. *'The husband is always the last to find out.'* But still, Ross refused to think people would believe that of Carla. Or him, in fact. They had only been married eight months.

The second option was to call some friends, to ask if Carla was with them. If he did eventually call the police, it was the sort of thing they'd have expected him to do.

And the third was to sit tight, do nothing, see what the morning brought. Definitely an option but it would make it a long night.

Ross gazed round the kitchen, it had Carla written all over it. Not a frill in sight, spartan would be a reasonable description. She had been extremely precise in her directions to the kitchen installer, six months previously when the house was built. Come to think about it, she was extremely precise with everyone, including him. He couldn't help smiling as he recalled the ding-dong arguments she had with some of the tradesmen. But in the end they always fell into line, sooner rather than later.

Black polished granite worktops, pale cream glossy doors. Not Shaker. *'Those little ledges just gather dust,'* was her opinion. Brushed chrome hob and double-oven, and definitely no microwave. *'That's not proper cooking.'* The kettle, toaster and all the other accoutrements followed the brushed chrome and cream theme. Carla had spent ages trawling the internet to find the perfect match for everything. Ross didn't do internet, at all, but was dutifully dragged round all the posh kitchen shops in Edinburgh. On weekends away, they rummaged in Glasgow, Manchester and the boutique areas of London like Camden Town and Brick Lane. He didn't really understand this fastidious attention to detail but it was Carla's one weakness and he was happy to indulge her. Yet, oddly enough, the other rooms were furnished in a fairly straightforward, almost perfunctory manner.

He made himself another coffee, and sat down at the table again.

Ross was by nature an ordered, logical person. Twenty-odd years as a corporate accountant testified to that. As he sipped his drink, he compiled a list of everything he thought he should do before he finally accepted he had no choice but to report Carla missing. As far as he could remember he hadn't ever reported *anything* to the police, far less a missing wife. So he was reluctant, let's make no bones about that. He really did *not* want to call the police. He knew the time might come but, as yet, he couldn't bring himself to do it.

But it *was* time to call some friends. There were two couples they were reasonably friendly with, although, thinking back, Ross realised it had been several weeks since he and Carla had socialised with either of the pairings. But they were certainly an option if Carla *did* need somewhere to go. To lie low, as it were.

He looked up their numbers on his mobile and wrote them down. He wanted to keep the mobile clear for incoming calls so he plucked the landline from its base, and dialled the first one.

'Hello?'

'Amanda, hi, it's Ross here. How are you doing?'

Dead silence.

Ross checked the display on the phone but, no, the line hadn't dropped out. *Maybe she didn't hear me.*

He was just about to say *'Hi,'* again when Amanda spoke. 'Fine, Ross.'

And that was it. No *'How are you?'* or *'It's been ages.'*

Flat, dead tone. No inflection in her voice whatsoever.

Flustered, he launched himself into the pool of silence, feet first. 'Sorry to bother you but have you seen Carla this evening at all?'

'Carla?' Then, heavy on the derision, 'And *why* would *Carla* be *here*, of all places?'

He noticed he'd made a couple of muddy scuffs on the tiles near the door. *What on earth does she mean by that?*

'Well, em…' He was confused now. Amanda was normally perfectly friendly towards him, they weren't exactly best mates but they'd always rubbed along just fine.

The truth wasn't going to cut any ice so he opted for the sympathy vote. 'The thing is, it's really quite late and she was due home a while ago but she hasn't turned up.'

Amanda's next statement hit him like a baseball bat. 'Well, I can't say I'm surprised, Ross. You reap what you sow and all that. I'm just amazed it took her so long.'

And before he could formulate any sort of reply she hung up on him.

This time he *had* been cut off.

He didn't move for a few seconds then carefully, as if its case was constructed of eggshell, he placed the phone safely back on its station. Over the course of the next minute or two, he glanced at it a few times as if to ask, 'What the hell was *that* all about?'

But it was merely a lump of dumb plastic and circuitry.

And dumb, it remained.

6

Miroslav was standing at his office window gazing over at the bridge. There was no question Danijela's news had made him angry but, as with any other crisis, this view always soothed him. The office was on the third floor, just high enough for a decent view over the plane trees that lined the street below. It was a narrow street and only the occasional vehicle used it as a rat-run, probably because of the suspension-endangering sleeping policemen that had been recently installed. These monstrosities were appearing all over the city, and he detested them with a passion.

The daylight was fading fast, and a mist was forming, wisping above the river like steam from a simmering pan. The streetlights, white translucent globes suspended from old-fashioned lamp standards, were popping on in banks of a dozen at a time.

The afternoon tourists were heading back to their hotels to soak their aching feet. An hour's respite before drinks and dinner, and possibly an evening at the opera. The younger ones would hit the pubs, then the clubs. Just then, a cackle of girls appeared on the bridge, arm-in-arm in a line of five as they tramped across. The one in the centre was festooned in a veil, home-made L-plates, and a host of party-shop accessories. The temperature was still well below double digits but all five wore short skirts and flimsy tops. The bridge was relatively quiet but a lone cyclist had to swerve close to the balustrade to bypass the group. She was wearing a skirt and pumps, and her long dark ponytail bobbed about under her cycle helmet.

His discussion with Zelenka would be brief so he too would soon be walking across the bridge for a relaxing beer on his way home, and not in one of the many tourist traps that surrounded the square. No, a few streets further away he would drop in to a locals' bar, where the draught beers were half the price and many times more flavoursome than the fizzy piss-water the visitors assumed was the country's genuine article. He'd have one, possibly two, then hop a tram back to the outskirts of the city where he lived a quiet, unobtrusive life. A far cry from this few square kilometres of year-round madness, of gangs of inebriated youngsters, of still-life statues and their ever-increasing ingenuity, and of beyond-tacky souvenir shops.

* * *

Miroslav had been born in Prague in 1976 to Czech parents, Marta and Filip. His mother was a native of the city, his father hailed from Bratislava. If they'd produced their only offspring fifteen years later, they would have been Czech and Slovakian respectively.

Filip was a reader and a dreamer who would have loved to travel the world but for the majority of citizens in post-war Eastern Bloc countries, Soviet rule decreed that to be impossible. He was a skilled carpenter and contented himself with exploring his own country, picking up work where he could. While he was working in Prague he met Marta, who, after a brief dalliance in a park on the outskirts of the city, had fallen pregnant.

Filip considered himself to be a man of honour so he did the right thing, he stuck around and married Marta. Two days after his son was born, and very much the worse for wear having celebrated the new-born's arrival to an excessive degree, Filip fell underneath a tram on the corner of Mala Strana Square leaving Marta to raise her son on her own.

* * *

The office door swung open behind him and interrupted Miroslav's reverie.

Danijela walked across the carpeted floor and gave her friend a quick hug. Just the wrong side of forty, she was the product of a Czech father and a Finnish mother. She'd got her name and an occasionally stratospheric temper from her father, and a full set of Scandinavian genetics from her mother. Right down to the grey-blue eyes and the poker-straight Nordic-blonde hair. Danijela was tall, but the scales had never registered an ounce over nine stone despite possessing an appetite that could euphemistically be described as healthy.

Normally, they would shoot the breeze before getting down to business but not today. Social niceties flew out the window and floated away on the Vltava when treachery was involved. Especially when money was part of the equation.

She reached over and pushed a couple of buttons on the loudspeaker unit. 'Jarek?'

'I'm here.'

Jarek Zelenka's preferred language was Polish but all three were comfortable in several Eastern European languages. They settled easily into Czech.

'I would prefer to brief you in person,' said Miroslav, 'but there is very little to say. I need you to deal with this operative who has abused my trust. Dani has provided you with information about him and where he is located, yes?' He looked at Danijela as he spoke.

She nodded, and Jarek replied, 'She has.'

Miroslav continued. 'How you choose to carry out this assignment is, as always, entirely up to you. But there is one thing I would like to be clear about.'

Miroslav paused. The line remained silent. He leaned in a little closer to the speaker.

'I wish to send a message. A public message. One that involves the media. Newspapers *and* television networks. And one that Jean-Luc Dornier's colleagues, whether they are personally acquainted with him or not, will understand. Without any shadow of doubt.'

'Understood.'

'And, I wish this to happen in days, if not hours.'

'Will there be anything else?'

'Just one thing. Jean-Luc Dornier is not to die.'

Miroslav paused before adding the other half of the equation. 'It is imperative he lives to reflect upon the consequences of his treachery.'

7

'Sally, how are you? It's Ross.'

Again, there was a definite pause before Sally spoke. 'Hi Ross, yes, I'm fine thanks. We all are. Well, by all, I mean Robert and I. Or is it better to say Robert and me? Och, listen to me, I'm blethering on. How are you, darling?'

Ross took the phone away from his ear and looked at it. *Has Sal had a few?*

'I'm fine, Sal.' The automatic response. 'Listen, is Carla with you, by any chance?'

Another hesitation. 'Carla? Why would *she* be here? I mean, without you?'

'Ah. Yes. Of course. It's just... it's just that, well, she's not here and I'm trying to find her.'

'Well, no, she's not here either, Ross. Carla never comes to our house, not on her own. When you say you're trying to find her, has something happened? Have you pair fallen out or something?'

He rather blurted out his response. 'No, Sal, nothing like that. It's just that she's...' He groped around for an excuse. 'Very late, that's all. Really sorry to bother you. I'll have to go now, and I'll ring you later. But if you do hear from her, ask her to call me straight away, will you?'

'Of course I will. But are you sure everything's okay? Would you like to come over? Robert's away, you see, and I could do with the company. It would be lovely to see you.'

'I don't think so, Sal. But thanks. Speak to you later on. Bye for now.'

As he ended the call he heard her saying something else but he was already hitting disconnect. Like most men, apparently, he wasn't all that talkative on the phone but he found conversation with Sally particularly stressful. For good reason.

They had been friends for ages but a couple of years back, before he met Carla, Sally had made a real fool of herself with him, although, as far as he was aware, no one else knew about it. Seven of their crowd had gone back to Sally and Robert's after a spectacularly boozy Saturday lunch and had carried on drinking, yacking and listening to loud rock music, in that order. Ross had gone to the loo and was just closing the bathroom door when Sally slipped into the room behind him. She snicked the catch over, locking the door, and before his jaw had time to drop she was all over him like a rash.

Ross was stunned into immobility at first but he backed off pretty damn fast when she began fumbling at his flies while planting wet sloppy kisses all over his chin and lower lip. She was just over five feet in her socks, and had laid waste to the better part of two bottles of wine so accuracy definitely was not her strong point. His full-scale retreat was brought to a crashing halt when he bounced his skull off the sloping roof that formed part of the staircase above. Then his left foot scattered a miniature aluminium dustbin across the tiled floor, and at the same time he elbowed a canister of Forest Pine air freshener off a shelf. It flew in a perfect arc, directly onto the rim of the washbasin before it continued its lazy spiral onto the floor, where, naturally, it collided with the aforementioned miniature aluminium dustbin. AC/DC in their pomp would have made less noise and he was certain Robert would come to check what on earth was going on in his downstairs loo. Which, thought Ross, would be nothing short of a disaster. Luckily for them, no amount of din would have penetrated the racket the rest of the gang were creating.

Ross put both hands on her shoulders and none too gently pushed her away, which disengaged the limpet action of her mouth, and, painfully for him, ripped her right hand away from his balls. In her mightily pissed state she probably considered that to have been a caress but the piercing ache in his gut disproved that theory.

'Sally! What the bloody hell are you doing, for God's sake?' he hissed through clenched teeth, figuring he couldn't risk actually shouting at her. 'Robert, in fact everybody, they're just next door. Someone will come.'

'Aye. Me with a bit of luck. Then you can too, of course.' Neither of Sally's eyes were focussing particularly well and her speech was rather impaired. Ross's arms had relaxed as he leant forward, and she took this as an invitation to resume her assault.

Ross's state of panic was off the scale and all he could think was, get me the hell out of here! He performed a side-step that any matador would have been proud of, which left Sally groping thin air. He rattled the catch to what should have been the open position, only to realise she hadn't locked them in at all. 'Shit,' was one of the few things worth saying. After two or three more attempts he managed to open the door without crashing it back off its hinges, or into either of the metallic objects currently roaming the floor.

No way could he go straight back to join the others so he immediately ran for the stairs, figuring he would head up to the family bathroom and leave her to it.

'Ro-oss, could you close the loo door, plee-eese.' Not quite believing his ears, he took one glance back in Sally's direction, just in time to see her hauling her jeans and pants down in one unsteady, lurching movement before plopping her somewhat generous arse onto the toilet seat.

Ross had always considered himself to be the perfect gentleman but in this instance he grabbed the bannister and took the stairs two at a time. *You're on your own, pet. I am nowhere. To. Be. Seen.*

As he recalled that potentially calamitous episode he could feel his face burning red, and thanked the Lord the effects of excessive alcohol meant that if anyone apart from him or Sally had noticed anything amiss, they had all been too pissed to remember. Certainly he didn't ever mention it again, especially after she sent him a text the following morning: *Don't be such a tease next time. You know you want it as much as I do. S xx.*

The next couple of times they'd been in company, he imagined she'd been looking at him rather hopefully but there was no way he was giving her any encouragement.

He shook his head to disperse the memories.

But now he had a decision to make? Stick or twist?

No question.

Stick!

8

In the last couple of hours before the supermarket closed to customers, the aisles were usually quiet enough for the staff to do some cleaning. Anything they could do now might mean they didn't all have to stay till the end of their shift, officially one o'clock in the morning.

But even then, that depended upon which Store Manager was on duty, and if there wasn't a manager on shift, an early finish would be down to whether the supervisor was a complete tosser or *one of the lads*.

As it turned out, Steve Carroll had gone home and the supervisor, Declan, was indeed one of the lads, who could be relied upon to have them all out of there and heading for the clubs as early as humanly possible. But Declan wasn't a total pushover. He wanted everything done that needed to be done, *then* they could all go clubbing.

The gangly youth with the long straight jet-black hair and the bum-fluff moustache wouldn't be joining his mates as he could never pass for twenty-one and he was always skint. But he was still in a hurry to head back to his flat where his most recent girlfriend was waiting for him. He was fairly certain they wouldn't be an item for terribly much longer as she had told him more than once she wanted to enjoy life, and she loved constant change. In where she lived, what she did, and who she did it with.

So he was making hay because this girl was hot. Therefore, the earlier he was home the better, just in case tomorrow turned out to be the day she decided to split.

Declan had tasked him with cleaning and polishing the floors in the clothing section of the store so he was manoeuvring the machine up and down the aisles, sweeping it from side to side. As part of this task he should first have swept under the front edges of the racks with the wide flat mop, before polishing the tiles. Had he been doing his job properly he may have found the object that was key to solving the mystery that was Carla, and a lot quicker than was eventually the case. But he desperately wanted back to his flat, back to his girl and back to his bed, so he cut corners and only used the polisher, whose rotating circular brushes clipped the object and spun it further under the racking against the back wall.

Much further.

The good news was, his girlfriend didn't move on the following day.

But, the day after that, sadly for him, she did.

9

Amanda's comments invaded Ross's brain like a boll-weevil on speed. *'You reap what you sow and all that.'* And worse: *'I'm just amazed it took her so long.'*

He was wandering around the kitchen now, phone switching constantly from hand to hand, repeating those two phrases over and over while demanding to know, at top volume, just what the hell she meant. He must have asked himself that a dozen times before he sat down at the table with such force the chair moved about a foot, and he belted his knee off the table leg. Strangely enough, he barely registered the pain, so consumed was he in his own personal tirade.

'I'm going to phone her and ask what the hell is wrong with her. Or maybe I'll go over there and ask her to her face.' But his phone was now a few feet away on the worktop, and as his temper gradually subsided, his backside remained glued to the seat. Truth was, Ross didn't have much of a temper and he generally avoided confrontation at all cost. So there was no chance he would be phoning Amanda, and he certainly wouldn't have gone to her house.

He thought she'd probably just had a bad day at work and resolved to call her again tomorrow. Bottom line was, he'd asked the only two people Carla might have gone to, and both said she wasn't with them.

While the kettle was boiling for yet another coffee he walked out the front door and looked around for any sign of life. Their house was the last one in the street, a small detached villa hemmed in by a narrow piece of woodland about 30 or 40 metres deep that concealed a primary school. Or at least it concealed the view of the school but it did precious little to muffle the shrieks and screeches of the children in the playground. The noise always made him smile. It made him feel good to hear the kids enjoying themselves. *I wonder if it's still called a playground in these modern times, where political correctness has gone quite mad. Probably an External Exercise Environment or something.*

27

The wood was a popular destination for local dog-walkers, but not this evening. He craned his neck one more time to confirm the street was empty before closing the front door.

As he was stirring his coffee he briefly considered making something to eat but he couldn't stomach anything.

He took his coffee into the living room, lifting a coaster from the stack on a side table and carefully placing the coaster and mug centrally on the table. He well remembered the bollocking Carla had given him not long after they moved in, when he put a glass down without a coaster to protect the table. He flopped into the chair and glanced at the clock. It was after ten.

Without taking much of it in, he gazed around the room at the pale carpet and walls, the contrasting sofas and armchair, with colour-coordinated blinds covering the bay window. The longest wall had plenty space for a fireplace but as the house had been built without a chimney, Carla had decreed they wouldn't have one of those fake fireplaces with matching fake fire so she'd made the focal point of the room an artistic arrangement of candles bought from one of those overpoweringly smelly shops in town.

Apart from the modest flat-screen TV in the corner, the only other piece of furniture was a low unit below the bay window. It held a DVD/CD player, two small speakers that produced a surprisingly rich sound, and two framed photos, one on top of each speaker.

His coffee forgotten for the moment, he levered himself out of the armchair, moved across to the window and using two hands he gently lifted the photo from the left speaker. He buffed the glass with his left sleeve and stood, transfixed on the image of the elfin woman captured there.

She looked to be in her late twenties, her hair was short, blonde and cut in a bob that framed her face. She was wearing a pale pink summer dress with matching sneakers, and a collection of pink and white bangles on her right wrist. The woman was sitting on a child's swing in a playpark, her feet crossed underneath her. She was only holding on with one hand, causing the swing to rotate slightly to the left, which she was counteracting by pressing her toes into the ground. She obviously had good legs but holding herself in that pose brought out the definition of her calf and thigh muscles, which made her look athletic, despite her seated position.

She was laughing uproariously while pointing, jabbing even, at something behind the photographer. Or even at him because Ross had taken the snap. He couldn't remember what had caused the hilarity, which, staring at the picture now, caused him no small amount of regret.

He carried the photo back to his chair and sat with it balanced on his thighs, leaning forward with his arms folded under his ribcage. Tears brimmed on his lower eyelids and two drops, one from each side and perfectly synchronised, landed on the grass at the woman's pink-sneakered feet.

Quickly, as if those two tiny splashes of water would cause her harm, he blurred them away with his cuff only for them to be replaced immediately by several more.

Ross leaned all the way back and stared directly at the plain white ceiling.

'Liz.' He spoke softly, his voice catching on that single syllable. 'Liz, darling. This can't be happening to me.'

'Surely, not again.'

* * *

While Ross was navigating his way through the drink- and drugs-fuelled experience known as Edinburgh University Fresher's Week, he met a fellow newbie called Martin in a pub somewhere on Rose Street.

The boys became best buddies. Ross was studying accountancy while Martin, well, Martin tried two or three different courses, dropped out of them all and eventually realised employee status was never to be his destiny. After a few short-term ventures that promised far more than they delivered, along came this dazzling new toy called *The Internet*, which didn't so much push Martin's buttons as zap them repeatedly with a Taser. He was in on the ground floor and from that day on, he rode a series of rising business escalators to different floors in the Information Technology domain, keeping pace with innovation as effortlessly as a Formula One supercar running alongside a rusting old banger. Website design, PC installation and repair, mobile comms, Wi-Fi, tablets, cloud computing. Each one propelling him on to the Next Big Thing.

In their second year they shared a flat in Marchmont, prime student territory and Hedonism Central. While Ross was fairly diligent in his studies, his pal sowed more wild oats than a hundred farmers. Ross was quite used to the revolving door to Martin's bedroom and didn't bother trying to keep track of who his flatmate was shagging that week. 'Hi. I'm Ross,' became his signature phrase to a succession of women he either met in the kitchen or passed at the bathroom door. Some of these women were stunners, some not so much. But Martin's key criteria, as he so eloquently put it, was they all had to be willing to drop their drawers. None lasted longer than a few nights, and rarely did any of them prevent the boys having a few beers, playing tennis or going to the football.

Then Liz turned up and blew the whole dynamic to bits. She stayed for a few nights, then a few nights more, and then she and Martin were in *a relationship*. Ross went to the football on his own, only occasionally played tennis, and met other people for beers. He couldn't stand the sight of Liz. She treated him like The Invisible Man.

Then, about nine o'clock one midweek evening, he was walking home from the university library when he saw Liz crossing from a side street up ahead, obviously heading for the flat. He immediately slowed so she would arrive there well before him. No way was he holding doors for that frosty-faced cow.

Two lads in their early to mid-twenties, smartly dressed but weaving a bit, passed Liz just before she reached the short flight of worn sandstone steps that led up to the tenement door. Ross heard one of them passing comment but he didn't quite catch it. But he certainly did catch the, 'Fuck off, wankers,' that Liz tossed over her shoulder. Then it all kicked off.

One of them took a few quick strides back, grabbed Liz by her shoulder, flipped her round and aggressively pushed her against the railing that guarded the basement flat. The polythene shopping bag she was carrying clanged against the ironwork, and the contents began to spill into the void. 'What did you say, ya wee whore?' he yelled, spittle flecks spraying her face. In certain parts of Scotland, *whore* is pronounced *hoo-err* but that doesn't dilute the insult in the slightest.

The shock on Liz's face was evident and Ross, to his surprise, found himself running towards the scene. Both lads turned at the sound of Ross's trainers slapping along the paving slabs and immediately dismissed him as any form of threat. 'Come on, guys, leave the lass alone,' he pleaded, his voice just a tad too squeaky and effeminate for the effect he was trying to create.

'Beat it, Sir Galahad. This has got fuck all to do wi' you,' said the one standing nearer to him in precisely the correct tone: threatening, with a coating of malevolence.

'Look, this girl's a friend of mine. Just leave her alone, will you?' Ross was facing this second lad now but he was leaning slightly back, both hands up, palms forward. The bag containing his coursework and library books slid from his shoulder and caught in the crook of his arm, pulling it down and making him appear smaller than he already felt.

'I told you, pal, keep walking or you'll get a smack.'

'I... I can't do that. Please, just leave her.' Ross's legs were wobbling now, and he began to think he might fall over. He hadn't ever been in a situation like this before, and he had no idea what to do apart from try to reason with them. He steadied himself on the railing.

'Come on, Danny,' said the first. 'Let's leave fuckin' Superman here with his wee slag. He can tell his arsehole student mates tomorrow about how he rescued her from the big bad wolves.' They both started laughing and moved to walk away but Danny stopped and put his left hand on Ross's shoulder.

'You all right, pal? You're looking a wee bit shaky there.'

Ross looked bemused. 'Yes. I'm okay. Thanks.' He hitched his bag back onto his shoulder.

'That's good.' Danny paused for half a second before head-butting Ross so hard that he staggered back, his feet skittering in an attempt to maintain his balance. Danny then thumped the heel of his hand into the student's chest causing him to tumble backwards into Liz, and they both fell in a heap. Arms, legs, bodies and bags all jumbled up together.

Cackling and back-slapping, their two assailants wandered off down the street. They passed through a pool of yellow light and disappeared from view.

Disentangled now, and both leaning against the railing, Liz's voice was quavering. 'Are you okay, Ross? Why did he do that? That was just awful.'

'Jesus. That was fucking sore.' Ross's voice was muffled because his hand was across his mouth and nose. Amazingly, there was no blood but even this soon, he could feel his forehead swelling up.

'Let's go upstairs. We should maybe phone the police.'

He fished his key out of his pocket, and they helped each other up the broad tenement staircase to the second floor. Their flat was the middle one of three, with an original, scarred, solid wooden door with brass accessories that probably hadn't been polished since the fifties. Liz didn't have a key to the flat so Ross let them in. They closed the door behind them and both leaned back on it, their bags sliding to the floor in unison.

Liz switched feet to stand in front of Ross, put her palms flat on his cheeks, fingers up into his hair and kissed him quickly on the lips. 'Thank you, Ross. You were very brave.'

He nodded as he didn't trust himself to speak without bursting into tears, then Liz pushed herself away and turned round.

The entrance to the flat was a square hall, about 12 feet across. The doors to the two bedrooms, living room, bathroom, kitchen and two storage cupboards all led off this space. There were so many doors and they all looked the same. *Chipped dirty off-white* would have been the paint colour. It had taken Ross and Martin weeks to sort out the doors and the corresponding rooms in their heads so God help visitors. But Liz knew exactly which door was her boyfriend's bedroom and she took one pace towards it before stopping dead, one foot placed in front of the other. Ross wondered why for just one second, then he got it.

From behind the door, they heard several sounds mingling together. The slow, rhythmic thumping of wood against plaster and the tell-tale creaking of well-worn, second-hand bedsprings. But worse, far far worse, feminine gasps and squeals that couldn't possibly be misinterpreted. Liz didn't need a picture to be painted.

She marched the two remaining steps to the door and, without pausing, turned the handle and pushed the door away from her. The female in question was on the bed facing the door, on her knees and elbows, with the left side of her face on the duvet, which was concertinaed at the foot of the bed. She had long, wavy, brown hair that had fallen forward, revealing the back of her neck and all the little bumps on her spine. Her backside was in the air, higher than her shoulders.

Behind her, also facing the door, Martin was right in the moment. His eyes were closed, face raised slightly towards the ceiling, and he and the girl were both, clearly, accelerating towards the conclusion of this particular act.

Ross had walked forward like a zombie, his mouth and eyes wide open, staring into the room over Liz's shoulder. This was a motorway pile-up just about to happen and no one watching would be able to prevent it.

At that very second, Martin opened his eyes. He made one more thrust before he registered the pair of them framed in the doorway, their expressions like two teenagers who have just encountered Freddy Krueger halfway down a dark alley. He was shocked to discover the brakes had failed and the traffic up ahead was stationary. All his energy disappeared like cakes at a kids' party.

The girl pushed back once or twice, realised her partner was no longer contributing to her pleasure, turned her head and screamed at him, 'Don't fucking stop now! I'm gonna *come*.'

Liz lunged forward. 'That *will* be fucking right!' She grabbed two handfuls of long brown wavy hair and with an impressive show of strength, yanked the girl off the bed where she tumbled in a naked sweaty heap at Ross's feet. Astonished, and with no comprehension of what had happened to her, she found herself flat on her back, legs splayed wide apart with everything on show. With her clothes on, Ross would never have been able to pick her out at an identity parade.

Martin was frozen in time, still on his knees and still with his hands where the girl's hips had been not ten seconds before. His dick was encased in a bright orange condom that was, in tandem with its contents, deflating rapidly. He said nothing, he just stared at Liz, at Ross, and at the feet and calves of his illicit shag.

Liz knelt down till she was almost nose to nose with the startled brunette. 'I don't know who you are but you're fucking welcome to him. Sorry for interrupting.'

Then she stomped back into the hall and snapped over her shoulder, 'Ross, we're out of here.' She grabbed her bags up off the floor, hauled him away by his wrist, and they left Martin to pick up the pieces.

10

Ross opened Carla's bedroom closet and scanned the selection of her clothing hanging on the rail and folded on the shelves. There were no obvious gaps.

His wife didn't possess an extensive wardrobe. She had workwear, casual clothes and what she called *nice* things. She bought mostly from the internet, but she was far from compulsive.

Carla was employed by an offshore oil-services company headquartered in Texas but under Venezuelan ownership. For several years she'd worked a three-on, three-off rotation as a Deck Officer on a supply vessel in the North Sea. If Ross was honest, he really wasn't sure what that entailed. According to Carla it was twenty-one twelve-hour shifts full of endless paperwork and keeping balls in the air. Ross felt seasick if he even saw a boat so was appalled at the prospect of earning his living at sea but Carla said it wasn't too bad unless the weather took a severe turn. Apparently, every time she sailed, she threw up once within the first hour and was fine after that. He'd heard the pattern wasn't uncommon among seamen, even those who'd spent their entire careers afloat.

Ross knew his wife kept all her work clothes in one place, hanging on a rail in the spare bedroom. But, as far as he could tell, there appeared to be a full complement of coveralls, polo-shirts, fleeces and waterproofs. There was a boot bag containing a pair of steel-toed Timberlands, so no clues there either. But she wasn't due back offshore for another ten days or so, Monday week, so checking for missing work gear *was* a bit of a long shot.

He'd taken a couple of steps downstairs when he jammed both hands, stiff-armed, on the handrails, and hung there, leaning forward at an angle with the ball of one foot planted on the third step. One more option had just occurred to him but the butterflies in his stomach took flight again. He wasn't sure what he'd find but he had no choice but to look.

He lifted the L-shaped bar from its hook in the airing cupboard and clicked the hexagonal end into the slot on the underside of the hatch that gave access to the attic. He hesitated at the prospect then turned it anti-clockwise, releasing the ladder, which slid on well-oiled rails till the rubber feet rested on the carpet. It hardly made a sound on its descent, and one side of Ross's mouth lifted ironically. This had been one of Carla's ongoing battles with the joiner. She'd been blunt. *I do not want my teeth jangling like a cartoon character every time we use that ladder, so make certain it is installed properly.*

The joiner's first attempt hadn't met Carla's exacting standards, and neither had his second. But by golly, after two hours of tweaking and finessing by an increasingly irate tradesman, it glided up and down with less noise than a cat tiptoeing on a shag-pile carpet. Carla declared herself satisfied, and the joiner packed away his tools and left the house without a word, *and* without closing the front door. The next time Carla called the site agent to send a joiner, it was a gentle old man with bottle-bottom glasses and a limp. Attila the Hun couldn't have fallen out with him.

But there they were, Ross and Carla's full and only set of matching luggage handily placed for lifting through the hatch: one large Samsonite, one medium, two flight bags, and a soft leather valise with combination locks that Carla carted along on every trip.

And the butterflies settled down again. For a while at least.

11

Jarek Zelenka looked like he worked out but not excessively so. He was couple of inches short of six feet, with a physique that was tight and defined rather than overtly powerful. He always wore outdoor activities clothing and had a strong aversion to formal attire. His short fair hair had a hint of red, gradually balding from the crown. He was from strong Slavic stock so he didn't consider himself to be particularly handsome. That didn't stop women being drawn to him but he had never been interested in long-term relationships.

By nature, Jarek was not a violent man. But, early in life, he had discovered that he possessed a propensity for calm, controlled ferocity. It wasn't ever gratuitous, he only displayed this particular characteristic when the situation demanded.

Jarek had been born and brought up in the industrial city of Ostrava, about 300 kilometres due east of Prague, and within spitting distance of the Polish border. It was 1969, the same year that a student called Jan Palach set himself on fire in Prague's Wenceslas Square to protest against the invasion of his country by the Soviet Union one year earlier.

In 1979, aged ten, he was walking out of the school gates when an older boy tried to steal his jacket. Jarek was small for his age and his mother had bought the jacket for him to grow into. He knew she had saved hard for it. He wasn't giving it up so he told the boy to leave him alone, and tried to walk away.

The would-be thief grabbed Jarek by the collar and attempted to rip the jacket from his back, but the youngster wrestled free and punched his assailant on the nose. He meant it to be a warning but it wasn't heeded. The teenager came at him, arms windmilling and feet kicking out, as young boys often do. Jarek kept his eyes open, remained focussed, and let his attacker take a few fresh-air swipes. Then he stepped inside and hit his assailant with two hard lefts to an already tender nose. A thumping right uppercut laid the boy flat out. Then, to the astonishment of the circle of schoolchildren watching the fun, Jarek lifted the dazed boy's right hand and bent back his little finger until it snapped with a crack. That silenced the crowd.

Then he knelt down on the asphalt surface, close to the boy's ear and spoke to him. The goggle-eyed kids surrounding them couldn't hear what he said. The boy's screams probably had something to do with that.

As Jarek walked away, he thought about the coup-de-grace he'd just administered. He hadn't planned it, it just happened. So he stopped thinking and walked off home.

Even at such a tender age, the incident forged his reputation as someone not to be messed with. And no one did until six years later. During a chemistry exam, a fellow student whispered across the gap between their two desks. He wanted help with a formula. Jarek ignored him and carried on working. After the exam, the youth and two of his friends were waiting outside. Jarek had topped out at about five ten but these lads were all over six feet. The student who'd asked him to cheat was clearly angry and looking for trouble, while his two friends were trying their best to look mean. Unfortunately for them, they couldn't quite carry it off.

Jarek acted quickly, before the trio could react. He ran straight at the ringleader, who, caught by surprise, made the mistake of adopting a fighter's stance, raising his fists and leaning forward on his left leg, his knee bent to support him. His stance left him vulnerable. Jarek slammed a ferocious kick directly onto the knee, which collapsed under the assault and took its owner down with it, screaming from the intense pain of ruptured ligaments and a shattered patella. Jarek silenced the noise with a single kick to the fallen boy's jaw.

The attack was over in seconds but that was enough time for one of the other two to disappear. The third boy was rooted to the spot, arms by his sides, staring down at his unconscious mate. Jarek wasn't of a mind to be generous. Seconds later, there were two bodies lying there, out cold, and Jarek was walking calmly away through the throng of departing students. Most of them were utterly oblivious.

But the event that cemented him in the role of enforcer for hire happened many years later in 2009, the eve of his fortieth birthday. He'd lived in Prague for over a decade and was walking along a street near the Old Town Square, hand-in-hand with a woman he'd only been dating for a few days.

Her name was Erika and she was quite a beauty. Dark hair, darker eyes, high cheekbones, slender without being thin. In his opinion she was way out of his league. Erika was a friend of his cousin, who'd told him Erika was single.

This wasn't strictly true.

Neither Erika nor his cousin had thought to tell Jarek that he was the catalyst for her to dump her current boyfriend, Emil.

And, to top it all off, Emil was a nasty piece of work who was seriously pissed off at his newly single status.

The couple had been to a chamber music recital and were now heading for a late-evening supper. They turned a corner and found their way barred by Emil and several of his cronies. Erika helpfully whispered in Jarek's ear who this man was, and why he was standing in the middle of the pavement pointing a knife at them.

Jarek spotted immediately that Emil was the only one who was armed. He also detected a tremor in the aggressor's knife hand. Jarek didn't give Emil any opportunity to think. He didn't take any time to discuss, negotiate or plead. He simply launched his attack, specifically against the hand holding the knife.

Moments later, Jarek was entitled to assume that with Emil prostrate on the ground with a broken wrist and a lacerated forearm, his band of henchmen would melt away into the night. Not so. Two of the younger men flew straight at him, presenting more enthusiasm than danger. Jarek nullified the threat quickly and easily. It turned out those two were the infantry, the sacrificial lambs. The heavy artillery, in the shape of the remaining three, advanced on him with serious intent.

Although Jarek now had Emil's knife, the odds were stacked heavily against him. So this time he chose an alternative strategy, albeit with a high level of risk associated. Quickly appraising the two who had most recently fallen, he made a snap judgement on facial similarities between the nearest unconscious body and one of the advancing thugs. He knelt down, placed the knife against the teenager's throat and stared directly and evenly at the centre one of the three. 'Your brother, by any chance?'

Thugs two and three hesitated while they deferred to number one. 'He's my cousin. Hurt him, and you are a dead man.' He didn't look like he was bluffing.

The teenager was on his back, right arm splayed out across the cobbled street. The sleeve of his plain black t-shirt had ridden up, revealing his arm almost to the shoulder joint. Jarek moved his blade so it rested horizontally against the inside of the upper arm. He pushed hard enough to split the skin, which produced a light weal of blood along the line of the blade. 'Under here is the brachial artery. If I slice through it you'll have a choice. You can save him, if you're quick…' He paused to let that sink in. 'Or you can leave him to die while you come after me.'

The teenager's cousin glared at him. 'You wouldn't have the balls.'

Jarek cut the artery. Then a few things happened in rapid succession. A spurt of bright red arterial blood arced from the boy's arm; Jarek stood up and sprinted off in the opposite direction; the other man screamed and ran towards his cousin; and his two sidekicks froze solid, as if all their muscles had calcified.

It was only then that he realised Erika was nowhere to be seen. He stopped and spun round in a circle to try to locate her, but she had vanished. He jumped when a voice spoke to him from the shadows. A male voice. 'I wouldn't hang about if I were you, my friend. They'll get their act together in a minute then you will be in trouble.'

Jarek looked up to see a man, a few years his junior, leaning nonchalantly against the side wall of an alley that led off the street. His arms were folded casually and he wore an amused expression. 'I suggest you follow me. They're not likely to check up here.'

Jarek glanced past him. It looked like the alley came to a dead end against a brick wall a few metres in, but a dark slash to the left of the wall revealed a narrow exit. He hadn't a clue where it led but a chasing pack would almost certainly miss it. 'Why should I trust you?'

'Whether you do, or whether you don't, it's your call.' And with that, the man pushed himself away from the wall, turned and disappeared through the gap.

Jarek glanced back. All three men were crowded round the stricken teenager. Emil was struggling to his feet, his wounded arm held against his stomach. It wouldn't be long before they would begin looking for him so he walked into the alley and slipped through the gap.

12

Ross couldn't think of anyone else to contact. With Carla working out of Aberdeen, she had no work colleagues in Edinburgh. As was standard in their industry, when the team arrived back onshore they all went their separate ways, some via a multi-pint stopover in the pubs near Aberdeen railway station. Others flew further afield, even abroad, as Aberdeen was simply where they picked up the chopper that would take them to the vessel and bring them back again three weeks later.

So Carla didn't ever go to a work night out or even a Christmas party. Occasionally, senior management would issue a three-line whip to attend what they called *town hall* meetings, usually held in one of Aberdeenshire's more salubrious venues. She'd explained to Ross that she found these events totally irrelevant to her job but she had no choice so every now and again she'd disappear for a few days.

All this meant he hadn't met any of her co-workers. He assumed there were other husbands and wives in other locations in a similar position to him.

Carla had often spoken about a friend she met at spin classes down at the local gym but Ross struggled to recall her name. Ellie, was it? Or Ellen? He tossed them around for a few seconds and settled on Ellie, it sounded right to him. Not that it made any difference of course, he knew nothing about this Ellie, nothing at all.

His phone was charged again so he called Martin. Their friendship had endured through thick and thin since their student days. It was almost twenty-five years later when Martin found out his wife, Naomi, had been having an affair for over nine months. He told Ross about it the following day. '*Her tennis coach! How fucking clichéd is that?*' Funny thing was, both men had always thought the coach was as bent as a fiddler's elbow, so it just goes to show. The supreme irony was they were eventually caught *in flagrante* by one of Martin and Naomi's twin daughters, Beth, who was fifteen at the time. She'd asked her father to drive her down to the tennis club late one evening to pick up a racquet she'd left there, so Martin was sitting outside in the car when she came flying back out of the club, without her racquet. Although Beth was both angry and upset, she told her father in explicit terms what she'd just witnessed.

Martin drove his daughter home, preferring to distance her from such a distressing experience and from the confrontation he was about to have with his wife. But, minutes later, Naomi rushed in, concern for her daughter and guilt at being caught fighting for supremacy like two gladiators.

Through sheer bloody-mindedness, Martin offered Naomi the opportunity to explain herself, which she tried to do. Then he threw her out on her ear immediately she ran out of pathetic, lame excuses. Beth and her twin sister, Gail, decided in an instant to stay with their dad, and the coach dropped Naomi like a handful of molten glass.

'Hi. Martin Redpath's voicemail. If you want me to call you back, leave a message.'

Ross garbled a few words then regretted it immediately. He hoped he hadn't sounded too desperate and prayed Martin wouldn't call back that night, because his friend's off-the-shelf solution to most personal crises was booze, and usually enough to submerge a nuclear submarine.

He switched on the outside lights, opened the living room blinds, moved the armchair into the bay window so it faced the street, then switched off the lamps and settled down to wait.

If Ross thought he was going to be able to sit in that chair, waiting calmly for Carla to come home, he was way off the mark. Within seconds he began to imagine the worst possible outcomes. Carla was having an affair; Carla had been kidnapped; Carla was never coming back.

Carla was dead.

That one kicked him right in the nuts. He stood up and paced the room, trying to evade this constant barrage of dread. He tried changing the subject in his head, talking loudly over the possible Carla storylines, trying to chase them away.

And it worked.

Just not in the way he'd hoped. Because, what bubbled to the surface instead was the other major memory strand in his life: Liz.

And if the Carla thread was bad, that one was worse.

So much worse.

* * *

Ross was momentarily cheered as he recalled the time he and Liz had caught Martin humping that girl in their student flat. Liz recovered from that surprisingly quickly, but ripped the piss relentlessly out of her ex for wearing the bright orange condom. *'Carrot cock,'* she called him, whenever she felt like razzing him up.

After they stormed out of the flat they headed off to Liz's bedsit, about fifteen minutes away in Viewforth, on the other side of Bruntsfield Links. En route, they bought a bottle of vodka and some beer. There was about an inch left in the vodka and one unopened beer remaining when they crashed out.

The following afternoon, sporting matching hangovers, they went out for a long walk and discovered they were far closer to being kindred spirits than they'd ever imagined. Ross stayed the night, moved in to her flat a few days later and their relationship grew arms and legs from there.

Martin confessed much later that the girl, Cindy, had given him one hell of a bollocking because he'd promised her in the pub that he was single. Almost before the echoes of slammed doors from Liz and Ross's departure had died away, she was on her way downstairs leaving Martin sitting on the edge of his bed, staring at the open door.

Two years after Liz and Ross graduated, they were married and Martin was the best man. Liz refrained from saying anything untoward to his plus one, but late on she spotted him dancing with a different partner. His hands were everywhere and the woman didn't seem put out at all. She probably *will* drop her drawers, thought Liz, with a wry smile.

On a dismal dark December night, the eve of their twenty-third wedding anniversary, Ross was driving Liz home from a weekend in Perthshire when he misjudged the access lane to a contraflow set up for overnight construction works for the Queensferry crossing. Their car spun off the road into a stack of concrete pipes.

There didn't seem to be a mark on either of them but Liz took a bang to the temple from the doorpost of the car. She was unconscious for no more than a minute but recovered, apparently with no ill effects. The paramedics wanted to admit her to hospital for tests but she refused. 'Thanks for being so caring but I'm fine, honestly I am.'

They went to bed a few hours later but when Ross woke up in the morning he couldn't rouse her. An ambulance arrived within minutes and took her into Edinburgh Royal Infirmary, blue flashing lights and sirens all the way.

Just after eleven, the doctors told Ross and Martin that Liz had died without regaining consciousness. The post-mortem showed the cause was a subdural haematoma, almost certainly sustained as a result of the impact.

Ross buried his wife in a tiny churchyard just outside Gullane in East Lothian, overlooking the Firth of Forth. It was a horrible, windy, rainy day and Martin drove him home.

It was several months before he could bring himself to sit back behind the wheel of a car, and in his own words: 'I drive like an old woman now.'

* * *

So, between old memories of Liz and new fears about Carla, it turned out to be a long, long night for Ross, his spells in the armchair interspersed by short trips to the kitchen, the bathroom and the window. He didn't plan to sleep, he didn't want to sleep, but sleep he eventually did. But only for about an hour. Then he was awakened by a gentle, insistent tapping on the living room window.

The time was eight minutes past six.

13

When Jarek emerged into the open no one hit him on the head. He took that as a good sign. He was on the edge of a small courtyard. Pale lights from some rooms above cast a dirty glow, picking out broken glass and other detritus deposited there over the years. His mysterious benefactor was waiting at a wrought-iron gate on the opposite side of the area, which guarded a covered passageway between two buildings. As soon as he saw Jarek was following, he ducked through the gate, disappearing from sight yet again. This two-man, follow-my-leader procession continued for another few minutes as they crossed streets, courtyards and patches of waste ground before they eventually pushed through the back door of a long narrow bar. The two men slid sideways into a dimly-lit booth, which afforded uninterrupted views of both the front and back doors.

Neither man spoke while a po-faced, emaciated barman, wearing an apron that looked as though it been dragged behind a garbage truck for a week, dumped two beers on the table, muttered a few words in a dialect totally alien to Jarek, and stomped off.

Jarek raised his eyebrows and said, 'Na zdraví,' as he took a long slug of his beer.

'Cheers yourself. You're buying.'

'Fair enough, but there are a few things I'm curious about.'

'And they are?'

'Who are you, where did you spring from, and did you see where Erika went?'

'Ah. I'm sorry to say your date deserted you as soon as things kicked off.'

Jarek considered that. 'Her loss.'

'Not really.'

Jarek looked at him, one eyebrow raised.

'You're just a pawn, I'm afraid. Erika's done this several times over the years. Dumps Emil for a new boyfriend then goes back to him after a few days. He thinks he's controlling her but it's actually the other way round. Sadly, Emil hasn't worked that out yet.'

Jarek was warming to this stranger, whose amused expression seemed to be a semi-permanent fixture. 'And you know this Emil… how?'

'I've known him since we were kids. He was a year above me at school till he was put back a year for being stupid. He's an evil little shit and always has been. Why Erika sticks with him for any length of time, I have no idea. Anyway, earlier on, I dropped into a bar for a beer after work and there was Emil banging on about how some ugly-looking tosser, that would be you I suspect, has stolen his woman. And Emil wants to teach him a lesson. But Emil being Emil, he's too much of a coward to do it himself. He needs to be mob-handed. So he rounds up a posse, offering beers all round as a reward, and half a dozen of his mates tag along, thinking all they have to do is help kick some poor sap's head in, and then it's back to the bar on Emil's tab. Happy days.'

Jarek glanced around the bar. The place really was a dump. 'So you tagged along as well?'

'I did.'

'But why? If I'd been toiling, would you have jumped in?'

The other man shrugged. 'Who knows? But as it turned out, I didn't need to.'

He rocked his empty bottle back and fore on its base as he studied Jarek closely. 'You certainly know how to handle yourself. Impressive.'

Jarek tilted his head to one side and lifted his drink, acknowledging the compliment.

'And, I especially liked the trick with the artery.'

Jarek winced. 'I figured the leader would stop to help his cousin and not think to tell his goons to come after me. Luckily I wasn't dealing with the brightest bulbs in the chandelier but there's no doubt a severed artery creates the most dramatic effect. They got to him quickly, he'll be okay.'

Jarek now looked directly at his new companion. 'Well, you helped me out of a jam so I guess I should say thanks.' He held his hand out. 'Jarek Zelenka. I owe you one.'

'Miroslav Stepanek. You can start by buying me another beer. And while we're here, I have a proposition for you. From what I saw tonight, you have precisely the skill-set I need for a certain, how shall I put it, position within my organisation. Let me tell you about it...'

* * *

It had been over seven years since Miroslav had spelled out his proposal but Jarek had never been offered a position of any description. The name of the man from Ostrava didn't appear on personnel lists, in telephone directories or on any payroll run. But, then again, neither had any of the ninety-six operatives that Miroslav and Danijela had *employed* since their partnership began.

Of those ninety-six, almost all had been scrupulously honest in their dealings with Miroslav. But a handful had been caught with their fingers in the cookie jar. Jarek had paid them a visit to demonstrate the error of their ways in a fashion that could not be misunderstood. More frequently, relatives and friends of the operatives' victims intent on investigating Miroslav's business too closely had to be dissuaded from doing so. Most recently, this *dissuasion* involved two people in England. One had fallen from a high ladder and died, impaled on a spiked railing. The other had suffered a nasty fall in the street and succumbed to severe head injuries a few days later.

Jarek made a call to a close associate. The eighteen-hour drive to this place called Quimper, in the northwest corner of France, followed by an operation that was delicate in nature, was definitely a two-man job and one that required his colleague's specific skillset.

He stood up from the kitchen table, stretched and scratched at his chin. Then he opened the internal door to his garage, where he began gathering a comprehensive collection of hardware he would need for the next few days.

14

Saturday

Ross hadn't fully surfaced as he tottered towards the front door on legs that, following several hours in the armchair, hadn't quite grasped the fact their main purpose in life was to propel his body in a horizontal direction. A precious few seconds fell by the wayside while he fumbled his keys into the lock.

He yanked the door open to find his elderly neighbour, Joe, backing away from the doorstep as fast as his little legs could carry him. Ross knew Joe was the wrong side of seventy but probably attracted a quizzical look when he handed over his OAP card. This morning he was dressed for the elements: a red Berghaus jacket, grey fleece and black walking trousers. He never wore a hat. Even at his age he still possessed a full head of wiry white hair.

Joe wore a rather surprised expression, and, as he was reversing, his feet became entangled in his dog's lead. Bella, an ageing but still excitable Border Collie, yelped a couple of times, circled round and neatly extricated herself. Ross stepped forward to offer a steadying hand to save the old man from ending up on his backside.

'Morning, Bella.' He scratched the dog under her chin. 'Sorry, Joe. Didn't mean to startle you there.'

Joe tried to pretend nothing untoward had happened. 'I saw your lights were on so I came over to have a look, then I saw you sleeping in the chair. I just thought, better check he's okay. Sit, Bella.' And Bella sat. 'Good girl.'

'Thanks, Joe. Didn't quite make it to my bed last night.' Ross stopped there because he didn't know what to say next.

'Well, as long as you're okay.' Joe turned to walk away with Bella, who hadn't sat still for long. Then he stopped and half turned back, looking down at the doorstep. 'Joan said…' A glance up at Ross. 'Oh, never mind what Joan said. You're both all right, you and Carla?' He took a quick squint up at the bedroom window, where the curtains were still open. Their two houses were the same configuration so he knew perfectly well the master bedroom was to the front.

'Aye, Joe. We're fine, thanks. Everything's good.' Ross knew that was bullshit, and so did Joe, but Joe didn't bat an eyelid. He held his neighbour's gaze for just one second, tapped his index finger against the side of his nose then walked away down the path.

'I'll see you later, Ross. Shout if there's anything I can do. Come on, Bella, let's see if there's any rabbits about yet.' Bella immediately gave up on the bush she was sniffing and shot off towards the wood, extending her lead to the max and making Joe accelerate for a few steps.

Ross closed the door and switched off the outside light.

Don't think I'll be needing that.

15

RECEPTION DESK NOT MANNED. PLEASE RING BELL FOR ATTENTION.

Ross hadn't been able to duck the issue any longer, it was time to contact the police.

For over two hours that morning, he avoided the unavoidable. He made deals with himself. *I'll call them after I've had a shower. I'll check the local news first to make sure she hasn't been found wandering around Leith with amnesia. I'll wait till after eight o'clock because the shifts will probably change about then.* He knew his delaying tactics were all ridiculous, particularly the last one because he hadn't a clue when the Leith police nightshift knocked off.

So his phone remained untouched but he looked at it plenty. He tried to figure out what he would say to whoever answered his call. It would probably be a call centre, a back office function staffed by civilians, people whose partners hadn't ever gone missing. No, he didn't feel able to do this by phone.

He waited till half past eight and cycled the mile or two into Queen Charlotte Street, where the police HQ had been since way before his time. It was one of those crisp clear February mornings. The sun was still low on the horizon and the shallow angle meant it wasn't generating much in the way of heat.

He chained his bike to the spiked railing that separated the grimy Victorian sandstone building from the street, popped his cycle clips and helmet over the handlebars, and straightened the seams on his trousers before entering the building through a heavy revolving door.

He hesitated again before sticking his finger out to press the bell, and nearly jumped out of his skin when a female voice said, 'It doesn't bite, you know.' She had come through an open doorway to his left and was now standing behind the counter. She was tall, dark hair down to her shoulders with one side tucked behind her ear. Early forties, somewhere. 'How can I help you?'

Ross wasn't ready to answer questions quite as difficult as that. She smiled. 'Cat got your tongue?'

'I can't find my wife.' *God, that sounds so stupid.* The words had hardly cleared his teeth when the next lot came tumbling out like a bunch of skinny kids from a water flume. 'I mean, she's lost. We were in the supermarket, and she disappeared while I was picking up cashew nuts, and I can't find her. Anywhere.'

She must think I'm a complete fruit-loop. Ross, for heaven's sake, calm down.

She spoke in a quiet steady voice that was solid and reassuring. 'Let's have some details from you first, sir, and we'll take it from there. Okay?'

While she was rummaging around for a pen that worked, Ruth explained she was a civilian working with the police. She asked Ross a series of simple, logical questions that established the broad sequence of events beginning Friday evening. She then explained she would raise an incident with the control room, which would lead to uniformed officers visiting Ross to investigate. At this stage, the status was classed as a *Concern Call*. But if Carla didn't turn up, or if events escalated, she might be classed as vulnerable and the Concern Call would be upgraded to a Missing Person's Enquiry. At that point, the police would open an electronic missing person file.

He patted all his pockets for a tissue as it began to hit home that Carla was considered to be a missing person. 'We need to use that term to keep things straight, sir. And no, it's not too early to report your wife missing. You've done the right thing by coming in to see us this morning.'

Ruth explained the control room would make the area sergeant aware, and he would allocate a unit to attend at Ross's home address. The PCs would ask more detailed questions and conduct a search of the premises.

Ross hadn't even considered the police would need to visit the house but when Ruth told him why, it made perfect sense. 'You don't have a photo of your wife with you, and we'll need one to show staff at the supermarket. And, regarding the search, have you checked your garage or any other outbuildings?'

'But surely missing people don't turn up in their own garage, do they?'

Ruth's reply made his eyebrows lift. 'You'd actually be surprised how many times someone is reported missing, and they're in the garden shed all the time. In a huff, usually.'

Ruth didn't think the PCs would be at his house much before eleven but Ross said he'd go straight home anyway. He thanked her profusely for her kindness but she told him she was, 'Just doing my job.'

Outside, Ross felt so much better already. *At least something's happening now.*

He spun his bike in the direction of home, and was slinging his leg over the saddle when the lightbulb clicked on. He tapped his knuckles on the top of his helmet. *Wait a minute, why didn't I think of this before?* He turned the bike round again, picked a gap in the traffic and cycled off in the opposite direction.

* * *

Ross stepped aside to let a tall, athletic blonde wearing spray-on pink and navy-blue Lycra squeeze past on her way into the gym. She disappeared through a pair of frosted-glass swing doors leaving him loitering uncertainly in the foyer.

When Carla wasn't offshore, she visited the gym every Saturday morning for some class or another. He didn't think there was any chance she would be here this morning but it was certainly worth a try. He might also be able to find out if Ellie, or whatever her name was, attended the same class.

He heard a cough from behind the reception counter. All pale wood, glass and chrome, it was about four feet high including a shelf with gym literature and other paraphernalia. It took a second before he realised that a sphere that poked up from the middle of the desk wasn't pale wood, it was the shiny bald head of a very small man. Ross walked over to discover the bald head possessed glasses, and behind those was a pair of little beady eyes that did not transmit a welcoming air.

'Yes?' Blunt, and to the point.

'I'm trying to find out if my wife's here this morning. Her name's Carla McKinlay, has she come in?' Ross tried a smile in case that might help. He needn't have bothered.

'Heard that one before. Can't help you.'

Why on earth do people with the social skills of a football hooligan take jobs where they interact with the public? 'Look, I'm only trying to find out if she's here. Can't you check a register or something? It's really quite urgent.' Ross was annoyed he'd adopted a slightly pleading tone.

'There's no register, it's all electronic. Swipe cards. So, I don't see their names, therefore I don't know their names.' He leaned forward on spindly forearms, which pushed up the sleeves of his polo shirt to reveal biceps like pipe-cleaners. 'And you know what? I don't care what their names are, either.'

'Well, could I just take a quick peek in? Just to see.'

'You're not a member here?' Ross shook his head. 'Then no, you can't. And anyway, it's a ladies' class. They'd probably think you were some sort of pervert.' And with that, he turned his attention back to the red-top he was reading.

Ross was unable to form an appropriate retort, decided the conversation with this little ray of sunshine was going absolutely nowhere fast, and elbowed his way out the door. And, just to cap it all, the sun was posted missing and it had begun to rain. *Well, that's just bloody typical. Cheers!*

While cycling home through the steadily growing puddles, it dawned on him that he should have asked to speak to a manager or supervisor. But far too late, unfortunately.

And I didn't ask about Ellie. Buggeration!

* * *

Ross had been home for only a few minutes. He was in the bedroom with one leg out of his sodden trousers when the doorbell chimed. From his side of the bed he was just able to see the blue sign on the white roof of the police car. The rain was bouncing off it. *Perfect timing guys. Thanks.* He pulled his trouser leg inside out in his haste to drag them off, chucked on his dressing gown and rushed downstairs to the door.

Looking at the two policemen on the step he realised he must look a right dearie, standing there in his dressing gown, shirt and one sock. 'Sorry, I'm just in. I was out on my bike.' Both sets of eyebrows raised themselves below peaked caps as Ross ploughed on. 'I was at the police station. Well you know that of course, then I went to the gym. Not for exercise you understand, it was to see if my wife had gone to her class this morning.'

Jeez, Ross! What is it with the drivel?

He stopped then, to take a breath more than anything else.

Warrant card to the fore, the bell-ringer said, 'I'm PC Devlin, and this is PC Thomas. It's your wife we've come to speak to you about.' He paused. 'But do you think we could come in please, sir. It's kinda damp out here.'

'Of course. Sorry, forgot my manners. Just pop into the living room and make yourselves comfortable. I'll put on some clothes.'

When he walked back into the living room, PC Thomas was perched on the edge of the sofa. Fresh-faced was a perfect description. He had that still shiny appearance which suggested he hadn't been in the job that long. His older colleague, PC Devlin, although a good three inches shorter than Thomas, was carrying about three stone more. His bristly moustache made his face look round. He'd make a solid contribution to any police cordon.

Ross noticed that the officers had equipment hanging off several points on their uniforms. He wondered briefly if he was being filmed by one or both of their body-cams but chose not to ask.

Devlin was just replacing the photo of Ross and Carla on the speaker. It had been taken on the steps of the Registry Office in Leith eight months ago. Ross was wearing a morning suit while Carla looked radiant in a lilac skirt and jacket, with a cream silk camisole underneath. Her hair was up, and she was clutching a bouquet of cream roses in her left hand. Her right arm was hooked through her husband's left and she was goofing around, trying to avoid the deluge of rice and confetti being dumped on them by their wedding guests.

'That's Carla, my wife,' Ross said, stating the bleeding obvious yet again.

PC Devlin was clearly taking the lead. He snapped open a well-thumbed black notepad at a clean page, lifted a blue and silver Parker pen from a pocket in his gilet, clicked the top and positioned the point on the pad. 'I'd just like to confirm what we know already, Mr McKinlay, then we can move on. Okay with you?'

'Yes, certainly. But please, Ross'll do fine.' He sat down in the armchair.

'Happy to keep things informal, Ross. I'm Dave, and...' pointing, 'this is Lee.' A notepad and pen had appeared in Junior's hands too.

Dave Devlin positioned himself opposite Ross and spent the next few minutes reviewing what Ross had told Ruth at the station.

He asked Ross to describe Carla, so Ross gestured at the wedding photo. 'That doesn't tell me much, I'm afraid. You told Ruth that Carla's thirty-eight, five foot six, about nine and a half stone, and dark hair. But I'll need some specifics.'

So Ross told him that Carla was Italian, from the small town of Cervaro in the Lazio region to the south of Rome. She spoke English like a native, lightly accented but fluent. She had no relatives in the UK, just one sister back home but Ross hadn't met her or her family yet. Carla wore glasses for reading but not contact lenses. No distinguishing features, no tattoos, no piercings.

Then Devlin asked for their back-story. He explained they had met a year past Christmas, at his work's bash in a hotel on George Street. It was one of those horrific bring-a-party-to-a-party things, she'd been in a different part of the room, and they met at the bar while he was ordering a round. It turned out they were both bored witless, they had a couple of sneaky shots at a little side bar then came over all rebellious and did a runner to one of Rose Street's more raucous establishments. A real pub, with real ale and real people. They discovered they had a lot in common, hit it off immediately, met again the following night in the same bar, and that was that.

'So if that was Christmas 2014, when were you married?'

'Last July, 2015.'

'So,' Devlin did the maths, 'about six, seven months later.'

'That's right.' Ross knew what was coming next. Most people followed a similar line.

'You didn't hang about then?'

56

'What can I say? We met, we fell in love, we got married. At our age there was no point in a two-year engagement, was there?'

Devlin then asked if there was a photo he could borrow. Ross angled a hand towards the unit under the window. 'That's the only one I have. She detests her photo being taken and if we go anywhere, Carla uses her phone. She's the photographer in the family but she tends to take photos of scenery and buildings, not people.'

'What about a wedding album?'

'They don't do that in Italy, apparently. Or at least they don't where she comes from, so she didn't want one. And don't get her started on wedding videos.'

'Is she on Facebook or Instagram?'

Ross hesitated. 'I don't *think* she's on Facebook. And I've never even seen Instagram, so I wouldn't have a clue.'

Devlin pointed at Ross's mobile. 'None on your phone?'

'I know the phone has a camera but it doesn't really interest me so I've never used it.'

Devlin drew his head back a little and blinked a couple of times. Ross gestured towards the device. 'My old mobile was a Nokia, had it for years. It did all I needed it to do. I could phone people and send texts. Carla's always nagging me about how old-fashioned I am, and she's right. She pestered me to upgrade to an iPhone or something but I didn't want one, didn't see the need. Then I lost the Nokia somewhere so I had to buy a smartphone.' He smiled. 'Well Carla bought it for me, actually. But I still just use it for phone calls and texts. I could probably send an email if I tried but I haven't bothered.'

Devlin suppressed a smirk. *Christ, the guy's only fifty. It's not true what they say, dinosaurs aren't extinct after all.*

The policeman moved on. 'Can you describe what your wife was wearing in the supermarket, please?'

Ross leaned down and picked a crumb off the carpet. 'This is going to sound daft but, apart from her black jacket, I honestly can't be certain.' He looked at Devlin for some sign of empathy but the PC's face was totally expressionless.

'I'll need a description, Ross. Please try to remember.'

Ross gave Devlin a blank look so the constable tried prodding him. 'Anything missing from her wardrobe, for example? A coat hook without a jacket, maybe? It's winter, so would she have had boots on?'

Ross nodded and stood up. 'Give me a minute, I'll go upstairs and check.'

The two PCs shared a glance. 'Dodgy?' said Thomas. Devlin just shrugged.

Ross was speaking as he came back in. 'She was definitely wearing her black Puffa jacket. It's not upstairs. Probably jeans too, but I can't be certain. And I can't see her black ankle boots. They're suede, or nubuck, or something like that.'

Devlin looked up from his notepad. 'What about a scarf? Hat? Gloves? Handbag?'

Ross thought for a few seconds. 'She doesn't wear scarves so that's a no. I seem to think she had a pompom hat on. But hats are one of Carla's things, she's got a drawer full of them. I'd have absolutely no idea if one was missing.'

'What colour?'

'Again, not sure. I don't think she had it on in the store, you see. Probably stuck it in her pocket. Same with the gloves.'

'Handbag?'

'A little black rucksack. Leather, not a sporty one.'

After his last entry, Devlin wrote: *Monochrome!*

But at least they now had something to work with.

Then he asked Ross to talk them through the events of the previous evening, starting from when Carla disappeared inside the supermarket. He asked for the names of the staff but Ross had only registered the manager, Steve Carroll. He described the friendly redhead with the pierced gum but he couldn't remember much about her polar opposite on Customer Services.

'We'll visit the supermarket later,' said Devlin. 'Find out who you spoke to.'

Ross told them about meeting Joan but as it had been such a brief discussion, Devlin didn't seem all that interested although he did jot it down. He became slightly more animated about the phone calls to Sally and Amanda but that tailed off when Ross explained neither of them had seen Carla recently.

Then Devlin asked about their car. Ross told him Carla definitely had the key because she had driven to the supermarket.

'Would she normally be the driver?'

Ross stood up and dropped the crumb into a wicker bin. 'We kinda share it, but Carla drove last night because she picked me up from the house. She'd been in town, shopping.' He dropped back into the chair.

'And where did you park?'

'Out in the open area, a couple of rows away from the building.'

Devlin was familiar with the car park. He knew it had a covered section at ground level and an open area about twice the size. 'That seems a bit strange, if you don't mind me saying. It was pouring down last night but you didn't park under cover?'

'It's usually much busier under cover and the spaces are tight because of all the pillars. My wife's not the best at parking so if she's driving, we're always outside.'

Then the PC asked Ross to describe everything he'd done after returning home from the supermarket. At one point, Devlin paged back through his notes. 'You've mentioned Joan from number seventeen but did you check with any of the other neighbours?'

Ross felt the blood surging into his cheeks. 'Em. Well, no. I haven't, actually.'

Devlin had been leaning well back on the sofa, one leg crossed over the other. But now he sat forward, elbow on his knee. Thomas also seemed to be paying much closer attention. Devlin tapped his pen against his top lip. The room was so silent they could hear the kitchen clock ticking from two rooms away. 'Why not, sir?' The last word of Devlin's question hung heavily in the air.

Ross had been trying to present an air of calm but that swiftly evaporated. The seam on his trouser leg became terribly interesting, as he plucked non-existent pieces of fluff from the grey material. He looked up at Thomas, then at Devlin. 'I don't know. I really don't know. I didn't think of it.'

The two PCs didn't speak, they just waited to hear how Ross would follow that up. Elbows on the arms of the chair now, he turned both his palms up. 'Honestly, it just didn't occur to me.' Back in control again, he continued, tapping each of the fingertips of his right hand with his left index finger. 'Next door's empty. It's never been sold. Joan and Joe? Well, she's just a nosey old bat so I don't speak to her if I can help it. And Carla can't stick her, either.' He pointed out the window to his left. 'The couple who live over there are French, I think. But I've never spoken to them apart from good morning. Stuff like that.'

'Barry at number eighteen, single guy. I play tennis with him on a Saturday and sometimes during the week. But Barry goes out on the town every Friday night, without fail. I suppose I knew he wouldn't be in so I didn't even consider asking him.' Ross waved his hand further to the right. 'I don't know anyone else in the street. I wouldn't recognise them if I found them in my soup. It's a new development, this area, and some families moved in over the winter, so there haven't been too many opportunities to meet people. And that's pretty much that…'

His voiced tailed off as he looked at each of them in turn, settling back on Devlin.

'Okay. No worries. We'll be speaking to the neighbours.'

Ross had anticipated they would but still he groaned. It was bad enough that Joan would find out. The woman would be in her element. But he did feel guilty he hadn't told Joe what was going on.

Devlin picked up again. 'You said you went to a gym. Why was that?'

Ross told them all about the jobs-worth he'd spoken to. 'A right pain in the backside, he was.' He also told them about Carla's friend but had to confess he couldn't remember if her name was Ellen, Ellie or something else entirely.

'We'll ask for their membership records.' Then added, with some feeling, 'He'll talk to us.'

Devlin tried another tack. 'Have you called her sister?'

That was easier for Ross to answer. 'I couldn't even if I wanted to. For one thing, Caterina, that's Carla's sister, she doesn't speak English. And Carla always called her from her mobile so I don't even know the number.'

'She didn't come over for the wedding?'

'No, Caterina and Allesandro have four young kids and they couldn't afford it. We offered to pay but they wouldn't hear of it. Too proud to accept, I think. We're planning to visit them for a couple of weeks in the summer, when Carla's back onshore.' Ross broke eye contact and scratched at his cheek. 'I've to meet the whole family, apparently there's dozens of them. Quite a daunting prospect.'

'What about her work colleagues?'

Ross told them about Carla's job offshore and that none of the people she worked with lived in Edinburgh, or anywhere nearby. He gave them the name of the offshore company but explained that Carla was technically employed by an agency. She was contracted out but he couldn't remember the name of the agency off the top of his head. Devlin looked him in the eye. It seemed to him there was a lot that Ross couldn't remember.

Ross quickly said he'd find a pay-slip and hand it in to the station.

The policeman put his notebook and pen away and stood up. He placed his hands in the small of his back and stretched out a bit. Thomas followed suit but without the stretching.

'I think I have enough information for now, but I'd like to look around the house and the garage. By the way, do you have a garden shed?' Ross nodded. 'We'll have a quick look in the car too.' Ross began to stand up but Devlin put out his hand. 'Just on our own this time, if that's okay.'

Ross started to speak but Devlin continued, 'Tell you what, you fetch the keys and we'll be back in a jiffy.' He jerked his head in Thomas's direction, and the two of them disappeared into the hall and up the stairs.

After a few seconds, Ross followed them out the door. He heard them moving from room to room, opening and closing doors. When they came back down, Devlin had a cursory glance into the dining room.

Ross handed over the keys then leaned against the sink to wait. When the PCs came back in, Devlin dropped the keys in Ross's outstretched palm. 'Everything looks neat and tidy upstairs. Even the bed's made, clearly you're very domesticated. Wish I was.' A short pause. 'The wife wishes I was, too.'

Devlin sniggered at his own joke but Ross was in no mood for humour. *At least you know where your wife is.*

'Can you tell if any of her personal things are missing? Work clothes, cases, anything like that?'

'Nothing as far as I can see. Her work clothes are all in the back bedroom, and I've checked all our bags are in the loft.'

'Do you know if her passport's in the house?'

That hadn't occurred to Ross. She used it all the time for work but he had no idea where she kept it when she was home. 'I don't know. I'll have a look and let you know.'

Devlin looked over at Thomas, and they started to leave but Ross stopped them. 'Hang on a minute, will you? What happens now? What are you going to do next?' He jerked his thumb at his chest. 'And what about me? Is there anything I should be doing?'

Devlin turned halfway back towards Ross. 'We'll go and talk to your neighbours, and ask if they saw Carla at any point yesterday evening or this morning. If they're out, we'll leave a note asking them to contact us. Then we'll go to the supermarket and talk to the staff.' He ticked off a third finger. 'And, we'll have a word with mister Grumpy at the gym.'

Devlin then suggested Ross should do whatever he thought was right. Check with their friends, try to think of anywhere else she might go, and look for her if he wished. Or he could stick close to home. It was entirely up to him.

Devlin handed Ross a card. 'If your wife turns up, please let us know. But we'll be back in touch anyway. Possibly tonight, more likely tomorrow. It really depends.' He paused for a second. 'I hope she does turn up, and soon. Make sure to let us know if she does.' Devlin then offered his hand, Ross shook it, and the PCs went out to their car.

Ross didn't trust himself to speak so he mumbled his thanks at their departing backs. He closed the door behind them, slid down on his haunches with his back against the door, and stared into middle distance for what seemed like a long, long time.

16

Half an hour later, Ross was back at the kitchen table writing a list of things he thought he should do next. He'd had a minor meltdown, and might well have another but once he regained equilibrium he gave himself a talking to and decided he needed an action plan.

He scanned his list, and typical of Ross, he numbered the items in the order he intended to attack them. He was satisfied he'd covered everything, and could see how his afternoon was panning out, which gave him a positive buzz. *Right, let's crack on.* He climbed the stairs to their little office where Carla kept the household filing, leaned his shoulder against the door jamb and gazed into the room without really registering anything.

When he and Liz had graduated, Ross had gone straight into a corporate position with an accountancy firm based close to the west end of Princes Street. The company was safe, solid, steeped in tradition, and structured so tight it could hardly breathe. It had suited Ross down to the ground and he stayed there for the next twenty-five years. His rise in the company was gradual rather than spectacular although he didn't make partner and had no desire to.

Liz had piloted her career through different waters. With her degree in Marketing and Business Management tucked safely in her back pocket, she knew from the outset she wanted to start her own business and be in charge of her own destiny. For three years she had a part-time job in a marketing and design company on the south side of Edinburgh, where she learned every aspect of that operation. In parallel, she worked a series of short-term jobs in recruitment, personnel, sales and operations, which gave her a fully rounded view of how to run a business. Liz worked in bars and restaurants during any gaps, and Ross supported her by covering almost all the domestic chores and responsibilities.

When Liz felt she possessed all the ingredients necessary to be successful, she jumped straight in and launched her business. She raised some seed capital from grant funding,

Ross was able to contribute and they borrowed a small amount from the bank.

Ecosse Business Development Ltd was born in spring 1993 and hit the streets at a canter. Liz had been stockpiling a warehouse of strategies, concepts and ideas, and she immediately started hiring the best people, and cultivating her most fruitful contacts. Her business soared like an untethered hot air balloon, practically from day one. She loved the work and she loved business but it had a voracious appetite for consuming time and energy. Weaker marriages would have gone under. But Ross was always willing and happy to play the support act to her rock celebrity because they were orchestrating a plan that was designed to come to fruition in time for their fiftieth birthdays.

With the prescience of a world-class mystic, Liz sold out to a competitor in early 2008 while the world's most devastating recession lurked in the tall grass like a leopard waiting to pounce on an unsuspecting goat. Liz pocketed just short of one and half million then, uncharacteristically, dilly-dallied over where to invest her windfall and it was still in a high interest current account when the leopard struck. The value of investments worldwide plummeted but her money sat there in cash, untroubled by the financial crash. A classic piece of fannying about, according to Martin.

Kismet, however, was on hand to bring the curtain down. Through an over-reliance on financial institutions, Edinburgh suffered that particular recession far longer than other UK regions and just as the city was beginning to emerge, bleary-eyed, from beneath a suffocating blanket of austerity they were involved in that terrible car accident. When Liz died in 2014, the money was still in cash. A few months later, Ross instructed their financial adviser friend to: 'Stick it somewhere safe. I'll decide what to do with it at some point.'

Several months later he met Carla, and when they set up house together after they were married, Ross was delighted that his new wife took over most of his domestic responsibilities. '*The woman runs the house. The man takes care of the woman,*' according to her late mother, apparently.

Carla's filing system made a Swiss bank look like a model of chaos so it only took him a few seconds to locate her latest pay-slip from the agency. Based on the top line, Carla earned a decent salary but her take-home pay didn't reflect that. She told Ross that for several years before she met him, she'd paid a hefty premium into a personal pension plan because her view was quite clear. Look after number one because no one else will. Particularly the government. *Difficult to argue with, that one.* He was openly pleased she'd adopted such a pragmatic view.

Next stop, her passport. He'd made a quick appraisal of Carla's wardrobe the previous night but knew he'd been in a flap. *This time I'll check a bit more thoroughly.* He looked through her clothes and shoes again but came to the same conclusion. Nothing significant was missing.

He opened the chest of drawers below the window. Four of the six drawers contained her scarves, gloves, hats, socks and woolly tights, and underwear. He ruffled through the first three without hesitation but paused in the act of opening the fourth drawer. When Ross folded the laundry he didn't ever put her underwear away, he left it stacked on a chair for her to file accordingly. Privacy was something he cherished and this felt like an invasion. Not Normandy Landings in scale, but still…

He breathed in once, tugged at the handle and the drawer slid towards him on steel runners, bumping to a stop against his knee. He ran the palm of his hand lightly over the pool of colourful satin and silk items neatly ordered from left to right. Bras, panties, camisoles. Then things became more interesting. Basques, suspenders, stockings, a sheer white nightdress. The left side of the drawer was distinctly pastel, the right side mainly pinks, reds and blacks. But no passport.

Only one place remained and he never, ever looked in there. But he knew he had no choice. Perched on Carla's side of the bed with his right foot tucked underneath his left thigh, he hesitated for even longer before leaning forward and reluctantly opening the only drawer in her bedside cabinet. His conscience nudged him in the ribs. *'You're not supposed to be in here.'*

Batting the thought away to left field he opened his wife's personal drawer for the first time. A disparate collection of items returned his gaze: lip balm, hand cream, a blue foil sachet containing a flavoured condom, a sleek black and chrome vibrator, a silver Papermate pen, a plastic wallet containing coffee shop loyalty cards, a string of rosary beads. And, tucked inside a white A5 envelope, an embossed burgundy booklet with gold writing on the front cover:

UNIONE EUROPEA; REPUBBLICA ITALIANA; PASSAPORTO

Ross didn't know whether to laugh or to cry. So he indulged in a little bit of both, more or less at the same time.

17

PC Devlin had suggested earlier that if Ross thought he should go out searching for Carla he should do exactly that. So he debated what his wife might do if this was a normal day. Clearly this day was far from normal but as he was trying his best to remain positive, he intended to follow up on Devlin's suggestion.

There was a limit to how far he was prepared to venture from home but he couldn't see the point in sitting around staring at however many walls the house possessed. *Anyway, what would I do? Wash the car?*

Although Ross realised it was a faintly ridiculous idea, he reasoned if Carla was to be anywhere in public she would head for the bustling New Town enclave of Stockbridge, one of her favourite haunts. Originally a small outlying village, Stockbridge was incorporated into the City of Edinburgh in the nineteenth century. If you asked a native of the city to define Stockbridge, they would probably mention Raeburn Place, with its eclectic assortment of boutiques, arty-crafty little shops, cafes, restaurants, pubs and general bourgeoisie. But on the other side of the Water of Leith is St Stephen Street, choc-a-bloc with yet more niche establishments selling second-hand designer clothes, vinyl records, more antique shops than you could shake a stick at and the fantastically-named Mr Purves' Lamp Emporium.

Yes, if I'm going to look for her, Stockbridge is as good a place as any.

He left another voicemail and sent another text but only because he thought he should. His heart certainly wasn't in it. He scribbled a note to say where he was heading, and propped it up against the kettle.

He wheeled his bike out of the garage and had yet another pointless look up and down the street. He didn't see a soul as he cycled off.

After he handed Carla's passport and payslip in to the police station, Ross worked his way across town in a series of gradually rising zigzags, and about quarter of an hour later he was pedalling along Henderson Row, past the dramatically named Saxe Coburg Street, and into Stockbridge proper.

He chained his bike to the bridge, a stone structure over two centuries old that had replaced the original *stock brig*, the Scots words meaning timber bridge, from which the area took its name. While he debated where he would look first, Ross recalled the TV and film cliché, where the hero, searching for his damsel, would spot someone who looked exactly like her from the rear. He would run across and place a mightily relieved hand on the woman's shoulder only to discover, surprise surprise: mistaken identity.

Ross was under no illusions. There would be no false sightings, and so it proved. Moving at window-shopper's pace he looked in every shop, every café, every pub. Nothing.

He decided to hang around the area for a while so he stopped in at a coffee shop. He only intended to have a coffee then he realised just how hungry he was, and a chicken and bacon panini seduced him from the front row of the chilled cabinet. The young barista who served him was a bit flash, spinning the crockery and cutlery up onto the tray with a magician's flourish, and topping off the coffee with an intricate fern pattern. But he was good fun, and so unfeasibly happy in his work that Ross couldn't stop himself laughing at the lad's patter. *How do they keep these kids so motivated on such crap wages?*

From his seat at the window he could keep watch along the pavement to left and right. Legions of shoppers, mostly well-laden at this late stage in the day, traipsed past the window but none of them were Carla. He began to feel a little cheated. *Not even a vague resemblance. Not like on the telly.*

Definitely the longest of long shots, he thought to himself as he freed his bike, swung his leg over the frame, and debated his next move. Amanda's offhand comments on the phone still rankled and although the prospect made him anxious, he called her again.

'Hi. Amanda, Tom and the boys can't take your call just now. Leave a message, and one of us will call you back. Thanks.'

Ross had his elbow on the bridge parapet, and the palm of his hand flat against his forehead as he listened to her voice.

He had no clue what to say, and he hesitated for so long the voicemail system beeped twice and cut him off.

'Oh, shit!' to himself, and, 'Oh, sorry,' to an elderly lady who was glaring daggers as she side-stepped him on the pavement, pulling her tartan shopping trolley behind her and bashing it off his bike. Ross dropped his phone into his pocket, paused, and lifted it straight back out again.

He mulled it over for a few seconds, then redialled. 'Amanda, hi, it's Ross. Listen, Carla still hasn't come home and, well, obviously I'm really worried. As you can imagine. I've been to the police so they're... making enquiries.' *Well what else do you say?*

'Anyway, if you know where she is, could you call me right away please?'

Now the tricky bit. 'And Amanda... last night... on the phone... I didn't know what you meant by... well, I just didn't know what you meant. So can we talk please, one way or the other? Thanks.'

Ross had trouble disconnecting the call. His hand was shaking like an alcoholic coming off a three-day bender. But he'd overcome another hurdle, one he knew he'd been avoiding.

He looked down at the phone to turn the screen off. His recent calls were still showing and in the list above Amanda was House. *Worth a try, I suppose.* But the house phone remained unanswered. He'd probably have fallen into the Water of Leith through shock if Carla *had* picked up.

With nothing else to do but head for home, Ross bumped his bike onto the road and joined the rush-hour traffic. Which was the main reason he didn't hear his ringtone.

18

'You calling him back?'

Tom had been down at the playing fields earlier to cheer on his son's football team and hadn't yet changed out of his t-shirt and tracksuit bottoms. He needed a shave too but hadn't bothered as he and Amanda weren't going out that night.

He was leaning against the frame of the kitchen door, arms folded. He arched an eyebrow at his wife, knowing his question was as good a way as any to waste four words.

'Am I hell.'

'Do you know where Carla is?'

'No idea. And even if I did, I wouldn't tell *him*.'

'And the reason?'

Amanda wasn't long back from lunch with her sister. She hadn't changed yet either but had put on a green cotton apron to protect her dress jeans and red sleeveless top. She'd tied back her shoulder-length red hair while she prepared dinner. She swished some onions round a sizzling pan, tutting as a crescent of miniscule spots of oil sparked onto the gleaming brushed aluminium hob. She ripped a sheet of kitchen paper from the roll and smeared the oil away.

'Do I need a reason?'

'It would make more sense if you did.'

'Oh. So I'm not making sense then, am I?'

Joy, thought Tom. Another enthralling evening looms. 'Suit yourself.' He lifted the *Edinburgh Evening News* from that day's stack of pre-recycling and headed for his recliner in the den. His younger son, Richard, was in there too. Wired for sound, scribbling in a school notebook, and intermittently watching recorded highlights of Tottenham Hotspur playing some Portuguese mob.

'What's the score, Rickie?'

'Two-nil, Spurs. A penalty and an own goal. Dodgy ref.'

Tom smiled and ruffled Richard's hair. The kid can listen, write, watch and speak. All at the same time. 'Aren't they all?' he said, as he settled down to read the paper.

Back in the kitchen, Amanda had watched her husband going into the den before eventually uttering: 'Arse.'

She threw some mushrooms in the pan and reached for the kitchen roll again.

19

'So, what's the story with the missing Mrs McKinlay then, Dave?' asked Divisional Sergeant Ronnie Cockburn, full concentration on his keyboard as he tapped out an operational report.

Cockburn was short for a police officer and had clearly ceased any form of aerobic exercise a long time ago. Even on a cold day he sweated buckets. Very thin on top, his hairstyle comprised half a dozen strands of slicked black hair running from back to front.

He was also one of police life's little mysteries. He hardly ever looked up from his desk, rarely ventured out from behind it unless summoned from above, yet he knew every damned thing that was happening on his patch. And well before anyone else, it seemed. His nickname was Radar, after Walter Eugene *Radar* O'Reilly, the apparently psychic corporal from the legendary film and TV series: M*A*S*H. Radar's party piece was to report he'd just completed an assignment for his commanding officer, just as the CO was about to issue said assignment to his clairvoyant subordinate.

So PC Dave Devlin had no idea how Ronnie knew he was even in the Area Control Room, or that Dave would be reporting in on his and Lee's activities that day. Dave had been trying unsuccessfully to catch Ronnie out for months, sneaking up on him from all directions in vain attempts to reach the desk unnoticed. One time, he entered and crossed the room, hidden all the way behind Mick Moffat, a six foot seven giant of a PC, who, as part of the subterfuge, was carrying a huge empty cardboard box. Just as their little caravan was on final approach, Ronnie piped up without a trace of humour, 'Shift your arse out the way, Mick. I need Dave to update me on that assault in Admiralty Street.'

While PC Thomas had been driving them back to the station, Devlin had radioed in his report to one of the Control Room team. Normally, he would also have updated his own sergeant but the officer he spoke to explained that Devlin's supervisor was out, investigating the death of a young woman whose body had been found in a lane behind the Leith Malmaison. The controller asked Devlin to come into the Control Room and update Sergeant Cockburn himself.

Devlin was nothing if not efficient. He described everything he and his colleague had done starting with their canvass of the residents. As he'd imagined, not many of Ross's neighbours had been at home, only Joe from those that Ross was acquainted with. Joan was away for the weekend visiting her sister in Crieff. No one had seen Carla. Devlin planned to make another sweep in the early evening, and had typed up notes to drop through the letterboxes of anyone who still wasn't home, asking them to contact the station if they could help.

'The first place we checked was the gym. The guy on reception wasn't the most helpful but he confirmed Mrs McKinlay is a member.' Devlin checked his notes. 'She was there for a spin class last Saturday morning, and again on Tuesday afternoon but she hasn't been in since.' Devlin turned a page in his notebook. 'McKinlay mentioned a woman his wife was friendly with. He said Ellie or Ellen but they don't have an Ellie or an Ellen on their membership. Two Helens, though. I have their numbers and I'll follow them up this evening too.'

But Devlin's next statement certainly captured Ronnie Cockburn's attention. 'Mr McKinlay's tale has a wife-sized hole in it, Sarge.' The sergeant stopped typing immediately and swung round in his chair as his officer continued. 'We spoke to the Store Manager, who seemed really switched on. He thought McKinlay was genuine. But then we had a look through the footage from the car park cameras. McKinlay told us his wife drove to the store but it was him that got out of the driver's side.' He paused for an instant. 'And no one got out the passenger's seat, as far as we could see.'

Cockburn made a *hmmm* sound, patted down an errant strand of hair and waved Devlin to keep talking.

'But, it's fair to say the quality of the film's not brilliant, Sarge. The lighting in the car park's not the best, he parked about as far from a security camera as he could, and it was pissing down at the time.'

The sergeant held up a hand. 'Are we suspicious about where he parked? I mean, how's the coverage in the car park?'

'I don't know about suspicious. It *was* Friday evening, which can be a busy time. That could've been why they parked outside.'

Cockburn rocked his head from side to side, indicating he was at least considering the idea as a possibility.

'Okay, Dave. Still doesn't explain why he said she was driving, though.' Cockburn pondered for a few seconds. 'What about the instore cameras?'

Devlin hitched his bum onto the edge of the sergeant's desk. 'According to McKinlay, they didn't get very far through their shopping before she sent him to pick up these cashew nuts.

'And those first few aisles were busy?'

Devlin nodded. 'But he's quite obvious, appears a few times going up and down the aisles, but not her. As far as I can see, anyway. According to him, his wife was wearing all blacks and greys like any number of other women in those aisles. She might have had a hat on, she might not. Can't remember, he says. But, from what we saw, he looks like he's on his own in the store.'

'Right. Put that to one side for the moment. Let's imagine she has actually gone missing. What've we got?'

Devlin checked his notes. 'Including when he said they first arrived at the store, McKinlay appears on video at the entrance at all the right times, both coming in and going back out. There's a second exit that opens onto a walkway to the car park. Video quality's not so good there, one of the lights is bust. But in the timeframe he says she went missing, no females fitting her description left through either door. There were several couples as you would expect, but they were all either pushing trolleys or lugging bags. No sign of anyone coercing a woman to leave.' Cockburn had gone back to typing his report but Devlin knew to keep talking. It would all be sinking in.

'Hospitals?'

'They've all been checked out. No women recently admitted who fit Mrs McKinlay's description. But they know we're looking, and we'll try them again tomorrow, just in case.'

Cockburn bashed the *Enter* key and sat back with his hands clasped behind his head, looking up at Devlin. 'So, what are you thinking?'

Devlin rubbed his chin. 'Apart from this discrepancy about who was driving, and the fact we can't identify her in the store, in truth, we've nothing concrete to go on. There's absolutely no evidence any crime's been committed, so it could still be something domestic. Or he could be a nutcase who's made the whole thing up, but I don't think so.'

'Could she have a bit on the side?'

'There's always that chance, Sarge. After all, she's about twelve years younger than him. Italian, and a bit tasty too, from what I could see.'

'Okay, Dave. Well done. You leave it there and let me think about it. Before you finish tonight, call McKinlay and remind him to let us know if his missus turns up. Pick it up again when you come back on shift in the morning, and if she's still missing we'll pass it to CID.'

'Will do.' Dave Devlin turned away, wondering just how the bloody hell Cockburn knew he'd swapped for a morning shift, considering he'd only arranged it with a colleague about fifteen minutes earlier.

'I'll just need to get up earlier,' he sighed, as he pushed his way through the swing door to leave the Control Room.

20

Ross's route home to Newhaven from Stockbridge was fairly flat so his progress was relatively speedy. Once he crossed Ferry Road, a four mile long, poker-straight road that connected Leith with Davidson's Mains, another of Edinburgh's original outlying villages, he passed through the expensive suburb of Trinity, where Amanda and Tom Duncan lived. As he was cycling down Trinity Road he stopped at a junction, their detached sandstone villa was only a couple of streets to his left.

There was definitely something up with Amanda, that much was obvious, and Ross knew he needed to find out what it was. There was a good chance she and her husband would be home right now. Both were creatures of habit. For years Tom had coached the junior football teams at the local school, while Amanda ferried their children to and from their various sporting and social activities. But it was common knowledge that around five o'clock virtually every Saturday, the car keys were ditched and a minimum two bottles of red wine, and frequently more, were consumed in the Duncan household.

He steered his bike in the direction of their house but after only a few metres, he abruptly changed his mind and chickened out. He made a tight turn in front of a driveway that curved through rhododendrons to a small Victorian mansion, typical of the area. Ross was disappointed he'd bottled it, but he reasoned that whatever Amanda's problem was, it might be resolved by tomorrow. *I'll definitely go and see her on Sunday.*

He had just finished executing his U-turn when his phone rang. As far as Ross knew, it was the first time since Carla had gone missing. He nearly jumped out of his shirt. He jammed on the anchors and grabbed for his pocket, but his woolly-gloved fingers didn't have a proper grip and the ringing phone squirmed from his grasp, collided with the bike frame and landed with a plasticky slap in the gutter. He was aghast as the phone broke into its three main components: front, back and battery. He was slow to react as the battery skittered towards a grating. At the last second, he stuck out a foot and prevented it from plopping into the mud-laced water but the scraping sound the battery made under the sole of his shoe left him wondering if it would survive his attempt to save it.

He laid his bike down, whipped off his gloves, and gathered up the three pieces, carefully wiping mud away from the battery terminals with the fleecy lining of his sleeve.

Desperate to find out who had called, he snapped the phone back together. He turned it over and tapped the screen to check for the missed call. When the phone didn't respond, he thought at first it was broken. *Muppet. It's powered off.* Ross jabbed at the switch and waited for the better part of an eternity before the home screen appeared, then several seconds more before the signal bars became visible.

Two missed calls? How the hell did that happen?

He navigated through the menus till he located the calls log, then selected the missed calls list. Ross didn't do shortcuts. There was one number he didn't recognise, while the other one read: Martin Mobile.

He tapped the first number. *Please God, let this be Carla calling from another phone. And by the way, God, if this turns out to be one of those flamin' PPI calls, I'll go absolutely apeshit.*

He could feel his pulse thumping at his temple as he clamped the phone to his ear. 'Come on, answer the bloody phone.'

'Hello. PC Dave Devlin speaking.'

The tension in his gut dissipated like dust falling through chicken-wire. 'Oh. Hi, Dave. It's Ross McKinlay here. I see you've called my mobile. Sorry I missed your call.'

Sorry I missed your call? What a terminally stupid thing to say.

'Aye. No worries, Ross. Just a quick update.' Ross knew people's ears didn't actually prick up but if they were capable of that, his would definitely have done so. 'Although, I'm sorry to say I've nothing new to report.' Devlin carried on to relate more or less the same story he'd told Ronnie Cockburn earlier, that he'd spoken to more neighbours who hadn't seen Carla, and that he'd tracked down two Helens who hadn't met her at all.

He could have saved his breath: Ross had hardly heard a word the policeman said after *nothing new to report*.

Devlin closed by promising he would call again in the morning with any further updates, and extracted a similar promise from Ross that he would contact the police if Carla came home. Ross mumbled his agreement and disconnected.

This tidal surf of emotions, hope and expectation, followed by despair and disappointment, repeat as necessary, was beginning to wear him down and his eyes brimmed up again. A black BMW X5 drove slowly by and while the driver paid him little attention, his female passenger wouldn't need a photo to recognise him again. Ross moved over to a hedge, out of the light, not considering that this might make him look even more suspicious.

His phone beeped its voicemail tone, a reminder that Martin had called too. 'Hi Ross. Sorry it's taken me ages to phone back but I was out for dinner with the girls last night, then my phone was on the charger and I forgot. Anyway, humble apologies, my man. Call me back. Cheers.'

Ross hit Martin's number, and didn't beat about the bush. 'Hi. It's me. Listen, something crazy's happened. Carla's missing. She's been missing since last night and I don't know where she is. I'm scared, Martin, and I haven't a clue what to do. I've been to the police and everything.'

'Fuck! Missing? Have you two had a barney or something?'

'No. We haven't. Definitely not.'

'Where are you now?'

'On my way home. Just a few minutes away.'

'Right. I'm coming over. Ten minutes, tops.'

21

Sunday

Ross opened his eyes.

Not normally a huge deal but on this occasion, that basic automatic response took the better part of half a minute. It was akin to dragging open a dungeon gate, rusty and seized solid after decades of non-use.

By degrees, he allowed painful chinks of light to filter through. He lifted his hand to add another layer of protection against the assault on his sight.

He discovered he was back in his armchair, and now that his eyes were open his ears followed suit.

There was a tapping noise.

Gradually, reluctantly, and desperate for lubricant, the gears in his brain began to mesh, and he isolated the tapping to an area over by the window. It was the best he could do. Then Ross groaned. A croaky, larynx-made-of-broken-glass type of groan as it dawned on him he was experiencing his own personal *Groundhog Day*.

He flapped a weak, wavery hand towards the window. Joe waved back and walked away down the path with Bella. His watch said it was six o'clock. Now he knew how Bill Murray's character felt.

It was pointless denying the truth. Ross felt like shit warmed over, twice. All the lights in the living room were on. The hot, solid mass of pain bolted to the back of his skull discouraged him from looking up, but vision at the horizontal was just about achievable and that brought three things into soft focus. A crystal glass containing less than an inch of rich, amber liquid. An empty bottle with *Talisker* on the label, horizontal on a side table. A small, dried-in ragged brown stain, pooled on the carpet below. The other side table was also on its side, and sported two crystal glass-sized rings that would take some shifting. *Shit!*

He groaned once more but decided he wouldn't do that again. It really wasn't worth it.

Pushing gingerly with both arms, Ross arrived at something approaching vertical. He ignored the carnage. *Later, it can wait till later.* He shuffled towards the door like a ninety-year-old with bad cramp and knackered kneecaps. He switched off the lights in the room but that didn't seem to make any difference. *Where is all the bloody light coming from?* Standing in the doorway, now he could see that practically every light on the ground floor was burning brightly. The place was like Blackpool Illuminations, and the pain in his head had escalated to molten metal. Next stop, nuclear fusion.

He clicked off light switches, and pulled doors closed. The front door was unlocked. His keys were lying on the floor of the vestibule and he knew, he just *knew*, the next manoeuvre would hurt. Straight-backed, down on one knee, he managed to lift the bunch, and lock the door at the first attempt. *Result!*

Upstairs now, and hit the pit. Ross was moving slowly, one hand on the bannister. A bit unsteady, but getting there. He was just thinking about congratulating himself when his mouth flooded with saliva, and his stomach lurched in that familiar dread-inducing fashion. He almost made it to the WC. Almost, but not quite. That was a clean-up job he couldn't defer.

Ross sat with his forehead on the cool rim of the sink, and splashed a little water over his face. He feared he would probably vomit again, and about five minutes later he did. Trusting that would be it, he brushed his teeth, threw back two paracetamol with some water, closed the curtains, took off his clothes and slunk under the duvet.

He was the equivalent of comatose within seconds.

* * *

Ross had been lying awake, well, half awake, when the doorbell chimed. He felt marginally more alive than five hours earlier but there wasn't much in it. He'd been piecing the Saturday night jigsaw together as the fragments of his memory slowly returned like a herd of lost cows ambling back to the barn. There were still a few bits to find, never mind fit, but Ross reckoned the sorry tale read something like this. Martin turned up at the house, a mixed bag of booze clanking in his hand. They had a couple of beers each first, while the wine was chilling in the fridge. A Chinese carry-out merely stemmed the flow, the wine took a hammering, and finally, out came the whisky. Swiftly followed by Martin wandering off home and Ross heading for oblivion.

Martin. Last night. Deep and meaningful discussions. Questions.

'But Ross. Why would she just disappear like this? Without any warning.'

'I honestly haven't got the foggiest notion.'

'Definitely no signs?'

'No. Nothing at all. Everything's been so... so... normal.'

Questions, questions, questions.

But no answers.

And now someone was ringing the bell and as much as he didn't want to, Ross creaked out of bed, made himself relatively decent and headed downstairs, descending each step with care as if he might crack bones in his feet.

'Okay, okay, I'm coming.'

To most people, Edinburgh may not seem particularly far north but, perhaps surprisingly, the city is north of Moscow, and lies at a significantly higher latitude than Edmonton in Canada. So the winter sun can be a bitch at certain times, and when Ross opened the door he couldn't immediately see who was on the step because the low-level rays were lancing straight into his eyes. A hangover of gargantuan proportions didn't help of course, and neither did scrunching up his eyes in a vain attempt to see who was standing on his doorstep.

Ross moved to the side to place the door as a shield against the sun, and was now able to separate the two shapes into a woman in her mid-thirties and a sharply-dressed man about eight or ten years younger. They were holding up Warrant Cards.

'Mr McKinlay, I'm Detective Sergeant Melissa Cooper, and this is Detective Constable Andrew Young. We've come to speak to you about your wife, Carla McKinlay. I understand she's missing from home.'

Ross motioned the police officers into the house. He was concerned his voice, unused since he'd puked earlier, would sound like Tom Waits with emphysema. And so it proved.

'Yes. That's right. Come in, please.' DS Cooper winced visibly and indicated the closed door to the living room. 'Yes. In there's fine.'

The police officer was first into the room. The reek of stale booze hit her like a slap from a barman's cloth. She moved a hand over her crinkled nose, and gazed around. Her colleague stopped at her side, and spoke over his left shoulder in Ross's direction. 'Had a bit of a party, have we, sir?'

Ross had forgotten this piece of the jigsaw but given the state he was in when Joe tapped the window, he could be forgiven.

He had his eyes closed, fingers and thumb massaging his temples, his still bleary vision obscured by his palm. 'Not a party, no. My mate Martin came round. Way too much to drink. Stupid really, but...' He stopped there, didn't see the point in explaining any further. The officers had eyes after all, and what had caused this mess didn't need pictures to be drawn. 'I'll clean this up later. We should go through to the kitchen instead.'

Previously at the rear, now in front, Ross opened the kitchen door. He stopped dead. If the other two had been walking any faster, they'd have piled into the back of him. 'Oh, shit!'

The worktops and the table were awash with the relics of last night's session. Food containers, some empty, some not. Plates and cutlery encrusted in dried rice. Congealed pools of Oriental gloop, one as crimson as a sunburned tomato. Beer bottles, wine bottles, glasses. The works, really.

'And it was just the two of you, sir?' said DS Cooper.

Ross confirmed with a jerky nod. Then his embarrassment galvanised him into action, like an old-fashioned wind-up toy car let loose on linoleum, with its wheels already spinning.

Problem was, his whirling-dervish clean-up act caused more mess than it resolved. He managed to spatter sauces all over the worktop. He tried to cram the white plastic containers into an already overflowing bin but a lid came pinging off and the rice inside sprayed across the floor, bouncing and tinkling around like hailstones on a tin roof. Finally, when he knocked over a beer bottle and the dregs ran down the front of a cupboard door, DS Cooper stepped in and placed a hand gently on Ross's forearm. 'Mr McKinlay.

Just leave it for now. It's just a bit of untidiness, you can sort it once we've gone.'

Ross bowed his head, mortified. *Carla will go bonkers if she sees this. She'll hit the piggin' roof.*

'Tell you what,' she said. 'Why don't you get dressed, and I'll make us some coffee. How does that sound?'

Ross knew he looked a mess. His vision hadn't cleared, principally because his headache was back, although the term seemed well down the scale for what he was suffering. *Eyes like piss-holes in the snow, I imagine.* He hadn't shaved for two days but even had he been tip-top in all other aspects, as often as not his natural state was borderline scruffy.

'That would be great. Black please.' Then, as an afterthought: 'And two sugars.'

* * *

Now washed, and dressed in navy cords and a dark green sweatshirt, Ross had taken a few sips of hot, sweet coffee. He felt slightly worse, which didn't seem fair. *This'll be a peaks and troughs day, I suppose.* His gaze switched back and fore between his two visitors, waiting to hear what they had to say.

Melissa, or Mel as she preferred, was a cheerful looking woman with medium-length, mid-brown hair in no discernible style. It had a fairly serious kink just above her right eyebrow that had defied most hairdressers' attempts to tame it. The style of her skirt would allow her to negotiate low walls, steep stairs and muddy puddles if necessary and her shoes were more Marks and Spencer than Kurt Geiger.

But Andrew Young, he was quite the opposite. His hair and clothes were right on the money. Tie perfectly knotted over a crisp white shirt, a sharp suit that looked fresh out of the box, and shoes that would earn him a gold star from the most demanding of parade ground sergeants. The men on the team had immediately pinned the *pretty boy* badge on him but they only used it in fun now. He'd proved time and time again he was smart, loyal, and tenacious in securing justice for victims and against perpetrators.

Ross assumed that as Mel was the senior officer, she would take the lead. So he was taken aback just a little when

Andrew kicked things off. Mel relaxed into her seat, tapping a pen against an empty page in her notebook, which rested casually on her knee. She wore a gentle smile but her eyes were focussed on Ross, as if Andrew was just an audio input to the discussion.

'First thing to say is PC Devlin has completed his enquiries. Unfortunately, he hasn't been able to establish why your wife might have disappeared so our Detective Inspector has instructed us to take on the case. As you've already been advised, Mrs McKinlay, Carla, is being treated as a missing person, and we are taking her disappearance seriously.'

Ross didn't really know how best to respond to that so he just nodded and waited for Andrew to continue.

He opened a pale blue folder containing a few sheets of typed A4. 'Your wife's file has all the information PC Devlin collected but there are some points we'd like to discuss with you in more detail.'

'Whatever you need to know, just ask.'

Mel interjected. 'I should just explain something first, Ross. Andrew will be asking you some fairly direct questions. He won't beat about the bush. That wouldn't help us at all.'

Ross was looking alternately at Mel and Andrew, still nodding. She continued, 'You may feel that some of the questions are personal, and think, I'm not answering that. But we need you to be as honest as you can. It's the only way.'

'I appreciate you warning me. But we're all grown-ups here and I'll do anything at all, answer any questions, if it will help you find Carla. But would you mind if I asked a question first, please?'

'Shoot,' said Andrew.

'Am I a suspect?'

'A suspect in what?' Mel came back this time, making Ross swivel again.

'Well, in Carla's disappearance.'

'Why would you think that?'

Ross could feel the temperature rising. 'Em, I don't know. Don't you always look at the husband first, in crimes like this?'

Andrew now. 'Has there *been* a crime, Mr McKinlay?'

'No, of course not. I didn't mean to say crime, I meant case. *Cases.* I'm sorry, that just came out all wrong. It's just… you

84

read things, you know? And hear them on the news.' Ross took a deep breath and sat up straight. He made a *time-out* signal with his hands. 'Please just ask your questions. That was a stupid thing to say.' If he hadn't been shaking his head and studying his slippers he would have noticed the matching glances making semaphore between the two officers.

Andrew didn't comment any further, he just launched in with the questions. He asked Ross to describe the days leading up to their supermarket trip. What he and Carla had been doing, was there anything untoward, who had they seen, had Carla been anywhere without him? Just a standard week, was the summary of Ross's reply.

'Now, talk us through the whole supermarket visit, in your own words, starting from when you left the house. Then take us right through your evening.'

Ross didn't object to the repeat performance of his discussion with PC Devlin, he saw it as a necessary evil. Occasionally, Andrew or Mel interrupted to clarify certain points, often related to the timings of each stage. But largely, they let him speak.

They asked him about Liz. He explained how she died just as all their plans were coming together, and how his own mortality had been brought into sharp focus. He told them he was approaching fifty, and any signposts to indicate where his life was heading had been mown down as if by an articulated lorry with its brake lines cut. Carla had been a sharp, frosty breeze cutting through his musty existence, and he'd fallen hook, line and sinker. He missed Liz like crazy, of course he did. But he was absolutely certain she would have told him just to get on with it. So he had, he and Carla had, and if anyone didn't like it, well, that was just tough titties as far as he was concerned.

'What's your relationship like, you and Carla?'

The question sparked a wisp of a memory from the previous night.

'But that's why I'm so confused, Martin. This has come right out of the blue.'

'Has something changed, then? Because you pair always seem so good together.'

'Nothing's changed, everything's been just fine.'

And that was Ross's answer. He didn't hesitate. He told Mel their relationship was perfect, they had no problems whatsoever. She could ask anybody.

Andrew tugged Ross along a different path. 'So things have been fine this week. Has she ever done this before?'

Ross looked at the collection of candles arranged by the wall. None of them had ever been lit. 'Of course she hasn't! Why on earth would she?'

Andrew treated the question as rhetorical and carried on. 'Okay, so can you think of any reason, any reason at all, why she would stay away from home? Money perhaps, or family reasons? Something to do with her work?'

Ross told him they were comfortably off, he had no family anywhere close. Carla only had one sister and she lived in Italy. Her job was full-on while she was there but she switched off completely when she was home. He explained about Carla's job just before he was asked, so Andrew left it there.

Mel took a turn. 'What about you? I think you said you were, what, comfortably off? What do you do for a living?'

'I was an accountant.' She nodded a few times. 'It's that obvious?'

She waggled her right hand from side to side above her knee. 'I wasn't thinking stuntman, put it that way.'

'I wish. No, accountancy, I'm afraid. Not exactly exciting but there you go. I'd earned a fair amount over the years, and with no kids to spend the ill-gotten gains, we were able to put a decent amount away. Liz's business did incredibly well right from the off, really, so we both had well paid jobs.' Ross's voice caught, and he rubbed below his eyes with thumb and forefinger.

Mel gave him a few seconds. 'What about now, are you still working?'

'I packed in the accountancy after Liz died.' Ross swallowed, jutted his chin out and soldiered on. 'They gave me a redundancy package, which was very good of them, and then it took me a few months to sort things out. To sort myself out actually. I was never going back to my old life but then my best mate, Martin, he runs his own company and it turned out their bookkeeper was leaving to have a baby. He asked me if I would help out. I'm not sure he actually needed the help but it was good of him to offer. So I've worked there part-time ever since. A job-share. No pressure, easy work, suits me down to the ground.'

'So, Martin, he's your best friend, did you say?' Ross nodded. 'And have you seen him since your wife disappeared?'

'Oh yes. He was one of the first people I called. He came round last night with some booze.' Ross waved a hand in the general direction of the kitchen. 'Martin is fifty per-cent, no, make that seventy five per-cent responsible for the carnage through there.'

'So what did you two talk about?'

'The fact she's gone, it's not something to do with Liz, is it?'

'Liz? Of course not. Why the hell would it?'

'I don't know, mate. I'm just asking, that's all.'

'No, Not Liz. Definitely not. Now, can we change the subject?'

Mel spoke again. 'And what time did you two call it a night?'

Ross laughed out loud, albeit without a trace of humour. 'Have you seen the state of this place? I'm sorry, but I haven't a clue.'

'We'll ask him.'

The smile was genuine this time. 'Good luck with that.'

Mel changed tack. 'What about money, Ross? Have you checked your bank accounts to see if your wife's made any withdrawals since Friday?'

'Well, no, I haven't. But it's Sunday now, the banks are closed.'

'Internet banking?' said Andrew.

'I don't do internet banking. I'm an old-fashioned type of guy. If I need money, I go to an ATM. If I need to pay a bill, I go to the branch or post a cheque.'

Andrew almost sighed, he would never have made a poker player. He took a more considered look at the other man, who'd just risen from his bed and was palpably hungover. Ross was about average height and although he was quite trim, the sweatshirt, cords and slippers combo was doing him no favours today. He tuned back in as Ross continued.

'I'm not a complete Luddite. I use Excel and other programs for work but I've no interest in what you'd call the social side of computers. They're a tool to help me do my job, that's all.' He shrugged. 'So, no, I've no idea if Carla's withdrawn any money, it just didn't occur to me.' Andrew found himself gazing at the older man again, almost transfixed, as if Ross had just presented him with irrefutable evidence that Santa Claus had been caught climbing out of a chimney.

'But I'll phone the bank first thing tomorrow morning and check. Deal?'

'Deal,' said Andrew, who rarely entered a shop, never mind a bank.

The policeman didn't miss a beat on the next one. He had solid eye contact with Ross when he hit him with: 'Have you ever suspected your wife might be having a relationship with someone else?'

Ross sat a little straighter. 'Absolutely not! For goodness sake, we've only been married seven months. Only been together a year. When she's home, we spend most of our time in each other's company. She goes to gym classes that are all female, *and* she works offshore.'

They shared a few seconds' silence, while that last comment bounced around the room. Andrew was writing so Ross switched over to Mel, who raised an eyebrow. 'What?' he barked. 'Oh, come on. What are you saying?'

'I'm not *saying* anything, Ross. But *you've* just said your wife works offshore, in a male-dominated environment, where none of them see their partners for weeks at a time. Andrew's only asking the question because it's something we have to rule out. Carla's an attractive woman. Is there any possibility at all she could be having an affair with someone from work, and that's why she's not at home? Because after all, her colleagues would be on, what would you call it, shore-time too.'

Ross was now sitting like he had a snooker cue up his backside. 'The answer's still no. There would have been some sign, and there hasn't been. So, no. Definitely not. Can we move on now?'

Ross exhaled heavily and sat back, and Andrew picked up again. His next fusillade of questions were all answered in the negative. No mental health issues, no recent arguments with anyone, no one had upset her prior to the supermarket or while they were inside, no urgent family calls from Italy, no disasters at work, no problems with anyone in the street, no suspicious activity around the house or the gym. A big fat series of blanks. Nothing happening here, folks. Time to go home.

There was a lull in the Carla Q&A. Andrew was running the tip of his pen back through his notes as he checked them, fiddling with the end of his nose, tapping his foot on the floor.

Ross's phone beeped twice. He looked at it and experienced another flashback. And this one hurt.

'Martin, I really don't know if I could survive something bad happening to Carla.'

'Oh, come on, pal. Don't think like that. It'll be fine. I'm sure it will.'

'But what if it's not fine? What if... what if this is Liz all over again? I've met another woman that I love and she... she...'

But Ross couldn't remember what Martin had said after that.

'Who was that, Ross?'

'Martin's surfaced.' He checked his wrist. 'And it's still morning, just. I wonder how *he's* feeling.'

'Want to call him back?'

'Not yet. He'll need some serious caffeine before he can have a lucid conversation. I'll catch him later.'

They dredged up a few more possibilities. Did Carla meet anyone she knew in the supermarket? No. Did she make or take any calls? No. Did she send or receive any texts or emails?

Ross fell silent.

Mel had the eyebrow thing going again. 'Ross?'

'It's possible. I can't say yes or no to that. Here's the thing, though. Carla was always on her phone. I don't mean talking, she didn't make many calls but the bloody thing was never out of her hand. I used to joke...' He caught himself as he realised it was the first time he'd used the past tense in relation to Carla.

Mel noted it but didn't comment. She prodded him. 'It's okay, Ross. Now, what were you saying? About Carla's phone?'

'I used to joke that bloody iPhone was stapled to her hand. Carla used to say...' he mimicked a snotty, girlie voice, *'It would not be possible to put a staple through a phone.* Just one of those stupid-things-we say-in-our-house exchanges. But it's true, she was...' he caught himself again, 'she is... addicted to her phone. Texting people to meet for gym classes, what's on at the cinema, booking the seats, restaurant tables, who starred in such-and-such a film or TV programme. If a question came up, Carla was on it. Internet, work, emails: everything.' He paused mid-tirade. 'She even put her shopping list on it, so the phone was in her hand all the time we were in the store. She could have taken any number of texts, and I wouldn't have had a clue.'

'And you told PC Devlin she's not active on social media.'

'No. Not as far as I know.'

There was a lengthy pause in the conversation while the two officers digested what Ross had said. Then, after the briefest of glances between them, Andrew came straight out with his next point.

'Just going back to the supermarket car park for a moment, you told PC Devlin your wife drove to the store.'

Ross blinked at the unexpected tangent. 'Yes. She did.'

'You see, Ross, that's curious. Your car's a standard UK right-hand drive. Yet, when PC Devlin reviewed the CCTV at the store, he saw you getting out of the driver's seat.' Andrew had his gaze fixed on Ross, who looked rather startled at this revelation.

'Furthermore, he didn't see anyone leaving the car from the passenger side.' He left a couple of seconds of silence. 'Care to explain, Mr McKinlay?'

Ross looked everywhere other than directly at either of the two police officers, who waited patiently for him to speak.

Then Ross threw himself back in his chair, hands in the air. 'Jeez! What a plonker. I completely forgot. It *was* me who drove that night.'

Andrew's expression said: *Go on, then. I'm looking forward to this.*

'Sorry. I remember now. Carla intended to drive because she was going on somewhere afterwards. But I forgot and got in behind the wheel and drove after all. Then Carla stayed in the car to make a call, and caught up with me inside the store a few minutes later.'

'Who did she call?'

Ross blinked. 'I've no idea. Something to do with work, I think.'

Andrew didn't look impressed then Mel changed the angle again. 'This is maybe a woman thing, but once you got home from the supermarket would she have left you to put away the shopping?'

'Oh no. No way. Carla would never let me do that myself.' He smiled. 'I'm always getting into trouble for putting things in the wrong place.'

Andrew this time. 'So, let me get this straight. Your wife was going to drive to the supermarket. Then home. Then she was going to come inside to put away the shopping. Then she was going off somewhere else. Yes?'

'Well… yes.'

'Where?' said Mel.

'Where what?'

'Where was she going?'

Ross hesitated for a second. 'I don't know. She didn't say.'

He looked at Mel and Andrew in turn. The expressions on their faces couldn't have been misread. But before he could qualify his answer, Andrew spoke again.

'Was it raining when you arrived at the store?'

'I think so. Why?'

'I just wondered why you would have parked out in the rain when there's undercover parking.'

Ross made a face. 'The spaces under there are quite tight, and there are pillars everywhere. I pranged the car a few months back, and ever since then I've always parked outside.'

Andrew thought that was a reasonable response, if a bit girlie. He glanced at the pale blue folder before continuing. 'The Store Manager told us you were going home to have dinner after you'd both been shopping.'

'That's right.'

'But you've just told us your wife was going on somewhere else.'

'Yes, you're right, I did. But she wasn't going to be long. The plan was, I'd make dinner in time for her coming back.'

'But you don't know where from?'

Ross snorted. 'Look, I've already told you I didn't know. It was just an errand or something banal like that. She didn't say, and I didn't ask. She often popped out for short periods. I didn't quiz her on it. Why would I?'

'What were you going to have?'

'Eh?'

Mel spoke slowly, as if she were talking to a small child. 'You said you were going to make dinner. What were you going to cook?'

Ross rubbed his hand across his eyes. 'I don't know. We'd have picked something up, I suppose. Or pasta. Or...' He stopped. 'Like I said, I don't know.'

Mel surprised Ross by jumping to her feet. 'Would you mind if I took a look around?'

Andrew spoke fluent Mel so understood that he and Ross should stay exactly where they were.

She came back a few minutes later, her arms extended. Balanced in her palms were five small green and yellow polythene bags that made crinkly-crackly noises.

As she walked across the carpet and stood in front of the candle display. 'How many did of these did your wife send you for?'

'Two'

'There were already three packets of cashew nuts in your kitchen cupboard, why would you need two more?'

Ross shrugged. A big, exaggerated shrug. It seemed to take lots of effort. 'You tell me.'

Mel was shaking her head.

'That's not how it works, I'm afraid. Not how it works at all.'

22

'So, what are you thinking?' asked Mel, studying the top of Andrew's head as he tied his shoelace. They were standing outside in the bright winter sunshine.

They'd taken a quick tour round the house, stuck their noses in the garage and the garden shed, and quickly checked the car, popping the boot open for no other reason than to say they had. Ross would have had to be an eighteen-carat idiot to leave Carla's body in the car but Mel had a couple of ex-colleagues who'd missed worse. Which is why they were ex.

Andrew squinted over at her from his perch on the nearside wing of their pool car. He'd wiped it with a tissue before trusting his worsted-wool-clad bum to the surface, which amused Mel as they'd picked up the Mondeo straight from the car-wash in the police yard. 'If we assume Mrs McKinlay *was* in the store, and we don't know that for sure, then the cashew nut thing was probably a ruse. Some sort of distraction while she buggered off. Dave checked the security videos, and didn't see anyone leaving the store who resembled her. But we should have a closer look, see if we can spot her either entering or leaving.

'Dave also called her number and left a voicemail message. I'll do the same, for all the good it'll probably do. Ross can't think of any reason why she would have left him, and there's nothing here to suggest why, either. Plus, all his timings check out.'

She nodded in agreement, looking down at her feet. She rolled a small pebble under her sole, from left to right, then front to back before toe-poking it into the gutter. 'No bad vibes, then?'

'I have to say no. His story about who drove to the store is more than a bit iffy, I have to say. But, having said that, there's something telling me he's okay. There's no question he was a bit nervous, hesitant's probably a better word, but that could be because he was talking to us. The past few years have dealt him a dodgy hand but he seems fairly level-headed to me. And I can't see him bumping off his wife of, what, seven or eight months when there's no apparent motive. So, my finely-tuned gut says whatever's happened to his wife, it's not down to him. What about you?'

'While you were asking your questions, I was having a really good look at him. And my first impression is he's straight. Old-fashioned, sensible, a bit of a relic. In fact, the only thing that's bugging me is the number of times he said he didn't know something, like what they were having for dinner or what her mystery errand was all about. They're fairly minor points, I suppose, but he also couldn't tell us what his wife was wearing. Mind you, it *is* a bloke we're talking about here.' Mel pondered for a moment. 'No, I'm with you. The driving bit aside, I kinda believe his story.'

Andrew continued, 'The answer's somewhere but it's not in that house. So, we need to look elsewhere. What do we have?' Mel moved over to beside her younger colleague, rested her backside over the wheel arch, and angled her head to read his notes. He carried on speaking. 'Back to the supermarket to pick up the CCTV footage. Catch the neighbours Dave missed out on. The two couples Ross phoned. His mate, what's his name again: Martin?' He peeled onto the next page. 'I don't suppose Mrs McKinlay's agency will be open on a Sunday, so that's a job for tomorrow. Ross's work too, obviously. Anything I've missed?'

He looked at Mel who studied the list again, flipping the page back to double-check. 'I'm nit-picking here but maybe we could find out where he plays tennis, a club I suppose, and ask around there. And possibly talk to the guys he goes to the football with. But apart from that?' She shook her head, and screwed up her nose.

Andrew snapped his notebook shut. 'And after all that, if we're no further forward, it's bank statements and phone records. Yeah?'

'Yeah.' Mel pushed herself upright. 'Right. Who's first?'

'The French couple at number twenty. Then his tennis pal, Barry, number eighteen.'

'Let's crack on then.' She turned to Andrew, holding her right arm out towards him. They locked hands on their respective forearms, and she made a great show of pulling him to his feet.

He placed his hand in the small of his back, and groaned for effect. 'Cheers, Mel. Wasn't sure I'd have managed that myself.'

'I could see that.' She was already marching off across the road. 'You need to work out a bit more, my boy.'

He just grinned, their banter was well-worn by now. He straightened the seam of his left trouser leg, brushed away a tiny speck of lint and followed her towards the next house. 'Hang on, Mel. Not quite so fast if you don't mind.'

'Forever in my shadow, Andrew. Forever in my shadow.'

Andrew just grinned. Again.

* * *

Mel pressed her nose against the bay windows of number twenty. She'd rung the bell twice but the front door remained firmly closed. 'Two cars on the driveway though. Round the back?'

'Might as well. We're the police, we can do stuff like that.'

They walked through a tall, wrought-iron gate between the garage and the side of the house. She turned the corner, and stopped dead in her tracks before she walked smack into the side of a massive conservatory that extended practically the full width of the house. If Andrew hadn't been alert he'd have bounced her forward a couple of feet. 'Fuck's sake, Mel. What are you playing at?'

Inside, a couple in their mid-to-late twenties were lounging on low, pale-grey, leather sofas reading what looked like the heavyweight Sundays. The woman had straight dark hair in a rough ponytail, several strands had fallen loose from the clip. She was wearing a dark blue lightweight fleece and white jogging bottoms, nothing on her feet. Her partner had on black shorts and a white sleeveless tee-shirt. In the USA they call them *wife-beaters*. His hair was dark, wavy, with a central parting. They both sported tans they certainly hadn't picked up in Leith. On the laminated wooden floor between them were several small white coffee cups, and a couple of plates containing the remnants of a continental breakfast.

The woman glanced up and spoke a few words to her partner, who raised an eyebrow then turned to look at the two police officers standing outside. He sat up straight, spun his magazine onto the pile and rose slowly and smoothly to his feet. He sauntered towards the glass, a genuine *well, hello there* grin spreading across his face to reveal sparkling white teeth.

She too stood up, stepped over the papers, and turned round to shuffle them into one sloping pile, bending forward from the waist to do so. Andrew remained silent but he missed nothing. Mel hated her on sight.

The patio door glided open on silent runners, and the man spoke. 'You have surprised us. The gate to the garden, it is normally locked.' He looked at each of them in turn. 'How may I help you?' He was still smiling.

He was tall, and clearly no stranger to the gym. He rubbed his hand up and down his left cheek. It made a faint rasping noise. He gazed serenely down at Mel from his elevated position.

'Ah. Yes. Sorry about that. We're the police.'

'I only have your word for that.'

They produced their warrant cards. He hardly glanced at Andrew's but scrutinised Mel's as if it were a winning lottery ticket. He held her hand from underneath for several seconds, while he continued to speak. 'I am Didier, and that is my wife, Amelie. Again, how may I help you?'

Andrew spoke up. 'We tried ringing the doorbell but there was no answer.'

Didier was still facing Mel. 'We do not answer the door. A new house, always someone trying to sell us carpets or blinds or plastic grass. Or something. But clearly you are here for a reason. What would that be?'

Mel this time. 'The lady who lives at number nineteen is missing from home so we have some questions to ask you. To ask all the neighbours, in fact.' She could feel her cheeks glowing, and not from the chill in the air.

'Please, come inside.' Didier led them into the conservatory and invited them to sit.

Amelie sat cross-legged on the floor while Didier flopped down on the sofa opposite Mel. He lifted one ankle and rested it on his other thigh.

Amelie looked up at Mel. 'What is it you would like to ask?'

As it turned out, they weren't a tremendous help. Amelie and Didier Marconnet hardly ever used their front door, preferring to access their garage and cars directly from the rear of the house. They didn't walk much, hadn't been in any other house on the street, and apart from Barry next door, they had spoken to only a handful of people since they'd moved in. But Didier did confess that Carla had been in their house on a couple of occasions, both in the afternoon. 'We drank some coffee. Chatted for a while. Nothing of any significance.' He was nonchalant about it.

Mel looked over at Amelie, who said, 'I wasn't here. On either occasion.' Her tone was a little more firm than before. Mel kept looking, expecting more. Amelie drew her knees up to her chest, wrapped her arms around her shins then turned and gazed out of a window.

Despite their conversations, the fact Carla was Italian seemed to be a surprise to Didier, who also had Ross and Joe mixed up. And Amelie was allergic to dogs, so that ruled Bella out too.

Didier walked them to the end of the driveway and shook hands with them both, Andrew before Mel. 'I apologise we were unable to help you. I hope you find the lady.' He let Mel's hand drop away, eventually. 'Please feel free to come to see me again.'

'Thank you Monsieur Marconnet. We may take you up on that.'

She turned away to catch up with Andrew, who was heading for Barry's house.

'So what did you think of Amelie?' she asked him. 'Apart from the bloody obvious, that is.'

Andrew smiled. 'I think, given her reaction, there could be just a tad more to Didier's afternoon conversations with Carla than he told us in there.' He put on a mock French accent. 'And I do believe Monsieur Marconnet has a small soft spot for you, ma petite Mel.'

'I'm not sure I noticed.'

'Lying cow.'

'Guilty.'

* * *

Barry Taylor opened his front door within seconds of Andrew ringing the bell. His garden was still in the design stage so perhaps *he* was keen to meet a plastic grass salesman. Barry was about five nine, slender, his blond hair in a stylish razor cut. He had a cheeky, infectious grin under bright blue eyes, and his accent, combined with the black and white striped football top he was wearing placed him as a son of Newcastle-upon-Tyne. Ross had said his tennis partner had just turned thirty but, based on his appearance, he could have been five years younger at least.

Mel explained the purpose of their visit and confirmed Barry hadn't seen Carla that week. She asked him how well he knew the McKinlays.

'I know Ross quite well, he's a good lad. We play tennis most weekends, Saturday mornings usually. I always get stuffed.' Andrew sniggered. 'No, he's top class. Played loads when he was younger apparently. He's not that quick any more, obviously, but he plays some brilliant shots, always hits the angles. He can move me all over the court whenever he likes, especially on his serve.' Barry added in some tennis-swing actions. 'He can slice it way out to my backhand, what with him being a leftie…'

Mel could see Barry was settling in to yap away for hours, and Andrew would have loved to join in but she had her *bored now* face on, so she butted in. 'And what about Carla?'

'I don't think she plays tennis.'

Andrew laughed out loud this time, and Mel cut him off at the knees with a *don't be such a tit* look.

Barry was utterly oblivious. 'Anyway, she goes to a class on a Saturday morning, I think.' He grinned again, clearly delighted with his reasoning.

'What I meant was,' said Mel, her teeth not quite close enough to grit, 'do you socialise with Ross and Carla as a couple?'

'Not as a couple, I'm single you see.' Mel leaned over to her right, and looked pointedly at a black and gold Michael Kors handbag on the floor by the side of the sofa. She raised one eyebrow as her gaze swung back towards Barry.

If anything, his grin was wider now. Ear-to-ear didn't quite describe it. 'Ah, well, I was single when I went out last night. Tomorrow, who knows?' He glanced up at the ceiling as a new sound vibrated from one of the bedrooms. Shower-pump, thought Mel.

Barry wasn't embarrassed in the slightest. 'Ross and I go for a pint sometimes but only if she's away. Carla, I mean.'

'Only if she's away?' asked Andrew. 'Is there something behind that?'

Barry's perpetual grin faltered. He focussed on the handbag, rather than look at either of the two officers. 'Let's just say, Carla and I didn't get off to a particularly good start so we don't speak now.'

Mel leaned towards him. 'So, tell us about the *not particularly good start*, Barry.'

He looked up again. 'I don't think Ross knows about this, though.'

But Mel didn't say anything. She left him to fill the silence, which he did a few seconds later.

'Look, I don't think it's a big deal. It's just…'

Still she remained silent. Andrew was adept at reading her signals and kept schtum.

'Christ, you don't give much away, do you, bonny lass?' It was the first piece of genuine Geordie vernacular he'd used in their presence.

'No, I don't. So you might as well tell us what happened.'

Barry shuffled in his seat. 'I moved in about a fortnight before Ross and Carla so I was kinda sorted, and I invited them over for a drink. I don't know why people say that, do you? Come over for a drink. I mean, nobody ever thinks it's just for one, do they? Anyway, we had quite a few. A skinful, actually.' He paused at the memory then carried on quickly, as if the faster pace would help somehow. 'Ross had done most of the removal work cos Carla had been offshore, and he was quite boozy fairly early on. Maybe because he was knackered, I don't know.

'I had been thinking it was about time they hit the trail because Ross had passed out on the sofa.' Mel's eyebrows rose. 'Well, passed out is possibly an exaggeration but he certainly fell sound asleep.' He patted the couch next to him. 'Just here as it happens. Carla said, what about one for the road, and when I went through to the kitchen to fix the drinks, she followed me.' Mel figured out what was coming next and he didn't disappoint her. 'Not to put too fine a point on it, she came on to me. Strong, like.'

'How strong?' asked Andrew.

Barry hesitated again then jumped right in. 'She was standing behind me. She put both hands round my waist and started pulling at my zip. I got a hell of a shock. I mean, that doesn't happen every day, does it? Anyway, before I could react, she had her hand down the front of my boxers and, well, you know...'

'So what did you do?'

'Do? Jesus! I grabbed her hand and pulled it out. I asked her what the bloody hell she was playing at, with her husband in the next room for Chrissakes.'

'What did she say?'

'Something like Ross wouldn't mind, they had an open marriage, crap like that. I didn't believe it for a second and I told her that. Poured the drinks down the sink, and said they should probably leave.'

The shower-pump stopped and three pairs of eyes turned upwards before Mel asked, 'And did they?'

'Too right, and sharpish. She hauled Ross off the sofa, and dragged him out the door. He was all over the place, and Carla was clearly pissed at me. But in a cold, silent way. Know what I mean?'

Mel nodded. 'And since then?'

Barry shrugged. 'Hard to tell, really. Ross has been fine, which is why I think he hasn't any idea what Carla did. Perhaps they do have an open marriage after all. It's not something I would ask, would I? But she hasn't spoken another word to me since that night, and I'm fine with that. Life's too short.'

Andrew stepped in. 'So you wouldn't have any idea why she's disappeared, or where she's gone.'

'None.'

'And Ross hasn't said anything to you?'

'Nope. Nothing.'

Andrew glanced over at Mel. She gave a slight shake of her head and picked up her bag. He flipped his notebook closed and popped his pen into his inside jacket pocket.

Having said their goodbyes, they walked out to the pavement and took a few paces down the street before stopping to face each other. 'Interesting,' said Andrew.

'Mmmm.' Mel jammed her hands into her pockets. 'So now what do we have? Do the McKinlays have an open marriage, or not?'

'Not. He just doesn't seem the type.'

'Is there a type?'

'Probably. But not Ross. He's just too… too…'

'Boring?'

'I was about to say staid. And I know Carla's quite a bit younger than him. But no.'

Mel agreed. Like most successful partnerships, she and Andrew often knocked stuff about like that, if only to rule things out. 'Bearing in mind what Barry's just told us about Carla and the boxers incident, do you now think she and Didier did more than drink coffee on their afternoons together?'

'Definitely a possibility.'

She laughed. 'Glad you're so certain.'

'Well, Amelie didn't exactly sound delighted.'

'She didn't, did she? And do you think Barry's story holds water?'

'I do, actually. If he was a braggart or a story teller, he would have said he wiped the floor with Ross at tennis, not the other way round.'

'Fair point,' Mel conceded. Then, after a pause, 'Carla McKinlay's beginning to sound like she throws it about a bit.'

'Indeed. But now it's the older couple at number fifteen. Let's see if she threw any in Mr Jones's direction.'

'That paints a lovely picture, Andrew. Thank you for that.'

'My pleasure, Melissa. Any time.'

23

Ross had been sitting in his armchair all this time, watching. And thinking.

He watched the two detectives walk down the side of the Marconnet house. Then he watched till they reappeared on the driveway.

He watched them going into Barry's. And he watched them coming out again.

He watched them while they had their chat on the pavement, although he had to lean way over on his left elbow to do that.

He watched them crossing towards Joe and Joan's house until they disappeared from sight.

And when he had nothing more to watch, he leaned back in the armchair and closed his eyes for a few seconds.

Finally, he picked up his phone, scrolled through the few contacts he had logged, and made a call.

24

'Thank you, Mr Jones. If you would ask your wife to call me in the morning, I'd be grateful.' Mel leaned down to rub Bella's ears before walking over to where Andrew was waiting by their car. He was smirking.

'What?' Mel demanded.

'Not too much of a tart then. Poor old Joe, the only bloke at this end of the street who isn't getting any.'

'Enough, Andrew,' but she was smiling too. She pulled back her left cuff. 'It's nearly three. What else can we do before we knock off?'

Andrew looked at his list. 'How about you drop me at the supermarket then when I get back to the station we can compare notes and update Jeff.' He was referring to Jeff Hunter, their DI.

'Sounds good.'

* * *

'Hi. Barry. It's Ross here.'

'Ross. How are you, man? I've just had the cops here, asking about Carla. They said she's disappeared. Is that right?'

'I'm afraid so, Barry.' Ross went on to relate the bones of the story since Friday night. 'So that's about it. And listen, I'm really sorry you had to find out from the police. I would have told you myself but it seems like I've hardly had a spare minute since...'

Ross shuddered before picking up again. 'Anyway, part of me says this is all a storm in a teacup. Something's caused Carla to stay away from home but it's nothing major and she'll come back. Then, whatever's wrong, we can sort things out and get back to normal. But then, there's the other side, the other possibility. And I don't really want to think about that.' Ross paused because he feared he might lose it, then recovered enough to continue. 'Until I absolutely have to, that is.'

'What are we like here, Ross? We're like two bloody women nattering away on the phone, when we live across the road from each other. Do you want to come over, or how about a pint? Maybe go for some food, or something?'

Ross was moving through the house as they were talking. He leaned against the kitchen door, surveying the debris from the previous night's shenanigans. 'Thanks Barry, but I have a fair bit of tidying up to do. Martin was here last night, and we had several over the eight. A pint's the last thing I need just now. Sorry.'

Barry laughed. 'Enough said. I'll leave you to it but shout if there's anything I can do, or if you change your mind. I'm in all night. And obviously, this goes without saying, let me know when Carla comes home, will you?'

Ross noticed his friend had said *when* instead of *if*, and realised he was definitely about to lose it this time. So he huckled Barry off the phone, promising to keep in touch.

Then, with tears nearly blinding him, he ran the hot tap into the kitchen sink, and began clearing a space to work in.

25

'Mel. Come and have a look at this, will you? I think I might've spotted something.'

When Andrew had come back into the station he told Mel that the supermarket could only provide an excerpt from the car park CCTV. There had been a technical issue involving the in-store footage but the stores IT support expected to have a DVD ready at some point the following day. Then Andrew had sat down to review the external footage.

Mel spun her chair round, and zipped the short distance across the floor to her colleague's desk. His monitor was displaying a grainy image of the car park and he moved to one side so she could see it. He left it paused while he explained to Mel what she was looking at.

He pointed his pen at the screen. 'That's the McKinlays' Golf. It's just been driven into the car park, and the driver will reverse it into that space there. The quality of the image isn't brilliant, mainly because of the distance from the camera but also because of the rain. But you'll be able to see the driver getting out of the car and walking directly towards the camera.'

Andrew pressed play, and Mel watched the scene unfold to where Ross walked out of shot at the foot of the screen, leaving the car isolated in its spot. The passenger door remained closed. After a couple of minutes, the camera panned to cover a different area of the car park. After a similar time period, it returned to its original position, bringing the Golf back into view.

Mel shrugged, but kept her eyes on the film. 'Okay, maybe it's just me, but what am I supposed to be seeing here?'

Andrew ran the footage back to the car reversing into the space. 'It's not what you do see, it's what you don't.' He used his pen as a pointer again. 'Watch. The car's in the space now, Ross gets out, walks away. Now, keep an eye on the back of the car. With most cars, when you lock them with the remote, the hazards blink.'

After a few moments, Mel smiled. 'But not here, suggesting he didn't lock the car, because someone was still inside.'

'Precisely.'

'And that particular car's lights definitely flash when you lock it?'

'They do. I just called the VW dealership down at Seafield. They told me the Golf has had flashing indicators on remote locking for at least nine or ten years.'

'So maybe our Mr McKinlay's telling the truth. His wife *was* still in the car.'

'Well, there's no footage of her getting out but as you saw, that camera covers two different parts of the car park so she could have got out while the camera wasn't on the car. Plus, I've watched it for a good ten minutes after this. There was a big Tonka toy in the way for a while, the driver made a right pig's ear of parking it. And a couple of supermarket vans drove past too.' He laid his pen down on the desk. 'So, not conclusive.'

'Maybe not. But that was a good spy. Well done you. Now, let's go and speak to the boss, so I can tell him what a clever little detective you are.'

26

Detective Inspector Jeff Hunter was one of those impossibly tall, spare men, who seemed not to be carrying a spare ounce of fat. When he sat down, as he was just now, it seemed to take an age for his legs and arms to arrange themselves into their resting positions. His right foot looked as though it was looped at least twice round his left ankle, and his shoulders appeared no wider than his hips. His face was a collection of angles and planes, all of them severe. He wore wire-framed glasses through which, hazel eyes gazed benignly at their subjects. His mind was far from benign, however, as many a suspect or interviewee had discovered to their cost. Often fatally. Jeff had listened intently while Mel and Andrew updated him. He asked questions at key points, and was satisfied with the answers.

A mutual respect existed between Jeff and his team. He gave them just the right amount of rope but always stepped in immediately if any of them were likely to end up with their necks stretched, and their feet dangling and kicking. In return, they gave him zero crap, kept him well in the loop, and knew not to bug him with every if, but and maybe.

Mel was his senior DS, they'd worked together for several years and rubbed along just fine. They disagreed plenty but hadn't ever fallen out. She was correct far more often than not, but that didn't stop Jeff hitting her with Devil's Advocate questions. Because if she could convince him she was correct, on whatever count, they could both be fairly certain she was on the right lines with her investigations. That suited them both perfectly and kept their clearance rates high enough to avoid hassle from above.

Jeff had been impressed with Andrew since the young DC had joined the team six months earlier. He could see Andrew was benefitting from Mel's mentoring, they were developing into a terrific pairing.

Mel looked out the window at a pair of gulls squabbling on the roof opposite while her partner explained about Ross parking the Golf.

'Nice one, Andrew.' Jeff tapped his lip with a pen. 'It's a strange one, then, eh?' He went quiet for a few seconds. 'Let me see if I understand all this, and you tell me if I'm off-beam anywhere.' He carried on without waiting for them to concur.

'Right from the outset we've got things that are a bit odd. McKinlay says his wife drove to the store but we've got film of him walking away from the car, driver's side. No one got out of the passenger's seat, and it appears he didn't lock the car. He parks outside in the rain just because he pranged it against a pillar sometime in the dim and distant.' Jeff raised his eyebrows before carrying on with his summary.

'We can't be certain that Mrs McKinlay, Carla, was even in the store because we don't have her on the external CCTV, and none of the staff you've spoken to actually laid eyes on her. So, questions. Does he strike you as being scatty enough to forget who drove?'

'No.' Mel saw no need to elaborate.

'Is it possible she *wasn't* in the car but he deliberately didn't lock it to *suggest* to anyone looking at the CCTV that someone was still to get out? Also, did he park away out in the rain because he knows the camera angles? Is she in the car and knows when to get out unobserved? Are they in cahoots, and setting something up together, or was McKinlay deliberately drawing attention to himself in the store? And, if he did lock the car, how come he told the manager he didn't have the keys? And then he walked home in the pouring rain. What, to prove a point?'

Jeff was smiling. 'Even to me that all sounds a bit far-fetched. What's your take?'

Andrew glanced at Mel before replying. 'We might be able to answer some of those questions tomorrow once we collect the internal CCTV footage. That should prove one way or another whether she was actually there. However, based on the discussions we've had with McKinlay and his neighbours we've no reason, thus far, to suspect him of anything untoward.'

'Okay. Let's assume she was there, and then she vanished like he said. But we've no idea why. Background checks?'

'Clear,' said Mel. The gulls had flown off to continue their scrap elsewhere.

'Their relationship's fine. No alarm bells?'

'Nothing.'

'And no money worries, as far as we know?'

'No. But we'll be looking into that tomorrow.'

Jeff nodded and continued with his mental list. 'But the husband can't say if she's made any withdrawals. That seems a bit odd, in this day and age.'

They had already described Ross's dinosaur tendencies so Mel didn't bother answering that one.

'And apart from this cashew nuts thing, nothing obviously untoward happened at the supermarket?' Andrew shook his head as Jeff continued. 'But she could have taken a text or a phone call. We don't know.'

'Yet.'

'You'll start looking at phone logs, voicemails, emails and texts tomorrow too?'

'They're on the list.'

Jeff leaned back, disentangled his arms and stretched them way behind his head. Andrew was surprised the photo of his wife and kids hadn't ever been knocked from its perch on top of the filing cabinet behind his boss's desk.

Clearly the next question was mystifying Jeff. 'But what's she been playing at with the neighbours, especially the blokes, hey? Lived there for five minutes and apparently, apparently I say, tried it on with two guys younger than her.' He looked at Andrew. 'Now Barry Taylor is single, which is one thing. But Didier Marconnet is not. And his wife, Amelie is rather attractive. Is that right, Andrew?'

'Can't say I noticed, actually.'

'A great pity, as you're principally employed to notice things.'

Andrew laughed and held up both palms. 'That's a fair cop.'

'It is indeed, but you get my drift.'

Then they reviewed the actions planned for the following day.

'All sounds good to me.' Jeff paused for a moment before changing direction completely. 'Two suggestions concerning the supermarket, Andrew. If Mrs McKinlay was inside, she definitely left by a public exit because there were no alarms at any of the service doors. She's not Harry Houdini, meaning she walked out but she wasn't recognised. So, check with the manager to see if there were any security alerts, of the shoplifting variety, in the immediate period after she disappeared.'

Andrew saw where Jeff was heading, but thought he had it covered. 'You're thinking she could have stolen, what, a hoodie or something? We did check the video for women wearing one, just in case.'

'It's the *just in case* I want to eradicate. She could have cut a tag off a hoodie, and popped it in someone's bag, or in a kid's buggy. Watched them walking out, and when the alarm goes off and there's, hopefully, a security guard rummaging about in some poor sod's shopping…'

'She waltzes out at precisely that moment, which gives us the exact time she left the store.' Andrew scratched at his ear. 'But not what she was wearing.'

'I was coming to that. Instead, maybe she just cut or ripped a tag off a hoodie to disguise her appearance and dumped it on the floor. Ask the manager how often they sweep for these tags under the racking.' Andrew looked a little bemused until his boss explained that most security tags were simple magnets but he'd heard about a new generation of tags that contain details of the item, like size, colour and price. Plus, they emit a radio signal meaning they can be detected anywhere in the store, not just at the security scanners at the front door. 'If they can find the tag, it'll probably still be attached to some material.'

Andrew felt like kicking his own backside. 'Meaning we'll have a clear description of what she was wearing.'

'That's right. Now, did you say she was wearing a Puffa jacket?'

This time Andrew managed to get ahead of Jeff. 'She's not going to put a stolen hoodie on, then walk out with the jacket that would identify her. So, she dumps it on a rail somewhere, a member of staff picks it up, and it ends up in lost property.' He jotted down a note to follow that up.

'With a bit of luck.'

Mel smiled openly then immediately wished she hadn't as Jeff turned to her. 'The gym. I've been thinking.'

Oh bloody hell. My turn to look stupid now.

Jeff continued without a hint of superiority. 'You've been looking for this *friend* of Mrs McKinlay. Ellie, or Ellen. Perhaps even Helen. But no joy?'

'No joy at all. We found two Helens but neither of them knows Carla.'

Vehicle horns blared down in the street. A different type of scrap, perhaps.

'A pity. But how many adult female members are there?'

'Nearly four hundred.'

'So you've been running search queries against their membership list?'

Mel nodded. She could see where Jeff was going as he pushed on.

'Against first names, and similar names?'

'Yes. And hyphenated names like Sue-Ellen. Even diminutives, like Ellie as a short form of Elizabeth. Although that's a bit tenuous.'

Jeff stretched again. 'I guess that's the problem with search queries. The limitations. Things they can't possibly find, like nicknames, or anglicised versions of foreign names. You never know, someone might use their middle name but register with their first name because that's what's on their driving license.'

'You think I should check every name on the database. Manually?'

Jeff lifted his shoulders but only by half an inch. 'It's your call. After all, whoever this woman is, there's only a small possibility she would be able to help. You can let me know what you decide.'

Mel knew that was her cue. 'Okay, Jeff. Thanks. We'll take another look at all of these things.'

As she and Andrew were leaving, they exchanged we-should-have-thought-of-that-ourselves glances and, unusually, neither was able to lord it over the other. This time around.

* * *

DS Hunter's phone trilled about half an hour later, a welcome interruption to the dreary task of reviewing operational procedures.

'Hunter.'

It was Andrew. The supermarket had reported no alarms in the hour prior to Carla's disappearance but there was better

111

news concerning the security tag. They'd conducted a quick sweep in the ladies' clothing aisles and found a tag that had been cut off a navy-blue hoodie. It was one of a batch only put on sale that day so reasonable to assume Carla had stolen the garment. Andrew said he'd check the DVD extracts when the store handed them over. The Puffa jacket hadn't turned up yet but apparently most of the bigger supermarkets sent lost property to a central location. It normally took forty-eight hours for items to be logged in their system but he'd asked them to expedite it.

Andrew also relayed that Mel had been right through the membership list but nothing had jumped out at her. It looked like this was going to be a dead end.

'Ah well, Andrew. Some you win, some you lose. You can update me in the morning if anything new crops up. Good night.'

Jeff Hunter smiled briefly then carried on with his review.

27

'That's better.' Ross made the statement to convince himself because there was no one in the kitchen to hear him. The dishwasher was gurgling away, doing whatever dishwashers do behind their inscrutable white doors. The worktops were clear of all clutter, he'd put all the rubbish and recycling outside in the wheelie bins, and as far as he could tell the floor was now free of fried rice.

He had already checked he'd put the living room back to rights but made one more tour just to satisfy himself. He bent down and plucked a morsel of dirt from the hall carpet. *Probably came from the tread of a copper's shoe.*

It was just after seven so it had been a bit of a cleanathon but he was happier now. *Spotless, Carla. Just how you like it.* But there was no Carla. Not yet, anyway.

His stomach had been rumbling for a while and although he wouldn't have minded cooking he didn't want to mess up his newly cleaned kitchen.

Chip shop for you, Ross, my boy. Then you'll only have to wash one plate.

He grabbed a jacket and his bike helmet, and lifted his wallet from the little alcove next to the kitchen door. He knew he was short of cash so he pocketed the wallet and headed off out.

It was a beautiful winter's evening. Clear and sparkling with not a cloud in the sky, and just a light breeze. He hopped on the bike for an easy five-minute run to the fish and chip shop on Newhaven Road.

Ross ordered haddock and chips, and while it was cooking he walked across the road to the bank. He slid his card into the ATM, keyed his PIN and waited for it to prompt him with the usual array of options. But when the screen changed, it stated:

**THERE IS A PROBLEM WITH YOUR CARD.
FOR YOUR SECURITY, THE CARD HAS BEEN RETAINED.
PLEASE CONTACT YOUR BANK IMMEDIATELY.**

And with that, the screen reverted to its default setting ready for the next customer. Ross just stood and stared at it, completely nonplussed. *Oh, that's just piggin' marvellous, that is.*

This was a totally unexpected turn of events. He jabbed at the *Cancel* button a couple of times but knew he was farting against thunder. He should have turned away immediately but he lingered a few seconds longer than was necessary.

Then a voice from behind him growled, 'Fuck's sake, pal. Shift yer arse.'

Ross startled, threw out an automatic, 'Sorry,' and stepped aside. A young lad wearing a grey Adidas tracksuit stomped past him.

As he trudged back across the street, he pondered why the ATM would have swallowed up his card. Eventually he decided it was a waste of energy, he'd just go to the bank the following morning and sort it out.

At first he was no more than mildly irritated but then he realised he wouldn't be able to pay for his meal. Approaching the shop, the lad from the ATM nipped in front of him and barged inside. Without looking behind, he let the heavy glass door swing shut. Ross had to put out an arm to stop it crashing into him. His carton of food was perched on a heated shelf, and the female shop assistant broke away from greeting grey-tracksuit-boy long enough to say, 'Haddock and chips, six pounds fifty, please.' She slapped her hand, palm up, on the counter. The girl was still a teenager and clearly she frequently sampled the cooking from her own shop. She was wearing a grubby blue-striped apron over an equally soiled short-sleeved tee-shirt, exposing most of her fleshy pink arms. They appeared to wobble for at least two seconds after she thumped the counter.

'I'm really very sorry but there's some sort of problem with the cash machine, and I can't withdraw any money.' He put on his most charming smile, but he may as well have been talking to the food for all the good it did.

'No cash, no supper.' The girl whipped the carton away below the counter at twice the speed of light.

'Is there any chance I can come back and pay you tomorrow, then?'

The girl leaned forward, her elbows on the worktop below the counter, and glared at him. She worked her lump of chewing gum over to one side. 'Do you think I look stupid?'

Ross took that as a *No* but he had one more option at his disposal. 'Do you take cards by any chance?'

This time there was no verbal response, just a greasy, stubby finger poking at a sign she'd made a couple of weeks earlier. It stated bluntly:

CASH TRANSACTION'S ONLY

Defeated now, Ross turned away and swung open the door. From behind him he heard, 'Go, Candace. Ya beauty.' It was followed by the greasy slap of a high-five.

A match made in heaven, he reckoned, picturing several small soiled chubby children wearing matching naff grey tracksuits, and raised with a total inability to use apostrophes correctly.

Seriously grumpy now, he cycled home and settled for cheese on toast.

I'll go in to the bank tomorrow. See what the problem is.

For the umpteenth time he checked his voicemails. But there was only one. From Martin, in death-warmed-up mode.

Ross headed off to bed, ever hopeful that Monday would turn out to be a better day.

28

He almost put his back out in his haste to reach the phone before voicemail cut in. It hadn't helped he was dozing on the sofa when it rang.

'Hello?'

'Hi, it's me, just checking in. Are you okay?'

He hadn't spoken to his wife for a few days, and he was really pleased to hear her voice. He just loved her to bits and although he wasn't happy they had to spend time apart, phone calls were the next best thing. So he was delighted and relieved she had called. 'Yes, yes, I'm fine. All good here. And what about you, did everything go smoothly? All your, eh, arrangements work out?'

'Uh-huh. No problems at all. Am I interrupting anything? What are you doing just now?'

'Well, I was reading my book but I think I drifted off. Had a wee snooze.'

'Honestly, what are you like? It's only what, just after nine?'

'Five past, according to the clock.' They had been chatting for a few minutes when he sensed the background noise from her end had become muffled. Then he heard her speaking, but not to him. He couldn't really make it out so didn't bother trying. He waited patiently till she came back on.

'I'm really sorry,' she said. 'I thought I was free to talk but something's happened here, and I have to go and sort things out.'

'It's okay. I understand. I know you're under a bit of pressure, and calling me isn't the priority. As long as I know you arrived there safely, that'll do me.' He didn't mean it, of course. He'd have talked to her for hours, given half a chance.

'Look, I'll call you again tomorrow. I'll have more time then. Promise.'

'It's all right, pet. Don't worry. Love you.'

'Love you too. Bye.'

'Bye bye.' He didn't know if she'd heard him or not. He walked over to the base unit and was just placing the phone back on charge when he felt a warm, soft pressure running from his calf round to his shin. He bent down and scooped the furry bundle up to his face, coming eyeball to eyeball with Tess, his tortoiseshell cat. Tess immediately turned on the purring after-burners, and bumped noses with him.

'Hungry again, Tess? I don't know why you're not the size of a small hippo. Come on then, let's see what's in the kitchen for you.' The cat squirmed out of his grasp, bounced once off the arm of the sofa, and set off across the floor in front of him, her tail in the air and her ears doing the radar-sweep thing that cats do.

Dennis knew she'd played him like a fiddle: again. But he didn't mind. She was his little pal, and he loved her as much as he loved his new wife. He bent down and opened the cupboard door below the sink. 'Okay, Tess. What's it to be? Chicken, or lamb's liver?'

Tess didn't care, really, but she kept the purring going anyway. Just to make sure.

29

Monday

Mel placed her pen deliberately and carefully on the interview table, and sat back in her seat. She looked at Joan Jones sitting opposite, dressed in a dark blue winter coat, still tightly buttoned and belted almost fifteen minutes after its owner had arrived in the station.

'And you're absolutely certain about this, Mrs Jones. You couldn't be mistaken.'

The woman adjusted her two-handed grip on the straps of her handbag, which rested resolutely in her lap. 'I certainly am not mistaken, Detective Sergeant Cooper. I clearly recall the event.'

'Fair enough. And just to confirm, this was in late September, last year.'

'The twenty-eighth, Detective Sergeant. I keep a journal.'

Mel looked up at the ceiling, there were more cobwebs than a kids' Halloween party. She smiled. 'Mrs Jones. Joan. There's no need to keep calling me Detective Sergeant. Mel or Melissa will do just fine, honestly.'

'I prefer to maintain the appropriate formality, *Detective Sergeant*. This is,' she paused, 'a formal investigation, is it not?'

Mel had tried to soften up Joan Jones several times during their conversation but the lady wasn't for being softened. She gave up. 'Yes, Mrs Jones. It is.'

'Well, then.' Joan Marjorie Jones (née Farningham) savoured her small but important victory. She didn't like Melissa Cooper. Not one little bit.

'So you didn't believe Mrs McKinlay's explanation.'

'I most certainly did not. I may be elderly, Detective Sergeant Cooper, but I am neither stupid nor gullible. But if you don't believe me, I suggest you speak to their friend, Amanda. I don't know her surname but I'm sure even *you* could find out.'

Mel gave a minute shake of her head. 'I'll do that, Mrs Jones. Thank you ever so much for your help this morning. I'll take you back down to reception now.'

'You are most welcome. I trust you will keep me informed.'

She escorted Joan to the station door, and hurried back up the stairs to Andrew's desk on the first floor. He'd been studying the internal CCTV footage he'd collected from the store first thing that morning.

'Any joy?'

But she knew the answer already. Her colleague was staring at his monitor, elbow on the desk, his chin cupped in that hand. The fingers of his other hand drummed on his mouse mat.

'I've been through it twice. As far as I can see, she's not there.' He sat back, his hands linked behind his head. 'How did you get on with Joan Jones?'

Mel just rolled her eyes. 'Not the most fun conversation I've ever had but she did tell me something rather interesting.'

She talked Andrew through the interview with Ross's elderly neighbour.

When she had finished, Andrew rolled his chair back. 'Well, well, well, Detective Sergeant Cooper. I didn't see that coming, did you?'

Mel tilted her head back, peered down her nose and raised her voice an octave or two. 'I most certainly did not, Detective Constable Young,' in her best posh-Edinburgh accent.

Andrew laughed. 'Did you believe old Mrs J, then?'

'I did. Because despite all that front she isn't stupid, and she's certainly not gullible. But I do get the feeling there's nothing she'd like better than to see Ross in a spot of bother. I might be wrong… but I don't think so. We'll need to follow this up anyway, make sure she isn't spinning us a line.'

Mel consulted her notebook then called Ross's friend, Amanda. Following the introductions, she said, 'The reason we'd like to speak to you and your husband… it's Tom, isn't it? Yes, well, it's because, as you may already know, Carla McKinlay has been missing since Friday, and we're becoming extremely concerned for her wellbeing. We also need you to corroborate, or otherwise, some information we've just received.

'Now, I understand you and your husband work together so would it be possible to come over to see you?'

She listened for a few seconds. 'Now, actually. Yes.'

She closed her eyes, clearly exasperated. 'I do appreciate you're busy, aren't we all? But I'm sure you can also appreciate how important it is that we speak to you both, as soon as possible. Is Tom there at the moment?'

'In that case, there's no time like the present, is there? Where can we find you?' She scribbled on her notepad. 'Thank you, Mrs Duncan. We'll be there around eleven.'

Andrew leaned over to read the address. 'Southside Business Park, That's on the old Dalkeith Road, if I'm not mistaken.'

'It is. And handy if we do need to pop into ERI.' Mel was referring to the Edinburgh Royal Infirmary, situated on the same road, near the city boundary.

They grabbed notepads, keys and jackets, and headed out the door.

30

The rustic city of Quimper, pronounced Kham-perr, is the capital of the Finistère department of Brittany, in northwestern France. It's a beautiful place, sitting at the confluence of three rivers: the Steir, the Odet and the Jet, with a pedestrianised old town and an atmosphere that is more rural community than urban landscape.

For Jean-Luc Dornier, life wasn't *just* a bowl of cherries at the moment. Those little dark-red fruits were floating in a rich liqueur sauce with a healthy dollop of fresh cream on top. Now in his late forties, this was his third *assignment* and the most enjoyable by a distance, principally because it was so undemanding. His new wife, Giselle, was trusting, loving, docile and breathtakingly boring. She was more interested in helping out at their local church than being the centre of any social whirl, or, heaven forbid, indulging in anything but the most perfunctory of bedroom athletics.

Jean-Luc had a dark complexion, hair and eyes to match, and teeth so unnaturally white his friends dubbed him Colgate. His trademark was a battered cream Fedora he'd bought in Saint-Tropez as a teenager. It was decorated with a red tartan band that had come from his cousin's wedding cake.

Naturally, he had wooed Giselle with flowers and other empty romantic gestures but she had genuinely shocked him in bed on their wedding night when she stated, matter of fact, that as long as he loved her and treated her well, there was no need for him to prove it. Physically speaking. Furthermore, she didn't give one jot if he sought his pleasures elsewhere, as long as he was discreet. Then she jerked at his dick for a few minutes until, despite himself, he spattered across the underside of the duvet, leaving just a dribble on her white cotton night-dress. She lifted a couple of tissues from her bedside cabinet and dabbed at the little stain. She kissed him on the cheek, and switched off the bedside lamp before immediately falling fast asleep. Within minutes she was snoring heavily and Jean-Luc was heading for the hotel bar, looking for some action.

He found it in the shape of Giselle's close friend, Abigail, one of several wedding guests staying at the hotel. Abigail was recently divorced and the complete antithesis of her prematurely ageing chum. She made it abundantly obvious that if action was what he required, she was just the lady to satisfy his demands. And, in the four months since the wedding she had been doing precisely that, at least a couple of times a week. His new wife knew exactly what was going on. Neither she nor Abigail would allow the small matter of an extra-marital affair to spoil a lifelong friendship.

It was to Abigail's house that Jean-Luc was heading now. This was on the pretext of picking up one or two things from town and spending some time at the local library. 'Take your time, my darling,' said Giselle, wondering, not for the first time, what went on between lover-boy's ears. 'I'll be at the church most of the day, helping to organise next week's fete.'

By road, Abigail's house was only a few minutes' drive but by crossing a wide footbridge over the Odet, and walking along the tow-path for a few hundred metres, he could cut through to her street and be in her bed in less than fifteen minutes.

It was a bright, sunny morning with just a gentle breeze and Jean-Luc was enjoying the walk. He could feel the excitement building in his genitals as he strode along the path. The kids were already in school and their parents had gone off to do whatever parents do, so the tow-path was relatively quiet. He had just turned right off the bridge when he met an elderly lady dragging two yapping terriers in her wake. Swaying branches, his ankles or bits of foliage blowing about, they didn't care as long as they had something to bark at. He smiled at her. She grimaced back, clearly intent on reaching her destination as quickly as humanly possible.

Further along, a gentleman wearing a cream, wide-brimmed hat was cycling towards him rather unsteadily as the bike looked far too small for him. Jean-Luc stopped and stood well to the side, giving the cyclist plenty of room to pass. An image appeared in Jean-Luc's mind of the chap over-correcting a particularly severe wobble and sailing off the path into the river. The Laurel-and-Hardy-esque cameo caused Jean Luc to smile as he waited for the man to ride by.

Jean-Luc lived for another four years before he eventually took his own life. He could never have imagined at that moment on the tow-path that the smile he was sporting would be his last. A few metres before he reached Jean-Luc, the cyclist stood up on the pedals and pumped them like a sprint finisher on the *Tour de France*, accelerating dramatically and directly at his target. Jean-Luc wasn't expecting this so he had no time to avoid the front of the bike crashing straight into his groin and lower stomach, while the rider quite deliberately launched himself at Jean-Luc's head, butting him into instant and bloody unconsciousness as cyclist, cycle and pedestrian collided with a sickening crunch.

Jarek Zelenka regained his feet in an instant, checked around quickly to see the only other person visible was just disappearing from sight with her narky little mutts, before disentangling the recently-stolen bike from the crumpled figure of Jean-Luc Dornier and heaving it over a hedge. At the same moment, a plain white Mercedes van sporting stolen plates skidded to a dusty halt beside Jarek, throwing up a cloud of dried grass and pebbles. The driver jumped out, slid open the side door with a screeching metallic crash, and helped toss a groaning Jean-Luc into the van. Jarek jumped in after him, the driver slammed the door shut and climbed back behind the wheel. At a slightly less frantic pace, he turned the van round and headed away from town. He followed a carefully planned route to the Brittany coast and its innumerable inlets, dunes and patches of woodland that would provide the privacy they needed.

And, apart from a cream Fedora with a red tartan band lying in amongst some flattened grass and wildflowers, it was as if Jean-Luc had never existed.

31

Ross had had an awful night's sleep.

He woke up just after four, and that was pretty much that. He knew instantly that Carla wasn't sleeping beside him. There was no warm bottom, no cold feet, no soft breathing.

At eight o'clock he gave up, and apart from the mechanics of shower and breakfast, he spent the rest of the morning wasting time.

Eventually, not far short of two in the afternoon, he set off on his bike for the bank. He used the branch near the foot of Leith Walk, or *The Fit o' the Walk*, as it's known to Leithers. He parked his bike and walked in through the swing door, which opened automatically as he approached. Now standing in a wide open space, he blinked in the bright fluorescent lighting, surprised to see he was the only customer. *One of the upsides of internet banking, a branch all to myself.*

A young woman swished across the floor towards him, all smiles and red corporate clothing. Her bright red lipstick and short blonde hair matched perfectly with her scarlet and white cravat. Her badge read: Amy.

'How may I help you today, sir?' She seemed genuinely pleased to see him.

'My name's Ross McKinlay. I tried to withdraw cash from the ATM on Newhaven Road last night but it swallowed my card. Said there was a problem with it. Could you check it for me, please?'

'Certainly Mr McKinlay. If you come over to the desk, we'll take a look.' She led him behind a shoulder-height room divider that matched the colour of her skirt, slid in behind the desk and offered him the seat to her right. He gave her his account details, she bashed some keys at lightning speed, asked him a few verification questions then angled the monitor so they could both look at the screen.

Amy used a pen to indicate a ticked box. 'According to our system, Mr McKinlay...'

'Please, just call me Ross.'

'Okay, thanks. Our records indicate your card was reported as lost on the nineteenth of February at 20:08. Friday evening.'

'But that's ridiculous!' Ross didn't splutter but it wasn't far off. 'Reported as lost? By whom?'

'The cardholder, according to this.' She turned to face him. 'I see the account is in your name only. You didn't report it?'

'No, I certainly did not. Why would I, when I still had the card in my possession last night when I tried to use it.'

Amy sat for a few seconds, thinking. Then she reached for the mouse and logged out. 'Let me go and see if I can figure out what's happened. Are you happy to wait?'

Ross said he was. He declined the offer of a coffee, moved over to a couch near the front door, and tried to make himself comfortable.

Amy came back about quarter of an hour later. Although the desk they'd used earlier was still free, she took him to a small meeting room on the first floor. The point wasn't lost on Ross. 'I'm guessing this isn't good news?'

'I'm not entirely sure, yet. Here's what I've managed to find out.' She explained she'd confirmed his card had indeed been retained by the ATM on Newhaven Road the previous evening. Ross was relieved, it proved he'd told the truth.

Amy told him she'd listened to a recorded call that had been made to the bank's helpdesk the previous Friday evening. It was a man's voice, difficult to place the accent, but definitely not Scottish. He said he'd lost his wallet but couldn't be sure where. Amy said she had just placed a stop on the account because it now appeared the call was fraudulent.

'Could it have been a mistake?' said Ross. 'He gave the wrong account number or someone took down the wrong details, and that's all it is?'

'I'm afraid not. The caller gave your name, your contact details, and was able to answer our security questions. So, I'm suspicious, and while you're here I'd like to look at all your accounts. Just to check everything is as it should be.'

Ross felt a little tingle running up his spine, which then cascaded down both of his arms and chilled his fingers. *This is not good.*

'But before I can do that, and I'm sorry to ask, do you have photographic ID with you?'

He produced his driving license and Amy pulled up all his details on screen. Ross wasn't wearing his reading glasses, and he deliberately chose not to put them on. Something told him that for the next couple of minutes, blurred vision might not necessarily be a bad thing. He wanted Amy to read the screen, tell him everything was absolutely fine, that a genuine, honest mistake had been made, and he'd be on his way in a few minutes. That was what he *wanted*, but he didn't think for a single second that would be the case. He kept his gaze on her, and studiously avoided looking at the monitor.

Amy noticed, and read out the number of his personal account. 'Is this the account you planned to withdraw cash from?' And when Ross confirmed it was, she asked, 'Approximately, what would you expect the balance to be?'

He looked down to his left. His brow became furrowed. 'I can't be certain, but probably a bit less than £2,000.'

'Hmmm.' Amy *was* studying the screen, and Ross detected a certain tension. 'I'm afraid there's nothing like that in the account. As of today, the balance is only £6.82.'

He thought he'd misheard. 'I'm sorry. Say that again.' Amy repeated herself, and now Ross was studying the screen intently, glasses or no glasses. 'But that can't be right. My salary went in at the end of last month, and I certainly haven't spent it already.'

Ross patted pockets for his spectacles case.

Amy waited while Ross polished his glasses. She pointed to an entry near the top of a column. 'On Thursday, the balance on the account was £1856.82. But on Friday, £1850 was transferred from your personal account, to this account.' She clicked again. 'A joint current account with Mrs C McKinlay.'

Ross brightened visibly. 'Ah. Okay. That's my wife, Carla.'

'Did you make the transfer? It was done online.'

'No. No, I didn't.' He didn't feel the need to tell this bright young thing that he and internet banking rarely shared bedspace. 'I don't know why she did that, so can you just move it back please. That'll solve the problem.'

Amy clicked several more times but didn't key in any figures. She continued to study the screen.

Ross leaned forward. 'Is there a problem?'

'These are the three accounts associated with your card. Your personal account, the joint current account, and a joint savings account also with Mrs McKinlay.'

Despite his attempts to concentrate, he was struggling to make sense of the figures.

Amy looked directly at her customer. 'I'm not able to transfer the amount back, because the combined balance of all three accounts is less than £100.'

Ross had never been kicked in the stomach by a horse but he imagined this was what it felt like. 'But I don't understand. If the £1850 was only transferred into our joint current account on Friday, why is the balance so low?' His mental processes were beginning to reform. 'I mean, that account should have three, maybe four thousand in it. And that's not including the transfer.'

Then Ross processed what Amy had said about the combined total of *all three accounts* being less than £100. 'The joint saver. It can't possibly be that low either. That's our savings, the money we have ready access to.' He looked around for a few seconds. *Why do they keep these offices so bloody hot?* He flapped his jacket in an attempt to offset his rising temperature. 'Last statement I saw said there was nearly twenty thousand in there.'

Amy walked Ross through a series of transactions, step by step. She wrote the details down as she spoke, and paused at the end of each statement to let him assimilate the information.

'Friday, joint current account balance: £3814.20.

'Then, add £1850, transferred from your personal account, into the joint current account. Making a balance of £5664.20.

'Also on Friday, joint savings account balance: £18,300.

'But, again on Friday, £5600 was transferred from the joint current to the joint savings, making £23,900.'

Then she asked him: 'Did you make any of those transactions?' But she already knew the answer.

Ross took another kick to the solar plexus from that damned horse. He could see the balance of the savings account was low. Very low. 'The twenty three thousand odds… it's not in the savings account, is it?'

'I'm afraid it's not. No.'

Amy had been through the bank's customer care training. She often had to tell people things they didn't like to hear. She didn't relish that part of her job but she definitely had the aptitude for it, instinctively able to pull together just the right combination of words, tone and facial expression to put her message across. This was now a time to utilise those skills.

She clicked through to a different screen. 'These are the last few transactions on your joint savings account.'

Ross was momentarily confused. He pointed at a credit of £14,000. 'Where's that come from?'

'That's an online cash transfer from your credit card. That transaction was made early on Saturday morning, just after midnight.' This time, she didn't ask if Ross was responsible.

He pulled his jacket together across his body. His eyes blurred over. He couldn't speak. His index finger wavered at the last transaction on the screen. He stared, pleadingly at Amy.

'That's an international transfer to Banco Iberia. 'I'm fairly certain it's a Spanish bank. The transfer was made on Saturday morning, at nine-thirty-two. It's for £37,900.'

She paused again. This last part was going to be so, so difficult to tell him. 'Virtually the entire balance from all your accounts, plus the credit card transfer.'

Ross felt he was about to disintegrate. 'But this is all wrong,' he croaked. 'I don't know anything about all this. And I've never even *been* to Spain.'

He stared in Amy's direction for several seconds then slumped back in his chair.

Why, Carla?

What did I do to deserve this?

32

Mel showed her ID to Ashley, the teenaged receptionist at Thomas Duncan Joinery. Ashley wouldn't have reached five feet even if she had stood on a box. She was pretty in a just-out-of-school way, with long straight brown hair. And a fringe. Most definitely a fringe. Mel imagined she'd probably had the same hairstyle since she was about six years old. 'Detective Sergeant Cooper and Detective Constable Young, to see Mr and Mrs Duncan.' She smiled at Ashley but the young girl looked rather too scared to smile back.

Mel reckoned she could have popped a DVD onto each of the teenager's eyes, so she smiled again as if to say, *'Earth calling Ashley.'*

This jolted the girl back into receptionist mode. 'Hold on one moment, please. I'll check to see if they're free.'

Mel smiled once more. 'They *are* free. We're expected.'

'Oh. Okay. Please sign in and take a seat. I'll call them both now.'

The detectives sat on low, functional purple seating in a semi-circular area that faced Ashley's desk. All around were working models of window frames in different configurations. Trade magazines and journals flooded the coffee table in front of them. The *Scotsman* newspaper lay open at the football section. Apparently only one side of the city would have been celebrating at the weekend.

An internal door thumped open and a tall redhead in a charcoal pin-striped business suit marched across the floor. Her heels rat-a-tatted on the laminate floorboards. Ashley began to make the introductions but the woman silenced her with the palm of her left hand, which then swung round in one movement to point at another door. 'Amanda Duncan. We'll use this room.' Her multifunctional and overworked hand slapped the *Vacant* sign across so it now read *Meeting in Progress* then banged down on the handle and pushed the door open. She stood with her back to the door, leaving barely enough space for Mel and Andrew to squeeze past, and before they had sat down, she closed the door with enough force to flutter the blinds on the window opposite.

'Tom's on his way over from the workshop. He'll be here in a minute.'

Having made this statement, Amanda virtually turned to stone. Mel was unconcerned by the silence so made no attempt to fill it. *We'll just play you at your own game, my lady. Yes, indeed.*

Not long after, Tom Duncan came in and introduced himself to the two detectives, shaking their hands. He wasn't quite as tall as Amanda in her heels. He was dressed in work gear: overalls, a tan leather work-belt, and bright blue plastic overshoes that protected the carpets from his sawdusty, size ten Timberlands.

When he realised he hadn't interrupted any conversation, his blank look was as telling as any display of shock or surprise. He jumped straight in. 'I gather this is about Carla being missing from home. How can we help you?' Tom took a seat next to his wife, whose arms were folded so tightly Mel was surprised she could take a breath. The woman's expression suggested she'd just discovered a warm turd in the breast-pocket of her jacket.

'You knew she was missing, then?' asked Mel.

'Ah... umm... well, yes, we did, as it happens.' He threw the first of many glances at Amanda, whose gaze was fixed on a point on the wall above Andrew's head.

'How did you find out? Have you spoken to Ross?'

'Yes. No. Em, not exactly.'

'And which one is it then, Mr Duncan?'

Tom was looking more uncomfortable with every tick of the clock. 'We haven't spoken to Ross but he left us a message on voicemail. He sounded quite agitated.'

Mel didn't let him off the hook. 'And when was that?'

'Em, Saturday, I think. Amanda?' But Tom received no support from that quarter, 'Yes, about five o'clock on Saturday.' He pulled a faded red handkerchief from one of his many pockets and swiped it across the top half of his face.

'Did you call him back?'

Tom risked another glance at his wife, who blanked him completely. 'Ah. No. No. We didn't, actually.' Out came the handkerchief again.

Andrew picked up from there. 'You're friends with the McKinlays, aren't you?'

'Well, yes. I suppose we are. Yes.' The daggers from Amanda missed their target because Tom appeared to be trying to focus on a point somewhere beneath the floorboards.

Andrew tightened the screws. 'So your *friend*, Ross, calls you, what, a day and a half ago? He tells you his wife's gone missing. He sounds, in your words, quite agitated.' He waited till Tom looked up at him. 'And you haven't called him back?'

The Sword of Zorro wouldn't have been sharp enough to cut the silence in the small meeting room but Amanda soon changed that. 'Oh, for fuck's sake, Tom! Would you stop beating about the fucking bush?' Her voice was about one decibel short of a yell.

Mel's view through the glass panel on the door meant she could see Ashley at her desk. She was pretending to concentrate on her monitor but Mel feared if the young receptionist strained her ears any harder, she would need an operation to fix them back in place.

Amanda continued, the decibel level gradually reducing. 'What my husband is trying to say, although at this rate it'll probably be about midnight before he gets there, is we *were* friends, close friends, with Liz and Ross for almost twenty years.' The order in which Amanda listed their names wasn't lost on Mel. 'Then poor Liz passed away, and within five minutes…'

'Oh come on, Amanda…' Tom protested.

'Okay, make that ten… he takes up with that Carla, and one whirlwind romance later,' she snapped her fingers. 'Bingo! They're married.'

Mel spoke. 'Do I take it you're not keen on Carla, then?'

'You take that absolutely fucking correctly.'

No sooner had the words left Amanda's lips when she leapt from her seat, snatched the meeting room door open, and launched herself into the gap, one hand still on the door handle and the other on the jamb. The decibels had made a comeback. 'In case you've forgotten, young lady, you're employed here to perform reception and administration duties, not to eavesdrop on private conversations. Especially *my* private conversations. Now get your bloody head down and do your *work*.' Ashley gulped audibly and tears sprang into her eyes. She nodded furiously and somehow became even smaller than four foot odds.

As Amanda slammed the door closed again, Andrew opened his mouth as if to protest but her frosty glare stopped him dead. But strangely enough, she seemed much calmer. It was almost as if the outburst had shattered some sort of high fever she'd contracted.

'I'm not keen on Carla, as you put it. I tried, I really did. We both did, for Ross's sake.' She sat down. 'And I know Liz would never have wanted him to mope about or be lonely but it was just too quick. Far too bloody quick.'

'So why did you stop trying?' asked Mel.

Some of the fire returned to Amanda's eyes but her voice remained even. 'I'll bet the only photo you've seen of Carla is that wedding picture in their front room. Yes?' Both Mel and Andrew nodded. 'All prim and proper. Little Miss Italian bride. Like butter wouldn't melt. Well let me tell you, that is not Carla. That is *not* who she is.'

'Amanda,' said Tom, in a warning tone. 'Do we *have* to go through all this again? I don't think this is the time or the place.'

She blanked him again. 'When Carla's in company, any company, she wears short skirts. Very short skirts. *And* she shows more cleavage than bloody Playboy Mansions. Now maybe they don't wear bras in Italy, I don't know, but at least it's bloody warm there. She came to our house on Christmas Day. Freezing cold, white top, no bra.' Amanda jerked a thumb at her husband, who had his head in his hands. 'The boy wonder here had had a few by then. When she took her coat off I thought he was going to pass out on the spot.' Mel gave Tom a pitying look as Amanda continued, 'Mind you, she had the body to go with it. In fact, if I were that way inclined I'd shag her myself.'

'Amandaaaaa!'

But Tom's pleading, whining voice cut no ice with his wife, and she turned on him. 'Don't you Amandaaaaa me, you bastard. If you'd spent less time ogling her tits and giggling like a little schoolboy every time she fluttered her eyelashes, I might have some respect for you.' She turned back to Mel. 'I could have walked about naked that day and he wouldn't have bloody noticed.'

'Fat chance of that,' Tom muttered, suffering yet another malevolent glare from his wife.

Mel considered yawning. 'This is all enormously interesting. But if you two could cut it with the major domestics for a minute...'

Amanda looked back at Tom but this time there was nothing in her eyes. He leaned down and adjusted the elastic in his right boot-cover.

Mel had their attention, even if the couple were clearly nursing open wounds. 'So, I get it that you've cancelled your membership to the Carla McKinlay Fan Club but there is one question I'd like to ask you about her.'

Amanda actually said, 'Go on then,' but her expression clearly stated: *If you must.*

'We interviewed Joan Jones this morning, Ross's neighbour, and she told us something that was quite a surprise. She suggested we speak to you about it.'

Amanda and Tom both wore quizzical expressions. Neither one spoke so Mel pushed on.

'Back in September, when Carla was admitted to A&E with a suspected broken cheekbone and bruises on her face, did you *also* think Ross had physically abused her?'

33

Amy explained to Ross that she was unable to answer his two key questions: why was this allowed to happen, and will the bank be able to recover the transferred money. She brought him a mug of coffee, and went off to speak to her manager.

Ten minutes later she was back with a serious-looking young man wearing a white shirt with the obligatory red tie. His hair was tied back in the tiniest sprig of ponytail Ross had ever seen.

He introduced himself as Simon, and they sat across the table from Ross.

'Right, Mr McKinlay. We're almost certain the phone call to report your card as lost was fraudulent. Unfortunately, the number was withheld so there's nothing we can do about that now.'

Ross's expression had *c'est la vie* written all over it, and Simon carried on.

'As I see it, we have four separate issues here. First, we have the internet banking transfer from your personal account to the joint current account with Mrs McKinlay. Now, can I just confirm you didn't perform this transaction?'

'No. I didn't.'

'And, apart from Mrs McKinlay, is there anyone else in your household who could have done so?'

Ross was distracted for a moment. A line of four seasonal prints decorated the wall behind Simon. The second one from the right was seriously squint. Autumn.

'No. It's just me and Carla at home.'

'So, reasonable to assume your wife transferred the money?'

'I suppose so.' Ross knew what was coming.

Simon didn't miss a beat. 'To do that, she would have had to know your login details.' A statement, but the tone suggested a question, which Ross didn't answer. 'Did you reveal your security credentials to Mrs McKinlay?'

Ross knew the truthful answer was also the dumb answer but there was no point in denying it. The dumb answer it had to be.

'You know I did.' He looked at Amy and Simon in turn. 'Doesn't everybody? Carla did all the internet banking in our house. So, yes, she knew my password.'

Simon shuffled a little in his seat. 'Let's come back to that, shall we?'

Ross didn't really want to leave it there but thought it best to let the bank manager run with it. *May as well hear all the bad news at once. See where I stand.*

Simon was clearly of a similar mind. 'Next, the transfer from your joint current to your joint saver. If we assume that was Mrs McKinlay again, and we leave aside the password issue, the transfer from your personal account is technically fraudulent because that's your money. But *this* transfer is quite legitimate.'

Ross butted in. 'Because Carla's a joint holder on both accounts.'

'Exactly.'

Ross barely registered the interjection. 'But the cash transfer from the credit card… oh shit!' Realisation dawned. 'Because she has a card for that account the transfer is also legitimate, isn't it?'

Simon deliberately softened his voice and his tone, 'I'm afraid it is, yes. As a cardholder, she has the same authority as you do. But whether she does, or she doesn't, if she had your ID and password…' He left the obvious conclusion unsaid.

Ross waved it away. 'Let me think for a minute.' His eyes flew about the room but there was nothing to see. A windowless internal room with stark natural light. And one squint painting. He looked back at Simon as a darker thought surfaced. 'All these transactions were made online, yes?'

'Yes.'

'I've never made an international bank transfer personally but would that be done online?'

'Under most circumstances, no, it wouldn't.'

'So it was made in person. By my wife. And that was…' Ross leaned forward and dragged the monitor round. Two pairs of hands shot towards it as it almost toppled over. 'That was on Saturday morning. So Carla must have been in the branch. Was she? You'll have security cameras so she'll be on film. Can I see it? You'll have to let me see it to prove it was her.'

He was now staring wildly, pleading with Simon to say, 'Yes, Mr McKinlay, of course. Just sit there for a minute and I'll organise that immediately.'

But Simon didn't say that at all. He just held up both palms, and spoke in an even softer tone. 'Mr McKinlay. Please. Slow down. I can appreciate this is a terrible situation for you and I don't want to make it any worse by promising you something I can't deliver on. We do have security cameras, and we *will* review them but I'm not permitted to show any film to a customer.' Ross began to protest but Simon did the palm thing again. 'I would be breaching the privacy of anyone on that film.'

'But,' Simon continued, 'now that you know what's happened with your accounts, may I suggest you discuss this with Mrs McKinlay? Are you able to speak to her about this?'

It hadn't ever occurred to Ross that he would need to explain why that wasn't possible to these, well, *strangers*. He'd always imagined the problem with his card was a glitch. Some sort of software bug. He sighed and looked down at the floor. 'No, I'm not. She's missing you see. No one's seen her since Friday.' He elbowed his jacket aside and pulled a crumpled tissue from his trouser pocket. He blew his nose quietly. He never could understand all those trumpeting nose-blowers who regarded anything less than a hundred decibels as an evacuation failure.

Amy spoke up. 'I don't mean to pry but have you talked to the police?' When Ross confirmed he had, she glanced sideways at Simon, willing him to pick up from there.

But Simon surprised them both by shooting to his feet, 'Why don't you just sit tight for a few minutes, Ross, while I go downstairs and check some things out. And Amy, could you bring us some fresh drinks please?' He held the door open and they both disappeared, leaving Ross rather startled at the speed of their vanishing act. He sat still for a moment, trying in vain to make sense of things. He walked round the table and adjusted the misaligned print.

He had just sat down when Amy came back with three mugs of coffee. Simon wasn't long after her, carrying a printout. 'As we said earlier, international transfers above a certain amount must be processed in branch. This is the form that was completed. Is this Mrs McKinlay's signature?'

The manic scrawl was instantly recognisable. Ross had often joked that Carla's signature looked like the tracks of a pissed spider that had just staggered out of a pool of ink. 'Definitely.'

'I've just spoken to the teller who dealt with the transfer. She had no reason to believe it wasn't your wife because all her ID checked out. But here's the thing, with international transfers we always ask the purpose.'

'And?'

'She *said* it was the deposit for a holiday home on the Costa Brava.'

'But like I said to Amy earlier, I've never even been to Spain. I've no desire whatsoever to buy a property in Spain. I don't even like Spanish food for God's sake. Why the hell would she say that?'

'I'm supposing because the transfer is to the Banco Iberia, and I don't mean to prejudge your wife's actions but her explanation would have had to hold water. After all, it's for about the right amount. Ten per cent on a property of about 400,000 euros. A villa, perhaps?'

Ross was immobile. *This cannot be happening.*

But his wheels started spinning again. 'Can you stop the transfer?'

'I'm afraid I can't, no. The whole process is electronic so if it left here on Saturday morning, the transfer would have been completed, at the latest, by *this* morning. And, according to my teller, your wife asked for it to be expedited to meet a deadline for bids on the property.'

'When *is* this deadline?'

'She said it was four o'clock...'

Ross glanced at his wrist. 'But it's only just after three now. Don't you still have time to check?'

'Sorry, no. I was about to say four o'clock *Spanish* time, and they're an hour ahead of us so the deadline's passed. I wouldn't normally be disappointed to admit we'd been efficient but, unfortunately, we processed it in time.'

Simon anticipated the next question so he answered it anyway. 'And, it's highly unlikely we'll be able to reverse the transaction.'

'But why the fuck…' Ross glanced at Amy. 'Sorry. Why not?' He detested the whine that coated his voice. He thought he sounded like a bearing, bereft of lubricant.

Simon took a few seconds to consider his words. 'Because, all the indications are that this is fraudulent activity. It's organised.' Ross gasped at the word as if he'd been slapped. 'We'll make enquiries of this bank but I would be surprised, astonished in fact, if the money was still there.'

Ross had his head in his hands now, both elbows resting on the table. 'Go on. You may as well tell me.'

'If this is what I think it is, the money was sent to an account in Banco Iberia. Then it would have been transferred immediately to a different bank, most probably in a different country. Then the account in Banco Iberia would have been closed. Repeat several times more, and the audit trail becomes virtually untraceable. And even if we could trace it, we're unlikely to receive cooperation from the banking authorities in some of the countries the money will have passed through. If I'm right, it would have been routed through somewhere like Albania or Belize at some point, and the trail would hit a brick wall.'

Ross stayed silent, and the others followed suit. Eventually he stood up and walked behind his chair, placing both hands on the curved back. 'I think I know the answers to my next few questions but I should ask them anyway.' He deliberated for a few moments, gathering himself. When he spoke his voice wavered at first but gradually grew in strength. 'So, my wife has maxed out my credit card, and more or less emptied all our accounts to the tune of, what, £38,000 in total? Give or take.'

'That's correct.'

'And we stand little or no chance of recovering it.'

'I don't believe we do.'

'And technically, no crime has been committed because they are joint accounts.'

'Technically, no.'

'Including the £14,000 from my credit card.'

'Yes.'

'Now, I'm guessing here… but I would say it's unlikely the bank will reimburse me for my losses because, *technically*, there's been no crime.'

Simon hesitated. 'I can't say that for sure. The bank treats cases like these on their own merits so I'll seek guidance on that. It's not my decision.'

'But if you were a betting man?'

'I'm not. Like I said, it's not my decision.'

'I'll assume you're *not* going to reimburse me.'

The bank manager didn't respond to that. And Amy was concentrating on *not* looking at either man.

Ross picked up again. 'My losses are my losses, I can see that. But then there's the credit card withdrawal. I'll have to pay that back because I won't have any consumer protection, will I?'

'I don't think you *will* have any consumer protection, no. And I'm afraid, with regard to the £14,000 drawn from your credit card, it's likely either the full balance will have to be paid, or the monthly interest.'

'And because my wife's not here,' Ross's voice caught for an instant. 'And not liable to be coming back, paying off the balance will be down to me. That's right, isn't it?'

'Again, I'm afraid that's most likely to be the case. The reason is because of something known as…'

Ross finished Simon's explanation for him. 'Joint liability.' Both Simon and Amy looked a little surprised until Ross said. 'I'm an accountant.' There was a collective pause. 'I know. Hard to believe but there you go.'

Ross finished summing up. 'So, in a nutshell, Carla's disappeared, and if she stays disappeared then I'm solely liable for the full £14,000.'

Simon's silence told Ross everything he needed to know. He sat down again. 'So where does that leave us?'

'You said you'd spoken to the police. But of course, they don't know about any of this, do they?'

'No. I only discovered the problem with my bank card last night, and I came here without talking to them again. But I will let them know, obviously.'

'Well, tell them I'll be happy to make myself available.'

'Thanks, I'll do that.' Ross swept his hand in the direction of the printouts and the monitor. 'What will happen now with all this?'

'Leave it with me. I'll have to talk to our banking fraud department. But, and I'm sorry to ask in these circumstances, do you have ready access to any other funds?'

'I hadn't given it a minute's thought. Not ready access, no.'

'Okay. In which case, Amy, can you set up an overdraft on Mr McKinlay's account...' He slapped his forehead, and lost his professional air for once. 'Oh what a bloody plonker. That would be a really stupid idea, wouldn't it?' Amy started laughing but jammed her hand over her mouth. Then she saw Ross was laughing too so that made her feel better.

Simon recovered his composure. 'Cancel that. Suspend all three accounts, and set up a new one in Mr McKinlay's name. Put an immediate overdraft of £1000 with no charges, and interest free.' Amy was smiling openly now.

He addressed Ross directly. 'And if you make an appointment to come in and see Amy in the next couple of days, she'll help you sort out any standing orders and direct debits.'

'Thanks, Simon. I appreciate that.'

The manager smiled. 'I think, given everything we've discovered this afternoon, I can hardly send you out the door without some help. There's still a lot to sort out but that should give you some breathing space.' Ross started to thank him again but Simon brushed it off.

'There is one thing I'd like to say before you go. Please try to understand that you're the victim in all this. You haven't done anything wrong. Unfortunately, this sort of thing happens to lots of innocent people, and the bank must follow the formal line.' He indicated his colleague. 'But we, Amy and I, we have to deal with the personal impact, with real human beings, and we'll do all we can to help. I honestly can't say how it will all pan out but let me ask the questions anyway.'

Ross just nodded, not trusting himself to speak. Simon shook his hand and left the room, striding out along the corridor. Amy and Ross stopped off at her desk and made an appointment for later in the week.

Outside, he looked around for his bike, forgetting for a moment where he'd left it. As he was preparing to cycle away he recognised his afternoon at the bank had been a tough hurdle. But he was safely over it, and now he felt able to move on to the next stage.

His next thought was less positive.

And as for you, Carla, you evil bitch, I'm going to fuckin' swing for you!

34

Throwing a quick, 'Back in a minute,' over her shoulder, Amanda hurried from the meeting room.

A few minutes later she reappeared carrying an iPad. She walked briskly past reception, where Ashley was doing her best to morph into her monitor. Amanda halted, took a few steps back to lean over the reception desk, and spoke quietly and earnestly to her for about thirty seconds. Just before she moved away, she placed her hand gently on Ashley's forearm. The girl nodded briefly, as did Amanda. Mel couldn't be certain but she thought Ashley was sitting a good deal straighter than a few minutes previously.

Amanda positioned herself between Andrew and Mel. She accessed Facebook then swiped and tapped for a good few minutes.

'Hang on,' said Mel. 'Is Carla on Facebook?'

'Yes,' said Amanda. 'Why do you ask?'

'We understood she wasn't.' Mel glanced at her partner, who shook his head.

'Well,' said Amanda. 'I don't see posts from her every day but she is on there. Anyway, I'm about to show you something on her timeline. And I should warn you, it's not pretty.' She tapped on a collection of photos then sat back.

Mel looked at the screen. She could sense her expression was revealing her feelings like a bad gambler's tell.

She pointed at an image, the largest one on the screen. 'And that's Carla?'

'It's a selfie so it's not the best quality but you get the picture.' Amanda put on a wry smile. 'No pun intended.'

Mel scrolled up and down. There were half a dozen similar images taken from different angles.

Tom moved round the table to stand behind Mel. 'What the fuck happened to *her*?'

Mel had only ever seen Carla dolled up in her wedding photo so she didn't know what the woman looked like normally. But whatever *normal* was, this wasn't it. The face staring at her resembled a testing ground for one of Andy

Warhol's more garish colour palettes. Mustard yellow and midnight blue for the half face bruise that ran from the left side of Carla's throat to her hairline; Burgundy red for the livid scab that snaked down the ridge of her nose; charcoal for the deep smudges under her eyes; and blazing green for her right eye, which glared in silent defiance at the lens. Carla's left eye was swollen and half closed so its colouring could only be assumed.

Amanda pointed at the caption but Mel had already spotted it.

'This is me, two days after my 'fall'. My husband is unusually attentive.'

The inference wasn't subtle.

Below the photo were several messages of support, a continuum that ran from outrage to revenge. Conciliation and reason were conspicuous by their absence.

'Do you know any of these people?' Mel twisted her neck to include Tom.

'I didn't post,' said Amanda. 'I'm a bit of a lurker on Facebook. But that one's Sal, a friend of ours.' She moved her finger down the list of comments to one posted in Italian. 'I imagine that's her sister but I don't know any of the others.'

Andrew leaned over and pointed at a comment, glancing meaningfully at Mel.

'Get yourself out of there, girl. Luv Ell xx.'

She nodded, then asked Amanda, 'Do *you* think it was an accident?'

'That's what's tearing me up. I've known Ross for twenty-odd years. He wouldn't hurt a fly. I've never seen him lose his temper. *Never.*' She smoothed out her skirt with her palms. 'But I tell you, that Carla, she's a right madam. And it wasn't just my old man she flirted with. Anything in trousers as far I could see. So maybe, just maybe, he'd had enough of it and had a pop at her.' Mel raised an eyebrow, and Amanda shot straight back with: 'But I can't see it. Not Ross.' She turned to her husband. 'Back me up here, Tom.'

He didn't hesitate. 'Ross wouldn't have done that to her. No way. I'm positive about that.'

It was the only civil exchange between the couple that Mel and Andrew had witnessed all morning.

* * *

'Right, my boy. This is growing arms and legs. I'll do the talking, you do the thinking.' The two detectives were sitting in their car. Mel fiddled with her seatbelt. 'First, do we think he put her in hospital?'

'The Duncans say he didn't. Carla's Facebook post *hints* he did but she doesn't actually *say* he did. Not outright, anyway. And there's nothing about Ross that suggests to me he would do that, unless he's Laurence Olivier in disguise'

'So, we should speak to A&E. And her GP. Do we know who that is?'

Andrew flicked through his notes. 'We do.'

'Good. Now, what's behind all this flirting?' She slapped the seat beside her. 'No, bugger flirting. This is much more than that. We now have three guys, minimum, she's tried it on with to one degree or another. What do you make of it?'

'That's been bugging me too and I think it's all a smokescreen.' Andrew twisted sideways and rested his elbow on the steering wheel. 'It's entirely possible she's deliberately pissed Amanda off by dressing provocatively in front of Tom.'

'Who took the bait, as it happens.'

'Indeed. And if you look at who she's tried it on with, the two nearest neighbours and one of his oldest pals, I definitely think she's gone out of her way to alienate people. Friends and neighbours Ross is close with, or might become close with in the case of the French couple. In fact, is there anyone else who's close to him she hasn't had a go at?'

In unison, they both said: 'Martin.'

Mel clapped her hands together. 'Right. We were planning to speak to him anyway so let's do that sooner rather than later. Now, who's this other friend of theirs, the one that Amanda recognised on Facebook?'

'Sally.'

'We need to talk to her but not right now. But there's someone I do want to talk to.'

'And who's that?'

'Carla's agency. It didn't seem so urgent before but something tells me it is now.' She deliberated for a few seconds. 'Anything I've missed?'

'I don't think so. But I want to go back and look at the supermarket CCTV again.'

'Why? What are you thinking?'

'I don't know. There something bothering me about it. Something nagging me.' He shook his head. 'Can't explain it, really. I just want to check it again with fresh eyes.'

They both paused as a delivery van swept into the car park and blocked them in. The driver was in the building for less than twenty seconds before he was off again, bumping out of the car park and over the pavement in a manoeuvre that wasn't exactly legal.

Mel just shrugged. 'Fair do's. We'll head back to the station at some point but A&E is on the opposite side of town, and we're right in the middle. Marvellous. Where's the GP?'

'Colinton.' Andrew named a residential area on the west side of Edinburgh. At the third point of a city-wide triangle and also miles away from where they sat.

'Flamin' typical. And where's Martin's office? On the bloody moon?'

'Near enough. Cramond Village.'

'You must be fucking joking. A scenic tour of Edinburgh? That'll be bloody right. I'm not driving all over town just to speak to three people.'

'Actually, you're not driving. I am.'

'Don't be such a wanker, Andrew. It doesn't suit you.'

'There are just too many answers to that... but I won't bother. Right, where first, boss?'

Mel was decisive. 'To the GP. And don't spare the horsepower, my man. I'll make some calls.'

As they drove across town Mel phoned the station. She spoke to a PC who was seconded to their team while she recovered from a broken ankle, sustained while *'Chasing some ned'* across a building site. According to Steph, the PC in question: *'I nearly had the wee bugger.'* But sadly a half buried lump of concrete had intervened.

Mel asked her colleague to contact A&E admissions at the Edinburgh Royal Infirmary to see if they could track down who'd treated Carla. She also requested that Steph get the ball rolling on Carla's and Ross's mobile phone records, and Carla's email activity. Next, she called Martin to say they would be coming over at some point.

Finally, she rang Carla's agency and introduced herself. 'This is just an initial enquiry. Do you have a Carla McKinlay on your books?' She quoted Carla's address and her employer. After a couple of minutes' wait, she spoke again. 'Could she be registered under her maiden name? She's not been married that long.' She whispered to Andrew. 'What *is* her maiden name?'

'Marinello.' Mel relayed that to the agency.

'And you're sure about that. No chance you've missed something?' A car pulled alongside, hoping to switch lanes but Mel gave the driver the evil eye. He braked, trying to squeeze into the gap behind. 'So who do I speak to about that?' A pause. 'Okay, thanks very much. You've been very helpful.'

'Do you want to guess?' she said to the windscreen.

'Carla McKinlay isn't registered with the agency.'

She sighed. 'I don't suppose it was a difficult question.'

'Not exactly Mastermind level, admittedly. So what next?'

'I'll need to speak to Steph again.' Mel called her colleague and explained that all North Sea offshore personnel carried a Vantage card. The card is linked to a person-on-board, or POB, database that holds up-to-date information on offshore workers' survival training records, medical certificates and, most importantly, a complete history of their trips offshore. Every time Carla checked in at the Aberdeen heliport, her card would have been scanned. So even if Mel had called the wrong agency, or quoted the wrong employer, if Carla worked offshore she would have had to show her card. Mel also told Steph the company that administered the POB database on behalf of any organisation, worldwide, that had people working in the North Sea. Steph said she'd get on it immediately.

While Mel was on the phone, the supermarket's lost property office called Andrew on hands-free. No one had yet handed in a black Puffa jacket but they would keep in touch.

He was pulling up outside the Colinton Medical Practice when Mel's phone rang. 'Steph, what've you got for me?' Her colleague had quite a tale to tell. Mel listened intently, jotting down the odd note and asking one or two questions. She finished with, 'Thanks, Steph, you're a wee star. I'll probably be back to you soon.'

Andrew arched an eyebrow. 'Well?'

'We've caught a break here. The A&E doctor who treated Carla back in September is on duty this afternoon. I'll ring her before we go into the GP.'

'And the Vantage card?'

'Whatever the missing Mrs McKinlay does for a living on her three weeks away from home, she does not work offshore.'

'Oh ho!' But Andrew was unable to say any more as Mel was calling A&E. After several minutes she thanked the doctor for her help, and ended the call.

'Right. That was Hannah White. She remembers Carla, even though it was four, five months ago. She said it was mainly because of the way Ross behaved.'

'Meaning?'

'Apparently, in her experience, when a couple come in to A&E, and there's even a *suggestion* of domestic abuse, the husband, partner or whoever he is, tends to display specific behaviours. They might be completely uptight and say nothing, but the vibe to the woman is crystal. Keep your mouth shut. And, he won't let her out of his sight.'

'And if the partner behaved like that, the doc would be fairly sure he'd knocked her about?'

'Let's just say she'd be more than a bit suspicious. Or, it could be that the partner is fawning all over the woman, making a huge fuss, sucking up to the medical staff, as if he's trying way too hard to convince everybody his lady's injuries are a total accident.'

'That sounds realistic. What about the third type?'

'Apparently they *look* as guilty as sin but they keep absolutely schtum, so it's difficult to tell one way or the other.'

'Okay.' Andrew looked puzzled. 'Where does that leave Ross?'

'Well that's the reason Hannah remembered him. Apparently he was attentive and concerned but not overly so. When Carla was called through into the treatment area, he *asked* her if she wanted him to come too. Seems like they agreed he would just wait where he was until she'd been seen. Then, when she came back out with the doctor, he asked specifically where he should take her for any follow up treatment. A&E, or her own GP, or what.'

'And all those things pointed towards him being innocent, in the doctor's eyes?'

A young woman with a toddler appeared in Mel's wing mirror. Mel tensed as the child made a bid for freedom but the woman was on it, scooping him up in a bundle and making him giggle. His feet hit the deck as they drew level with the car then turned into the surgery.

Mel breathed. 'There's a bit more to it than that. When Hannah was examining her, she asked Carla how she'd hurt herself. Carla said she'd fallen down the stairs so Hannah asked if Ross had been there at the time. And this is where it becomes interesting because at first, Carla said no, it was her own fault, Ross had been in the back garden. It was just an accident.'

'And then?'

'Hannah had accepted that but then Carla brought it up again by saying something like, I'm *sure* it was an accident. Then when Hannah asked her what she meant, she clammed up.'

'Okay. But thinking aloud, might that not suggest Ross *could* have hit her, and Carla was trying to say that, then changed her mind?'

'Possibly. But Hannah's obviously highly experienced and it just didn't ring true to her. She told me she makes a point of accompanying any woman who comes in with injuries like that, back to her partner, so she can assess if the woman's likely to be in more danger. Because A&E have a duty to report these injuries back to the patient's GP with recommendations to follow up. And, as you know, if the GP thinks it's serious enough, they'll report it to us.'

'I'm guessing Hannah didn't make that recommendation.'

'No, she didn't. When they went back out to the waiting area she had a good look at Ross and it was obvious from the state of his clothes and his hands that he'd been gardening. Then, once they were back together, apparently he gave Carla a big smile and a real, genuine hug. And, the clincher I guess, Carla hugged him right back. Hannah's seen plenty women who are kind of stiff towards their men when they see them again. Almost like they've recovered some courage and just want out of there, away from prying eyes. Especially eyes with a degree of authority.'

'Like a doctor?'

'Like a doctor.'

'So, it looks like it really *was* an accident? Carla thought she might be able to put the blame on Ross, started down that road then chickened out?'

'Exactly. Hannah was spot on, in my opinion. Now let's see what the GP did when the report was sent in from A&E.

35

It was a Monday, and only just gone four but Ross decided Jimmy Buffet was right: It *was* 'Five O'Clock Somewhere'. The large G&T he was demolishing was hitting the spot. Plus, the bottles and the slices of lime were still on the worktop so it didn't look like Ross would be stopping at one.

Like a tennis ball in a long rally, his emotions bounced back and fore between raging internally at Carla and wondering what in God's name had possessed her. Printouts from their bank accounts lay face down on the table. He'd given up looking at them. The terrible tale they told never altered.

He'd also stopped castigating himself for leaving the field clear for her to rip him off. There was no point, he rationalised. She was going to do it anyway. If he hadn't made it so easy for her, she would just have found another way.

Organised. Isn't it bloody ironic that a common or garden verb with generally positive connotations can turn out to be so fucking destructive, once it's paired with the word crime.

Ross didn't swear all that much but today he felt completely justified. Then the doorbell chimed. 'Who the fucking hell is that?' His outburst made him smile, despite the situation. He opened the front door.

It was Martin. 'Hello, sunshine. How's tricks?'

Ross's best mate didn't exercise much these days as his waistline clearly demonstrated. He was a master of the permanent three-day-stubble look, and possessed a cheeky grin that no one had ever wiped off. Martin had started going bald in his twenties so he bought an electric shaver, and hadn't paid for a haircut ever since. He loved jackets, jeans and buttoned down shirts, and possessed a wardrobe comprising more combinations than there are snowflakes on an Alpine ski-slope. Today's ensemble included an ancient pale blue Ben Sherman with red pinstripes he absolutely refused to throw out, despite its rapidly advancing years.

Ross held up his glass of watery ice and lime. Martin grimaced. 'Ah. That good, is it? Well, I may as well join you. Can't have you drinking on your own, especially at...' He pushed his sleeve up. 'Christ, Ross. Half four?' He slung his jacket on the back of a chair. 'No ice for me, thanks. I'll need to use your loo. You make the drinks, then you can tell me all about it.'

They were on their second round by the time Ross finished updating him on Sunday and Monday's events. Martin kept asking questions beginning with *why*, but Ross was unable to enlighten his friend.

'Have you told the cops?'

'Not yet. I'll call them tomorrow.'

Martin swallowed some gin to save spluttering it all over the table. 'Tomorrow? Why not tonight? In fact, why not now?' He'd been wondering if this was why the police wanted to speak to him but it couldn't be if Ross hadn't told them.

'You know, Martin, I just cannot be arsed. I've been in the bank most of the afternoon, I've been back through the whole story with you, and I can't face going through it all for a third time in one day. I've just about had enough, so tomorrow will do just fine. And anyway, it's not as if the police will be able to do anything.' He indicated the bottle of gin. 'I'll have one more of these, then something to eat, and then I'm planning to have an early night.'

'Very sensible, my man.'

'Not really. It's just that I only have enough tonic for one more.'

And for the first time since Martin had arrived, they both laughed out loud.

* * *

Mel swung her feet into the car, slammed the passenger door shut and immediately turned to her partner. 'Thank God I'm not one of their patients. And who the fuck does that Practice Manager, what was her name, Norma, think she is?'

Andrew enjoyed her little tirades. Hardly a day passed without one, and he'd soon sussed it was pointless interrupting her, or trying to adopt the voice of reason. When she was on a roll he found it easier, and far more entertaining, just to let her rattle on. Other drivers, jaywalkers, cyclists, snooty shop assistants, music on hold, people who took ages at an ATM. You name it, Mel would rant about it.

'Frosty-faced, jumped-up, old bag!'

There was no doubt the Practice Manager had been less than cooperative, throwing up all sorts of reasons why she couldn't help the detectives as quickly as they would have liked. It wasn't till Mel played her *obstructing our inquiries* card that Norma shifted, reluctantly, out of first gear. They saw the report from A&E about Carla's injuries, with a flag to indicate her GP should follow up with the patient. However, the practice's records showed that Carla had made and then subsequently cancelled an appointment. When Mel asked why they hadn't followed up a second time, Norma became all defensive. Lots of patients, lack of spare appointments, doctors run off their feet, patients have every right to cancel, and we don't have time to chase them. All just a series of excuses as far as Mel was concerned but at least they now knew why the incident, if there had been one, had turned into a dead end.

'I've been thinking,' said Andrew. 'Do we really want to be speaking to Martin right now?'

'Explain.'

'Well, Ross and Martin are really close. Anything we say to Martin will go straight back to Ross. And if we ask if Carla ever tried it on with him, or ask him about her injuries...'

'He'll call Ross, who doesn't know we're looking at either of those two things yet.'

'Precisely.'

She grinned at him. 'You're not as stupid as you look, are you?'

'Couldn't possibly be.'

'Right, let's forget Martin. We'll go back to the station. You can check out the CCTV.' Mel screwed up her face. 'And I've got some paperwork to catch up on. Bummer!'

But if Mel was looking for sympathy from her younger colleague, she would be sadly disappointed.

* * *

'You beauty!' yelled Andrew, slapping his palm on the desk.

Mel was at his side in an instant. The fuzzy image on his screen was a view taken from above a supermarket aisle.

Blurred shoppers studying shelves and pushing trolleys were posed, facing in all directions.

'Come on then, super-sleuth. What've you found?'

Andrew explained the film jumped about a bit because there were different cameras involved. Then he clicked his mouse, and the film jerked into action. This time his pointer was a crimson HB pencil, with a lead that could have performed open heart surgery.

'There's Ross coming through the front doors, it looks like he's on his own.' The view changed abruptly. 'In this one he's back there, quite far from the camera, with no one nearby that resembles his missus. A different angle this time but it still looks like he's not with anyone. Now there he is again, a couple of aisles later. The traffic's a bit busier here but still, it appears, no Mrs McKinlay. It's fairly crowded in this view but you'll see him pushing his trolley through in a second. There.'

At one point, Mel pointed at a woman who was just walking out of shot. 'Is she wearing a Puffa?'

Andrew reversed the film, and paused it. 'It looks like it but she's far too tall. But, it's February after all. Lots of women in dark padded jackets.'

From time to time, the recording would focus on particular individuals or groups. Andrew explained that the base footage might be determined by a security operative tracking suspicious shoppers, meaning everyone who had been in shot moved on, and might never appear again. There was nothing they could do about that.

They'd been watching for only a few minutes and Mel's eyes had remained glued to the screen. Eventually she sat back. 'So, does this mean he actually *is* on his own?'

'It would *appear* so.'

'Andrew,' Mel growled, as she watched three more shots of Ross captured from different angles. 'Get to the punchline or your next career move will be chasing sheep-shaggers in Shetland.'

Andrew had had his fun but now he dropped back into professional mode.

'I'll run it all again. What you're going to see is very clever. Cunning, even. Now, this time, ignore Ross. Just watch where I point.'

After a few seconds, Andrew's pencil picked up a woman wearing a light coloured jumper, or possibly a fleece. She was carrying something quite bulky down by her side. She had dark hair, in a ponytail. As she turned the corner at the end of an aisle, she tugged at the back of her hair. It fell down to her shoulders. Just as she disappeared from sight, she pulled something from her back pocket.

The camera angle changed. The woman was now walking down an aisle towards the camera but she was quite far away. As she came closer it became apparent she was now wearing a bobble hat with a Fair Isle pattern. She passed in front of Ross and his trolley, paused for an instant then walked on. The camera didn't follow her.

They watched as the screen changed once more. Yet again, the aisle was busy but the woman didn't seem to be in view.

'Where the hell is she?' said Mel.

'Look more closely. The other side of that young couple.'

'You sneaky cow.' But Mel sounded quite impressed. The woman they presumed to be Carla had taken off her hat but now she was wearing a dark coat, and the bulky item was no longer under her arm. But the coat wasn't fastened. She seemed to be deliberately holding it open to reveal the lighter top she wore underneath. As she passed closer to the camera, she rubbed her forehead with her forearm and turned away.

Mel slapped the desk. '*She's* done that to keep her face hidden.'

They watched for another couple of minutes. The woman continually changed her outfit so she was wearing the hat, the coat, and sometimes the hat *and* the coat. Sometimes the coat was open, at other times it was zipped up. Even the ponytail put in another appearance.

Then, the film ended. Mel turned to Andrew. 'Don't tell me.'

Andrew's expression matched his shrug. 'Sorry, but that's it. The cameras don't pick her up again after that.'

'So she vanished.' Mel snapped her fingers. 'Just like that.'

'Just like Ross said she did.'

Mel pushed her chair away from the desk, to create some space they could talk across. 'So… let me think this through. That woman was fairly close to Ross for several aisles. She just has to be Carla. But what other reason could she possibly have for changing her appearance so many times, apart from trying to hide in plain sight? I'm supposing, of course, that she's not a complete nutter who does this every time she goes shopping.'

'I'd be surprised.'

'So, she must have been doing it this time because she knew she was going to pull a vanishing act from inside the store.' Mel scratched her head like some oddball scientist trying to work out an elusive formula. 'Is it now safe to assume Ross didn't lock the car because she was still in there? But, if she was going to do a runner, why not do one from the car park? Why go inside at all?'

Andrew raised an index finger. 'Maybe whatever triggered the runner, happened after she left the car.'

Mel rocked her head from side to side, like an Indian gentleman saying yes. 'Could be. But she started the hat off, hat on, coat off, coat on routine, more or less in the first aisle.'

'She did. And if we base our suspicions only on her behaviour, it definitely looks like she's up to something. But remember, one of Jeff's suggestions was the two of them could be in cahoots. It could be some sort of scam that involves both of them being inside the store, but Ross ends up on his own, and pretends to anyone who'll listen that his wife has gone missing.'

She looked at Andrew across the space. 'Well. It's your theory. How does it sound to you?'

His reply was typically forthright. 'Flaky. But it's all I've got at the minute.'

'I guess the one thing we do know is the missing Mrs McKinlay is simply that. Missing. She isn't propping up a patio, and if she is, Ross didn't dig the hole. And it's now a matter of record that Ross was still in the store long after she left it.'

Mel stood up. 'Right. Before I go home to my beloved and our two darling offspring, let's go and update Jeff. We'll go and see Ross first thing in the morning and show him the video. Check for certain it's Carla.'

36

Just after nine the following morning, Mel and Andrew were driving over to Ross's house. Mel had called from the car to check he was at home. He sounded like he was about to launch into a great long story but she cut him short, telling him the call was breaking up.

'Breaking up?' Andrew snorted. 'Does anybody still fall for that?'

Mel looked embarrassed. 'Probably not, but I don't see the point in blethering away to him on the phone when we'll be meeting up in five minutes.'

Behind the scenes, Steph had been hard at work tracking down and analysing the McKinlays' phone and email records. She raised a request with the Police Communications Unit, who, in turn, had contacted the internet service provider for Carla's email. Ross didn't have a personal email address. As part of the same request, they had contacted both their phone providers but the overall result was a big fat zero.

Carla's phone hadn't been used since about two hours before she disappeared, her last call was to her husband's mobile. In the two weeks since she allegedly returned home from working offshore she'd only made calls to Ross, his office, their home and the gym. Apart from junk emails, there was nothing interesting in her email account. It hadn't been used for at least a week. Her last text was older than that, a message to Ross to say her train was approaching Edinburgh.

Carla's Facebook account would take longer, and a lot more work. Mel had given Steph the names of Carla's Facebook friends and Steph had carried out what is known as an open source check but hadn't been able to come up with anything else on Facebook that was new. If they wanted to extract more information from the social media company they would require a warrant. Steph had made an application to a Sheriff, and was waiting for a response. Once the warrant was signed off, it would probably take at least a week for the results to filter through. In truth, Mel wasn't particularly hopeful but they had to follow it up.

They were all savvy enough to recognise that Ross couldn't yet be excluded as a suspect, no matter how innocent and genuine he appeared to them. So Jeff had suggested they eyeball Ross when they told him Carla didn't work offshore at all. His reaction to the Facebook photo and the supermarket video might also be revealing.

'How do you want to play this?' Andrew asked

'I've been thinking about that. Sounds like he has something urgent to tell us, so we could let him go first. Then tell him the whole A&E and Facebook story, and see how he reacts.'

'And what about Carla's behaviour with Tom and the others? Do you think we should mention that?'

'Hmmm, not sure.' Mel poked her little finger in her right ear and waggled it about furiously. She withdrew it and studied her nail, disappointed not to have unearthed a decent-sized lump of wax or some other foreign body. 'I might drop it in, just to knock him off balance. Let's play that by ear, see how it goes. Thing is, we've got one or two surprises for *him*. So, keep a close eye on his body language, see if he gives anything away.'

As they pulled up, Ross opened the front door. He waved to them, pointed at the phone he was holding to his ear, and disappeared into the house. Mel shrugged her shoulders and they followed Ross inside, just as he finished his call.

Ross was boiling the kettle. 'Cuppa?'

A few minutes later, they were all seated round the kitchen table. Mel was about to ask Ross what he wanted to talk about, but he jumped in first.'

'Any news? Have you found anything?'

'No. We haven't, I'm afraid. But there is something we want to ask you.'

That caught his attention. 'Fire away.'

'On the twenty-eighth of September last year, Carla was treated at A&E for a suspected broken cheekbone and other injuries to her face. Can you tell us how she sustained those injuries?'

Ross didn't speak straight away. He placed his mug deliberately on a table-mat, sat back and made solid eye contact with Mel. 'Yes. I can, as a matter of fact. She was carrying some bedding down the stairs, and she tripped and fell. She hit her head on the post at the foot of the bannister. Why do you ask?'

'Were you in the house at the time?'

'No. I was outside, gardening. Again, why do you ask?'

'Did you hear her falling? Did she cry out?'

Ross leaned forward, elbows on the table. 'Mel. Let's do a deal here. I will quite happily answer all your questions but, first, do me the courtesy, why are you asking me this?'

She mirrored his position. 'Sorry to say, Ross, but I decide the agenda here. And on my agenda it says, you answer my questions first. Then, maybe, I'll answer yours. Get it?'

Ross glared at her but he could see she wasn't going to shift any time soon. 'Fine. I didn't hear her falling. I was at the back of the garden, digging over the borders. The back door was closed because it was blowing a gale. Carla knocked on the window and waved for me to come in. It was quite dark in the kitchen and I couldn't really see her properly. I didn't realise she was hurt till I went inside. Actually, she gave me a bollocking because I didn't come running when she knocked.'

'You didn't?' said Andrew.

'No. I only had about a foot of the border still to do so I just finished up. But if I'd known she was injured, of course I'd have come in straight away.' He looked at the two detectives in turn. 'Ah. I see it now. You think I hit her, don't you?'

Mel lifted her phone and tapped at the screen. 'Have you seen this?'

'I don't know. What is it?' He peered at the device, struggling at first to interpret the image on the screen. Eventually, he twigged. 'Wait a minute. This is Carla!' He looked back at Mel. 'Where did you find this picture? I haven't seen this before.'

'You don't recognise it?' asked Andrew.

'Recognise it? Of course I don't bloody recognise it. I just told you, I've never seen it before. Now, tell me where it came from.'

'We were shown it by Amanda Duncan. Carla posted it on her Facebook timeline.' Andrew fixed Ross with a direct look. 'Are you sure you didn't know she had an account?'

'I didn't, no. I have absolutely no interest in social media. None at all.' He snapped his fingers. '*That's* why Amanda's acting strangely towards me! She thinks I did this to Carla. But why would she think that? We've been friends for God knows how many years. She knows I wouldn't ever raise my hand to a woman. *Any* woman. Never mind Carla.'

Ross appeared to collapse in on himself. 'Oh, God. This is ridiculous. Terrible. I can't believe it.'

For a few seconds, it appeared as though someone had pressed his *Pause* button. He spoke again. His voice was shaky. Frail, almost. 'I don't know what you must think but let me tell you this. I've never lifted my hands to anybody. I just don't have it in me. I'm not a violent person.'

He picked up his coffee cup and rocked it back and fore on its base. It clunked the table top every time he switched direction. Ross was at rock bottom but a flame that was about to succumb sourced some oxygen from somewhere and reignited.

He addressed Mel directly. 'There's something about all this that you don't know yet. And, it's a game-changer.'

Deep down inside, Mel didn't think Ross was at the root of his wife's disappearance but that was her opinion as a woman. As a police officer, she suspected everyone until she could prove their innocence. If she had half a dozen suspects, and she could prove five of them were innocent beyond any doubt, the sixth, the perpetrator, would inevitably land safely in her lap.

'Do tell, Ross. We're all ears.'

Feeling like he had a hand full of aces, Ross related the whole story about his bank accounts. To the officers, his revelations placed Carla's disappearance in a completely different light and, being realistic, made it even less likely that he was guilty of any wrongdoing.

Andrew had reassessed the situation and picked up the threads. 'So, there's a possibility your wife was in the bank on Saturday morning.'

'Well, someone was. But I'm not allowed to see the video so I don't know if it was Carla.'

'And the bank manager doesn't think the money can be recovered?'

'No. He doesn't.'

Ross told them that Simon had offered to help them in any way he could and obviously, he would release the film of Carla or whoever it was to them. 'So will you go into the bank this morning? Because obviously that might help you find Carla, yes?'

'Possibly,' said Mel. 'We'll see.'

Ross stood up and moved away a few steps before turning to face her. 'What do you mean, you'll see?'

But it was Andrew who replied. 'Something's just occurred to me. You've been reasonably successful in life. You've had a well-paid job. Your late wife sold her business for a fair amount of cash. You don't have any kids. You've no dependants.' He swept his arm in an arc. 'And although this is a nice house, it isn't… well… a mansion. Is it?'

'I don't follow, Andrew. What's your point?'

'My point is, you don't appear to have an extravagant lifestyle. Not a huge house, five-year-old Golf sitting outside, and only twenty-odd grand in the bank? And you need an overdraft to keep the wolf from the door?'

Ross stood stock-still, his eyes locked on Andrew. Mel leaned slowly back, watching intently.

Andrew carried on. 'The missing twenty-four k, that can't be every penny you have, surely.'

Ross sat back down with such a thump, the front legs of the kitchen chair cleared the floor, and the back legs scraped a few inches towards the wall. 'No. I have other money. It's in investments. I don't touch it so I didn't even consider it.' His complexion looked like someone had opened a tap connected to his jugular. Chalk white wasn't even close. 'You don't think…'

'You should check, Ross,' said Mel.

He didn't say anything for quite a few seconds, and when he spoke it was as if the syllables were swimming through heavy syrup. 'I'll need to ring my financial adviser.' He lifted his phone and rose from the chair. Struggling to focus on the screen, he swiped and stabbed at it several times before dropping it back on the table. 'Her number's not on there. It was on my old phone but when it went missing I lost some of my contacts.' He leaned over, opened a drawer and rustled about inside. 'I'll have to look it up.' Ross closed that drawer and tried two more. 'Where the hell's my address book?'

The two detectives just looked at each other. Andrew mouthed: *his address book?* Mel had to turn away.

Ross had gone back into statue mode so Andrew, mobile in hand, stepped in to help. 'What's the company name?' Ross told him, he found their website with a few keystrokes and tapped the hyperlink to the phone number. He handed the ringing phone to Ross, whose expression was a mixture of bewildered and amazed.

'I'd like to speak with Sam Mitchell, please? It's Ross McKinlay.' He turned and faced away from the table. 'Hi Sam, Ross McKinlay here. Yes, fine Sam. Listen, I'm really sorry to be so abrupt but I need you to check something for me right away, and I don't have time to chat just now. I'll explain later.'

He rubbed his forehead and closed his eyes. 'The investments I have with you, Sam. Can you tell me, what's the current valuation?' He paused. 'No, if you don't mind, I'll hold.'

Several minutes dragged by and no one spoke. Ross paced up and down along the same length of laminate flooring. He made patterns with his steps to give him something to think about: a distraction. 'Yes, Sam. Those ones.' He stopped speaking *and* pacing. 'What do you mean, *were* held under the Trident platform?' He walked over to the window and put a hand on the sill. He slid an ornament from the centre to the left and back again. 'No, Sam. I didn't do that. When was this? What was the date?' He turned to face into the room. 'And you didn't know about it? No, of course, online transactions. You wouldn't have been aware.'

Now Ross was looking skywards. 'And you're not alerted in any way, an email or something?' Mel and Andrew were whispering to each other but Ross didn't notice. 'I'm sorry, Sam, I'd rather not say. But could you please find out the banking details and call me back on my mobile, please.' He listened for a few more seconds, confirmed his phone number, stumbled out his thanks and ended the call.

Mel spoke first. 'How much are we talking about?'

Ross sat down again before answering her. He smoothed out some creases in his trousers then squeezed his lower lip with his thumb and index finger. He looked directly at her, and spoke in a strong, clear voice. 'I forget the exact figure but it's about £390,000.'

'Shit!'

Mel now knew for sure that Ross definitely was *not* suspect number six.

37

Sabine Mathieu yawned.

Not a demure, ladylike little yawn, where one might politely shield one's open mouth with the back of one's hand. No, the yawn that practically consumed Sabine's entire body was an enormous, jaw-wrenching, arms-to-the-ceiling and feet-stretched-right-out yawn. It was accompanied by a vocal exhalation that travelled all the way from the soles of her size thirty-eight pumps. Anyone nearby wouldn't have been in any doubt just how exhausted the young woman was.

Sabine was overweight, her hair desperately needed a restyle and she was fed up wearing the same clothes all the time. Her problem was, funds were way past tight.

That particular Friday morning, it wasn't even seven o'clock. The thirty-four-year-old freelance journalist had just parked her car two streets away from her apartment on the outskirts of Quimper. Free spaces in this neighbourhood were as scarce as Shergar-shit.

Sabine had just pulled a long shift, almost twenty-four hours. She'd been chasing down a story she was *that close* to selling to the features editor of *Ouest-France*, a regional newspaper with the largest circulation of any journal in its home country and purportedly read by 2.5 million French-speaking people every day. So this was a biggie as far as Sabine's escalating credit card bill was concerned. In the next day or so she expected to be handed conclusive proof that several regional council officials had been in receipt of bungs in the form of plump envelopes, apparently eager call-girls and Mediterranean cruises on yachts belonging to the extremely wealthy, and the extremely grateful.

So when her phone trilled just as she was walking through the door of her apartment block, she assumed the call related to the bent officials. Sabine jammed the phone to her ear without checking the display and was surprised to hear what, on later reflection, sounded like a prepared statement read by a man with a Slavic accent. After several seconds of stunned immobility she snapped back into ace-reporter mode and left the door swinging closed as she shot back down the steps and set off on a breathless jog in the direction of her car. Her previously dog-tired state disappeared like the remnants of a pleasurable dream as she wondered if this might be a second story she could sell to that cheapskate features editor.

Within ninety seconds, a similar call was taken by a freelancer who worked almost exclusively for the Quimper sub-office of *Le Figaro*, a national daily. A third call was answered by the operations director at a local agency that supplied stories to the international news and current affairs channel, France 24. As a result of those calls, two reporters and a cameraman made rapid exits from their beds and charged off to the same location that Sabine was heading for in her decrepit wheezing Renault. *If I land both of these stories, the first thing I'll be doing is replacing this shit-heap of a car.*

The Credit Mutuel de Bretagne, or CMB, on Boulevard Dupleix is an elegant four-storey building. It is fronted by two small lawns, divided by a central path that leads to the entrance to the bank. Above the double doors is a semi-circular veranda supported by two stone columns, one either side of the door.

The morning sun was flirting with the horizon to the east as Sabine stood on the path in between the two lawns, gazing up at the building. She was frozen to the spot as if she'd just come second to Medusa in a staring competition. Standing next to her was Lucas Dufour, from *Le Figaro*. The two reporters had been firm friends for several years. They'd worked together, been drunk together but hadn't slept together. Yet, as far as she was concerned.

Sabine was clinging on to Lucas's left arm, to the extent his fingers were beginning to tingle. Behind them, a France 24 van bumped up on the pavement and a camera-man hopped out. He trotted forward to join them, followed their line of sight, and uttered two words: 'Jesus Christ!' In different circumstances, it would have been an outstanding pun. In the distance, they could hear a siren wailing as an ambulance made its way from the Centre Hospitalier de Cornouaille to this very building.

Later that day, having worked several hours past the end of her shift in the Critical Care Unit, or CCU, a nurse snuggled up to her husband on an over-stuffed sofa in their three-room apartment on the outskirts of Quimper. Her hair, still wet from the shower, hung down over the collar of a towelling robe that had once been white.

'I saw it on the news, Claire.' Her husband, Raoul, gave her shoulder a comforting squeeze with his arm. 'What on earth had they done to that poor man?'

Claire just shuddered and gripped her mug of hot chocolate even more tightly. But over the course of the evening, she told Raoul all about *that poor man*.

The three news-people had discovered Jean-Luc Dornier affixed to a rough wooden 'A' frame, its legs resting on the balcony of the CMB building. It was leaning against a decorative stone carving of the bank's logo, just below the roofline.

Jean-Luc was impaled to the legs of the frame by two long galvanised metal bolts, drilled directly through his shoulder joints. His head was supported by a sling, hooked over the peak of the 'A' and, curiously, padded with a hand-towel as if to prevent any damage to his neck and throat.

When the police checked out all the timings it transpired that following the initial three calls, exactly ten minutes later an emergency call was made requesting fire, police *and* an ambulance.

The fire crew and the medics had lowered the desperately injured and heavily sedated man to the lawn where the scale of his horrific injuries gradually became apparent. But it wasn't until he was admitted to the CCU that a hastily assembled emergency team would discover the full extent.

In addition to the holes drilled through his shoulders, he had similar injuries to his elbows, hips and knees. His pelvis had been broken in several places, and extensive bruising at the base of his spine indicated his lower back had suffered a similar assault.

His feet were in a terrible state. Both his big toes had been removed, and scans revealed most of his foot and ankle bones had been crushed. His eight remaining toenails had been ripped out. His hands had fared no better. All five fingers had been removed from his right hand, the thumb from his left, and again, the remaining fingernails from that hand were all missing.

Raoul was as shocked now as Claire had been earlier when Jean-Luc was wheeled into theatre. He commented that perhaps the injured man might be able to give the police some information concerning his assailants. She was unable to meet her husband's eye. She opened her mouth and, using her fingernail, drew a line across her tongue indicating that communicating by speech would no longer be an option for Jean-Luc.

As far as his face was concerned, it appeared at first as though no damage had been caused. But then the medical team discovered that most of his sparkling white teeth had been drilled out. Finally it was revealed that a strong acid had been dripped directly onto his eyeballs, penetrating all the way though the retina so his sight was completely and irreversibly destroyed.

But the one fact that Claire didn't pass on to Raoul related to something no man would ever wish to consider. Jean-Luc's torturers had cut off the end of his penis.

Later that evening, as they were closing blinds and turning off lights, Claire paused and turned to Raoul. 'There is something bizarre about this case. All of the man's wounds had been surgically cleaned and taped up. They had even hooked him up to a saline drip while he was hanging there. And looking at his body, despite all those unimaginable injuries, he had been kept well-nourished. Whoever did all that to him, they certainly didn't want him to die accidentally of an infection or dehydration.' She shook her head for the hundredth time that day, still unable to come to terms with what she had witnessed.

'But why was he crucified on the front wall of a bank? What's the symbolism there?'

Claire pulled the duvet up to her chin. 'We don't know. But there's obviously some connection to money. There was a huge euro currency sign on his chest. They branded it into his flesh, most likely with a lit cigar.'

38

The morning after Jean-Luc Dornier was found impaled, Dani was in her office waiting for Miroslav to call. She imagined today was probably a first. It certainly felt like it.

She'd come in for only one reason, to compile and send an email. This email could not be sent from her laptop or her phone. It required the higher security provided by their office servers, linked as they were to a chain of proxies located across Europe and beyond, that would ensure the email could never be traced back to them.

And the reason today was so unusual? Miroslav had insisted he read the email before she sent it. She was sure there had never been an instance where he'd even considered cross-checking her work and, as she thought about that, her mind drifted back in time.

All the way to 1996, when she had just turned nineteen.

* * *

Danijela was walking home from a party with two friends. Laughing and giggling like the schoolgirls they had been not that long ago, they were crossing a street close to Prague's main railway station, Hlavni Nadrazi. It was just before midnight. In most cities, these areas are hardly salubrious and the Czech capital was no exception. Think King's Cross in London or Rome's Stazione Termini. They were just passing an extremely dodgy-looking bar when the doors crashed open and a group of drunken young hooligans erupted onto the street, practically landing on top of the three girls. Danijela's friends recognised they were sitting on a fizzing powder-keg and immediately legged it, but she was so enraged at the men's behaviour she took it upon herself to berate the group. At first they appeared cowed, then they began laughing at the absurdity of the situation. Eventually one of the younger ones, awash with bravado fuelled by umpteen glasses of slivovitz, pawed at her and told her he'd give her a damn good seeing to if she didn't shut up. Danijela

167

turned on him, spat directly in his face and kicked him full force in the nuts.

If she had left it there, his friends might very well have carried her shoulder-high the full length of nearby Wenceslas Square in celebratory procession, and made her queen of their little gang. But, unfortunately, she'd partaken of a few slivovitzes herself and continued her verbal attack, choosing, regrettably, the group's leader as her next target. An ill-advised decision. Older than the others, and a violent man with a mean streak, he wasn't about to lose face. He belted her once across the jaw, hard, and dragged her, semi-conscious, into a darkened alley that gave access to the rear of the bar. It was a foul-smelling place, frequented by drugs users, prostitutes with their clients, and the occasional wayward drunk, caught short in between stops. While two of his comrades pinned her down, the leader used a knife to rip open her dress from breast to knee. He was about to repeat the motion on her underclothes when an empty steel beer keg came crashing down on the back of his head. He dropped to the ground like his heart had been ripped from his chest. And he stayed there.

The two lads holding Danijela turned quickly, rising to face their aggressor and ready to defend themselves, but stopped like they'd been tasered when they realised who it was. 'Are you fucking crazy?' one of them yelled at Miroslav, who was bent over slightly from the waist, still gently massaging his aching crotch.

He stared them both down. 'We'll all be crazy if we hang about here too long, you bloody idiots.' He gestured towards the girl but kept his gaze firmly on them. 'This is attempted rape at the least. What the fuck were you thinking of?' There was no reply, just the echo of dawning realisation in alcohol-sozzled brains. 'Now, help me get her out of here before *he* wakes up or a policeman walks past.'

In the movies, the heroine would probably have informed the hero in strident tones and in no uncertain terms that she was fully in control of the situation, thank you, and who the hell did he think he was, sticking his nose in where it wasn't wanted. Or needed.

But when Miroslav turned back to Danijela she was on the edge of collapse, weeping and shivering uncontrollably, whilst trying, and failing, to preserve her modesty. He wrapped his coat around her and all three men half walked, half supported the traumatised woman to the steps of a nearby church where, gradually, she calmed down.

Miroslav's jerked his head to indicate his buddies should clear off and they didn't need a second invitation. They jogged away down the street, anxious to be well clear of the area in case their erstwhile leader made an unwelcome return.

Later, Danijela was able to laugh at the circumstances of her assault on his wedding tackle, but she stopped short of offering to sooth his pain.

Over the next few months Miroslav and Danijela became close friends and, following the untimely death of his mother, they took off to see what the rest of the world had to offer. On their travels, they were occasional lovers but mainly for fun, lust, and sometimes just to keep warm. They loved each other but were not *in* love. Despite each of them having the occasional fling, by and large they stuck together. Danijela always maintained they were saving two other poor sods from a life of hell.

* * *

Danijela looked up. Blinked. Miroslav was standing at her desk.

'Dani.' He spoke softly, gently. 'Some of the things we have to do, the actions we have to take are somewhat… distasteful. But, they are also necessary.'

She made to speak but he held up a hand. 'I asked to see the email before you sent it, not because I wished to vet your work. No, I wanted… needed to see it so I could appreciate how you might be feeling after compiling it.'

He smiled at her.

She tried to return the smile but didn't quite succeed.

'Thank you, Dani. The email is perfect. It should achieve precisely what we need it to.'

He paused. Smiled again. 'Send it. Send it now, please.'

Then he reached out, cupped a hand on her shoulder, and walked out the door.

Danijela didn't react immediately. She too, paused, and thought for a while.

Then she hit Send.

The email's distribution list included all seventy-three of their active operatives. She had already closed down the Frenchman's email account and deleted all references to him. As far as the organisation was concerned, he had never existed.

The email was sent to recipients in Spain, Portugal, France, Germany, Italy, Switzerland, Austria, Scandinavia and the UK. It contained no text. That was *completely* surplus to requirements. But it did include several file attachments. Close-up images of Jean-Luc hanging on the 'A' frame, plus several others showing him in various states of consciousness in what appeared to be a dilapidated farmhouse. These were quite gruesome and left nothing to the imagination. Also included were links to articles in *Ouest-France* and *Le Figaro*, and to a video of a France 24 news bulletin.

The vast majority of the recipients found the content of the email abhorrent, and spent very little time studying either the still photos or the video before permanently deleting the message. If they said or thought anything at all about their critically injured former colleague, it was along the lines of *'Poor bugger.'* Only two or three people gloried in the content. Had it been possible to wear out a jpeg by looking at it, their file attachments would have been blank by the end of the weekend.

A similar number immediately revised plans they had been making to retire somewhere warm with healthy bank balances. *'Honesty is the best policy,'* became their new catch phrase.

But one person couldn't tear their eyes from the horrendous images. In their imagination Jean-Luc's face and body was supplanted by their own. They suffered, and continued to suffer several different inter-changeable emotions that looped in their brain like some macabre, uninterruptable slideshow.

As time passed, this person's abject terror convinced them their fate was already sealed.

There were only two questions to be answered.

When?

And how?

39

Three Weeks Later

In the intervening period, Ross pinballed between plummeting despair, mind-numbing pragmatism, and repeated short-lived attempts to regain some equilibrium. He was a frequent visitor to four of the five stations on the bereavement curve: denial, anger, bargaining and depression. His ticket didn't allow him to travel as far down the line as acceptance. Just as well, as he had no intention of going there anytime soon.

He couldn't count the number of times he'd thought or said, 'This just can't be happening to me.'

Denial.

And his own voices, internal and external, were beginning to irritate him no end.

The day after the bombshell about his investment portfolio being cleaned out, he went in to Queen Charlotte Street and was shown the CCTV excerpts. He confirmed without hesitation it was Carla on both films, despite the disguises: the blue hoodie in the supermarket and a wide-brimmed hat at the bank. When Mel asked how he could be so certain when the woman had been careful to keep her face hidden from view, he said he'd recognise his wife's walk anywhere.

'How does she walk?'

'It's not really a walk, it's more of a glide.'

'A glide?'

'Yes, I used to tease her about walking like a Dalek but she didn't know what a Dalek was.'

'They don't have *Doctor Who* on Italian TV then?'

'I don't fucking know, do I?'

Anger.

Mel also asked if he'd noticed Carla continually altering her appearance with her coat, hat and ponytail. Ross said he hadn't. Even Andrew arched his eyebrows.

Although they said they'd be continuing with their enquiries Ross considered that to be the ultimate exercise in time-wasting futility. He found himself constantly dwelling on how naïve he had been, berating himself for never giving a single thought as to why a pretty Italian woman, twelve years his junior, would fall for *a boring fucking accountant*. He felt massively humiliated, deeply embarrassed, and so, so disappointed with himself. There were periods when he felt utterly at a loss, unable to concentrate on anything.

Depression.

But his overriding emotion was shame. He was ashamed he'd lost all the savings he and Liz had accumulated during their all-too-brief life together. When Sam gave him the ball-crushing news that their long-term investments had been plundered, he wondered if his pain could *be* more acute. It wasn't simply the loss of the money, nor was it the discovery of yet another layer of Carla's betrayal. No, it was that he and Liz had worked relentlessly for two decades to accumulate, grow and safeguard their intended nest-egg, which his late wife didn't ever have the opportunity to enjoy.

More depression.

That bitch had schemed for over a year to steal it from him. And, she had stolen it from places he had assumed were the safest of safe havens. A bank and an investment fund.

His phone conversation with Sam had been so brief, he'd been so blunt, he called her to apologise, to explain and to ask her the question he was dreading asking. He couldn't say why, but he had deliberately avoided checking that the money from the sale of Liz's business was still safe. Mel and Andrew hadn't asked if Liz had left any estate. Ross thought that was either an oversight or they'd just assumed Sam was holding all his investments in one portfolio.

Either way, he had deliberately chosen not to mention Liz's money because he didn't want to admit to the police officers that he just hadn't considered it. The truth? He was absolutely terrified it had been taken, and was even more terrified to find out. He felt like some kid who was scared to look out from behind the sofa, even although his mum had promised him the TV monsters really *were* dead. Later, he decided he'd probably been trying to protect himself from more hurt. In the two years since he had instructed Sam to put it somewhere safe, he'd never considered touching it. In his head it was his wife's money, and the prospect of spending it was anathema to him. So, step one on the pragmatism ladder, speak to Sam, and *please, God, let it still be there.*

Bargaining.

Understanding the severity of the situation, Sam instantly offered to meet him the same day he called. He laid out the whole tale of Carla's deception then bit the bullet and asked his question. But she was one step ahead of him, and he didn't know whether to laugh or cry when she assured him Liz's money was fully accounted for. She showed him a statement, dated that day. The value of the fund had grown to just over £1.6 million.

Sam had also investigated how Carla had been able to steal the £390,000 held on the Trident platform. She'd established that Ross had, purportedly, written direct to Trident requesting online access, and had been sent the User ID, password and PIN. She explained to them that the request hadn't come from Ross, that the police were investigating financial irregularities, and asked them to escalate the issue through their internal anti-fraud unit. 'But don't build your hopes up, Ross. It could take years, and you might only recover a fraction of your money.'

Knowing Ross as well as she did, Sam hadn't ever suggested online banking. She couldn't have known what Carla was doing with the Trident fund but Sam had put Liz's money in a fixed interest Government Bond, which she controlled, so it hadn't been possible for Carla to pull the same trick. Ross laid it out, straight. 'No matter what, Sam, I will *never* want online access to this fund, so keep things just as they are. And, unless I ask you in person, treat any other request as bogus.' He finished by arranging to transfer £5,000 from the fund to his new current account. He expected the bank would eventually ask him to reimburse them for the credit card cash withdrawal but would deal with that as and when it became an issue.

Something else that was bugging him was the sex. Carla had been way out there on that front, encouraging him and being willing to do all sorts of unusual stuff. It had been sensational at the time but now he realised it had all been an act. She had played the part of a cheap hooker, tricking her john out of his money while he slept. *I was sleeping for over a year. Some bloody fairy tale, that.* He wondered now if she'd ever enjoyed any of the sex. He refused to consider it had been lovemaking.

A few days in, with hardly any thought and with zero conscience, he took all Carla's belongings and anything she had ever given him and dumped the whole lot in black bin liners. Only then did he notice she had very few personal effects. *Christ, Ross. Were your eyes and your brain disconnected or something?* His socialist principles stopped him throwing the bags into a skip, so the charity shops in Leith became the grateful beneficiaries. But the photograph taken on their wedding day, *another farce*, was a different story. He ripped that into tiny pieces, and binned them. He imagined he might derive some satisfaction from the act but he was wrong.

He moved Liz's picture to centre stage on the unit in the living room, angled it towards his armchair, and vowed he would never again compromise his love for her. The tears came again that day.

As arranged, he met with Amy, who sorted out everything to do with his accounts, standing orders and direct debits. She told him Simon was on the case regarding all the missing money and although she tried to sound positive, Ross considered pessimism to be the more realistic approach.

Eventually, he needed some shopping and drove to the supermarket. He saw no point in changing stores. After all, he knew where to find all his standard items. *Including cashew nuts.* Even the bleakest of circumstances will generate little gems of black humour, he thought.

Martin had told him to take as much time as he needed but he only took a week off work. After about an hour of his colleagues pussyfooting around him, he gathered them round and told them in very straightforward terms that he wasn't a leper, nor an invalid, and could they just start behaving normally. Please. His job-share, Elspeth, had no such hang-ups even though they hadn't worked together that long. When she came in on their crossover day she stomped straight up to him, enveloped him in a life-threatening hug, and murmured in his ear, 'If I ever meet that cow, I'll rip her bloody head off and bounce it off a wall.' Then she released him to breathe again and wandered off to make them a coffee.

Martin told Amanda and Sally what had happened. The girls turned up at Ross's house one Saturday evening, laden with food, wine and bucket-loads of remorse. Especially Amanda. They all had far too much to drink and just before midnight Amanda called for a taxi to take them both home. However, Sally declared she wasn't ready to leave. The other two were just about sober enough to exchange knowing glances.

At the cab, Amanda gave Ross a hug and a kiss on the cheek. 'Be careful there, Ross. You know Sal has the hots for you?'

He pretended to laugh off the remark but short of bundling Sally in beside her friend, he figured he was stuck with her for a while yet. 'Don't worry. I'll phone for another cab in a wee while. Time for some coffee now, I think.'

As he passed the living room door, he called out, 'I'll make us a coffee, Sal.' He carried on into the kitchen and busied himself making the drinks.

A few minutes later, carrying the coffees on a wooden tray, Ross nudged open the living room door with his elbow. He was surprised to find the room almost in darkness, only illuminated by a few flickering candles that Sally had obviously lit while he was out of the room. He felt immediate tension in the pit of his stomach, as if all his internal organs in that area had been shrink-wrapped. Sally was kneeling on the carpet, sitting back on her heels, her skirt flared out on the floor behind her. That was all she was wearing. Her recently discarded top lay in a crumpled heap on the arm of the sofa, one creased and crooked arm gesturing towards the floor. A cream-coloured lacy bra with enormous cups lay twisted on the carpet, a pair of matching knickers tangled in the strap. Sally wasn't a tall woman, barely five foot two, but she was carrying lots of extra pounds. She had a big bum, with the thighs and tummy to match. Her boobs were huge. To Ross, who hadn't ever experienced a woman of Sally's proportions, they looked like two flesh-coloured rugby balls.

'Sally, Sally, Sally. I'm sorry, pet, but this is just not happening.' He laid the tray down. 'I'll be back in a minute. Please put your clothes back on.'

Ross deliberately used the upstairs bathroom to kill some time and when he came back down, Sally was fully dressed and was calling a contract taxi. He tried to speak to her but she was having none of it, throwing a *talk to the hand* gesture at him. Ten minutes later he poured two lukewarm coffees down the sink.

What he couldn't have known was how intense her temper remained on her journey home, muttering things like: 'Fucking selfish rotten bastard. How fucking dare he turn me down. He doesn't know who he's fucking fucking with.'

The taxi driver was mightily relieved it was a contract hire. Had it been a cash fare, he wasn't sure madwoman in the back would have paid.

* * *

Martin and the twins came round for dinner too, a far more sedate affair. The girls loved their *uncle* Ross, and were glad to see he was almost back to his usual self.

He hardly ever saw Didier and Amelie but he knew they were still there, closeted behind their perpetually closed vertical blinds.

He resumed his tennis matches with Barry, had a few pints with his mates after a midweek football match, and told Joe that Carla was gone for good and wouldn't be back. When Joan heard the news, she adopted the snooty air she reserved especially for circumstances like this. 'I always knew she was just a gold-digger, and I'll be telling Ross that at the earliest opportunity.'

Joe told her she would be doing nothing of the sort and she should keep her nose out of other people's business: 'For once in your life, woman.' She wasn't happy, and started back at him, ready for an argument. Normally, he didn't argue back but this time was different. 'Joan, be quiet, and go and make the dinner.'

Martin organised a beer and curry team night out, which they did from time to time, so no one suspected it was mainly for his friend's benefit. Ross was grateful for the gesture, it gave him the chance to spend some social time with Elspeth. He normally only saw her on Wednesdays. They chatted for ages in the pub before and after the meal. He was in stitches at some of her stories, mainly concerning the bedroom and bathroom habits of her ex-husband. Some of them sounded quite disgusting.

Elspeth was in her early forties. She dyed her hair a silvery grey, and had a healthy suntan that, conversely, didn't look like it had come out of a bottle. In days gone by she'd have been described as buxom but she wore her clothes on the loose side to conceal rather than accentuate her curves.

While they were blethering away, Ross noticed her peculiar habit of ripping up beermats into odd shapes and arranging them on the table like soggy miniature jigsaws. At one stage, three of these pieces of art decorated the table-top in front of her. She slid them carefully to one side and swiped the last mat while Ross was taking a drink. He clanked his glass down on the unprotected table and scowled at her but Elspeth appeared oblivious.

A few minutes later, a young barman stopped to lift some empty glasses from their table. He made to sweep the torn mats onto his tray. 'Leave them!' said Elspeth, as if she were speaking to a misbehaving puppy. The barman froze, his arm held out, looking at her as if to say: *'Are you serious?'* She held up one stern index finger and kept it there until he walked away, shaking his head.

Scary lady, thought Ross. He was amused by this little quirk but didn't quiz her on it.

As he was walking home, Ross realised he had thoroughly enjoyed his evening and hoped Martin would arrange another event reasonably soon.

For their part, Mel and Andrew ticked off as many boxes as they could. They spoke to Ross's work colleagues, several players at the tennis club and tracked down Ross's fellow season ticket holders at Easter Road. Everyone sang the same song. Lovely guy, totally genuine, gentleman on court, doesn't even shout at the ref. Can't imagine he would hurt a fly.

Mel quizzed Ross about Carla's behaviour towards his male friends. Did he think it was over-friendly? But in Ross's opinion, it was simply the difference between the emotionally castrated British, and the Continental freedom of expression in relation to public affection.

Andrew was eventually able to contact Facebook, the warrant had done its job. An extremely cooperative lady with a strong Dutch accent and perfect English took responsibility for the enquiry and confirmed a few days later that most of Carla's friends appeared to be false, including her sister, Caterina. They were all tied in to random Hotmail accounts but emails to those addresses bounced back. Facebook closed down public access to Carla's page within the hour.

Andrew also canvassed a few of the gym classes. He spoke to women who said they knew Carla, but admittedly only to chat to. But there was something they were all agreed on: 'There's no doubt Carla could be a wee bit off from time to time.'

Andrew thought, no wonder. Maintaining the deception must have put her under a considerable amount of strain.

They also spoke to Martin. Had Carla ever made a pass at him? He was amused by the possibility but was forthright with his answer. 'No. And I'd have put my foot up her arse if she'd tried.'

Eventually, they dropped the whole idea that Ross had assaulted his wife. It just didn't hold water. Mel was secretly pleased.

Mel and Andrew discussed all this with DS Hunter, who congratulated them on being so thorough but then said exactly what they expected him to. Ross was almost certainly the victim of an organised crime group, or OCG, so Jeff told them to pass the case on to their colleagues in the Economic Crime Unit. Some of the older cops still called it the Fraud Squad. He agreed they should stay in touch with Ross, just in case anything new came to light, but this was definitely a backburner job from now on. They had other cases bubbling away.

And Carla's black Puffa jacket never did turn up.

One Friday evening, four weeks to the day that Carla disappeared, Ross came home from work. He sifted through the mail on his way to the kitchen. Two or three were advertising bumf, which he slung in the recycling. There was a postcard from Martin's daughter, Gail, who had been skiing in Argentière, in the French Alps. He'd never heard of the place but apparently the talent was, *'Hot! Hot! Hot!'*

The last item was an A5 white envelope with IMPORTANT: THIS IS NOT JUNK MAIL in bold across the envelope, front and back. *What's this then?*

Ross slit the envelope with his thumb, and flipped open the folded letter inside. His attention was immediately grabbed by the header. In red, bold and underlined, it shouted at him: *Payment Overdue. For Your Immediate Attention.*

Creases appeared on his forehead as he skimmed the page, hardly taking in the words. His entire body became a crazy, unfathomable mixture of freezing cold and roasting hot. He tottered over to the worktop, straightened the paper back against the fold and spread the pages out. Page two was a statement but he couldn't make sense of the figures.

He had to brace himself against the kitchen unit to stop himself collapsing. The bones in his legs felt like they had been replaced with liquorice, his eyes stung from the sweat that cascaded like liquid pepper from his forehead, and his elbows although locked tight, shuddered and trembled from the strain of holding him upright.

Ross forced himself to concentrate on the content of the letter. Finally, the fog dispersed and he was able to comprehend the story it told.

'Bitch!' he spat. 'Fucking, pox-infested, fucking, *bitch.*'

The kitchen surfaces, as usual, were totally clear of all accoutrements. Except for the brushed chrome and cream kettle. He picked it up, twisted round, and with all of his might he smashed the kettle into the fridge door.

The impact made one hell of a racket, and no small amount of mess, but Ross was way past caring.

40

A report with a clear Perspex cover and spiral binding lay precisely in the centre of the desk.

Miroslav didn't do *dress down Friday*. Today he wore a dark suit, immaculate white shirt and understated tie. He enjoyed the professional image his style portrayed. And although he was sure his new beard suited him he intended to keep it trimmed short. It *had* to complement his attire.

He pulled the document a little closer. It was an ad-hoc financial report, requested by him and prepared by his accountant. The first page was a summary. He ran his index finger down the right hand column. The individual totals were interesting, of course, but they were all bit-part players to the star of the show.

The 'A-list' celebrity on the page was the figure in the rightmost position on the lowest row. It was the cumulative profit for the 11 years since he and Danijela had launched their organisation and it had just passed a significant milestone. He'd known it was approaching fast, which was why he'd called the accountant.

He read the figure once, then checked it again. Just to make sure.

Then he leaned way back in his chair, raised his arms and locked his fingers behind his head.

* * *

The year was 1998, and Miroslav and Danijela had been bumming around Australasia and the Far East for about two years after they left Prague. It was a suffocating-hot night in Bali, and they were almost at the stage of checking for loose change down the back of the furniture. They agreed it was high time they devoted their energies not to survival but to prosperity. And they didn't give a toss how they would achieve that.

They were sitting on a low wall outside their crappy studio apartment when they spotted two stunning European women, wearing fewer and skimpier clothes than a Bangkok hooker. They were wrapped around two American businessmen with bellies that strained their shirt buttons to popping point. Curious, Miroslav and Danijela followed them. They watched, fascinated, as the Yanks lavished their dates with cocktails, a banquet meal that covered two tables, and enough wine to bathe a family of hippos. Sadly, and unbeknown to them, it was the men who drank most of the wine. And while one of them was arguing almost incoherently with the waiter over the composition of the bill, the two women flashed one last tantalising eyeful of cleavage at their hosts and disappeared off to *the bathroom*. From their viewpoint way out at a corner table on the terrace, this turned out to be a side exit from the kitchen. Danijela and Miroslav laughed as they watched the women putting plenty of distance between them and their soon-to-be-aggrieved married businessmen abroad. 'That must happen every night of the week in places like this.'

They watched the two men stomping around the restaurant becoming louder and angrier. But even in their advanced state of befuddlement, it eventually became obvious to them that they'd been well and truly had.

'Hmmm,' from Danijela. 'You don't suppose...?'

They couldn't see how they would be even remotely successful as a couple so they split up and agreed to meet back at their apartment at two in the morning: latest. Despite his tanned body and GQ front cover abs and pecs, Miroslav was home, somewhat deflated, by just after midnight. He'd chatted up dozens of women, from teenage to middle age, with absolutely zero success. Apart from a couple of quick gropes from a plastered English woman who was convinced he had played Dr Luka Kovac in the US hospital drama, *ER*.

At five past two, he was just about to go out searching for Danijela when she fell in the door wearing a grin as broad as a Sumo wrestler's backside. She was loaded up with a gigantic takeaway, two large bottles of full-fat Coke and a litre of Stolichnaya.

He stared at her, aghast. 'Where the fuck...?' But she silenced him with a flat palm in his face. She jammed her hand into her back pocket, swung it round in a wide flourish and tooted a fanfare as she dumped a fat, ragged bundle of mixed currency notes on the breakfast bar. Miroslav fanned them out. There were hundreds of New Zealand dollar bills, a healthy selection of Indonesian rupiah, some euros and, incongruously, a single UK £20 note.

Danijela planted a kiss on his cheek. 'I couldn't eat another thing so the food's for you. Get stuck in and I'll make us a drink.'

'How do you know I haven't eaten?' The huffy tone said it all.

'Fuck off.' Her laugh was both mocking and riotous. 'And while you're eating, I'll tell you about my evening.' The crappy studio apartment didn't stretch to ice or decent glasses so they made do with warm Stoli and Coke from chipped coffee mugs. But it tasted wonderful and didn't hit the sides. Danijela poured a second round and told her story.

Within minutes of leaving Miroslav she chanced upon a group of twenty-somethings, fresh off a flight from Heathrow and two stops away from Rat-arsed Central. They provided her first two cocktails and the £20 note when one guy told her his mates had bet him £50 he couldn't persuade her to flash her tits. He wasn't quite as pissed as the others, and reckoned this was a win–win. Several selfies later, and £20 richer, she left them waving after her like palm trees in a tropical storm. They were destined to crash and burn within the hour. Time to move on.

The cocktails provided Dutch courage so she slipped off her bra and jammed it into her shorts' pocket. A German tourist bought her a drink but as she was considering her next move, his wife turned up so that was that. Then a couple of Canadians chatted her up for a while but their wallets never saw the light of day. Time to split.

Finally, just before midnight, she pulled the lever one last time and a line of sevens came up. A group of New Zealanders crossed the road right in front of her and swarmed towards a restaurant with most of its tables outside. She couldn't explain where the idea came from but she allowed one of the tail-enders to crash into her. She made a meal of bouncing off the edge of a table and landing pseudo-heavily on the floor. Immediately she was surrounded by several burly rugby players, who sported steel thighs and biceps like cantaloupes. The men were most concerned about her welfare so they whisked her to their table and fed and watered her till she was fit to burst. When she explained in a deliberately heavily accented and sexy voice, while struggling to hold back fake tears, that she'd completely run out of money and would probably have to sleep down by the beach, they had a whip-round. She made her excuses and left. One of their number gallantly offered to chaperone her but his friends ridiculed him for his unsubtle technique, and dragged him off to their hotel.

Then, the icing on the cake. On her way back to the apartment she met one of the English boys from earlier. He was so pissed he could hardly see but somehow he recognised her, and told her in language that possessed hardly any consonants that she could have all the money in his wallet if she would, quote: 'Gimme a gobble.' Before her nerve failed her, Danijela agreed and helped him stagger up an alley to an empty car park behind a derelict hotel. She insisted he proved there was money in his wallet, which, after a serious amount of fumbling in various pockets he was able to do. He handed it over.

For an instant, with his wallet in her possession, she considered honouring her side of the deal. Instead, she thought: 'Fuck that.' One reasonable shove on his chest sent him tumbling backwards down a slope and into a bush. She walked smartly away from the scene and headed for home.

And from small acorns, mighty oak trees grow. Over the next six years or so, the couple conned their way through the world's major tourist destinations on every continent bar Antarctica. What started off with cocktails, the odd meal, and the occasional roll of a drunken tourist, evolved into an increasingly ingenious and sophisticated series of scams where they both played their part. Rich travellers were separated from their cash, wallets, jewellery, currency cards, passports. Sometimes they were deprived of their virginity, their manhood, their inhibitions. And often they were left feeling embarrassed, used, shamed, violated, cheated, distressed.

In that period their schemes brought in a significant amount of money but eventually they realised they would never be seriously wealthy unless they scaled up. And, late in the summer of 2005, on a genuine holiday in La Rochelle on the Atlantic coast of France, Danijela allowed herself to be seduced by a lonely English widower while Miroslav was out surfing. This gentleman had property in Brittany, Normandy, Kent and Hampshire, no children or close relatives, his sex life had withered and died on the vine, and he fell hook, line and sinker for a blonde, blue-eyed Czech goddess who, apparently, worshipped the ground he walked on.

Having left her hopelessly love-struck English gentleman poorer to the tune of well over half a million pounds, she had designs on repeating the caper. But Miroslav's fondness for Danijela dictated that he found the prospect rather distasteful, and he convinced her to concentrate on managing the burgeoning organisation.

Eleven years and one exceptionally lucrative international scamming operation later, Miroslav and Danijela had well and truly scaled up and their operation ran like a professional commercial organisation.

Which is precisely what it was.

* * *

Miroslav had read the bottom line on the financial report over and over again. But the story it told did not change.

Cumulative Profit: Five Hundred *Million* Euros.

He might have screamed and punched the air. Or pulled his shirt over his head and run round the room. Or danced a little jig behind his desk.

But Miroslav did none of these things. He just tapped his finger on the figure a couple of times, smiled, closed the folder and locked it in the top drawer of his desk.

He keyed a number on his phone and left a voicemail.

'Dani. Let's go for dinner tonight. Somewhere expensive.'

He thought about that for a second then added: '*Very* expensive.'

41

Ross was exasperated.

'Look. As I've already explained, I just need to speak to someone who can tell me what this is all about. Because I know nothing about it. Nothing whatsoever.'

The help-desk operator was trying to maintain her professionalism but she was struggling on this call. He was like a dog with a bone, and although he had been reasonably pleasant to her so far, she could sense his frustration was building and knew from experience it wouldn't be long before he snapped at her. 'As I've already explained, sir, I'm sorry, but unless you can answer the security questions, I'm not able to help you over the phone. Personally, I don't doubt you are who you say you are. But unless you're able to prove it, I can't... I'm not permitted, to deal with your enquiry.'

Ross's tone rose by a few notes. 'But I can't answer your damned security questions because I didn't set them. You've asked me my mother's maiden name, and I've told you it's Mathieson but you say it's not. Well, it is. I'm not likely to get my own mother's maiden name wrong, am I?'

'Of course not, sir. But that is not the name I have on my system.' She had asked Ross for the name of his first pet and his secondary school too, but Buster and Trinity Academy didn't cut the mustard either.

'In which case, may I speak to your supervisor, please?'

'Again, sir, I'm sorry but my supervisor will give you the same answers I have. I can only suggest you visit one of our branches and discuss it personally with an adviser. I can make an appointment for you now, if that would help.'

'Well, it would be the first thing you've done that's been even remotely helpful.' Ross regretted the comment immediately but there was nothing he could do. It was already out there.

There was silence from the other end but Ross didn't know she'd muted her headset, muttered the word *tosser*, before switching back to speech. Risky, but highly rewarding.

The atmosphere between them was now rather strained but she managed to keep her tone neutral while she arranged the appointment for three o'clock the following Tuesday. When she closed down the call she didn't ask if there was anything else she could help him with today. She was supposed to, it was part of the script, but she didn't see any point. She did, however, wish him a pleasant evening but that was just her being mischievous. She ticked the *Irate Customer* box on her screen, updated the record and saved it.

Before she picked up the next call in the queue she glanced at the time.

Only an hour till I'm out of here. Thank fuck for that.

42

Tuesday

'Please take a seat Mr McKinlay, and how may I help you today?'

Ross was teetering on a knife-edge. He had been all weekend. He was a hair's breadth away from yelling at someone, and the mortgage adviser with the Lancs and Cumbria Building Society was smack in the middle of the cross hairs.

He slapped the letter and statement on the meeting room table and stabbed it three times with his index finger.

'You can start by explaining why you've sent me this. As you will see, it's a reminder for the first payment against a second mortgage on my house. It's due on the fourteenth of March, apparently.'

Tim O'Keefe glanced down at the paperwork, clearly a little baffled by Ross's opening gambit. The man wore a pink striped shirt that had untucked from his belt as soon as he sat down. The collar gripped his neck as tight as a garrotte and there were perspiration stains under the arms. His florid features were dominated by a bushy greying moustache that seemed to jut out beyond the tip of his nose.

He took a few seconds to scan the documents, flipping the statement over to check the outstanding balance. It said Ross should have paid just over £350 for the first payment on an interest-only mortgage of £180,000.

'Have you made the payment Mr McKinlay?'

'No, I haven't. And furthermore, I have no intention of making it… or any other payment for that matter. No matter how many reminders you send me.'

Tim's level of bafflement increased by a couple of notches. Customers who'd been sent reminders for overdue payments usually weren't this bolshie.

But Ross wasn't being bolshie. It was bluster. Blind panic. Ever since he had opened that envelope, his words, thoughts, emotions, had been elbowing for supremacy like drunken shoppers when the doors opened at a Black Friday sale.

A second mortgage of £180,000? Of course, he knew exactly who was responsible but he was consumed by one question. How had Carla done it? Ross was way past why. He was sick fed up wondering why. Now, it was all about the how. *How* had she managed to falsify a loan of that magnitude against a property that barely covered it?

He also knew he should have contacted the police. He should have, but he hadn't. Ross preferred to cling to the faintly ridiculous and misguided notion that the letter was some sort of silly mistake. The mortgage belonged to someone else but an admin error had misdirected the reminder to him. His propensity for self-delusion had never been so acute.

Back in 1990, Ross and Liz eventually bought the student flat in Viewforth, where she lived when they started dating. About a year after he qualified, before they were married, their landlord had died. His only son had absolutely zero inclination to manage the portfolio of flats and small houses his father had accumulated all over town so he sold the whole lot for a song. If the sitting tenants could match the valuation, the deal was done. Theirs was a Victorian, three-bedroomed, top-floor tenement flat. Superficially it was in terrible condition, but behind the crappy woodchip and the layers of flaking gloss paint it retained all its original features including fireplaces, cornices, pitch-pine doors and skirtings. They scraped a deposit together and made the purchase. In those days, mortgages for three or four times earnings were commonplace, and Ross's salary just about covered it. They let out the other two bedrooms for a few years while they gradually improved the flat. Eventually, they owned a superb property in a desirable part of town, stylishly and sympathetically restored.

Their plan had always been to move to a house somewhere down the coast when Liz sold her business but her death put paid to that. After she died, Ross had no interest in fulfilling that dream and was content to stay put with his memories and Liz's spirit. Accordingly, when he started dating Carla, he didn't take her there. They always went to her place. A small, soulless box in a modern block near Saughton Prison, on the west side of town. She told him she was renting until she decided to remain in Edinburgh or move somewhere else. Ross now assumed this too was bogus, all part of the façade.

So when he popped the question, he reluctantly sold the flat and used the proceeds as a down-payment on the new house: a new start. Carla had offered to put in some of her *savings* but Ross, ever the gentleman, and gullible idiot it now transpired, wouldn't hear of it. He took out an interest-only mortgage to pay the balance, the basement-level interest rates of the time made the mortgage route to purchase a no-brainer. Certainly it would not have been prudent for Ross to dip into his investments. He told Carla about those, of course. There had been no reason not to.

'I don't really understand, Mr McKinlay. You've taken out a second mortgage on the property, we've asked you to make the scheduled payment, and you say you don't intend to pay. Why not? What is the issue here?' Tim sat back, his hands flat out on the table, palms facing upwards.

'The issue is I didn't apply for this second mortgage. This letter is the first I've heard of it.'

Tim O'Keefe had been a mortgage adviser with various lenders for approaching twenty years but this was a new one. But not much fazed him. He was also quite astute. He studied Ross for a few seconds, his head tilted over to one side. 'Clearly, there's something going on here. Something I'm obviously in the dark about.' He pushed the paperwork away to one side. 'So, why don't you enlighten me?'

'It's a long story.'

Tim glanced at his watch and shrugged. 'I'm in no hurry.'

While Ross was relating the whole sorry saga, Tim jotted the occasional note and opened a few windows on his PC. He didn't say much, preferring to leave his customer to speak uninterrupted but his eyebrows jumped up and down from time to time and he made genuinely sympathetic noises at all the key points in the story. And when Ross told him the total amount Carla had taken, he swore, then apologised for being unprofessional.

When Ross finished speaking, Tim looked up. 'My goodness, that's quite a tale. But bring your chair round and I'll show you what I've been doing while you've been talking.'

Ross moved round, Tim pointed at the screen and explained: 'This is your mortgage file, and here are all the documents associated with it. I've checked a few of them and, well, let's just say there are some things that don't add up. But to save us wading through all this on screen, I'll print them off. Back in a minute.' Tim clicked a *Print All* button, logged off and left the room.

A few minutes later he was back, carrying several sheets of A3 and A4 paper. Some of them were wedged in his armpit, and a couple swished their way to the floor as he was closing the door. Ross jumped out of his chair to pick them up. 'Cheers, thanks,' said Tim, as he tried to tuck his shirt back in.

For the next few minutes Tim explained the documents, some of which Ross had apparently signed. There was a second mortgage application, architect's drawings of a house extension, planning permission, building warrant, payslips for Ross and Carla, and savings and investment statements. There were letters to and from the building society, Ross, the Council Planning Department and a solicitor. There was even one from Martin, confirming how long Ross had worked in his company. And every single one of them was fake.

But the last item was the most interesting. A letter confirming an online payment for the full amount, £180,000 to a Royal Bank of Scotland account in joint names: Mr and Mrs R McKinlay.

Ross just looked at Tim. He opened his mouth as if to speak, and promptly closed it again.

'Just a wild guess. You and these documents are total strangers?'

'We've never even been introduced.'

Tim indicated the mortgage application. 'And although this is your signature, you didn't actually sign it.'

'No, I didn't.'

Now one of the drawings. 'Your house?'

'Similar, but no. The front elevation is near enough, but the rear elevation is the wrong way round. And our garage is wider than that so the extension wouldn't actually fit in the space.' Ross smiled. 'Might have been interesting watching them trying to build it, though.'

'The payslips. Are they accurate?'

'Maybe if I worked a seven-day week and had a couple of pay rises. But no. Fiction.'

Tim sighed. And it was a belter. He took a few seconds while he shuffled his thoughts around. 'Okay. Here's what I'm thinking.'

Tim explained he suspected the whole scam had been perpetrated online and by phone. Ross's signature was no more than a squiggle so easy to forge with the assistance of Photoshop. The drawings and other formal documents were probably forgeries too, it was likely they had been emailed and were therefore untraceable. Someone, possibly Carla, had visited the office to deliver the signed documents but this was a satellite office that didn't handle cash so security was light. There was no CCTV.

Assuming Ross's story checked out with the police, the building society would probably suspend the mortgage account and, for the moment, they wouldn't ask Ross to make the repayments. But Tim was equally clear, and he didn't sugar-coat it, that Ross may still be held liable depending on the outcome of their, and the police's, investigations.

Ross gave Tim Mel's contact details, accepted a warm handshake and left the office. It had been a good meeting, and now he didn't feel the same as with his other losses. Somehow, this felt like someone else's problem and his potential liability seemed to be distant. There was no point in worrying about it too much, for now at least.

When he reached home he phoned Mel. He told her things had kicked off again, and asked if they could meet up.

She said she would: 'Pop round in about quarter of an hour. Put the kettle on.'

While he was waiting, Ross calculated the full extent of Carla's scam on him, his savings, his and Liz's investments, his credit card, and now the building society. Almost £610,000.

'Jesus, Carla. Well, whatever you're spending it on, I hope you're fucking enjoying it.'

SPRING

SPRING

43

Six Weeks Later

'Is anyone else's Outlook playing up?'

Ross stuck his nose over the top of his monitor. Several of his colleagues were tap-tapping at their keyboards and another two were chatting by the emergency exit, clutching cigarettes and lighters in readiness for braving the elements. But heads were shaken and *Nopes* were uttered.

He spun his chair round and looked over at the company's newest, and youngest, recruit. Nineteen years old, and in third year at technical college, Wayne was desperate to create a good impression. So he was practically bouncing about in the hope that his polar opposite would actually ask him for help. For some reason Wayne was in awe of Ross, which no one else in the team could comprehend. But there was no point in asking the man himself. Typically, he was utterly oblivious.

But despite his undoubted enthusiasm for the task and trying everything he could think of, Wayne wasn't able to solve the problem for his uber-hero. The poor lad returned to his desk. Deflated wasn't even close.

Ross tried his PC again a few minutes later, with the same result. He didn't actually need Outlook or the internet for the rest of the day so decided to try again in the morning. He didn't know if that would make a difference.

As things transpired, it didn't.

* * *

Elspeth was at the desk opposite, peering at a spreadsheet. Tuesday wasn't normally a working day for her but she was banking some extra hours to take some time off later in the month.

'El, who do I report a faulty PC to?' said Ross. 'I can't connect to the network,'

195

Without looking up, she passed him a business card for their IT support company. Like most small business owners, Martin outsourced support for functions like IT. Glitches like this were handled by a local helpdesk so Ross made the call.

He explained the fault as best he could, and was relieved when the technician, Dexter, asked him a series of fairly straightforward questions in relatively plain English. Guided by Dexter, for whom patience definitely *was* a virtue, Ross checked basic system and hardware settings on the PC, and was more than a little chuffed when they discovered a network adaptor was faulty.

'I'm sorry, Ross, but I'll have to send out an engineer to replace the card. I'm afraid you'll have no email or internet access in the meantime.' Ross said he wasn't too concerned, especially when Dexter hoped the engineer should be able to attend later that day.

'Well, Mr Jobs,' said Elspeth. 'Have you cracked it?'

He didn't rise to the bait, mainly because he'd never yet won a battle of wits with Elspeth. She was sharper than a Turkish barber's razor. 'It's a hardware fault, apparently. They're sending someone called Alex to investigate. He'll run some diagnostics, I expect.'

'*Diagnostics.* Jesus, will you listen to him.'

'Can I help it if I'm down with the techies?'

'Oh, fuck off. And sort out some coffees while you're at it.'

* * *

Just gone three, his phone rang. 'Ross. It's Gloria. I have Alex from Esprit IT at reception for you.'

'Thanks, Gloria, I'll be right down.'

His office was on the second floor but he always used the stairs. For one thing it was quicker than the wheezing single lift that served the building, and he was taking every opportunity to work on his fitness. The tennis season was in full swing and Barry was pushing him hard.

He clicked the button to unlock the door to the reception area, and wandered over to the desk. He glanced around as he crossed the room and wore a confused expression by the time he arrived in front of Gloria. 'Has he gone to the toilet or something?'

Gloria hailed from Englefield, New Jersey. She'd visited Scotland a few years earlier to take in the Edinburgh Festival, and had never quite made it home again. Her sense of humour was dry sardonic with a side order of heavy sarcasm. She was face-slappingly rude to almost everyone but she was a top-class administrator and would help anyone with anything, at any time. To complete the paradox that was Gloria, she called everyone Sweet-pea, and possessed a smile that could light up the Arctic in the dead of winter. Everyone in the company just loved her to bits.

'Sweet-pea. I don't insist on you calling the pavement a sidewalk, and if you prefer rubbish to garbage well that's just fine by me. But that... that over there,' Gloria jerked her thumb at an internal door, 'is a rest room. Capiche?' She blitzed his eyeballs with a dazzling display of snow-white dentals. 'We don't *have* a toilet. Poor people have toilets.'

Ross was finding Gloria quite unnerving today so he just nodded, several times. She continued. 'Now, has who gone to the rest room, Sweet-pea?'

'The IT guy, Alex. You phoned and said he was here to fix my PC.'

She regarded him as if he'd just been found guilty of conning blind pensioners out of their life savings. 'What?' said Ross. She positioned her right hand as if she were about to karate-chop her desk-pad, four stiff fingers pointing directly at his chest. Then she flicked those fingers from left to right, until he cottoned on and moved out of her line of sight. Now she pointed.

'You see over there, on that sofa, in front of the window?'

Ross half turned, 'Yes.'

'There's your IT guy. Alex.'

He turned all the way round to find a brunette, about average height and wearing a black polo shirt, black jeans and bright-red Doc Marten boots. She was making tiny waving motions at him. Her smile didn't quite match Gloria's, but it was close.

'Alex is a woman?'

'Jeez. You didn't skip many human biology classes, did you?' Then, more softly, 'Or was it them titties that gave the game away?'

The woman negotiated the seating area and held out her hand. 'Hi. I'm Alex Mair from Esprit IT. Well, it's Alexis actually, but not many people call me that. Are you Ross McKinlay?'

They shook hands. 'I am. And apologies about the mix-up. My only excuse is I've never met an Alex who wasn't a bloke.' Gloria sniggered but he didn't react. There was no point giving her more ammunition.

'Och, no worries. It happens to me all the time. Thing is, Alexis is nowhere near cool enough for an IT geek.' She laughed. 'Especially a girl IT geek.'

Ross laughed too. He liked her instantly, she definitely had something about her. *An IT geek with a personality. Whatever next?*

As they walked to his office he explained all about the fault with the network adaptor. It was only when they sat down at his desk he realised she probably would have had all that information relayed to her by the helpdesk. But Alex was patient and polite, and listened carefully to him babbling away. Ross started off on another apology but stopped himself just in time. One grovelling per hour to a woman he hadn't ever clapped eyes on before was quite enough for now, he thought.

While she was working at his PC he fetched two coffees then left her in peace. He sat a few desks away and read a monthly trade journal from his local institute. It wasn't exactly riveting but he liked to keep up with the latest in accountancy. Elspeth binned them without so much as a glance and never seemed to come to any harm. Ross was way too cautious for that.

'Ross.' He looked over to see Alex beckoning him. 'Got a minute? I need to ask you something.'

'Sure.' He dropped the journal into a green recycling bin on his way over. 'How can I help?'

Alex twirled a chair from the desk behind, and patted the seat. 'I've replaced the network card and tested the internet connection. Both Outlook and your browser are working fine now. But I've spotted something that I wanted to ask you about.'

'As good a way to waste your breath as any other,' Elspeth cackled. 'Just watch for his eyes glazing over. We're talking seconds here.'

'Just ignore her,' said Ross. 'She's standing in for the office cat. But maybe keep it simple?'

'Will do.' Alex clicked on a window, and pointed at it with a black-varnished fingernail. She lowered her voice, and leaned closer to him. 'I've noticed your Outlook's set up to copy every email you receive or send, to a different account. It's not one of the company's accounts, it's a bog-standard Hotmail.' She showed him: **ross_mckinlay_1966@hotmail. com**

'That's not particularly secure so if you like, I can...'

He stood up abruptly, his chair shot back and crashed into a metal filing cabinet. Elspeth jumped in her seat, 'Jesus, Ross!'

He flapped a hand in her direction, and spoke quickly to Alex. 'Excuse me a minute. Just stay there will you? I need to talk to Martin.' He took a couple of quick paces before turning back. 'And just leave everything as it is for now, please. Okay?'

'Emmm... okay.' But he had hurried away.

She glanced over at Elspeth, they looked equally bemused.

* * *

Both men stood up as Alex walked into Martin's office. Martin to welcome her, and Ross to offer her the only spare chair. He perched on the edge of Martin's desk, almost knocking a leaning tower of paperwork onto the floor. He grabbed it just in time.

'Alex. Martin Redpath. I'm the MD here.' He sat back in his ancient cream leather executive chair. He loved that chair but it played havoc with his back. He shifted about, searching for a comfortable position. Alex looked at her two clients in turn, she was about as comfortable as they were. Clearly, she thought she'd done something wrong. She started to speak but Martin cut in.

'Looks like we have a bit of a security breach here, so I need to ask for your assistance and for your discretion.'

Alex breathed out. 'Of course. How can I help?'

'I won't go into any detail but Ross has been going through a... how can I put it... tricky time of late.' Ross raised his eyebrows at the massive understatement. 'And now, based on what you've just found it looks like that's possibly spilled over into the office.'

'You mean the emails being copied to the Hotmail account?'

'Exactly.'

'Ah.' One syllable, but it spoke volumes.

'Alex, I need you to have a good look at Ross's PC, his profile, username. The works, really. And could you also check Elspeth's PC, please.' She shot him a look but he held up both palms. 'No, no. I don't think Elspeth's involved at all. I appointed her for God's sake. It's just that she's Ross's job-share and if this is a business finance thing, perhaps her PC's been compromised too. Now, would you have the time to do that now, or does the helpdesk have something else lined up for you? Because I can make a call.'

'No. This is my last job before knocking off. I can easily stay on for a while, it's not a problem.' Alex smiled for the first time since she'd told Ross about his emails. 'I'll crack on. I'm guessing you'll be hanging around to see what I find?'

Martin looked at his watch, it had only just gone four. 'Definitely. And...'

'You'd prefer I kept this to myself for the moment?'

'I would indeed. Ross, ask El to pop in, would you?'

* * *

'There's nothing else on Ross's PC,' said Alex. 'And Elspeth's is fine too.'

Martin exhaled as if he'd been holding his breath for a week. 'You're sure?'

She'd been working for almost an hour, moving between the two PCs and her laptop, which she had hooked up to the office network. She was like a miniature black Merlin, her fingers a continual blur as she attacked each keyboard in turn. The only thing missing was the pointy hat.

'I'm certain. I have some really powerful software on this.' She held up a USB memory stick. 'And I downloaded a few extra utilities from our office server. There's nothing illegitimate on either PC, and both Ross's and Elspeth's profiles are clean too.'

'So no malware, no key-loggers, no little beasties hiding in there ready to come out as soon as our backs are turned?'

Alex ran her fingers through her hair, letting it flop back onto her neck and shoulders. Ross had noticed she did that a lot.

'No. They're totally clear.'

'So whatever, or whoever set up the email forwarding… that's all they did?' Martin glanced over at Ross, who studiously avoided his gaze.

Alex didn't miss the exchange. 'Unless they were incredibly sophisticated, yes, that's all they did.' She paused for a second. 'But one thing did occur to me.'

'What?' both men asked, perfectly in sync.

She held out a hand in Ross's direction. 'May I see your phone?'

Ross looked a little startled until Alex explained: 'I should check it too. If someone's gone to the trouble of hacking your PC, maybe they did something with your phone too.'

'It's in my jacket pocket. Back in a minute.'

'No need. I'll come with you. I want to connect it to my laptop.' She stood up to follow him out of the office.

'Alex,' said Martin. 'Thanks very much.'

She beamed back at him. 'No worries.'

They walked over to a coat-rack, Alex took the phone Ross offered her then sat down at her laptop.

About ten minutes later, Alex appeared in Martin's doorway, her laptop bag over her shoulder. 'Ross's phone's okay. It was a long shot but worth checking.'

'That's great. Thanks very much. And sorry you had to work on.'

'Ach, it's only what, half five? Not too bad. The overtime will come in handy.'

'Well I do appreciate it. Can I buy you a drink?'

She jangled a bunch of keys. 'Not tonight I'm afraid. I'm driving. Another time?'

Martin smiled. She was really quite cute but way too young for him. 'I'll walk you down. Gloria will have gone home by now so the front door will be locked.' He switched his PC to standby, grabbed his jacket from a hook near the door, and they both headed off towards the stairwell.

'I'll see you tomorrow, Ross,' Martin called. 'And we'll sit down and talk this through. I'm sure everything's okay. G'night.'

Ross flapped an arm in a get-out-of-here gesture. 'Night.'

He sat quietly for a while. He walked over to the kitchen, made himself a strong coffee, and sat back at his PC. He closed down all the applications with the exception of Outlook. He pulled some scrap A4 from a pile on the corner of his desk, and clicked on the first folder hanging off his Inbox. Abertay University. There were 18 emails in this folder, and God knows how many in all the other folders. But he decided he would spend the rest of the evening, or as long as it took, working through every folder and sub-folder, checking for any emails that might, if they fell into the wrong hands, cause damage to Martin, the company or their clients. It wasn't an insurmountable task. Ross's natural aversion to most things computing meant the emails numbered in the hundreds rather than thousands, and his one-finger typing style kept his output mercifully short.

He forced himself not to think about Carla. But she did encroach on his thoughts from time to time but just as it looked like she was about to sneak in past his guards, he blinked hard and swore at her until she buggered off again.

His phone rang as he was halfway through the Fs. Thankfully, no alarm bells had gone off yet. He looked at the display but didn't recognise the mobile number so he ignored it. *Some poxy cold-caller no doubt.* Then a double-ping sounded, indicating he had a voicemail. Ross hesitated then tapped the voicemail icon, and accepted the option to switch on the loudspeaker. *What a bloody job. Trying to sell people stuff they'll never want. They probably only sell about one thing a month, if they're lucky.*

'Ross. It's Alex from Esprit. It's just after six o'clock. Listen, I'm sorry to bother you but there's something I need to talk to you about.' A pause. 'I'm down the road in the pub. Either gimme a call, or maybe you could pop over. Cheers.'

Ross stared at his phone as the recorded announcement with all the voicemail options blethered away in the background. He hit three for delete then ended the call.

He checked a few more emails but found he could no longer concentrate. So he switched off his monitor, plucked his jacket from the coat-rack and headed for the door.

44

Dating back to Roman times and now one of Edinburgh's more expensive residential areas, Cramond sits on the Firth of Forth in sight of the famous rail bridge, at the point where the River Almond enters the estuary. Like Restalrig in the east and Corstorphine to the west, Cramond was one of the original villages that all eventually merged with the other districts to make up the city of Edinburgh.

Martin had moved his company into the des-res enclave about ten years previously. It had been an expensive option but it gave them a certain kudos, being the only major commercial enterprise in an exclusive residential area. The Edinburgh Council Planning Department must have been collectively drunk the day his Change of Use application was granted, to turn a decaying eighteenth-century villa into a high-tech IT office. The locals weren't exactly delighted but they soon changed their tune when Martin donated £10,000 to help the local boat club buy new hydraulic winches, and handed over a similar sum to the Cramond Kirk roof refurbishment fund.

Ross locked up his bike in the car park of the Cramond Inn and walked towards the bar, unzipping his luminescent green jacket as he did so. On warm summer evenings when Carla was away, he would often have a beer and a bar supper here before cycling home along the foreshore to Newhaven. And, being the pub closest to their office, he and his colleagues had spent more boozy evenings here than was good for them.

He found Alex sitting near an open fire. He signalled to ask if she would like another drink but she placed her hand flat across the top of her glass and shook her head. The barman knew Ross only drank Guinness and was already pouring it by the time his customer reached the ancient solid wood counter. 'Three-ten please, Ross. I'll bring it over.'

They made small talk until he'd taken his first drink of the coal-black beer then Ross said, 'You wanted to talk to me about something?'

'I did, yes.' She paused for thought, twisting a lock of her hair round her finger as she framed her response. 'But while I've been waiting for you I've managed to convince myself I'm probably way out of line so...' Her voiced tailed off and her eyes dropped away from him.

'Well, I'm here now so why don't you just tell me anyway, and we can decide if you're out of line or not.' Ross grinned at her. 'In the nicest possible way, of course.'

'Fair enough. I didn't mention this to Martin, and I've filled in the fault closure log for the office, and I didn't mention it there either. But here's the thing...'

It was all Ross could do not to yell out, *'For God's sake, woman. Just spit it out!'* But he could see she was struggling to formulate her words so the yelling remained inside his head.

'Probably it would be easier if I showed you. Can I see your phone again, please?'

Ross handed it over and watched, amazed, as Alex keyed in his security code. 'Hang on a minute. How did you know the number?'

Her pitying expression said, *'Oh puhleeeze.'* They were sitting at right angles to each other on an upholstered window seat, so she shuffled her bum round so she could be next to him. Her thigh was resting against his, so he waited a few seconds and adjusted his position to create the slightest of gaps.

'Like I said, I didn't mention this to Martin. He said earlier that you've been having a bit of a time of it recently.' She paused to look at him.

'That's putting it mildly.'

'So I wondered, if it was a personal thing, then maybe you wouldn't want other people to know about this.'

'Alex.'

'Yes?'

'You haven't told me what *this* is yet.'

'Oh. Well, you have a tracker app on your phone.'

'A what?'

She pointed at an icon. 'A tracker app.'

She could see the I-have-no-idea-what-you're-talking-about look on his face. 'It's an app that's enabling someone to track your phone by using theirs. They know where your phone is, so, as long as you have it with you, they know where you are too. All it needs is GPS to be enabled in the phone's settings. Parents use apps like this to keep track of their children. And,' Alex paused for effect, 'suspicious partners use them to keep an eye on other halves who they think might be, how can I put this… playing away from home.'

Ross grimaced, and shook his head slowly.

'You've never heard of them?' she said.

The look he gave her said everything.

'Sorry, I forgot you don't really do computers. But what about phones?'

'I make calls and I send texts, that's about it.'

Alex scrunched up her expression. It was all she could do not to sigh. 'There's another app on there. It's copying all your texts, incoming and outgoing, to another mobile.' She showed him the number but it meant nothing to him. 'That's why I thought it was personal but I didn't want to be the one to tell Martin about it. None of my business, really.'

Ross had forgotten all about his beer but now he picked up the pint glass and drained about half of it in one go. He stared into the fire. 'Jesus! What else is there?'

'Nothing I could see.'

'I didn't mean on the phone. I meant…' He stopped, and trotted out a phrase he'd used a good few times over the previous three months. 'Oh, never mind. It's a hell of a long story.'

He glanced out of the window in the direction of the Forth Rail Bridge, over 125 years old, with its recently refurbished deep red epoxy coating. He took another long draught of his beer, leaving only dregs in the bottom of the glass. 'I quite fancy sitting outside for a while. And I could go another beer.' He pointed at her glass, still half full of a clear liquid. 'What are you on?'

Alex put on an exaggerated petted lip. 'Water. I'm driving.'

'What time do you start work tomorrow?'

'Three o'clock. I'm on late shift.'

'So now that you're not working till three o'clock tomorrow, what are you drinking?'

A huge grin reached both her ears. 'I'll have a pint of Belhaven 80, please.'

'That's more like it.' Ross tossed his jacket in her general direction. 'You find seats outside, and I'll bring the drinks. Deal?'

'Deal. As long as I buy the next round?'

Ross signalled to the barman. 'Fine by me.'

* * *

Alex had found a table separated from its neighbour by a low hedge of potted shrubs, and had left Ross the seat with a view out onto the pale blue waters of the estuary. It was a calm evening, just about warm enough to sit without jackets but being so close to the water that was unlikely to last.

'So, is it a one pint long story or a few pints long story?'

Ross laughed out loud, startling a couple of sparrows foraging on the paving slabs around their table. They vanished into the shrubbery in the blink of an eye then hopped out the other side a few moments later to try their luck underneath another table.

'Christ! You don't beat about the bush, do you?'

Alex shrugged. 'Well, I kinda figure either you're going to tell me or you're not. And if you're not, it'll save me the bother of waiting. But I'd be lying if I said I wasn't curious. After all, it's not every day I meet a guy who's being spied on by his own phone.'

'Oh, what the hell.' Ross pulled his chair closer to the table, cradling his glass with both hands. 'But I do want to ask you a bit more about these two apps. I'm keen to find out how they work.'

'Sure. It'll be interesting to see how they fit into this story of yours.'

Including the time for all Alex's questions, the telling of Ross's tale took until well into a second round of beers and the light was fading fast. A row of spider's-web encrusted lamps on the external wall of the inn cast a glow so faint it wouldn't have attracted even a sharp-eyed moth.

'So, I could have mentioned your phone to Martin after all?'

'You could. And you wouldn't have had to set up this clandestine little meeting.'

'Are you sorry I did?'

'It was better than going home to an empty house.'

Alex spun a beermat at him, just missing his left ear. 'Cheeky bugger. And, might I remind you, I'm now miles from home, I can't drive my car because I'm well over the limit, *and* I'm bloody starving.' She turned to peer through a window into the pub. It was now far brighter inside than out. 'Are they still serving food in there, do you reckon?'

'Probably.' Ross grabbed a handful of his jacket and stood up. 'Let's go inside and ask. It's a bit cold out here now, anyway.'

Alex rarely felt the cold but she gathered up her things and followed him inside, at the same time telling him to: 'Man up, you big girl's blouse.'

While she was laying waste to a plate of steak and ale pie with all the trimmings, Ross sneaked a closer look at his dining companion. The general picture remained the same: brunette, cheery smile and an engaging personality. But now, some of the finer detail was beginning to emerge. He spotted her nails were painted black. It would have been impossible to have missed that. But now, he saw how perfectly manicured they were. No chips or scuffs as far as he could see.

At first he thought brunette but her hair was darker than that. Not quite black, almost a blue-black. *Highlights, possibly?* Ross had no idea if highlights that made hair darker were still called highlights, it simply had never occurred to him. He might have found her habit of fiddling frequently with her hair irritating in different circumstances but realised he liked the almost sensual movement it brought to her upper body. But no matter how much she messed with it, her hair always fell back into the same place.

They'd just finished their main course when the pub door swung open and a long line of women trooped in. The door was held open till the last one crossed the threshold. A cold draught slid in alongside them. From the snatches of conversation Ross picked up, the women had been at a talk on local history in the kirk up the road.

'Oh fuck, no. I don't believe it,' he groaned. The colour vanished from Ross's face.

Before Alex even had the chance to ask him what was wrong, one of the women detached herself from the line and arrowed for their table like a guided missile. She wore a dark grey jacket and skirt, and high heels that made her ankles wobble. An incredibly insincere smile was plastered to her face.

'Well, hello Ross.' Her smile morphed into a sneer as she looked Alex up and down. 'I hoped I might see you in here tonight but I didn't think you'd have company. And so *young*, too. Not learned your lesson from the last disaster then, eh?'

The combined heat from their faces would have melted a church candle at 50 paces, and while Ross was mortified and couldn't summon any form of cutting retort, Alex was raging internally. *You'll get a slap if you keep that up, you fat old cow.*

Ross cleared his throat as he sought to recover the situation. 'Alexis, this is Sally. She's, em, a friend of mine.' He waved a hand weakly over the table. 'Sally…'

But he didn't manage to complete the introduction as Sally butted in, clearly not interested in learning who his dining companion was. 'When Ross says I'm a friend of his, that's rather an understatement, you know.' She deliberately turned away from Alex. Sally laid her hand on Ross's shoulder. 'My husband and I have been friends with Ross and his darling late wife, Liz, for about… how long is it, Ross? Must be about twenty years, yeah?' Now she turned her head, and only her head, back to Alex. 'But I'm sure he will have told you about both of his wives, my dear, especially the foreign tart who conned him out of all of his money. She was probably about the same age as you, now I come to think about it.'

Alex had recovered her composure. 'Well, it's only our third date so I haven't heard all the gory details yet, Sarah…'

'It's SALLY!'

'Whatever.' Alex pointed, as the last of Sally's group crowded through a door marked Private Room. 'Better be careful they don't sneak out the back door while your back's turned, em…' She snapped her fingers a few times. 'Sally.'

The woman glared an arsenal of daggers then turned and barged off between the tables. 'What's *her* problem then?' asked Alex.

'Oh, that's just Sally. She's been a bit funny with me since Liz died. I've no idea why.'

'It'll be because she fancies you.'

Ross had just taken a drink, most of which he spluttered into the palm of his hand. 'What? Sally and me? What makes you think that?'

'It's a woman thing.' She picked up the desert menu. 'But be careful if you ever do hook up with her because that's some size of an arse she's carting around. Could cause you serious damage.'

Ross stifled a laugh, and studied her as she perused the menu. He noticed she had several piercing marks all down the curve of her left ear, yet she only wore one plain gold hoop in her earlobe. It was about the circumference of a £1 coin. The other marks didn't look as though they had healed up and he wondered just how many pieces of jewellery that ear would normally support. He would never have commented but as time passed by he identified similar marks on her other ear, below her bottom lip and on each of her eyebrows, which were also shaped beautifully. Ross figured, correctly, that multiple piercings and corporate image didn't go together.

So now he paid more attention to her face. Cobalt eyes, soft features and lips ideally suited for… *Well, let's not get into that, Ross my boy. She has to be at least fifteen years younger than you, and you know how the last one turned out.*

Then he caught himself scrutinising her as she walked to and from the ladies. And then he felt bad. Really bad. Alex was good fun, she had a quirky sense of humour, and he was enjoying her company. Of course, she couldn't know what he was thinking but she didn't deserve to be assessed like some prize ewe at a county fair. So he blushed, and the prize ewe clocked it immediately. *Damn!*

'Still thinking about Sally's arse?'

Ross suppressed a laugh and said no. Alex gave him an odd look but didn't pursue it. Then he remembered to ask about the tracker apps. She explained how they worked although she admitted she wasn't an expert. He asked if it would be possible to find out which phone his was linked to but she thought not. And although he would check if he had any record of the number the texts were being copied to, she was fairly sure it would be a Pay-As-You-Go SIM in a throwaway mobile.

'So, apart from actually finding these apps on my phone, there's nothing else we can do?'

'No. I don't think so.'

'Oh well. C'est la vie. Can you delete them?'

She laughed. 'Of course. Give me your phone again.' But as she took it from him, she paused. 'Are you sure you want to do that? Should you not report this to the police?'

'No, delete them. I'm fed up of all this crap. I just want them gone.'

As Alex was working on the phone, she looked amused. 'You really are a bit behind the times, aren't you?'

He grimaced. 'Massive understatement. Your average three-year-old is probably more tech-savvy than me. I just didn't ever buy into the whole computing thing. If it wasn't work-related, it sort of passed me by. And smartphones are just an extension of that so if computers weren't my thing...' He made a face. 'Apart from calling people, that is.'

'God! In a few years you'll be totally knackered then. Nobody will be making phone calls. That'll be so last decade. Or whatever.'

'But that's a problem, don't you see? If I keep avoiding technology, and that's what I do, I'll be totally lost. Because it's everywhere. And the non-technology options will gradually disappear. I won't even be able to go to the cinema or the theatre because box offices will be phased out. I really need to do something.'

'Well, maybe I can help. A friend of mine gave her grandma an iPad for her Christmas a couple of years back. She's seventy-eight.'

Ross immediately put on a *you're kidding me* look, but Alex came straight back at him. 'Listen. Don't mock, pal. After some excellent tuition from yours truly, she emails, does all her banking online, downloads music and films like there's no tomorrow, Facetimes her other great-grandkids in Canada and New Zealand: the works. And, as a result, all her pals at the old folks' home asked if I would teach them too. So I do one-to-ones called *Technology for the Totally Traumatised*. And if I was able to teach all those old biddies, you'd be a piece of cake. What do you think?'

'Well, I'd have to pay you.'

'You certainly would, I'm not a charity. £20 an hour, cash in hand.'

Ross scratched his ear. 'I'll think about it.' Just then, the bell sounded for last orders. 'A nightcap?'

Alex looked at her watch. 'Love to, but no. There's a bus at the top of the road in ten minutes. If I catch that into town, I can change buses or get a taxi home from there.'

Ross didn't ask how she knew the bus timetables, he was catching on. They handed each other their jackets, and shrugged them on. Outside, Ross hovered between heading for his bike and saying goodnight. Alex was far more decisive. She gave him the briefest of hugs, flung him a goodnight wave and disappeared off into the street. Ross waved at the space she'd just vacated, unlocked his bike and bounced it down the few steps from the car park to the foreshore. From there it was a flat run two miles east to Newhaven, where, a little unsteady on his feet, he pushed his bike the last mile through the quiet streets to his house.

He was almost home when his phoned cheeped. He stopped to check it.

Hi. It's Alex. That was great fun. Enjoyed your company and thanks for dinner. If you want to do it again or take pc lessons, call me. Take care. A

Ross dropped the phone back into his pocket. 'That's maybe not a bad idea,' he remarked to a ginger cat that was observing him guardedly from its perch on top of a nearby wall.

'Not a bad idea at all.'

SUMMER

45

Five Weeks Later

It was a Saturday evening in mid-June. Ross was sitting on the top deck of a bus, looking over at Edinburgh Castle. The dying rays of the sun were glinting off the temporary grandstands being erected on the Esplanade for the Military Tattoo, the main attraction of the world famous Edinburgh Festival. Not for the first time on the journey from his house into town, he pondered the wisdom of what he was about to do.

Well, if I'm not enjoying myself, I can always bail out. I'm sure Alex won't mind.

Alex. Despite several self-to-self lectures on the theme of once-bitten-twice-shy, he felt something was building between the two of them. He wasn't certain he wanted that, but equally he wasn't sure he didn't. But any tipping point was far enough in the distance that final decisions didn't need to be made, so he was on his way to meet her at a music venue in the depths of the Old Town.

The day after their bar supper in the Cramond Inn he phoned her to say thanks for finding and nullifying the apps on his phone, and to take her up on her offer to help him improve his IT skills. Alex came to his office the following Thursday after work and walked him through an introductory two-hour lesson in generic IT topics. To Ross's surprise, she held his interest throughout and he couldn't believe how quickly the time passed. Over the next half a dozen Thursdays he had one-hour lessons, covering different topics in more detail. Ross was quite amazed how she managed effortlessly to knit the whole subject together, and by the end of the final session he realised how much he'd enjoyed learning about all things computing and, more than once, he wondered why he hadn't ever bothered to understand it before. After each lesson they popped into the Cramond for one drink before going their separate ways but apart from friendly pecks on the cheek as they said good night, neither made any inappropriate moves.

Over the period, they settled into each other's company. Ross had told Alex about his back catalogue that first night and, gradually, she revealed more about herself.

Alexis had been born and brought up in Lairg, a small village in Sutherland about an hour north of Inverness. Despite being from a close-knit, loving family, as a sixteen-year-old she had rebelled against the claustrophobia of rural life, and had fallen in with a small band of other disaffected kids from the area. She described it as her wild-child period. Her schoolwork began to deteriorate and she refused to study for her exams. It wasn't a surprise when she failed most of them: badly. Trouble followed her and her gang around like an orphaned lamb. Then one night her father discovered her, stoned, in a tent with three of her *friends*.

Finlay, a mild-mannered Highlander who worked as an estate manager for the local laird, blew his stack completely and dragged her off home. Her mother had died when the girl was only twelve so Finlay had no choice but to deal with any and all problems involving his three children: all girls.

When Alexis surfaced the following morning, she expected to be read the riot act so she stayed precisely where she was, hoping to stave off the inevitable for a few hours yet.

A car crunching up the gravel driveway at the side of the house wakened her for a second time. She heard her father opening the kitchen door, then both male and female voices she didn't recognise. From the depths of her duvet, she figured something was up. A few minutes later, there was a polite knock on her bedroom door, which opened a crack. 'Are you decent, Alexis?' She grumped in the affirmative and pulled the bedclothes down as far as her nose, just in time for her father to plonk a gentle kiss on the end. He ruffled her hair affectionately. 'I'm sorry, pet, I'm afraid I have some terrible news for you.' He explained the police had come to the house to speak to her because about four hours earlier her best friend Maree had been found dead in the tent. He said she should come downstairs now. She turned away, chewing her lip to stop it trembling.

Alexis stared at the back of the door for a minute or two, pushed the duvet back and crawled out of bed. She was still wearing yesterday's underwear and one sock. Its mate lay crumpled on the floor at the foot of her bed. She noticed her jeans and t-shirt neatly folded over the back of her desk chair. *No way did I take them off.* She closed her eyes as a grainy image of crawling through a tent-flap flirted with her memory. The sequel involved playing-cards and a lot of shouting. She shook her head, then immediately resolved not to repeat that particular movement. For a while, at least.

Once the police had gone, she asked her father in a remarkably calm voice what had happened the night before. He told her another of her friends had called him to say she wasn't trying to cause trouble but she was worried about what Alexis and the others were up to in the tent. Finlay marched straight over to the field where the tent was pitched. He recognised Maree but he had his hands full with Alexis so couldn't take Maree home too.

Once he put Alexis to bed, Finlay called Maree's father but tragically, the poor man hadn't realised how potentially serious the situation was and didn't go out to bring his daughter home.

Alexis fell apart. She kept repeating the phrase: 'It could have been me that died.' It took Finlay most of the rest of the day to convince her she couldn't think like that. But, kind man and loving father though he was, he didn't let her completely off the hook. The following morning, he laid it out in calm but straightforward terms just how worried he was about her. He didn't mind she was pushing all sorts of boundaries, nor that she landed herself in the odd scrape. And while he positively encouraged experimentation he was damned if he would sit by and do nothing if any of his daughters were heading off the rails. Finlay knew he was taking a chance, that he might push Alexis further away but he had a sense that this rebellion was a fever that was about to break.

And he was right. Their conversation was stilted at first. Pulling teeth didn't come close to describing it. But gradually, the Berlin Wall came down, and father and daughter talked for several hours. Nothing was off the table, so some of the things she spoke about curled Finlay's eyelashes but he was prepared to accept the odd blush if it meant she would talk to him.

That night, Alexis gave her dad and her sisters several grizzly bear hugs then disappeared off to bed where she stayed for almost thirty-six hours, appearing periodically to be fed and watered.

By the end of the week she'd binned her erstwhile gang members, negotiated a rescue package with her head teacher, and enrolled in evening classes at the North Highland College, 25 miles away in Dornoch, with a study plan that would bring her back into line with her classmates. At Maree's funeral, Alexis silently promised her friend she would make the most of this second chance in life.

The following year, 1999, Finlay drove his daughter to Inverness to begin a three year course in Computer Science at the University of the Highlands and Islands, or UHI as it's commonly known. When she graduated, Finlay was the proudest man in the Highlands.

After a short period out of work, Alexis picked up the first in a succession of IT support jobs. She told Ross she'd always had a hankering to work in London and she was saving hard to make it happen. Her finances had been boosted over the past few months as her own flat was rented out while she was house-sitting for friends who were taking a gap year from work, backpacking through South America, Australasia and the Far East. They had invited Alexis but as she told Ross: 'At my age? You must be joking!' He thought this was highly amusing, a woman of thirty-five concerned about her age.

As the bus moved away from the lights, crossed Princes Street and began to climb up towards the castle, Ross reflected on how far his computing knowledge had come along under Alex's tutelage. Following that introductory two-hour session, and to help him build on the basics, she suggested they come up with a project he could use to stitch all the learning together. After a few false starts, he decided to design and publish a series of short travelogues about Edinburgh.

He bought an iPad online. He set up a Hotmail account so Alex could assign him tasks, and he could report back. He learned how to take pictures and videos using his phone and iPad, and how to upload them to the cloud. He researched facts and wrote scripts, recorded the audio and synchronised it with the video. Finally he added text and hyperlinks before publishing his work on YouTube.

As his computing confidence grew, he installed a few apps on his iPad, some music, eighties' crap according to Alex, and was currently watching box-sets of more eighties' crap streamed from Netflix. He was also using his phone to keep up with news and sport.

But where he steadfastly drew the line was internet banking. Alex asked him once, just to be sure but he refused even to consider it.

The Thursday after their final session, Ross was at work when he noticed the clock. It was their normal lesson time, and he felt at a loss. He considered calling her to suggest they should meet anyway, then changed his mind at least half a dozen times in the space of about ten minutes. Eventually he bit the bullet.

They agreed to meet for a drink in Leslie's Bar, a traditional pub not far from where she lived. Ross didn't even know it existed so he asked her for directions.

She giggled. 'Find it yourself. I'll see you there at half seven. We can have a couple then go for a curry.'

He found her sitting at a bench seat just inside the door. She had a pint of Guinness waiting for him. He eased himself carefully into the seat next to her, trying not to spill any of the beer. He didn't quite make it. She laughed at his clumsiness, pulled a pack of tissues from her jeans pocket and helped him to mop up the spillage. 'Did Mr Google come up with the directions then?'

'He did indeed, he's an incredibly clever chap that Mr Google. Seems to know everything.' They both laughed, which set the tone for the rest of the evening.

Walking her home, he asked her in a just-for-something-to-say manner, what she was up to at the weekend. 'I'm on late shift tomorrow, and I'm invited to a fortieth birthday party on Saturday. A friend of a friend.' He looked away and started blustering on about something inconsequential.

'Did you hear me, Ross?'

'Eh? What? Pardon?'

Alex sighed. 'I said, would you like to come?' Before he could chicken out and change his mind, Ross quickly said he would love to.

He stepped off the bus into the late evening sunlight, right into the midst of a noisy swarm of tourists charging towards the Royal Mile. He stood still as they parted like a fast-flowing stream round a half submerged rock. He waited till the tourists and the bus moved away then crossed George IV Bridge to walk down Victoria Street towards the pub/ music venue where Alex had suggested they meet. It was called Sneaky Pete's, just off the Grassmarket. This was yet another establishment that she frequented, which Ross had never been in.

Approaching the pub from the other side of the street, he hesitated before crossing. A group of smokers were blocking the entrance, and the music from inside was loud. Punk rock or something similar but he couldn't be sure. Mentally, he reviewed his chosen dress code for the evening: chinos, a navy-blue shirt and casual brown shoes. *You'll have to do, Ross. You can't exactly pop home and change, can you?* He manoeuvred past the smokers, and walked in through the open door before stopping dead in his tracks. He gawped at the scene in front of him. It was about as far removed from his comfort zone as Earth is from Pluto.

Oh, shit. What the fuck have I let myself in for?

* * *

Most of the punters in the bar fit the profile, *The Rocky Horror Picture Show* meets *The Crow* meets Kiss. There were a few people dressed reasonably normally but safe to say, the Chinos Club was represented by a membership of one. Ross's first reaction was he'd turned up at a fancy dress party, but Alex had neglected to tell him.

The place was heaving. He couldn't spot her so imagined she hadn't arrived yet. He worked his way to the bar and shouted for a Guinness. While his beer settled he listened to the music. He recognised the various bands from his teenage and student years: The Damned, The Cure, Bauhaus, Joy Division, Siouxsie and the Banshees. The overall atmosphere was on the lively side of raucous and he began to enjoy himself. But he kept an eye on the entrance, expecting to see Alex appear at any minute.

A surge of newcomers washed in, resulting in a fair amount of pushing and shoving as they battled their way to the bar. Ross lifted his beer, and moved so his back was against a pillar. He'd always enjoyed people watching and this place had it in spades, so it took him a few seconds to realise he was being spoken to by a familiar voice.

'Are you not talking to me, then?' He looked down. A woman right in front of him was laughing and waving her hand in his face. The music was too loud to hear a penny drop but drop it eventually did.

'Alex?' He wore a stunned expression on his face. 'Is that you?'

'Naw. It's Julie Andrews on a bad day. Of course it's me, you muppet.' She reached up and tapped below his chin. 'You're catching flies, Ross.'

He was used to seeing her with minimal make-up, wearing her Esprit IT corporate clothing, her hair wavy and natural. Tonight, well, he was quite simply gobsmacked.

The creature standing practically on his toes wasn't, as normal, six inches smaller than him. The black, leather, vertiginously high-heeled, platform-soled, knee-high boots with at least a dozen studded straps, meant she was close to looking him straight in the eye.

Horizontally slashed stockings, a black, crushed-velvet miniskirt, and above that a midriff-revealing lace creation that morphed into an equally black bustier. It was extremely low cut and scored high on the push-up factor. Alex's arms were wrapped in bicep-length lace gloves. Black: needless to say.

Ross had always wondered about her hair. What colour was it, really? Tonight it was blacker than a raven held captive in a nineteenth-century chimney. Furthermore, it was poker straight, cut to frame her face perfectly. Not a wave in sight.

He stared at her face, mesmerised. All her vacant piercings were now fully occupied with tiny silver daggers, studs that could have punched holes in solid steel, hoops so tight they looked painful and other pieces of metalwork possibly borrowed from a Marquis de Sade exhibition. But it was her make-up that was the ultimate accessory. She wouldn't have looked out of place on the cover of *Vogue*. Her eyelashes resembled black mascara needles, her eyebrows had been coloured and shaped as if by laser, and her complexion was alabaster-white. And her lips. Her lips looked like they'd had several coats of black enamel baked on.

The whole ensemble was finished off by a plain, black, satin choker. To Ross, the effect was jaw-droppingly sensational.

'Say something, then.'

'Jesus...'

'That'll do.' She stretched up on tiptoe, not easy in those boots, and kissed him full on the mouth. Slow, soft, with the merest flicker of tongue. She leaned back from the waist and considered his expression, the corners of her mouth upturned slightly. 'I'm assuming you *don't* have a beer bottle in your pocket.'

Ross put his hands on her waist, pulled her just a little tighter to him and kissed her straight back. When they broke for air, he said, 'I think that's just an indication of how bloody amazing you look. But, and apologies for my ignorance. Is it punk, or what?'

'It's a bit of punk and a bit of Goth. I like both and can never decide which one I prefer so I just mix it up. Now, what does a girl have to do around here to have a man buy her a drink?'

At just gone three in the morning, the pair of them fell out of the pub, laughing and giggling like teenagers. Ross had no idea how many Guinnesses he'd consumed but, pissed as he clearly was, from somewhere he found the sense to decline the several shots he was offered. He thought Alex was relatively sober compared to him but he couldn't imagine how that could be. She'd had a drink in every round, shots and all.

Alex had introduced him to the group. They numbered about six or seven but there was a lot of coming and going, and Ross found it difficult to keep track. Some were dressed like her and a couple were relatively normal. He spoke to them all at one time or another because Alex disappeared quite often to dance, usually on her own. She couldn't convince him to join her until the last dance: 'Dear Prudence' by Siouxsie and the Banshees. Not really a slow one but she draped herself all over him anyway. Bodily contact with her aside, he was secretly pleased. He was an awful dancer and was paranoid he'd look like someone's dad. But he had to admit he'd had a fantastic time. He had loved the music and the atmosphere, Alex's friends were great company and he couldn't take his eyes off *that outfit*.

They stopped several times on the walk home for some enthusiastic kissing sessions, with a fair amount of bump and grind involved. Now, standing outside her house, it was awkward time. *Will she invite me in? And if she does, should I accept? It's a first date after all.*

Later, when he confessed his indecision and insecurity to Elspeth she howled with laughter. 'Fuck's sake, Ross. Join the twenty-first century. These days, some people shag *before* their first date, never mind after it!'

Alex had guided him over to the gate and leaned in to give him one more kiss. She crossed her wrists behind his neck. 'I'd invite you in for a coffee, but...'

'No, no, you're quite right. This is just a bit too quick. It's probably time I was heading off home.'

She looked at him with some amusement. 'What I was about to say was... I'm not inviting you in for a coffee because, once we're inside, the *last* thing we will be doing is drinking coffee.'

She walked up the path, put her key in the door and turned round. 'Now. Are you coming in or not?'

46

Ross served his third straight double-fault to lose the game, the set and the match. Shoulders slumped, he walked up to the net and congratulated Barry, who'd never beaten him before.

'Jeez, man. 6-2, 6-1? You're clearly not yourself tonight.' They shook hands and headed for the clubhouse, waiting a few seconds for a break in play on the adjacent court before scuttling across at the net.

Sitting on a bench with his racquet propped up beside him, Ross leaned back against the wall and closed his eyes. Barry was practically bouncing round the room, he was so chuffed with his maiden victory. Ross smiled to himself as Barry recounted the key points in the match, all of them *unbelievable shots* by the man himself. Ross couldn't be annoyed with his friend. Even when Barry lost, he could always find at least one unbelievable shot to brighten up another defeat. Ross had long ago learned how to lose gracefully and Barry deserved his time in the spotlight. He'd probably lost about 15 or 20 times since they'd started playing each other.

'So what's up then, my man?' grinned Barry. 'Heavy night last night?'

Ross leaned down to untie a shoelace, grimacing at how dreadful he still felt, even though it was now just after nine o'clock on the Sunday evening.

'Indeed it was, Barry. Indeed it was.'

* * *

Ross waved after Barry's car as he cycled away from the tennis club. Normally he would ride his bike at a decent pace to prolong the exercise but on this occasion he meandered along, spinning the pedals when he needed to and coasting the rest of the time. He was in no hurry. He had a dilemma to resolve first, and that dilemma was Alex.

About halfway home, he reached a decision point on the route. He dug his phone out of his pocket and thumbed a number from his favourites list. 'Ah. You're in. Mind if I come over?' A brief pause. 'Okay. I'm on my bike so about a quarter of an hour.'

Bang on 15 minutes later, he rang the doorbell. A blurred figure approached the frosted-glass panel in the door and Ross knew exactly what to expect. Martin's traditional Sunday evening garb, born of post-Apocalyptic weekend student debauchery was a slobby t-shirt, shapeless tracksuit bottoms of indeterminate brand, and seriously down-at-heel slippers that looked as though they'd passed through a dog several times.

'Well, whatever's wrong, you'd better come in and tell me all about it.' Martin turned back towards the kitchen, leaving Ross to close the door. 'I'll put the kettle on. Can't have you pissed in charge of a bike.'

Now on the sofa with coffee in hand and his legs tucked under him, Martin said, 'What gives?'

Ross began by telling him about his Thursday evening with Alex, followed by the rock night in Sneaky Pete's. Martin mimed the whole: *You? In Sneaky Pete's? Until three in the morning?* thing. But Ross ignored him. Far more severe mockery would be heading in his direction all too soon. He paused the story at the door to Alex's friend's house. A couple of seconds passed while Martin waited for Ross to continue, then he broke into an enormous grin when he realised his friend had arrived at the crux of the tale.

He slapped his thigh in classic comedic style and cackled like a Macbeth witch. 'She dropped her drawers, didn't she?'

But Martin's laughter quickly subsided when he spotted Ross's downcast demeanour.

This wasn't Tales of a Goth/Punk's Boudoir after all.

* * *

Earlier on that evening, Ross had been well beaten by Barry partly because his younger, fitter opponent was improving steadily and partly because of his gargantuan hangover. But mainly because audio-visual flashbacks of last night's sex with Alex kept pinging into his brain.

Through the haze he could picture a trail of clothes hitting the floor at regular intervals between the front door and her bed despite buttons, zips and hooks that were determined not to play ball. There was a frantic and somewhat comical search for a condom, involving it seemed, every pocket, handbag and drawer. They attempted various positional changes that are made to look silky smooth in the movies but are rarely that in real life. Overall, it could be described as the fractured choreography of first time lovers, where the performance was both complicated and affected by a surfeit of alcohol.

Some time later, Ross was awakened by Alex slipping out of bed. 'Make-up,' she whispered, kissing him full on the mouth and moving smartly away as he reached out to fondle her breast. When she came back, smelling vaguely like coconut and cream, they made spoons and slept for several hours.

Now it was Sunday afternoon and he was walking home. He didn't think he would be able to suffer being cooped up in any form of transport, and it gave him time to think. He was confused. Hadn't he just had amazing sex with a woman 15 years his junior, who'd been wearing the remnants of an outfit loosely affiliated to bondage? Why wasn't he dancing down the street, twirling round lampposts, jumping and clicking his heels together like some latter day Gene Kelly in *Singing In The Rain?*

It was a long walk, almost an hour and a half and by the time he reached home he'd convinced himself the age gap was the issue. It just wasn't sustainable in the long term. Perhaps 15 years didn't matter too much when he was fifty, but what about at sixty? When he was seventy Alex would only be fifty-five. What if she wanted children? Then there was her desire to move to London. He certainly wouldn't be going with her. That was out of the question.

The Carla factor counted too. She'd disappeared four months ago and the scars were still livid. He wasn't sure they would ever heal. She had been twelve years younger so the comparisons were all too similar.

No. He would call Alex tomorrow, tell her he was sorry, that there was no future for them. *Oh God! What if she thinks it was only about the sex and now that I've had that, I'm off like a dirty shirt?* That troubled him. How would he navigate that particular minefield?

He explained all that to Martin, who sighed and scratched his ear. 'Listen, sunshine. I know I'm not exactly relationship counsellor material but really, what's the problem? You've just had great sex with a much younger woman, wearing kinky gear too I might add, and you're thinking of calling her to break it off?' Ross nodded but didn't speak. 'Anyway, you're asking my advice, and, for what it's worth, I think you must be out of your tree. I mean, I've only met her a couple of times but I wouldn't kick her out of bed for farting.'

Ross smiled at the image. 'But I just can't see it going anywhere.'

'So what? If it does, it does, and if it doesn't, it doesn't.' Ross shook his head slowly so Martin tried another tack. 'Okay, how about this. Keep things low key just now, don't go out in foursomes, don't invite people to dinner. Just go with the flow and see how it all pans out. If she does move to London things may just come to a natural end anyway.'

'But there's what happened with Carla…'

'Oh for fuck's sake…' Then, more gently. 'Look. What Carla did was total shit but, and I know it's easy for me to say, you can't let it affect other relationships you end up in. There aren't con artists hiding in every shadow, waiting to steal all your worldly goods when your back's turned. Alex seems like a lovely girl. She did you a favour with those phone apps, and the only downside I can think of is she's clearly into you so her taste's a bit suspect.' Ross tossed a cushion at his friend, who deflected it with his arm. 'And, she dresses up in S & M gear, which, I have to say, is a bit of a bonus as far as I'm concerned.'

Ross would have been surprised if Martin had managed to remain serious for too long. 'I suppose you're right. Ending it straight away would be a knee-jerk reaction. I'm probably just being a bit uptight about the whole thing.'

'Good man.' He hauled around at his tracksuit bottoms and gave his belly a good scratch. 'Now, I was just thinking earlier on, any more news from the police or the banks?'

'Not really. I was talking to Mel the other day. They've made a formal request to their counterparts in Spain, sent them an International Letter of Request or something like that. But apparently it could take months for any sort of reply to come back. Everybody knows the money was probably moved on to another country in a matter of minutes so what's the bloody point? And even if the Spanish authorities can trace it, Mel would then have to send another one of those letters to the authorities in the next country. And so it goes on.'

'Fuck's sake! Not exactly quick, are they? Do you stand *any* chance of seeing your money again?'

'I'm working on the basis I won't. Anything else is a bonus.'

'And what about the fourteen k she withdrew from your credit card? Will you need to reimburse the bank?'

'I don't know yet but it's unlikely. Eventually the police will decide I'm not the guilty party so when they confirm to the bank that I've been the victim of fraud, the bank will hopefully write off the debt.'

'And the fake mortgage?'

'Just exactly the same as the credit card, they're waiting to see what the police say. I'll lose all my own money but hopefully I won't owe the bank or the building society anything.'

'Well, that's something at least. Isn't it?'

Ross shrugged and turned his palms up. 'The only problem would be if the cops *can't* prove it's fraud. Because if they can't, I'll be liable for the debt.'

'Jesus! What a mess.'

Just as Ross was leaving, Martin said, 'Seriously, now. I hope everything works out with Alex, so stick in there, kid.'

Ross was putting his helmet on so he almost missed the follow-up. 'And you can let me know what she dresses up in next.'

But by the time he turned round to say, 'Bugger off,' he was saying it to a closed door.

He laughed to himself and pedalled off down the drive. No matter what, he'd always thanked his lucky stars he had Martin for a best mate.

Even if he is a complete tosser sometimes.

FALL

47

Seven Weeks Later

'Good game?' asked the barman.

It was just after five o'clock on the first Saturday in September, and Ross and three of his football-supporting friends had dropped in to their usual post-match haunt. The pub was far enough away from the stadium not to be mobbed with fans but close enough that they didn't have to walk too far for a beer. And, they could be reasonably sure of a table for their habitual dissection of their team's performance, and the rest of the day's football.

'Not bad, but I've no idea how we managed to only come away with a draw.'

The barman chortled as he poured the last beer. 'Let me guess. Hit the post, hit the bar, missed a few sitters, and their keeper played a blinder?'

Ross handed over the money, and picked up three of the beers. 'That's about right, Tommy. Never mind, there's always next week.'

'Ever the optimist, my boy. That's what I like to hear.' Tommy looked to the customer who was next in line. This was a proper pub and the patrons knew not to shout their order or try to jump the queue. Because if they did, they'd suffer the sharp edge of the barman's tongue.

Ross had delivered beers to his thirsty mates, come back for his pint and was walking away from the bar when he felt a tap on his left shoulder. He turned round to find an older gentleman smiling at him. The man was about Ross's height, maybe early sixties, bald as a bowling ball, bespectacled, trim and unusually well turned out for a Saturday tea-time. If Ross had been asked to find one word that described him it would have been *dapper*.

'Excuse me. It's Ross McKinlay, isn't it?'

'It is.' Ross instinctively switched his glass to his left hand. 'I'm sorry, have we met before?' He remained half turned away, still a little uncertain.

'No, we've never met but I wonder if we could have a quiet chat.'

Ross's first thought was, what are you selling? He glanced at the man's lapels, looking for a badge with the name of the charity he was using to fleece the Saturday evening drinkers. 'I don't know, what's it about? I'm having a drink with some friends.' He stepped to the side for a moment to let two men pass through the gap.

The man held up both hands. 'I don't want to interrupt your evening but I'm sure you'll want to talk to me.'

Ross was still smiling but not with his eyes. 'Okay. Two, no, three things. First, you know my name but I don't know yours. Second, you're standing in a busy pub, without a drink. What's that all about? And third, I'd rather not be rude but I'll be walking away this second if you don't tell me *what* you want to talk to me about.'

'That's fair comment. My name's Oliver. I'd prefer to stay sober while we talk but I'll certainly be enjoying a couple later on. And, I know exactly what you've been going through.'

Ross couldn't understand why but despite the man's outward appearance and his gentle, polite manner, he felt some anger towards him. He leaned forward, eyes narrowing, his brow lowered, and his index finger pointing at Oliver's nose. 'As you said, we've never met before. But you know exactly what I've been *going* through. What the hell are you talking about, *Oliver*?'

Oliver reached out and guided Ross's finger away from his face. 'I'd like to talk to you about your missing wife. And the reason I know about her is my wife went missing too.' Ross's pointing finger drifted gradually south as he stared blankly at the other man. '*And* I'm a few hundred thousand pounds down as a result.'

Ross looked like he'd just spotted John Lennon in the corner, sharing a joint with Jimi Hendrix. Oliver continued. 'So, I'll just order myself a soft drink and sit at that little table over there. Just come over whenever you're ready.'

And, with that, he walked off towards the bar, leaving Ross rooted to the spot in a space in the middle of the floor like the star-struck winner of a national elimination dance.

* * *

Ross could sense the confused stares from his three friends lancing into the back of his head as he sat down in the chair facing Oliver. There was a whole afternoon of football to be discussed, and now he was bailing out before a ball had been kicked. He hadn't even been able to come up with a decent excuse. 'Sorry guys, but I need to talk to this chap about, em, something.'

'Right.' Ross had his pint in front of him and his forearms crossed on the table. 'The floor's yours. But I want to know how you know me, and how do you know about my wife?'

Oliver pulled his chair in a little closer. He took his wallet from his inside jacket pocket and laid it on the table next to his glass of cranberry juice. Ross looked at the wallet, then back at Oliver, one eyebrow raised.

'I'll answer both questions in just a minute but may I tell you a bit more about myself first? It'll save me jumping about in the story.' Ross huffed a little but waved his hand in agreement.

'I'm sixty-two and my first wife, Esther, died just over four years ago. She'd been ill for a long time. We were quite well off. Decent jobs and no children, you see.' He looked at Ross for some sign of empathy but nothing came back. His mouth ticked up at the sides and he carried on. 'Less than a year later I began a relationship with a much younger woman, her name was Susanne. She had a French accent, *said* she was from Guernsey. Susanne was beautiful, energetic, vibrant. I was besotted, blind and, as it turned out, stupid. All my friends warned me she was a gold-digger but I didn't listen. Like I said, stupid.' Ross leaned back in his chair, arms crossed tightly, the head of his beer still level with the top of the glass.

'A few months later we were married so, of course, Susanne moved in. I didn't really notice but gradually she took charge of all my affairs. I was still working full-time, my job was pretty full-on, so it was a big help. I thought it was just boring stuff like household accounts, paying bills, banking. Esther used to do all that so I was just glad someone else was dealing with it.'

Ross was parched but still his beer sat there as Oliver continued. 'One day I came home from a business trip, I'd been away for a few days. Susanne wasn't at home. The car was still there so I wondered if she was just out for a walk or something. But the house felt a little… I don't know, different.' At last Ross took a mouthful of his beer and Oliver followed suit, sipping his juice. 'Then I realised things were missing. A couple of small antiques, a painting, all her jewellery including things I bought her. I couldn't find my good watch, an Omega. Then I noticed an open drawer in the study, where we kept household papers. The banking folder was missing too, and…' His voice croaked so he took another sip. He was struggling to retain his composure.

'She'd gone?' said Ross, and Oliver nodded. 'And you said earlier, you've lost a few hundred thousand?'

'No need to bore you with the exact figure but not far short of eight.'

They were both silent, lost in themselves. Ross spoke first. 'I'm assuming you're here because you've found out my wife did something similar to me.'

'That's right.'

'Okay. So, back to what I asked you earlier. How? How did you find out? How did you track me down?'

A cheer floated over from the bar and Ross glanced up. The television showed several footballers in white tops celebrating a goal.

Oliver's voice had regained its earlier strength, he sat taller in his seat. 'About nine months, a year after Susanne left, I was approached by two men who'd suffered the same. They'd met at a victim support group completely by accident, and between them they decided to try to track down the criminals.' He looked directly at Ross. 'You know it's organised crime, don't you?' Ross nodded as he was taking another drink. 'Then they found out about me, and a few others, and now we're a small group trying to pull together enough evidence to take to the police and the banks.'

'You *still* haven't told me how you tracked me down. And you need to tell me that or we're done here.'

'I get it. You're suspicious. You don't trust me, and you're quite right not to. Perhaps this will help.' He reached into his inside jacket pocket and withdrew two pages of A4, stapled together and folded in three. He smoothed out the folds, and pushed them across the table.

Ross read the first few lines. His eyes snapped up at the man opposite him. 'Where the hell did you get this?' It was a copy of a police report written by Mel Cooper concerning Carla's disappearance, including the full scale of the losses Ross had suffered.

Oliver picked his way carefully through his explanation. 'We have, let's just say, a *contact* in the police force who is willing to provide us with reports like that one. This person wasn't targeted personally but one of their close friends was.' Ross noted the gender-neutral terms Oliver had used but let it pass. 'Depending on how our conversation works out today I'll tell you more about other resources we have available to us but that's all I can say for now.'

Ross finished reading the document and spun the papers away from him. 'My problem is, I'm finding it difficult to trust you and, funnily enough, the fact you've got that report doesn't help your case. You've come out of absolutely nowhere so how do I know you're not part of this. That you're not a conman too.'

Oliver reached for his wallet, slid out a folded piece of paper and handed it to Ross. It was a newspaper clipping that showed Oliver and, inset, a grainy image of a dark-haired woman. Below was a report of Susanne's disappearance, suggesting there was a criminal element involved. It asked for anyone with any information about her to contact a helpline or a police station. Ross looked at the other man expectantly, pointing at several heavy black lines that obscured the couple's surname and the location of the police station. 'Why the redaction? It makes me wonder if this article is legit. After all, we're talking about organised crime here. A bit of Photoshopping wouldn't be beyond a gang of master criminals.'

Oliver wasn't perturbed about this line of questioning. It was as if he'd been expecting it. 'Again, you're right. I could have mocked it up but I didn't. All I can say is, it is genuine but at this stage I can't give you the proof you need.' Ross hit him with his best *oh really?* expression. 'And the names are scored out for your safety and security as well as mine. So I can't tell you my full name.'

'How mysterious. Why not?'

Oliver looked around to make sure he wasn't being overheard but most of the people nearby were concentrating on the game. 'I told you earlier we are a small group. At one time there were nine of us. Now there are only seven.'

'What happened to the other two?'

'They died.' Oliver paused. 'In circumstances that are, at best, unexplained.'

'And at worst?'

'They were murdered.'

48

Ross digested Oliver's last statement: that two of his fellow victims had perhaps been murdered. He was struggling to comprehend the enormity of this piece of information but he still wasn't one hundred per cent sure of the person sitting opposite him.

Ross drained his glass, and braced himself to stand up. 'This place is too busy to talk properly. There's a pub a few doors down on this side of the street. It's a barn of a place but it'll be quiet at this time of day. I'll meet you there in five but I'll need to tell my friends where I've gone.'

A few minutes later, they were seated in a soulless, plastic pub with a faux-Irish theme. It was popular with the 18 to 25 crowd, although everyone on this side of town knew the lower age limit was closer to 15. By ten o'clock the joint would be jumping but right now, only a dozy-looking barman with outlandish ear-tunnels was around to listen in. But he appeared to be lost in his own little world. The chances of him eavesdropping were slim to none.

Oliver allowed the silence to build. It was Ross who broke it. 'Being right up-front with you, I don't even know why I'm here. I've only known you five minutes, you're dragging me back into something I've been trying to put behind me, and now you're telling me that two people who were involved with you have been murdered. Now, based on things you *haven't* told me, like your surname and whether your *talented* friend is a him or a her, it's probably safe to assume that if I ask you for more details you'll come over all cloak and dagger again.'

Oliver spread his arms wide. 'Until I know you trust me, I won't be able to trust you. So until we reach that point, you're right, I do need to play my cards close to my chest. Because if I don't, we could both be in danger. I'm sorry, but that's the way it has to be.'

Having arrived at this impasse, Ross knew he had to fall down one side of the ridge or the other. A good couple of minutes passed, where both men allowed the other time to think. 'Okay, I'll give you the benefit of the doubt. For now.

But the only thing that'll keep me here for any longer is if you convince me that, beyond any shadow of doubt, you're on the side of the good guys.' Ross sat back and folded his arms. 'So, Oliver, you have one chance. Don't blow it.'

'Fair enough. If I can't convince you today that I'm the real deal, I'll walk away and you won't ever see or hear from me again. I'm going to start off by describing your profile, and what I think has been happening to you. You can let me know if I'm right.' Ross nodded his acquiescence.

'I imagine you're a widower, with no children or even close family relatives. If you died today you would have no one obvious to leave your estate to. Prior to meeting Carla, you won't have been widowed for long, possibly even less than a year. Carla will have come out of nowhere. Her background would have been vague, certainly no family anywhere nearby. She wouldn't have owned her house or flat. Perhaps she rented it or said she was looking after it for someone. Her personal possessions would have been few, no heirlooms or family photos or other mementos.' Ross's eyes widened but he didn't make any comment. Oliver noticed and continued. 'She may even have been reluctant to have her photo taken.' He paused for a second, received no reaction this time so carried on.

'Like I was with my wife, you were probably besotted by her and, I apologise for this, she could have been, em, extravagant when it came to sex. This is a major part of their MO. It's possible she made moves to alienate your friends, to narrow down your social circle, keep you closer to her.' Oliver considered asking, *How am I doing so far?* but Ross's expression suggested it wasn't a good idea.

The door swung open, someone looked in, and let the door swing closed again. Ross wasn't surprised, a funeral home would have more atmosphere.

Oliver continued with his analysis. 'I'm almost certain that you'd have been under some sort of electronic surveillance like tracking apps on your phone or tablet, key-loggers on your PC, possibly even hidden spy cameras.' Ross's eyebrows shot up as he'd never considered the possibility. Oliver continued quickly. 'I know that sounds a bit OTT but these things are dirt cheap, almost invisible and can be set up by practically anyone.' Ross shook his head, motioning Oliver to carry on.

'Now, your money. These people target men *and* women with a reasonable amount of personal wealth. Certainly mid-six figures at least. They don't single out Joe Normal. Or the rich and famous. That's too risky. They don't need the publicity nor do they want to antagonise powerful people. Obviously they're operating in the UK and definitely Europe but we don't know how far their operation extends. As my wife did with me, I think Carla would have gradually worked her way into your finances. Current and savings accounts are obvious targets but they're not usually lucrative enough on their own. That's not to say they won't empty those accounts, leave overdrafts and credit cards maxed out, but they're looking for bigger fish to fry. Investments, inheritances, things like that.'

Ross began fidgeting. The pub's windows were frosted part way up so people walking past were just a blur. He found this distracting and was struggling to maintain attention.

Oliver raised an index finger. 'Nearly there. The final sting usually happens when they secure a major cash amount like a big loan or a second mortgage. When that happens the operative disappears, completely without trace. And the police and the banks are powerless because the money trail goes cold.' Oliver drained half his glass and sat back as if to say, *'That's it. I'm done.'*

Ross had been desperate to speak so he jumped straight in. 'That was quite a speech. But, and this is a giant-sized but, if you *were* one of the bad guys, you'd know all those things. Most of your story is generic. It could apply to lots of people. So I'm afraid you haven't convinced me at all. Is this where you walk away?'

'Not quite, Ross. Most of the time I was talking, you kept a fairly neutral expression. Inscrutable, I would say. So I have a few questions to ask you now, and I suggest you keep that up. You don't want to give anything away and, actually, I don't want you to. Fair enough?'

Ross tilted his head a little to one side. He remained the epitome of inscrutability.

'One of the key questions is, do you think it's all over now?'

Ross's eyebrows lowered. 'Meaning?'

'Meaning, have they finished with you? Have they taken everything they can and they're not coming back for more?'

239

Ross's mouth opened a little as he considered Oliver's question. But he was careful how he phrased his retort. 'Explain.'

'If you do have more money, money they haven't taken yet, then it's not over. Now, I don't know if you have, and I don't *want* to know. But you can believe me when I say this or not, I actually hope you don't have anything left worth stealing. Because, if you have, they'll be back. That's if...' Oliver paused, trying to find an easy way to phrase his point. 'That's if they're not already back and preparing to try again.'

Ross, too, was struggling to reply while maintaining his mask of inscrutability, which he wasn't used to. He was the worst poker player in the world. Martin's twin daughters had been taking money from him at cards since their early teens, despite his best attempts to beat them.

Oliver helped him out by speaking again, this time without any eye contact. 'If you do have any more money hidden away, that you think is well protected, somewhere it can't possibly be hacked, then make damn sure it stays there. I didn't, and that's how I lost my last hundred and odd thousand.' Ross said absolutely nothing, just stared. 'Your silence suggests you have. Make bloody sure you keep it that way.'

Thoughts, suspicions, questions, ideas, were firing at Ross's brain like some souped-up version of *Asteroids*, one of his favourite arcade games from the eighties. He sat quietly, taking small mouthfuls of his drink while he sifted through this blizzard, trying to identify the nuggets, the items of real value. Eventually he found one. 'You said, and I quote, if they're not already back and preparing to try again. What did you mean by that?' He snapped his fingers softly a few times. 'What would that look like? How would I recognise it?'

Oliver didn't hesitate. 'In the last few months, since Carla disappeared, have you started a new relationship? Has anyone new come into your life?'

Ross's heart didn't actually stop. Time didn't stand still. The sun didn't stop shining for a few seconds. It just appeared that all three events had coincided. He instantly felt sick to his stomach. He couldn't look at Oliver. His gaze skittered around the pub, alighting on several locations, items and people, each for a split second before zapping off onto something else. He realised Oliver was speaking again, and had to interrupt. 'Sorry, what were you saying?'

Oliver knew just how traumatic all of this was for Ross. After all, he'd been through it. 'There is often what we term a secondary operative, who turns up at some point after the first one disappears. It's happened to five people as far as we know, and it's usually if they know the victim still has significant assets they haven't taken. On two occasions, they weren't successful but I was one of the unlucky ones. If it hasn't happened to you yet, you need to make sure it doesn't.'

To use an old saying of his father's, Ross didn't know whether he was punched, bored or countersunk. In his mind, he'd bottomed out and was coming up the other side. The nightmare was all over and he was recovering. His trust in people was beginning to return. *Surely Alex can't be part of this. I mean, the only reason I met her was because of a fault on my PC.*

He considered some of the assumptions Oliver had made. Alex *had* come out of nowhere. Her background wasn't vague but, on reflection, she hadn't ever suggested they visit her family in Lairg, and none of them had come to Edinburgh as far as he knew. But then again, he *had* taken Martin's advice to keep things low key so they hadn't socialised much with other people. She had seemed fine with that but perhaps it suited her to keep it that way for a different reason. Although she said she owned a flat, apparently it was rented out while she house-sat for friends who were on the other side of the world. *How terribly convenient.* And because she was in someone else's house, obviously it was full of their stuff, not Alex's.

As far as photos were concerned, she wasn't exactly reluctant to be snapped, they just weren't in the habit of taking photos of each other with their phones. Ross had taken lots of photos for his project but still wasn't anything like some people, whipping their phones out to take photos of anything and everything, where most of the results were probably blurred rubbish, fit only for Facebook fodder.

And then there was the sex... *What word had Oliver used? Extravagant?* There was no doubt Alex was experienced and adventurous, totally lacking in inhibition. They had only been together a few weeks but he thought about some of the things they'd done, and some of the places they'd done them. *But,*

is her attitude to sex extravagant or is she perfectly normal?
Am I the abnormal one? Or is she the same as Carla, using her
body to catch me off guard? He didn't know the answer to the
last question but he prayed it was *No.* He wasn't sure he could
survive a second betrayal.

Ross was torn. He was trying to find something
disingenuous about this stranger who had dropped into his
life less than an hour ago like a war-time parachutist. He
wasn't a psychologist but there was nothing about Oliver's
body language or expression that screamed *Suspicious!*

So Ross told Oliver all about Alex. He listened intently
before saying, 'She fits the profile.'

'Perhaps she does but I could come up with a counter-
argument for everything you've alluded to.' Then something
struck him. 'Wait a minute. I've just realised. Carla was able
to access my money because I was practically IT illiterate.
But Alex has been teaching me, and now I'm able to do all
sorts of things with my phone and iPad. Why would she do
that if IT was my Achilles' heel? It doesn't make any sense.'

'You're right. It doesn't. But the counter is, they wouldn't
attack you a second time in the same way. It would be too
obvious. Listen, I'm not accusing this woman, Alex, of
anything. I'm just saying that a second attack by a different
operative has happened a few times so I'm trying to prevent
the same thing happening to you.'

Ross swallowed some more beer and sat back. 'Ah, but wait
a minute, there's a big flaw in your theory about Alex being
one of these, what did you call them, secondary operatives.'

'And what's that?'

'Well, she first appeared on the scene when she was called
in to our office to fix a faulty network card on my PC. My
Outlook wasn't working, yet it had been fine the night
before. So, obviously, the network card must have gone kaput
overnight, and that's why we contacted the helpdesk. Which,
in turn, meant Alex turned up to fix the fault. That's one hell
of a coincidence, don't you think?'

Oliver made to reply but Ross was on a roll. 'If she is
involved, there's no way she was just sitting twiddling her
thumbs, waiting for something to go wrong with my PC so
she could come in and fix it. And then inveigle her way into
my life. That's just a total non-starter, isn't it?'

Oliver was finding it difficult to disagree. 'What if they somehow accessed your PC remotely? And engineered the fault that way?'

'I don't think so. I'm no expert, but if someone wanted to access my PC remotely would I not have to authorise access?' He paused, as another objection occurred to him. 'And anyway, I always switch my PC off overnight.'

Oliver began poking at his mobile phone. 'I don't know. But as the saying goes, I know a man who might.' He finished typing a text and hit send, before dropping the phone back into his pocket.

There was a lull in the conversation until Ross said, 'Going back to why you said you came here, to stop me being targeted by this secondary operative. That wasn't the only reason, was it?'

Oliver smiled again. 'No, Ross. It wasn't.' He leaned forward, folded his arms and rested his elbows on the table. 'What did Carla say she did for a living?'

'What the hell does that have to do with the price of cheese?'

'Please, Ross. Just humour me.'

'Well, she *said* she worked offshore but it didn't take the police long to discover she didn't.'

'What rota was she supposed to be working?'

'Three weeks on, three weeks off. Why do you... ah!' It was one of those light-bulb moments. 'I see where you're headed. If she was three weeks with me, what did she do in the three weeks she was allegedly working?'

'It's a pattern we've seen before. At the same time Carla was fleecing you, it's possible, even likely, she was working on some other poor soul. Otherwise, why would she not just stay with you all the time?'

Ross could have kicked his own arse. 'What a complete muppet. I've been wondering where she went while she was supposed to be offshore but it never occurred to me she was stringing another guy along.' It struck him that it hadn't cropped up in any of his conversations with the police either but that was a discussion for another time.

He slapped a hand on the table. 'And that's the real reason you're here talking to me, isn't it? You're hoping I'll help you to find this other,' Ross did the fingers-as-quotes thing, '"poor soul". So he doesn't suffer the same fate as me.' He corrected himself. 'As us.'

Oliver nodded.

Ross paused while the barman wandered past. He checked out their drinks to see if they needed a refill. Ross waited till he turned away before continuing. 'If you're right, and Carla's still in the UK, I don't see how in heaven's name we would be able to track her down. I mean, she, and this man, could be absolutely anywhere. Finding a needle in the proverbial haystack would be simple by comparison.' Oliver started to speak but Ross interrupted him. 'And, the sting could be complete by now. In fact, how can you be sure it isn't? In which case, she'll have disappeared again.'

'We haven't a clue whether the *sting*, which is as good a word as any, has been perpetrated. And as for how to track her down, or actually, track down the man and hope Carla's still with him, we think we've found a way to identify this gang's *likely* victims and then it's a case of checking them out. Trial and error, I'm afraid.' He paused, and gathered himself. 'So, Ross, it's time to stick or twist. Will you help us?'

Ross stood up. 'I need to go to the loo. Back in a minute.' He spotted the Toilets sign and headed off towards it. He didn't need to go at all. He just needed some time to think, away from Oliver's studied gaze. He walked through the door marked Fir, entered a cubicle, and locked the door. The tell-tale blue liquid in the bowl told him no one had been in there since the pub had reopened so he sat down.

A few minutes later, his mind made up, he returned to their table. 'Here's my main problem with helping you, Oliver. Since this all happened with Carla, I've been trying to get over it. To put my life back on track. So, do I really want it all to kick off again? Well the truth is, I'm not sure I do.'

'But are you not interested in finding Carla. In bringing her to trial? In giving the police some evidence that could disrupt or even close down this gang's activities?'

'With all due respect, I don't see how the efforts of a handful of middle-aged amateurs can possibly be successful against an organised criminal outfit. And a dangerous criminal outfit to boot. Maybe on TV but not in real life. And, as for Carla, I couldn't give a toss if I never saw her again. The money's gone. I'm reconciled to not recovering any of it. I'm trying to move on.'

'And there's nothing I can say to convince you otherwise?'

244

'I'm afraid not. No.'

Oliver sighed and shrugged. 'Oh well, that was my best shot. Shame it wasn't good enough.'

By now, Ross was satisfied Oliver was genuine so the two men sat and compared their experiences while they finished their drinks. He explained how things had all panned out with Carla just in case there was anything that might help in the future. As they were about to leave, Oliver asked, 'So, it was all financial then?'

'What do you mean?'

'Well, I told you earlier that Susanne stole some personal items of mine, like my watch, which I can't really replace. In a way, I'm glad all you lost was money. If that's not a stupid thing to say.'

Ross was standing by the table, one arm in his jacket, when for no apparent reason, he crashed back down in his chair. His complexion had changed to the colour of old snow. 'I've got to go,' he barked at Oliver. 'But how do I contact you?'

Oliver had no idea what had had such an impact on Ross, just as it appeared as though he had failed to win the younger man over. But this was the opening he'd been trying to engineer since they had first sat down. He fished about in a jacket pocket and produced a cell-phone, best described as primitive and only capable of phone calls and texts. 'Use this. It only has my number programmed in. Call me at any time.'

Ross grabbed the phone and rushed towards the door, an empty jacket sleeve trailing in his wake. 'I'll be in touch,' he yelled, vanishing into the street.

Oliver blinked a few times. The pub door was still swinging shut. *Well, well, well. There's a turn-up.* He checked his own phone was switched on and the ringer was turned up. *Time I had a beer, I think.* He walked over to the bar and pointed at a tap he was familiar with.

'A pint of that, please.' He gazed at the barman and wondered just how painful it must be to have those tunnel things jammed in your ears.

He'd just ordered a second beer when his phone rang. 'Hello?'

There was a brief pause before Ross spoke. 'Something's happened.' His voice caught a few times. He sounded as though he was under terrible strain. 'I'm going to help you track down that fucking bitch Carla and her bastard thieving gang of crooks.' Oliver looked up at the fake rustic ceiling of the bar, and joined his hands together in the classic *Thank the Lord* pose. 'Will you take a taxi over to my house straight away? Here's the address.' Ross hung up without another word.

Oliver took one gulp of his fresh pint, deposited it back on the bar, and hurried out the door. Two young lads in football tops and jeans standing further along the bar spotted his hasty departure. They instinctively judged it to be permanent, and quickly split the remainder of his beer between them. 'Shame tae fuckin' waste it, Deeks.'

His pal sported a grin that would have terrified small children. 'Too right, Gaz.' He slugged down at least half his share of their windfall. 'Wonder where the fuck *he* was goin' in such a fuckin' hurry.'

* * *

Ross had been desperate to get home. As soon as he hit the pavement he looked wildly around for a taxi. The pub was close to a major junction on Leith Walk and within a minute a black cab pulled up at the lights. He whistled shrilly, the driver spotted him waving and spun the cab round on a sixpence. Ross jumped in, shouted the address through the Perspex glass and slumped into the back seat. He didn't bother fastening the seatbelt.

Outside his house, he threw a tenner at the driver's cash slot and charged inside, straight past Joan and Joe who were walking Bella. Joan immediately started complaining to her husband about, 'Some people's manners...' but Joe had developed a fine line in ignoring during their marriage so her grumping was a waste of breath. But he did watch as the front door bounced off its hinges and failed to close properly on the backward swing. Joe stopped at the end of his path to see if his neighbour would reappear.

Now that Ross was actually inside, he moved like he was walking through setting concrete. He knew he had to look in a particular place but he was petrified because of what he might find. Now here he was, down on all fours, elbows locked and biceps vibrating with the tension. *After everything that's happened in the last few months, why have I never looked in here?* He had no idea what Oliver had said, what form of words he'd strung together that had kicked off the isolated spark in Ross's brain that had brought him rushing to this spot.

Fuck's sake! Open the bastarding thing. So he did, and the full range of his innermost terrors erupted like some unpronounceable Icelandic volcano.

At that instant, Ross Alasdair McKinlay roared with unbridled rage. He threw things across the room. Solid, heavy things that shattered mirrors and dented walls. He wept great gushes of tears and mucus, rendering his eyes and nose blotchy-red and swollen like he had repeatedly jammed his face into a wasps' nest. Then finally, he fell totally silent, catatonic, as if he'd been hypnotised. Only the occasional shuddering sob interrupted his trance.

Now Joe, his long-suffering and kindly neighbour, was crouched down beside him, his hand on Ross's shoulder. He spoke gently but insistently, coaxing the younger man to his feet and leading him downstairs, step by reluctant step to the kitchen. Then he sat Ross at the table and fussed around making coffee, pouring whisky and passing tissues.

For a long time, Ross paid Joe no attention. Then eventually, without altering his position one iota, or moving his focus from the blank section of wall not three feet from his face, he spoke. 'Thank you, Joe. You're a lovely man, and I really appreciate you looking after me. But can you leave now, please. I'll come to see you in the morning and explain.'

49

Ross had made a conscious effort to change his mind-set and was now channelling his rage into cold, rational thought with vengeance his only motive.

He was on his third whisky by the time Oliver arrived. They were having no effect. Joe had let the visitor in, hesitating at first but relenting and opening the door wide when Oliver asked, 'Is Ross all right?' Once Joe was satisfied he was there at Ross's request, he made himself scarce.

Ross excused himself to, 'Go and give my face a wash,' and returned wearing a fresh shirt and carrying a highly polished wooden box in his left hand. He placed it carefully on the table. 'When you asked me if it was all financial, that was when the penny dropped.' Oliver didn't need to speak. He could see what was coming. Ross turned the box so the brass metal catch was facing away from him. He flipped back the lid, pointing at the inset tray that formed the top layer. 'There's nothing missing from here. This was Liz's day-to-day stuff.' Oliver looked up at him. 'Liz was my late wife.' Oliver made an *I know* with his eyes.

Ross lifted the tray out and laid it to one side. The second layer had far fewer compartments than the first. There were only three, two square and one rectangular. All three compartments were empty. He pointed at each in turn, starting with the larger of the two squares. 'This one had all Liz's *good* jewellery. The expensive stuff. Things I bought her for anniversaries, special birthdays, Christmas.' His finger traced over to the rectangle. 'There was a diamond bracelet in here. Absolutely stunning, belonged to her mother. Her mum's rings were in here too: engagement, wedding, eternity. And a few others, I think, including a diamond solitaire.'

The only compartment remaining was the smaller square. He didn't bother pointing at it. 'The last one had all my mother's jewellery. Not so expensive but, well...' A single tear slid down his cheek, and he raised the back of his hand to smear away the chasing pack.

Oliver started to say something but Ross stopped him. 'I know, I know. How come it's taken me seven months to notice it was missing? Especially when it was so personal and so valuable.'

Oliver didn't speak, the younger man's distress was almost palpable. He waited while Ross gathered his thoughts, which came spilling out in random order. He rarely had occasion to open the jewellery box. After all, nothing in there belonged to him. The police *had* asked him if anything valuable was missing but for some inexplicable reason he had only considered possessions that were visible like limited-edition prints, a bronze figurine, and some bottles of rare whisky, all of which he had purchased as investments. He didn't look at the jewellery while he was with Carla because, somehow, that would have been disrespectful to Liz. But the main excuse he'd hidden behind was the collection was out of sight, and therefore, out of mind.

'Leaving aside the sentimental value, Ross, how much?'

'We had it all professionally valued about three, four years ago.' He looked out the kitchen window. 'I can't remember the exact figure but it was well into six figures.'

Both men fell silent till Ross spoke again. 'And what seriously pisses me off, is these thieving bastards will only pull in a fraction of that when they sell it.

'So I'm going after them, Oliver. I don't know how, or what it will cost. But I am. And this is not about money. Oh no. This is about Liz's memory, her mother's memory, and my mother's memory. Because that's what they've stolen from this box. My memories. And I would rot in hell if I didn't at least *try* to bring them to justice.'

The pitch of Ross's voice had been gradually rising but now it returned to a level that was almost a growl. 'Tell me how you think we can track them down.'

He put the stopper back in the whisky bottle, and settled in to listen to what Oliver had to say.

Oliver told Ross more about the members of his group. Including himself, there were seven, six of whom had been victims of the gang's activities. Most were in their fifties and early sixties. One was a woman. Their profiles were remarkably similar to Ross's. They had all recently lost their partners, none had any children who would inherit, relatively well off with cash or investment assets in the hundreds of thousands at least, and all had been flattered by the attentions of younger, attractive suitors. For the group's security and safety he used only their real first names. He was the only person who knew everyone's full name.

Ross asked, 'Are you able to tell me more about the two who died?'

Oliver said he was, Ross had every right to know exactly what he was signing up to. In chronological order, they had joined the group as numbers three and five. Both had been particularly bitter about the manner of their losses, and had been tenacious in their pursuit of the gang. Separately, they received late-night visits and were warned in blunt and unambiguous terms to back off. Cease all investigations. One, a man, said he would stop but didn't. The other, a woman, refused point-blank. A few days later, the man fell from a ladder at the back of his house and became impaled on a spiked railing. He died instantly, and there were no witnesses. The same day, the woman fell over on her way home after a night out, suffered head injuries and died from a cerebral haemorrhage. The post-mortem revealed she had been four to five times over the legal limit to drive but friends who'd been with her were stunned to hear that. Yes, she'd had a few drinks but she had been comparatively sober when she left the pub, which didn't reconcile with the reported blood alcohol levels.

The seventh and final person in the group was a younger woman whom Oliver described as being 'somewhat talented when it comes to accessing computer systems. Her name's Leona, and the woman who died was her Godmother.'

The deaths of their two comrades didn't ultimately deter the others in the group but they suspended all activities while they reviewed their personal security, their visibility to anyone trying to track *them* down, and their investigative methods. 'It sounds a bit melodramatic to say we moved underground but actually, that's what we did. And none of us has been threatened since we did that.' Ross nodded a couple of times and dropped his gaze to the floor, humbled by what he'd just heard.

A few seconds passed and Ross picked up the conversation again. 'So how on earth do you plan to find Carla and this person who could be her, what, second husband? I just can't see how it would be even remotely possible.'

Oliver took off his glasses and massaged the bridge of his nose. He replaced them and blinked a couple of times. 'It's quite complicated, and I'm not sure I fully understand how some of the technology works but I'll do my best to explain it to you.' He aimed a lopsided grin at Ross. 'I'm no expert, you see.'

'You and me both, Oliver.'

'Okay, here goes. For the past couple of years Leona has been running a daily search, Monday to Friday, against the online issues of most of Britain's major newspapers. Or, at least, those who print births, deaths and marriages. So we're talking papers like the *Times*, the *Guardian* and, in Scotland, the *Herald* and the *Scotsman*. I think there are about 20 in total. I should say, they're not all nationals, some of them are regional papers like the *Manchester Evening News*.

'The first search is against death notices. It specifically excludes any that contain words like father, mother, son, daughter, late husband, late wife. So it's designed to find people who've died, left a partner, but no close family.'

'So if there's no close family, it suggests the survivor is wide open to being exploited by the gang?'

'We think so.'

Ross scratched at his ear. 'But those searches must produce, what, dozens of names every day?'

'It varies, but there's usually well over a hundred most weeks. Having said that, the searches can't be guaranteed accurate, and we can usually rule out a few of the results manually.'

'Wow!' Ross did the maths in his head. 'If you've been running these searches for two years, they must have produced over ten thousand possibilities.'

'Something like that. But that number doesn't really matter because we run a second search in the same papers, against marriages this time.'

Ross had worked out what was coming next. 'So if a person appears on both lists, it's because they were married again quite soon after they lost their partner.' He drummed his fingers on the table. 'And you're thinking that some of these people have inadvertently married a Carla. Or the male equivalent?'

Oliver gave Ross the thumbs-up. 'That's the theory, yes. We know it's not an exact science, and we can't cover all eventualities because although most people post death notices, not everyone publishes the fact they're remarrying.'

Ross reflected on his own circumstances. 'Let's take me as an example here. I would have appeared on Leona's list because I put Liz's death in the *Scotsman* and… oh, hang on a minute, I remember now… I had no intention of posting a marriage notice but my friends said I should. I asked Carla what she thought but she wasn't bothered one way or the other so I put the notice in.'

He looked down at the table. 'But I'm still not getting it. Up and down the country there must be loads of people who remarry not long after being bereaved. There's no way you and your friends can check them all.'

'You're right. We can't check everybody and we don't need to. But we do when the deceased partner has made a will, and when their estate is worth a certain amount of money. That narrows the field down, quite a lot.'

Ross was out of his seat now, struggling to contain his energy. 'Liz and I both made wills. I'm no expert either but I'm assuming a will is a matter of public record so if you know where to look…' Oliver stayed silent, letting the younger man work it through. 'But from what I can remember about Liz's will, it didn't say there were specific amounts of money in the bank, or in investments, or whatever. So how did this gang make the leap that said I was worth targeting? That I had a certain amount of money?'

Oliver stood up too. 'Ross, this isn't a nickel and dime operation they're running. If you imagine what we've been doing with all these searches, the gang will have done all that, and probably much more, long before we did. Once they find a possible target, we think they would conduct a mountain of research on them to establish just how viable they are. So, initially, you were probably identified because of Liz's notice in the paper. But, and this is pure speculation, we think they were able to gain access to your finances, and that's what pointed them in your direction.'

Ross jumped in. 'Wait a minute. Has what's her name, Leona, been poking about in my finances?'

Oliver laughed and held up both hands. 'Definitely not. No. Although from time to time she does, em, *procure* information we shouldn't have…'

'Like police reports?'

'That's one example, yes. But by and large we can only work with what's in the public domain. Unless we have no choice, we try not to invade people's privacy.' He paused for a second and produced his phone. 'Oh, while we're on the subject of Leona, I nearly forgot. She sent me this earlier on. Take a look.'

Ross read a long text reply on the screen:

Yes, think h/ware fault could be engineered remotely. If pc is powered down but still switched on at plug, there is still a small amount of power going to pc. Power is enough to accept a 'wake-up' message from hacker eg in middle of night when nobody around. Hacker can then write temporary code to overload network card, then code to switch pc off. So when user switches pc on in morning, it comes on ok but card is u/s, and temporary code has been deleted – leaves no trace. Then, user calls helpdesk and technician ready (somehow) to attend and fix 'fault'. Think this is all feasible but never tried it of course J Shout if you need more. L.

Ross had to read the text a few times before he fully understood the meaning, both the technical content and the connotations. Hacking a PC while it was up and running was obvious even to him, but it hadn't occurred to him an expert could still exploit the contents when it was powered down. It still seemed rather improbable to him that Alex would be ready and waiting for a call that day, and would, somehow, have been able to insinuate herself into being allocated the job. But there was no doubt the logic was sound, assuming Leona's explanation held water. Ross imagined the IT woman would know her stuff so now he was faced with the unpalatable prospect that Alex may not be what she seemed. But he kept all that to himself.

'You were telling me about what you can find in the public domain,' said Ross.

'Ah, yes. Like everyone else we can access wills stored digitally. So, for you, we were able to check the National Records for Scotland. As you said, Liz's will didn't state specific values. Most wills don't. But there were enough keywords in there to make it worthwhile checking you out.'

'Keywords? So... I'm imagining words like investment, bond, savings, donations to charities and so on?'

Oliver nodded. 'We have a set of about ten or twelve but yes, you're on the right lines with those. Anyway, all we can do is make a value judgement but we're fairly certain the gang can take it a good deal further. We think they probably bribe or blackmail officials in banks and other financial institutions. Possibly even in the police.'

But Ross still couldn't see the full picture so he set off on another tack. 'I understand how the gang decided I should be a target but I still don't know how *you* found me. So I have to go back to the question I asked earlier. Why did you single me out?'

Oliver sat down at the table again and Ross followed suit. 'This is where my knowledge is a bit sketchy but suffice to say, Leona does something clever here with this subset of people.'

'And to make sure I'm still with you, by subset, you mean people who've lost a partner, remarried, their late partner had a will, and the value of that will makes the person a viable target.'

'Exactly. So she runs all the names in this subset against the newspapers' websites, and also sites like the BBC and the *Daily Mail.*'

'Looking for news articles about people disappearing?'

'Yes, and if the victims go public, articles about the resulting scams. The problem is, not everyone does...'

'Like me?' Ross hadn't ever sought any publicity. He couldn't imagine anything worse, his dirty linen being scrutinised by the masses.

'Sort of. Although you didn't trot off to the papers with a *Loving husband loses fortune to cheating wife* story, the press did put out two or three snippets but because neither you nor the police fanned the flames, they didn't amount to much.'

Ross was doing a lot of head-shaking tonight. 'But it was enough to bring me to your attention?'

'It was. Anyway, the output from all those searches is our final list of names. We call them highly probables. And at that stage we have no choice but to check them all out in person.' He sat a little straighter and levelled his gaze at Ross. 'Which is where you come in.'

'Ah. So these *highly probables* are men who might also be *married* to Carla, and, let me guess, you want me to check them out personally. Actually go and see if I can find her?'

'Eventually, yes. But there's another option first.' Oliver looked all around the ceiling, clearly struggling with what he had to say next. 'As I explained, we've been working on this for about two years, and all six of us have been travelling up and down the country checking out possibilities. But, we're only able to identify our own, em, wives. We can't tell if any of these women scammed someone else in the group. So we take photographs.'

'Which you have with you?' Ross was dreading the answer.

Oliver held up a USB memory stick. 'Do you have a PC or a laptop I can plug this into?'

Ross pointed at the kitchen worktop. 'Afraid not, just an iPad.' He'd always wondered why iPads didn't have USB connections, but right now, he thanked his lucky stars they didn't. He figured Oliver was hoping Carla would be the subject of one of their photos.

'Even better.' Oliver dashed Ross's hopes against the rock of technology. 'We can look at them online. May I?'

Ross began to work his way through an online photo album comprising hundreds of pictures. Some were of excellent quality, sharp and clear, and it was easy for him to say the subject wasn't Carla and move on. But a fair number were grainy, dark, blurred, and Oliver took note of the images where Ross couldn't confirm if the woman pictured was or was not his missing wife. There were 11 in all.

The task took the guts of an hour but finally he checked the last image. It was of a woman walking towards the camera from what looked like a country cottage. This was one of the clearer images and he was able to say straight away, 'No. That's not her, either.' He stood up, stretched his arms above his head, locked his fingers and arched his back. Once he regained his normal shape he walked over to the kitchen worktop and leaned against it. 'So, where does that leave us, Oliver? What happens now?'

'Well, as I said, my colleagues and I have spent a lot of time, travelled thousands of miles, checking possibilities.

And, not to put too fine a point on it, we've just about had enough. We need some fresh impetus, another body to share the load. Someone like you, who has a vested interest in first of all finding Carla, and secondly, bringing back pictures for the rest of us to look at. Because, if we don't find some help soon…'

'I understand.' Ross gathered himself, standing just a little bit taller. 'So, I'd need to check the 11 women from your album and, I'm guessing, you must have some names that none of you have visited yet.' Oliver nodded, so he carried on. 'I'm dreading asking but how many are there?'

'Thirty-seven in total, including the 11.'

'Thirty-seven? Jesus! And, dare I ask, where are they? None in Edinburgh, I'll bet.'

Oliver tapped on the iPad again, opening a different file from his iCloud account. He cross-checked the 11 names against a list, scribbled down the same number of place names, then switched to a different page on the same file. 'I knew there were none in Edinburgh but, funnily enough, none of them are even in Scotland. The closest one's in Durham.'

'And the farthest away?'

'Penzance.'

'Magic.' Ross reached for the iPad. 'Let's have a look.' He scanned the addresses. He didn't see any point in reading the names, they were all strangers to him. He pushed the device back towards the centre of the table. 'Two questions jump out at me.' Oliver spread his hands in a *let's hear them* gesture. 'I'd be surprised if I were the first, dare I say it, victim you've approached.'

'No. You're the fifth or sixth new person we've found since our group formed. But…'

'They turned you down?' And when Oliver nodded, Ross asked, 'Why wouldn't they help?'

'Various reasons. Ill-health, state of mind, didn't want to go there, too scared.'

Ross glanced up as a squall of rain pattered against the window. He reached over and closed the blind. He thought about these other victims and could see their point. All those reasons would have been high on his list if it weren't for the missing jewellery. 'Fair enough, I suppose.' He paused to think before framing his second question. 'So, all this effort, all this time, and two people dead...'

'You want to know how many fraudsters we've tracked down.' Ross waited for the answer. 'Only two.'

Ross felt like he'd been driving a car along a fast, smooth road, when, without any warning, the road surface changed to deep, soft sand and, simultaneously, the vehicle's tyres lost all their air. His motivation, enthusiasm and desire slewed to an immediate halt.

'And what happened to them?'

Oliver made a face. 'Both times, we took our evidence to the police but unfortunately they didn't take us seriously. Well, not at first anyway. We found the first one in Sheffield. A man who called himself Anthony. The local police told us they would investigate but they couldn't give it a high priority. We wanted them to carry out what's called arrest and detain, which is exactly what it sounds like. But what actually happened was they sent along an inexperienced PC, who, as far as we could make out, basically marched up to the front door and asked if Anthony could prove who he was.'

'It's stating the bleeding obvious, I know, but surely Anthony's fake ID would have stood up to scrutiny. Especially from a junior plod.'

'Of course. Yes. And while the PC was phoning his station for advice...'

'Anthony did a runner?'

'Precisely. So, when we found the second person, a woman this time, down in Buckinghamshire, we asked the local police to speak to their counterparts in Sheffield to try to stop the same thing happening again.'

'Let me guess.'

'Well, this time we were incredibly unlucky.' Ross wore a *how so?* expression. 'At the very instant the police turned up at the front door, the man of the house was on the phone to his wife. She was in town shopping, and had phoned home to check his collar size or something.' Now Ross had his head in his hands, peering at Oliver through meshed fingers. 'So the guy says, *"Honey, the police are here. They want to speak to you about something."*'

Ross couldn't help but smile. 'Another runner?'

Oliver actually laughed out loud. 'Yes. But apparently this woman stayed on the phone long enough to tell her husband he was a miserable little toad with bad breath and smelly feet, and she was glad she'd never have to give him a blowjob ever again. You have to see the funny side sometimes or else you'd go insane.'

'So, in both cases, the baddies just disappeared without trace?'

'Totally. And I suppose the only upside was that, because of our interventions, two people had narrow escapes. They didn't lose their life savings.'

'No. But how terrible must they feel? Their partners vanish. Their futures, their hopes and dreams are shattered. All their trust destroyed.'

'It's worse than that.'

'What do you mean?'

Oliver looked down at the table and took quite a while before eventually replying. 'Although I know the lady in Sheffield took the view she'd dodged a bullet, the chap in Buckinghamshire was so distraught he attempted to take his own life by jumping off a bridge.'

'Oh no.' Ross lifted a hand to his mouth. 'Is he okay?'

'Last I heard, he was in a coma. I've no idea if he'll recover.'

50

The two men talked until well past midnight, fortified by several rounds of coffee, sandwiches and biscuits. The whisky bottle wasn't called into action again.

They had no idea if Ross would ever find Carla because they couldn't be certain she *was* actively scamming another man. And even if she were, did her scam on Ross start first and she moved on to the other man, or vice versa? They had to hope it was the former or she was probably long gone by now.

Ross fetched a road atlas and they plotted all the locations from Leona's list on a one page map of England and Wales. The red circles were generally widely scattered but there were about a dozen in the south of the country spread across Hampshire, Dorset and Wiltshire. 'Lots of money down there,' he said.

'Yes. It's an affluent part of the country.'

Throughout their discussions, Ross's kept thinking about Alex, and the chance she could be involved. It was a possibility he steadfastly refused to accept. Oliver asked if he had been due to meet her that evening but he said no. 'When I've been to the match, and had a few pints afterwards, she isn't interested in me, quote, talking rubbish and breathing beer fumes all over her.' Oliver asked a few more questions about Alex, which turned into a debate that became quite heated. Ross eventually accepted he had no choice but to act as though she *was* involved as he couldn't run the risk of tipping the gang off about his activities, bearing in mind the fates that had befallen Oliver's two friends. Oliver also stressed that Ross should make sure he wasn't *off* with her, and not to ask her too many questions. Either might make her suspicious.

'And once I prove she's innocent, we can't even laugh about it later as she'll find out I suspected her. It'll probably wreck our relationship. Talk about lose–lose?'

'There's one thing we must find out, though. Are you certain your phone is not still being tracked? I know Alex found and deleted two apps but could she have left something else on there?'

Ross glanced at his phone and quickly looked away again, as if the device was listening to him. 'You're asking the wrong man, I'm afraid. Although I'm becoming more clued up about phones and stuff, I'm still a relative novice.'

'In which case, why don't you find someone you trust implicitly to check it out. But, if there is something on there, don't remove it. That would be a dead giveaway.' Ross nodded, but he was clearly unhappy about snooping on his girlfriend.

They also spoke about what he should say to Alex if she asked what he'd been up to on Saturday. After all, it was a natural question. They agreed the fewer outright lies Ross told, the better. So, if questioned, he would say he'd developed a blinding headache after the match, only had one drink, gone home and straight to bed. He'd say he felt fine when he woke up on the Sunday morning.

To move away from the subject of Alex, Ross said they should work out a plan of action for visiting this daunting list of locations. 'I'll need to make a series of road trips, and it makes sense to go to the closest places first. By my reckoning that's Durham, this place Pocklington near York, and Bainbridge in the Yorkshire Dales. Neither of which I've ever heard of, by the way.'

They discussed Ross's slight aversion to driving long distances but he said he'd just have to get over it. But they still didn't have an excuse lined up for him being absent for a few days. And that was only the first trip, possibly of many. Oliver asked if Ross ever travelled on business. 'Occasionally I travel away with Martin but usually it's just for the day. I think we did one overnighter in Manchester last year, but that was about it.' Ross said he would be speaking to Martin anyway, as he'd need time off. 'Martin'll help. I'm sure he'll come up with an idea.'

Oliver tapped a fingernail on the table. 'It's just occurred to me. If you're keeping your trip a secret from Alex, you won't be able to take your own car. If she *is* checking up on you, it's possible she's monitoring your mileage. In fact, your car may even be bugged.'

'Be serious, Oliver. This isn't a Bond movie.' Then Ross remembered Oliver's two deceased friends, and he instantly regretted his comment. He placed his hand on the older man's arm. 'Sorry. I wasn't thinking there.'

Oliver busied himself over the map. 'It's okay. I know I get carried away, conspiracies round every corner. But I'd rather say something stupid and be proved wrong.'

Then they talked about how Ross would need to spend some time at each location, watching houses from the car till he could see if each man's wife was Carla. Of course, if he were to be fortunate and the woman of the house appeared immediately, as if by magic, then he could set off for the next location. Otherwise he could be sat there for hours. 'Talk about tedious and uncomfortable. My car wouldn't be much good as a surveillance vehicle, it's far too low, and not enough bells and whistles. I could hire something more upmarket, I suppose, but something decent would cost a flamin' fortune.' Ross slapped his palm on the table, rattling the latest pair of coffee mugs. 'Oh bloody hell, I'll just buy one. Then it'll be the right spec.' He thought for a second. 'Aye, that's what I'll do. I can always sell it when this is all over.' Oliver didn't try to dissuade the younger man. It sounded like a sledgehammer to crack a nut but it was the ideal solution.

Oliver realised his coffee was empty, he walked over to the sink to make two more.

'Wait a minute,' said Ross. 'It's just dawned on me. There's a whacking great hole in this *check the wife isn't Carla* plan.'

'And what's that?'

'Well, imagine I'm sitting outside a house, doing my Secret Squirrel thing, and a woman comes out or arrives home or whatever. How do I know she's the wife? She could be the man's sister, or friend, or cleaner, or... bit on the side. She could be anybody.'

'It's a fair point, Ross, and it's come up before. We've all been in that position, and I'm afraid there's no real answer. It can come down to gut feeling, instinct, call it what you like. If the couple come out arm-in-arm, or holding hands or something, you can be fairly certain they're married. Is she wearing a wedding ring? What's her body language like? Does she look shifty? Or does she turn up, put on an apron and start hoovering or dusting in the front room? His bit on the side won't be putting out the rubbish, that's for sure.' Oliver gave an exaggerated shrug, where he held his shoulders up for half a second. 'Truth is, I just don't know. You'll be the man sitting there so it'll be down to your judgement.' He laid two fresh coffees down. 'Sorry, it's not much of an answer but it's the best I can do.'

'This isn't straightforward, is it? I mean, she could be away for a girlie holiday. I could sit there for days and not see any women at all.'

'It's possible. I went to a house in Leicestershire four times before the man's wife put in an appearance. God knows where she was all the time but I just had to wait it out. So no, Ross. It's not straightforward, it's grunt work. But your only chance of finding Carla, and possibly your family's jewellery, is checking out every woman in those thirty-seven houses.'

Ross had also been thinking about Carla's supposed shift pattern. 'Let's assume she's stuck with the same rota, to keep things straight with her other husband.' Ross looked back in his diary to January, when he'd marked in *Carla Offshore* against a three-week period. 'Counting forward in three-week blocks... she'll be due back with her other *husband* in nine or ten days' time. Well, that gives me time to sort myself out.' Then he calculated that if push came to shove he would probably spend, on average, a full day spying at each location. Not including travelling time that meant a minimum of thirty-seven days. Five or six calendar weeks.

Ross rubbed his forehead. Tiredness was setting in. 'Jeez! This is likely to take at least two of her rota changes, maybe three. I could still be traipsing around the country at Christmas at this rate. But thinking about it, if she *has* changed her rota she could be home at any time so let's just go for it. I'll start next week and take it from there.'

Oliver was delighted that Ross was so motivated. 'That sounds great. Better to crack on and cover them all off quickly. The longer you leave it, the more chance there is of Carla disappearing. And this time for good.'

'Just one final question, though. If I work through all thirty-seven and none of them is Carla, what happens then?'

'I guess you have two choices. Either you call a halt, and I wouldn't blame you if you did. Or you wait till we come up with the next list of highly probables, and you try again.'

Both men ruminated for a few seconds on what Oliver had just said. Neither was in any doubt that Ross would choose to call it a day.

* * *

After Oliver had gone back to his hotel, Ross was lying in bed with a fully paid-up membership to the wide-awake club. He was thinking about his relationship with Alex, what they had said and done since they'd met just four months ago. He was searching for any solid evidence that would prove, one way or the other, if she was this fabled secondary operative. Mentally, he added entries to the *For, Against,* and *Unproven* columns in the case: The Truth versus Alexis Mair.

Definitely listed as a *For*, she was teaching him IT skills. And why would she do that if she were snooping into his affairs? When he refused to even consider using internet banking, she dropped the idea immediately and didn't mention it again. She showed no interest whatsoever in his money or investments. The subject hadn't cropped up. And she actually had a job, a real job. This one wasn't a fabrication.

Against? He had to question whether she did have family in Lairg. Was she even *from* there? She spoke with a Scots accent but it wasn't particularly strong, not identifiable to a particular region. And she had shown no inclination to return to her Sutherland roots, not even for a visit. Yet she hadn't ever spoken ill of her family. In fact, she didn't speak about them at all. Now that he thought about it, that was a bit odd especially for a woman. Then there were her living arrangements. She'd said her own flat was rented out, but where was it? He remembered asking her about it. She told him it was near Haymarket but hadn't been specific. But there were thousands of flats in that area. Why hadn't she told him the address, even just mentioned the street name, rather than being so generic? He hadn't asked again, figuring it was rented so, out of sight, out of mind. And whose flat was she looking after? Friends? Again, so non-specific. Had he seen even a postcard from them? Well, no. But perhaps world travellers don't send postcards. Facebook or Instagram, probably. But again, hardly a mention. In four months?

Then those things that were neither for nor against. Plus nor minus. Not proven at worst, neutral at best. *Like photos. She's not that keen on being photographed. Well, guess what. Neither am I.* They didn't socialise all that much, but she didn't seem all that bothered. Another entry in the *so what?* category. Then there was The Sex. Was she some erotic black widow spider, using her body to snare him? Or was she just a single woman with a healthy, outgoing attitude to sharing her body, albeit with a bit of a kink thrown in for added spice?

He thought back to a conversation they'd had at another music night in town. She was dressed in full punk regalia, and had bought Ross a vintage *Clash* t-shirt and black jeans so he didn't stick out like a clown at a black-tie dinner. He asked her about this unusual punk/Goth affiliation, considering she was slightly too young to have been into those genres when they were in vogue, especially punk rock. She explained she'd had an older boyfriend at one time, who looked and acted like Sid Vicious with a migraine. She said she loved dressing up, and, *'Sex with the gear on is always fantastic.'* Something he certainly could vouch for.

But if indeed she was mixed up in all this, the one point he couldn't fathom was how she had managed to appear in his life to fix that fault on his PC. Leona's text had explained how the fault could have been generated but even with his new-found interest in all things IT, quite how a hacker was able to target his PC from all the others in the office when they too were powered down, was still a stretch for him. *Maybe I'll ask someone.*

The final mystery related to the age gap between them, almost 15 years. He'd confessed this concern to her while they were out walking on Blackford Hill, a vantage point to the southwest of Edinburgh that hosted the Royal Observatory. She was frank with him. His age didn't matter in the slightest. She had enjoyed a brief relationship the previous year with a co-worker who was just shy of his twenty-first birthday, and also had a fling with a widower in his fifties. She laughed as she told him she ended the first affair because, *'He just wanted to shag all the time,'* and binned the older man when she discovered his wife was alive and kicking, and working in Marks and Spencer.

Ross came to the conclusion that when he balanced up all the arguments and counter-arguments, all he had left was supposition and innuendo, with precious little in the way of fact.

He decided to text her in the morning to say he'd be watching football at Martin's house on Sunday afternoon, and would go to her place in the evening as previously arranged.

And then, considering how wound up he'd been for most of the evening, Ross dropped off to sleep and didn't awaken until his doorbell rang several times just after eleven o'clock the following morning.

51

Sunday

'You *have* to be kidding me.' Martin was incredulous. 'Not again!'

Martin had remained uncharacteristically quiet and serious while his friend related the events of the day before. Ross rounded things off by explaining it had been Joe who'd roused him late that morning. His neighbour was most concerned about Ross's welfare and, when Ross didn't go to see him as he'd promised Joe took matters into his own hands. He told Joe all about the stolen jewellery. The man deserved that for his kindness and compassion. But Ross didn't say what he was planning to do. That was a step too far.

'And what will you do if you find her?' asked Martin.

Ross stared out of the conservatory window. A football commentator prattled away on the TV in the adjacent room but neither man was remotely interested in watching the game. 'I honestly don't know. I haven't worked that part out yet.'

The blinds flapped against the windows and a door banged to the front of the house. Seconds later came raucous giggling and laughter as two bundles of energy and fun burst into the room as if they'd been fired from a cannon.

'Hey, Dad!' Gail hooted. 'What gives?' She flung her arms round her father's neck, and smacked a noisy kiss on his cheek.

'Uncle Ross!' from Beth, at a few decibels lower. 'Didn't know you'd be here.' She dished out similar hugs and kisses, then the twins swapped their attentions and repeated their enthusiastic greetings before collapsing onto the same end of one settee.

'Shift over a bit, fatso,' said Gail, linking arms with her sister. 'Gimme some space on here.'

'Who are you calling fatso, you skinny cow?' Beth retorted, shuffling her hips around in a vain attempt to budge her twin onto the next cushion. But she wasn't putting too much effort in. The girls would spend most of the day sprawled together, drinking, snacking and generally chilling out.

The truth was, Martin's daughters were neither fat nor thin. They still played hockey to a high standard for their school's Former Pupils team, and were on the fringes of the Scotland squad. Twenty-four now, it took a keen eye to figure out they had been split from the same egg. Both were reddish-blonde but Gail wore her hair long, usually in a pony-tail, while Beth sported a different style or colour every few months. Gail generally dressed in casual sports gear while Beth was Little Miss Trendy. So Beth, in heels, could usually claim a few inches on her sister and that, along with her preferred mode of attire, made her appear older. But today, it was jeans, t-shirts and sneakers all round. Sunday afternoon at Dad's was a regular feature and his wine-rack usually took a hammering, so the sneakers were for the walk back to their flat in Dean Village, on the edge of Edinburgh's New Town.

'And they both hold down responsible jobs too.' Martin shook his head.

Ross had his arms folded high up on his chest. 'Money under false pretences, if you ask me.'

'Not seeing the lovely Alexis today, Uncle Ross?' asked Gail.

'You tell them the abridged version,' said Martin. 'I'll open some wine.'

Ten minutes later, the mood of the camp was far more sombre. 'So let's make sure I've got this right.' Martin started counting off fingers. 'You only met this Oliver guy yesterday but he's convinced you it's a good idea to drive all over the country, on not just one wild goose chase but thirty-seven of the bloody things.'

'He didn't need to convince me. The fact that bitch stole my family's jewellery did his job for him.'

'Whatever.' Martin tapped another finger. 'You haven't driven the length of your arse since Christ knows when, and now Penzance and back seems like a good idea?'

'I have no choice on that one. Public transport would take forever and cost a bomb. Plus, I need somewhere to sit so I can watch the houses.'

'Oh aye, right enough. I forgot about you being Stanley Stakeout.'

Ross was bookended by the girls, their legs tucked under them on the sofa. 'But it does sound dangerous,' said Gail. 'Shouldn't you go to the police?'

'She's right, you know,' said Martin. 'Two people have died. You have no idea what you're dealing with here. And for some bunch of geezers you've never even met.'

'That's true,' Ross admitted, avoiding Gail's question about the police. 'But what if Carla *had* been in one of their photos. I'd know where she is now and it would all be down to one of those *geezers*, wouldn't it? So all I'm doing here is chipping in to help.'

It was Beth's turn to try to dissuade him. 'But you don't even know if you'll find her. It could all be such a waste of time.'

Ross stretched his arms wide and pulled the twins in close for another hug. 'But I have to try, girls. Don't you see that? I'd never forgive myself if I didn't even try.'

Beth twisted herself out from under his arm and kneeled to face him. 'But we're scared something bad might happen.'

He framed her cheeks with his hands. 'Aw, that's kind of you, pet. But where's the danger? I'll just be sitting in a car, keeping an eye out, taking some photos then driving off to the next *stakeout*.' He winked at Martin, who blanked Ross's anaemic attempt at humour.

'You'll probably be arrested as a Peeping Tom,' Martin growled. 'Anyway, I'll tell you where the danger is.' He spoke directly to his daughters. 'Your uncle Ross didn't tell you this part. He still can't be certain his phone's not being tracked.' He snapped his fingers at Ross. 'Give them the phone. They'll find out for you.'

Ross grumbled, but handed his mobile to Beth, who scrambled over to sit by her sister so they could study the screen together. After a few minutes, Gail pointed at something. Beth nodded, but didn't say anything as she swiped back a couple of pages then forward again. Then she turned the phone around and looked at the back. She scratched her ear and glanced at Gail, who shrugged and made big eyes. Beth held the phone up and pointed it at her father, as if she were about to take a photo. Then she tapped into the phone's settings, took another photo, seemed to reach a decision, and again, she looked at her sister. Gail smiled, then both girls turned to face Ross and Martin, still remaining silent.

Ross looked puzzled. 'Is this some sort of twin code?'

His friend laughed. 'Is it hell. They're winding you up. They don't believe in all that subliminal twin crap. Right, Beth. Spill the beans.'

Beth moved so Ross could see the screen. 'This is the first page of apps on your phone. And this is page two. These are all the standard apps and widgets that come with your phone. Ringtone, brightness, volume, all that sort of stuff.' She swiped again. 'Now here are some of the apps you've downloaded for your project. With me so far?'

Ross said he was. He could see his voice recorder, a photo-editor, Trip Advisor, and a few others that related to travel sites, local history and the Central Library. She swiped another couple of times. A row of small white dots at the foot of the screen indicated they were on page five of six. She pointed at an icon. 'See this one, *Flash-Enhance*? Any idea what it is?'

Ross looked perplexed. 'Something to do with the camera?'

'Good thinking. That's what we thought too.'

'Let me guess. It has nothing to do with the camera.'

'I have an app like that on my phone,' said Gail. 'It's called Flashlight. It's supposed to improve the flash on my camera, and, I can use it like a torch.'

'Hang on,' said Ross. 'I've tried to make my camera flash but it doesn't seem to work.'

'That's because,' said Beth, 'your phone doesn't *have* a flash. That's what I was trying to do when I was taking photos of Dad.'

He looked confused. 'So what does the app do?'

'It's actually a GPS tracker app, disguised as Flashlight.' She tapped the icon, which brought up a facing page, then she tapped *Settings*. 'Have a look at these.'

He began to read from the list. 'Panic Alert, Boundary Distance from Home, Location Sharing, Places, Emergency Contacts.' He stopped and smiled ruefully at Beth and Gail. 'Even I can tell these wouldn't be the settings for a camera app. Is it running just now?'

'Yes,' said Beth. 'And I think we should leave it running.'

'We should. Can we tell when it was installed?'

'No,' said Gail. 'Unfortunately you don't have an app manager on your phone. If you did, it would tell us when this tracker was installed but the tracker's own settings don't tell us that.'

'Pity. So it may not have been Alex who installed it?' Beth and Gail both shrugged. 'Either she installed it,' reasoned Ross, 'or it could've been there already and she just didn't notice it?' They nodded their agreement. 'In which case, it's inconclusive. We still don't know one way or the other if she *is* involved.'

All four of them glanced at each of the others in turn but no one could find any flaw in Ross's summation. 'I still think you should err on the side of caution,' said Martin. 'After all, you've admitted you're not totally certain about Alex.' He turned to the girls again. 'Yer man here has some doubts about whether she actually *is* from Lairg. Apparently they've never visited. Her family don't come here. In fact, she doesn't even talk about the place. Dodgy, if you ask me.'

The twins raised collective eyebrows at Ross. He shrugged. 'It's true. But I have to believe Alex is innocent until proven otherwise.' He paused as if to draw a line under the discussion. 'Anyway, last question, how did they change the name of the app to disguise it?'

'Ah,' said Beth. 'That, we don't know, but possibly by connecting the phone to a PC and editing the properties.'

'So whoever did install it, made the reasonable assumption I wouldn't notice.'

'They've sussed you out, then,' said Martin.

Gail was looking pensive. 'But if you do go away for at least three days the week after next, how will you explain that to Alex? And,' she pointed at his phone, 'if she, or anyone else for that matter is tracking that, she'll know where you are.'

'Aye,' said Martin. 'And if one of the women at one of those addresses is dodgy, they'll know right away that you're on to them. And that, my boy, could be a big problem.'

Grudgingly, even Ross could see he had a point. There was silence while they considered the implications.

'Ohh-kaaay,' said Martin. 'How about this for a plan?'

52

'Nothing.'

Even to Ross, his response to Alex's question sounded ridiculous because clearly there *was* something. It's the stock answer children trot out. 'What are you doing through there, Benjamin?' shouts Mummy. 'Nothing,' comes flying back automatically, but even Benjamin knows he must be doing *something*.

He'd left Martin and the girls after Sunday dinner, and gone over to Alex's house. Oliver's words were ringing in his ears. *'It's really important you continue to behave normally. You can't let her think we're suspicious of her.'*

Easy to say, Ross had thought. He knew he was unsettled, which translated into grumpy. His main problem was he really liked this woman and the prospect she might be involved with this criminal gang, doing the same as Carla, was devastating. He considered calling off. Coming up with some excuse. But he reasoned he would have to see her sometime so time to bite the bullet.

So there they were, sitting on the sofa, staring into space. Alex *had* asked how his day had been on Saturday, about the match, how many beers he'd had, and what time he'd gone home. Straight from the off he was forced to tell her about his mythical blinding headache. Lying to her didn't sit well with him at all.

Then she asked about his visit to Martin's, and specifically, which game had they watched. Trying to deflect her, he asked why she wanted to know. His tone was more than a tad defensive.

'Just making conversation. She dug her elbow gently into his ribs. 'Truth is, I don't really give a shit. I just pretend I'm interested in football for your sake.'

Ross huffed a little. 'Actually, we didn't watch the match after all. The twins came over so we just chatted away instead.' That wasn't a lie, which made him feel a bit happier. But not for long.

'How old are Martin's daughters?'

'They'll be twenty-five on their birthday. In February.'

Alex thought for a few seconds. 'So, they were about twenty-two when Liz died?'

He snapped his head round to face her. 'I don't bloody know! Probably. But why are you asking about Liz all of a sudden?'

She looked at him as if he were a stranger, and moved away to the far end of the sofa. 'Fuck's sake Ross, I'm just trying to make conversation. Jeez, you're like a bear with a headache tonight. Now, obviously something's wrong so either spit it out or bugger off home.' Alex picked up the TV remote, and began hopping through the channels.

Ross didn't want to leave. He'd always stuck to the maxim: never let the sun go down on an argument. His Auntie Irene had given him that piece of advice when he was a teenager dating his first serious girlfriend. So he stayed where he was, and slowly the atmosphere defrosted. Alex moved back to lean against his arm, and he eventually draped said arm over her shoulder. They watched TV for a while but nothing caught their attention.

Alex was bored so she switched the TV off. She began tickling Ross's chest, playing around with his shirt buttons and nibbling at his ear. He couldn't help but respond. Within seconds she stripped naked, and pulled and tugged at his clothes until he was in the same state. She made it quite clear she wanted sex and she wanted it right now, and right there on the sofa. She positioned herself on all fours, and looked back at him over her shoulder. She didn't say a word but her message couldn't possibly have been misinterpreted.

Ross knelt behind her as if to comply, he was certainly aroused enough. But his mood altered in an instant as a barrage of suspicions suddenly consumed him.

Wait a minute, you're just using sex to manipulate me.

It's been the Spanish Inquisition since I arrived. What's that all about?

You're as bad as her!

It was as if a cerebral switch had been thrown, immediately disconnecting the passion cortex. He sank to the floor and sat back on his heels, his hands covering his face.

Alex picked up her t-shirt and tracksuit bottoms, holding them against her body to shield her nakedness. She had a genuine look of concern on her face.

Ross's couldn't hold eye contact. His face was flushed, and not from any exertion. He was desperate to say something, to apologise. But he couldn't find the words. He started several sentences in his head but they all sounded insipid or defensive.

Now fully clothed, she knelt in front of him. She framed his face with her open palms and brought her nose right up close to his. 'What's wrong with you tonight, Ross? Please tell me.'

He averted his gaze again. He still couldn't muster a lucid, plausible response. He discarded the nuclear option: *'You're not having sex with me just to rip me off, are you?'* and settled on, 'I'm so, so sorry Alex. It's just... it's just...'

At that moment he desperately needed to get out of there. Away from the situation if not from Alex. He reached out, gently placed his hand on hers and summoned up a weak, watery smile from somewhere. 'I think I should probably go home now. I need some time to think.'

She gazed at him for a long moment then bent over to pick up a stray sock, and stood up. 'Okay, Ross. I've no idea what the hell's up with you tonight. But you go and have your time to think, and let me know the outcome.' She stood up straight and folded her arms as if to add emphasis to her closing statement. 'And, in person, please. If you get my drift.'

It was much later, while he was lying in bed replaying everything that had happened during what had been a surreal twenty-four hours, that Ross grasped her meaning. He reached for his phone and tapped out a text: *Sorry again Alex, I'll be in touch soon. R xx.*

53

Ross was behind the wheel of a nearly new, Nimbus grey, Audi SQ5, parked in the neck of a cul-de-sac in a residential area about three miles east of Durham city centre. It was Tuesday evening, almost ten o'clock, and there were absolutely no signs of life in the detached bungalow he had under observation. All the windows were in darkness but the curtains and blinds hadn't been drawn, suggesting the owners were due home at some point that night.

He stretched his arms up behind the headrest. 'Tell me again. Why did I let you talk me into this?'

His passenger sighed as he too adjusted his position. The SQ5 was undoubtedly a comfortable car but designed for driving in, not as a hide for two grown men. 'Because, my dear boy,' said Martin, 'I couldn't possibly have stayed home doing my knitting while you were travelling the country having such a blast. I mean, Tuesday night in some tacky housing estate in Durham. What more could a chap ask for?'

'Nobody calls them *housing estates* any more, Martin. Executive developments, at the very least.'

'Aye, right.' Martin jerked a thumb towards a house to his immediate left. The front garden was strewn with brightly-coloured plastic and ceramic paraphernalia so beloved of the terminally tasteless: windmills, bridges, water features, a life-sized crane, two foxes and more gnomes than the first audition for Snow White. 'Thank fuck we're not here at Christmas. We'd need bloody sunglasses.'

Ross smiled at the image. 'I guess at some point we should call it a night and check in somewhere.' He pointed at the car's satnav. 'Can this gizmo show hotels nearby?'

When Martin had outlined his plan to Ross and the twins a couple of Sundays previously, after the part where he said there was *no way* Ross was going on his own, he said it was pointless buying a car specifically for the purpose. Martin described his recently-purchased top of the range SQ5. 'It's the perfect motor for this sort of stuff. Privacy glass all round, high up for peeking over hedges, loads of bells and whistles. Just the job.'

Ross could see sense in Martin's suggestion, and warmed more to the plan especially when he heard what else his friend had to say. 'If you're likely to be away for three or four days on the trot, especially if it's during the week, you'll need a good reason. So, here's what I'm thinking…'

Martin explained it was common knowledge amongst the staff that he was planning to expand his business into other locations in the UK. England, in particular. Therefore, a few fact-finding missions with his in-house accountant shouldn't raise any eyebrows. Reminded about the GPS tracking app on Ross's phone, he said, 'Leave it on your desk under some papers or something. Once we're on the road, we'll call the office and tell them Ross the plonker has left his phone behind, and could they put it somewhere safe until we get back.' Ross pointed out that excuse would only work once but Martin just shrugged. They would come up with another reason the next time.

It had then occurred to Gail that perhaps her father's phone had also been bugged but they checked it out thoroughly and found nothing untoward. They did the same with his iPad, and she visited Ross a few nights later to check his tablet was also clean. Both men beefed up the access security codes on their devices. They knew that was only a deterrent but the girls promised to check them all at frequent intervals.

A young couple had just walked past the car, dragging a reluctant puppy intent on sniffing leaves when Ross tapped his watch. 'Almost eleven o'clock. We can't sit here much longer.' He gestured his impatience. 'Where the hell do people go till this time on a school night?'

'I don't know. The theatre or the cinema, maybe?' Martin shuffled in his seat. 'Let's leave it till half eleven, and if no one turns up by then, we'll call it quits.' He'd just begun pushing buttons and twirling dials to configure the satnav when Ross poked a stiff finger at his arm.

'Martin, there's a car pulling up behind us.'

Sure enough, a dark saloon was manoeuvring slowly around their car to allow the driver the widest possible turn into the bungalow's driveway. As it passed the gates, the motion of the vehicle triggered a pattern of lights sunk into the lock-bloc.

Between those and the glow from a nearby streetlamp, they could see a man was driving but his passenger was merely a shadow on the far side.

They both leaned forward in anticipation. 'Let's be realistic,' said Ross. 'It'll never be her. Not at the first house.'

The saloon pulled to a halt in front of a wide white double-garage door, integral to the house and topped off by what was probably a bedroom or a study.

'Come on, dear,' said Martin. 'Out you pop, and let's have a wee look at you.'

What happened next left the two men stunned, looking at each other in open-mouthed disbelief. The garage door opened automatically, the car was driven inside, and the doors slid slowly down over the boot of the car, swallowing it like a lizard taking an unwary cricket.

Martin, slumped back in the passenger's seat. 'Oh, that's just fucking wonderful.'

54

Wednesday

Ross gave out a long exhale. 'One down, thirty-six to go.'

It had just turned eight o'clock the next morning. They were driving south, away from Durham in the direction of Pocklington, a market town about 15 miles east of York. Martin checked his mirrors and accelerated past a delivery van and a double-decker bus making heavy weather of a long, steady incline. They were on the lookout for a breakfast stop having checked out of their hotel before the restaurant opened.

Before they'd gone to bed the previous night, they agreed to be back at the house by seven at the latest, reasoning not many people left for work much earlier than that, especially given the time Bob and Brenda Kelly had arrived home the night before. That logic had been rewarded at five to eight when the front door opened and a short dumpy woman, followed by a similarly-proportioned man and a decrepit English springer spaniel, toddled off for a walk in the pale morning sunshine. Arm-in-arm, the couple crossed right in front of the SQ5. They were still in sight when Martin hit the ignition and moved off. Ross had taken a couple of photos, and fully expected Oliver's database would contain one fewer name by the end of the day.

When the Kellys' car disappeared into their garage, Ross had said, 'Well, that really caught us out, didn't it? We'll need to plan our approach in a bit more detail from now on.' Martin had no choice but to agree and, talking about it on the short drive to their hotel, both men held their hands up. They had been naïve and ill-prepared. They didn't have any strategy to speak of, and they'd expected the answers simply to fall into their laps.

They discussed what would be the best time to be on watch at each house. Although, in theory, the lady of the house might be spotted at any time depending on her routine, if she had a full-time job there was precious little point in them sitting outside all day. And, as Ross pointed out, 'Most people work.' Because they hadn't left Edinburgh till gone four o'clock on the Tuesday afternoon, they hadn't arrived at the Kellys' until just after eight, by which time the couple had already gone out for the evening. So step one of the new plan was to try to be at each house by 07:00 if they were already in the vicinity, or by 16:00 if they had been travelling.

They had laughed at the irony of the couple driving straight into the garage but then they couldn't come up with a plausible excuse to knock on the door, given how late it was. As a result they'd dithered, and the opportunity was lost. They resolved that in similar circumstances at another house, whoever was the passenger would *shift his backside* out of the car to try to establish if the woman arriving home was Carla. A similar occurrence was probably unlikely but they were trying to cover all bases.

Suitably breakfasted, they'd set off again down the A1 towards York when Martin said, 'I've been thinking.'

Ross was reclined in the passenger seat with his eyes closed. 'Go on, then. What?'

'Let's say we *are* outside a house at the times we agreed, the woman might already be home, so who's to say that's not her in for the day, especially if the weather's pish. We could sit there for hours. She's inside, we're outside, and ne'er the twain shall meet. Then, when she does come out, and we discover she isn't Carla, we've wasted all that time.'

Ross nodded his agreement as he watched the gently undulating North Yorkshire countryside rolling by. 'Fair point. So what are you thinking? We just march up to the front door and ask if the missus is in?'

He glanced over at Martin, who was concentrating on the road. The A1(M) it may have been, but this stretch was only dual carriageway, and choc-a-bloc with articulated lorries heading south.

Martin paused to think. 'Let's work on the assumption that, more or less as soon as we arrive at a house, we *do* knock on the door so we don't waste time unnecessarily.'

'Unless we're there first thing in the morning. In which case, sometime after, say, nine o'clock?'

'Aye. Can't be before that,' Martin acknowledged. 'But either way, we'd need a damn good reason. Something plausible.'

Ross adopted a Jack-the-lad accent. 'We've noticed your windows are a bit dodgy, madam. Would you be interested in double glazing?'

'And perhaps we could tidy up your soffits at the same time, darlin'.' They both cackled like schoolboys, and would have kept up the sleazy salesman banter but Martin had to slow down to negotiate a busy roundabout.

'We're canvassing on behalf of the Conservative Party?' was Ross's next offering.

'Fuck *right* off.'

They eventually settled on the idea of a consumer survey but were struggling to come up with a realistic subject. 'It needs to be something that will bring the missus to the door,' said Martin. 'So, even if it's the old man we speak to first, he'll have to ask her to come out and talk to us.' He pondered the problem as they cruised along in the outside lane. 'What about internet shopping habits? We can ask if she shops online. How many times a week? Is it for clothes, groceries, blah blah blah? Even if the husband says he can give us the answers, we just say it's the female demographic we're aiming at, we're not allowed to record second-hand information, and what time will your wife be home.'

Ross picked up on the theme. 'I think that'll work. With it being internet related, it won't matter where we're canvassing. Rural, urban, suburban. It all fits. And if the woman isn't Carla, we can pretend the answers aren't what we're looking for and move on quickly. Do you shop online? If she says no, that's easy. If she says yes, we ask how many times a week? And whatever she says, it's the wrong number. We say thanks anyway, and bugger off.'

They both fell silent while they mulled over the idea but their nodding heads confirmed they were on to something. 'Hang on,' said Ross. 'What about ID? Canvassers always have a badge or a card or something, to prove they're genuine.'

'Hmmm. That's true.' Martin glanced at his watch. 'It's only half ten so we've got time to pop into York. We'll find a business centre or a stationery shop, and we can knock something up. We just need to print off a card and stick it in one of those Perspex holder things.' He thumped the steering wheel with the heel of his right hand. 'Bloody hell! You'd think one of us would have thought of this back in the office. No worries, we'll blag it this time and come up with something more professional in time for next week.'

Ross threw him a glance that said, *What do you mean, next week?* But Martin was oblivious. He took both hands off the wheel for a second to raise his palms skywards. 'We should've brought a clipboard.'

Ross laughed out loud. 'A clipboard?' He lifted his iPad from the pocket in the passenger door and waggled it in the driver's direction. Martin had the good grace to look embarrassed as his friend made an elaborate show of licking his index finger and drawing a large imaginary number one on the windscreen. Ross flipped the tablet open. 'You just keep driving, Grandpa. I'll make us one of them new-fangled online questionnaires.'

'Aye, you're right chuffed with yourself, aren't you? But, being serious for a minute, have you even considered what we'll do if one of these women *is* Carla?'

Ross took a few moments before replying. 'I guess if we spot her from the car, we'll have time to think about what to do. I'd probably phone Mel back in Edinburgh and tell her. If we're not too far away, she and Andrew might even come down to make the arrest. But if it's a case of bumping into her on a doorstep then I think I'll just grab her and dial 999.'

'And what's the husband doing while you're grappling with his missus?'

'I'll leave you to sort that out.'

'Thanks a bunch, mate.' Martin didn't mean it.

As things turned out, their fake internet consumer survey wasn't required for the couple in Pocklington. The house belonging to Harris and Lindsey Matthewson sat up on a large corner site with beautifully tended front and side gardens sloping down to the pavement. Two men were working hard, surrounded by gardening implements, bags of compost and an array of plants and shrubs. The older man was probably in his fifties and the other was his spitting image, almost certainly his son. As Ross and Martin sat watching from a couple of houses away, a woman appeared carrying a tray with three coffee mugs. The two men removed their gloves, the older man kissed her cheek, and the son gave his mum a shoulder-hug.

'They have to be family,' said Ross, just as a silver hatchback came along the road and parked outside the house. Two small boys aged about eight and six, and dressed in pale blue school uniforms, piled out the back and ran up the garden path. A young woman followed on, lugging a shoulder bag and three jackets. A bout of kissing, hugging and ruffling of hair then ensued before the women and the boys left the men to their coffees and vanished inside the house.

Martin tutted. 'I thought one of the criteria for being on Leona's list was no close family.'

'It is. But he also said the list couldn't be one hundred per cent accurate, and I guess that's what we're seeing here.'

Martin had taken photos *just in case* so there was nothing left for them to do but turn the car round and head for their next location. Bainbridge: a typically picturesque village more or less smack in the middle of the Yorkshire Dales.

Thirty-five to go.

55

Thursday

A serious crash on the motorway a few miles north of York caused a diabolical snarl-up of traffic, meaning Ross and Martin didn't reach Bainbridge until almost nine o'clock in the evening. Instead of going straight to the next address they booked into a hotel, enjoyed a bar supper and a couple of the local ales before hitting the sack early.

Apart from a teenage boy who cycled off to school at about eight o'clock, no one else crossed the threshold of Joyce and David Nisbet's Victorian detached villa before nine-thirty on a cold and misty morning. Feeling more than a little apprehensive, Martin led the way with their consumer survey dodge. It turned out Mrs Nisbet, who was wearing a t-shirt with the logo: *Dont misuse apostrophe's*, was something of an internet shopping demon. And that was proved when a delivery driver turned up just as they were making their excuses. Joyce took great delight in ripping open the parcel to show them her latest purchase. She told them it was a birthday gift for her eleven-year-old nephew, a three inch thick hardback copy of *The Complete Works of William Shakespeare*.

Martin could hardly stop laughing. 'I'd love to see the poor wee sod's face when he opens his present.'

They'd pointed the car in the direction of home when Martin spotted one of the addresses was on the edge of the Lake District village of Ambleside. He declared it, 'Ten minutes out of our way, so we may as well pop in.' They did, found the house all boarded up with a For Sale sign, and were standing outside wondering what to do when an elderly neighbour ambled by. Without any need for subterfuge, the lady told them poor old Mr O'Neill had passed away in the spring, Annabel had gone to live with her sister in Dorking, and the house was on offer at £395,000. But, to date, there had been no interest. They thanked her, had a late lunch in the village, and were back in Edinburgh by six o'clock.

The following week they set off on another supposed fact-finding mission. Ross couldn't pretend he'd forgotten his phone again so Martin faked an email to all staff advising of an impending audit of all mobile devices to upgrade software and antivirus, and remove obsolete or unauthorised apps. He knew the premise was thin but figured if he sent out a second email a few days later deferring the audit, the team would be relieved more than anything else. Then he'd just let it slide.

So Ross left his phone with Gloria just in case the *audit* took place while he was away. He texted Alex to let her know, which saved any potentially awkward conversations about his rather strange behaviour a few nights earlier.

On this trip they whittled Leona's list of addresses down to twenty-four. They knocked off five on a whistle-stop tour of Lancashire and Cheshire, one in the Peak District, another in the Lincolnshire town of Grantham, and finally, a memorable escapade in Stafford ticked off that particular box. They'd arrived at the address just as a Mercedes SUV turned out of the driveway, heading in the opposite direction. Neither man was able to identify the passenger. It could have been a man, a woman or possibly just the headrest. Ross was driving, and Martin uttered the immortal words: 'Follow that car!' Ross could barely speak for laughing and managed to stall the Audi in the middle of the road, no mean feat in an automatic. He broke several speed limits while trying to catch the Merc, eventually pulling into a restaurant car park on the outskirts of town, right on the bumper of the suspect vehicle.

'What now?' asked Ross. But Martin seized the day by following the couple inside and hovering behind them as they were welcomed by the Maître D'. Luckily, the man said something about, *'My wife,'* which was enough for Martin.

He'd just relaxed when the somewhat pompous Maître D' turned to him and asked if he had a reservation, looking him up and down as if to say, *'I don't care if you have. No way on earth are you coming in here.'* As always, Martin displayed his propensity for quick thinking by asking for directions to the town centre but would have been shocked if the Maître D' had believed him.

Finally, Martin checked a house in the Finsbury park area of North London while he was on a business jolly to watch Arsenal playing West Ham. Unfortunately, the wife was wheelchair-bound and not even *he* could find anything amusing to say about that.

One day, while Martin was at his desk, Elspeth nearly threw a spanner in the works. She tapped on the door jamb. 'Boss. Got a minute?'

'Sure, El. Come on in.'

'Sorry to bother you but I've been thinking about all these trips you and Ross have been making.'

'Uh-huh.' Martin wondered where she was going with this.

'Well it's just that it seems a shame Ross has to be away all the time. I've nothing much on at the moment so I could easy take a turn, if you like.'

Martin's first thought was, *'Oh shit,'* but he recovered quickly. 'Thanks for the offer, El. Actually, we only have one more trip, possibly two, and then we're done.' Elspeth looked quite crestfallen so he quickly followed up with: 'So, continuity's important but thanks very much for offering. Much appreciated.'

Then, against all his instincts, he turned back to what he was doing and sensed, rather than heard her leaving the room.

Martin did not like himself for how he'd just treated his employee.

Not one little bit.

56

'What's up, Sis?' asked Beth.

'You're my twin. You're supposed to know what's up.'

'Well, I don't. So spill.'

It was a Friday evening and the girls had met up for a few drinks after work. Not something they did often but Gail had recently ended a relationship, and Beth was *between men* at the moment. *'No change there,'* as her sister had been known to say.

'I've been thinking about Uncle Ross, and all this stuff about Alex and his phone. Did she? Didn't she? And all that.'

'You mean the Lairg uncertainty? Sounds like a Robert Ludlum novel.' Beth sniggered and dug an elbow into Gail's ribs. 'I'm so funny.'

'In *your* head.'

Beth sipped her wine. 'Strangely enough, I've been thinking about that too. Have you Googled her yet?'

'I've had a poke about.'

'And?'

'Nothing.'

Beth arched an eyebrow. 'Someone who's unknown to Google? They're slipping up, we should tell them.'

'When I said *nothing*, I meant nothing relating to Lairg. She's profiled on the Esprit IT website, and that's it.'

Totally at odds with the bulk of their generation, the twins weren't huge fans of social media platforms. They puddled about in them from time to time, more to be nosey than anything else. Beth listed the major ones in turn but Gail said she couldn't track Alex down in any of them.

'Oh, come on. Seriously?'

'Seriously.'

Then she told her sister she'd checked the Electoral Roll, trawled through the archives of the local paper and played about with a genealogy website. None of them had generated any information about Alexis Mair.

'So we know she's an IT technician,' said Beth. 'A graduate from UHI. Nothing on their website either?' Gail shook her head as Beth carried on with her list. 'She's house-sitting for some friends over on the South Side. And she *says* she's from Lairg.'

'Not much, is it?'

'Not really.' Beth finished off her wine. 'What are you doing this weekend?'

Gail placed her empty glass on the table and pushed it towards the centre with her fingernail. 'Actually, I was thinking of driving up to the Highlands for a couple of days.'

'What a coincidence!'

Beth's eyes sparkled. 'So was I.'

* * *

As the twins had travelled north from Edinburgh early the following morning, the weather through Fife and Perthshire had been dreich, a fabulous Scottish word that translates into *bloody miserable*. But by the time they drove over the Pass of Drumochter, at 1508 feet the highest point on the A9, the gunmetal skies were beginning to break apart suggesting a fine late summer's day was in the offing. Further south, they'd commented that the leaves were beginning to turn but at this altitude deciduous trees were few and far between. Rhomboid stands of forested pine and spruce pockmarked the lower slopes of the mountains to the west, with the occasional dusting of snow in the northern corries of the higher peaks.

They dropped into Newtonmore for coffee and bacon rolls just after nine, had cleared Inverness by half past ten and now they were parked at a view-point high on a soaring, twisting, hill-top road, known locally as The Struie. The girls had never been in this part of the country and they were in awe of the highland grandeur spread before them. The village of Lairg was now fewer than 20 miles to the north.

This was nothing other than a fishing expedition. Their chances of finding out anything about Alex in this remote highland community were low, but not so low it wasn't worth trying. They didn't think she'd been married so it seemed reasonable to assume Mair was her family name, although she might be divorced. The girls decided they would cross that bridge when they reached it.

The previous night, Gail had signed up for an online telephone directory, and subscribed to the Electoral Roll. So, flaky rural mobile reception notwithstanding, they at least had somewhere to start. Gail discovered only two Mairs with Lairg addresses and when she widened the search to include Sutherland, only one more name came up. They did consider calling the numbers but reasoned your average Highlander was highly unlikely to divulge family information to a cold-caller. Remote they may be. Stupid, they certainly are not.

Within an hour of arriving in the beautiful loch-side village with superlative mountain views to the south and west, the twins had visited all three addresses. Being Saturday, they were fortunate all three families were home but, unfortunately, none of these Mairs knew or had even heard of an Alexis. Ross had described her history so with a bit of memory-trawling on their part, they managed to recall her father's name was Finlay and her sisters were Nina and Janis. But still no joy. Blank faces remained the order of the day.

The Post Office seemed a reasonable bet but the cheerful lady behind the counter said to Beth, 'I'm sorry, my dear. I can't possibly divulge the names and addresses of my customers. It would be against the rules.' And when Beth tried turning up the heat on the charm offensive, she was told: 'Nice try. But I'm afraid the answer is still no. Now, is there anything *else* I can help you with?' As they turned away, Beth muttered that *any* help would have been a start.

Their next stop was the library but they were disappointed. Although it had been open for part of the morning, it was now closed for the weekend. As Gail said, disparagingly: 'Us city girls just expect everything to be open 24/7. Muppets!'

They'd brought some snacks and drinks and munched them by the edge of the loch, figuring out where to try next from the scribbled list of ideas they had conjured up on the long trek north.

During the afternoon they visited several local shops, the pharmacy and a tourist information point but were no further forward. One of the main factors working against them was the number of people they met who weren't originally from Lairg. They hadn't lived in the village long enough to be acquainted with the Mair family.

Earlier on, Gail had stuck her head through the door of the local hotel bar but pronounced it dead. Now, at just after four they found themselves outside again. 'May as well have a drink,' said Beth. It was her turn to drive so alcohol wasn't an option, and she was more than a little peeved when Gail chose a craft lager. With the frosting on the glass emphasising the pale golden colour of the beer, and the snowy white head on top, on this late summer's day Beth would cheerfully have mugged her sister for the drink. They sat at the bar, the place gradually filled up and within a short space of time the chatter had escalated to a healthy buzz.

Luke, the barman, a stick-thin lad wearing a burnt-orange t-shirt and barely out of his teens was overly attentive towards the girls, asking them several times if there was anything else he could offer them.

'Do you think we're his idea of an unfulfilled fantasy?' said Beth. She was nursing a soda water and lime and trying not to covet Gail's glass.

'Is that actually a thing?'

'Oh, probably. He's a bit young though.'

The object of their discussion lifted a couple of empty pint glasses from a couple of feet away and, yet again, tried to chat them up. They ordered two more drinks, and while he was pouring Gail's beer, he asked, 'What brings you to Lairg then?'

'We're actually trying to track down a friend we haven't seen for years.' Beth turned on full beam, just for the hell of it. 'Her name's Alexis Mair. Do you know her?'

Luke's complexion outshone his t-shirt as he pretended to give the question due consideration but the fact was, the name rang no bells whatsoever. What a pisser, he thought. He placed Gail's glass on a beermat and had no choice but to admit it. 'Sorry, I don't think I know anyone in the village called Alexis. But maybe Harry can help you.' He leaned on an elbow and called along the bar. 'Harry! You ever heard of an Alexis Mair living here?'

Harry had been perched on his barstool when the girls walked in. He looked as though he had been sitting there as the hotel was being constructed, and it had formed around him. There was a good chance he'd ordered the first pint to be poured. He folded his *Daily Record* and laid it on the bar.

'Possibly,' he drawled, looking sideways at the twins while tapping the rim of his empty whisky glass.

'Harry. Stop it!' Luke admonished him.

But Gail nodded to the barman and turned back to Harry. She scraped her barstool away from the bar to give Beth a clear view of the man on their left.

Harry had clearly worked a tough paper round. His hair hadn't seen shampoo for a number of days, his hands looked like they'd just dismantled a tractor engine, and there was faint whiff of bovine from his boiler-suit. No wonder he sat at the end of the counter. He studied his new-found benefactors over the top of his glasses, his gaze keen and sharp through surprisingly clear eyes.

'How many drinks is this likely to cost us, Harry?' asked Beth, as half his latest whisky vanished from the glass.

His expression was totally deadpan. 'Depends how long I can spin it out, lass.'

Beth shot him a *behave yourself, Harry* look. He placed a finger on his chin, and stared thoughtfully at the well-stocked gantry behind the bar. 'The Mair family? Aye, I remember them. Lived in that house on the bank overlooking the loch. It's a guest house now. Finlay was a good lad. Can't have been easy bringing up those girls on his own.'

Beth leaned forward, placing her hand on Gail's thigh to help her balance. 'What can you tell us about Alexis in particular?'

The remainder of Harry's whisky evaporated, and he looked pointedly down at the few dregs remaining. Beth nodded to Luke but when the drink landed on the bar she whipped it away and closed both hands around it. Harry had tracked the glass's route, an amused expression adding more creases to his weathered face. Beth was holding his gaze firmly. 'This is the last instalment, my man. And if it doesn't result in some concrete info, I'll drink it myself.'

'Fair enough.' Harry leaned back on his stool. 'But to save me wasting drinking time, tell me what you already know and I'll try to fill in the rest.'

Gail picked up the traces. She related as much of Alexis's back story as they knew including her teenage years, the tragic episode where her friend had died from an overdose, and how she had turned her life around to eventually graduate from UHI.

'This friend who died. What was her name?'

The girls turned to each other. 'Mary?' said Beth.

Gail snapped her fingers. 'Maree!'

'Ah.' Harry gazed longingly at the whisky glass. 'In that case, ladies, I'm afraid you're talking to the wrong person.'

'Oh,' said Gail. 'Who *should* we be talking to?'

He pointed over at a noisy bunch of locals occupying a corner at the far end of the bar. 'See the woman with the short grey hair, purple jumper, kiddie bouncing on her knee?'

The group was in Beth's line of sight. 'Yes. Who is she?'

Harry chuckled. 'That's Maree. And looking rather well, wouldn't you say?' Then he leaned forward, plucked the whisky glass from Beth's grasp, and opened his newspaper at the racing pages.

57

Monday

The door opened.

'Oh!' There was a brief pause before Alex said, 'This is a surprise, Ross. I wasn't expecting you. Sorry, did I miss a call?'

'No.' Ross pushed straight past her and into the living room, where he sat down heavily on the sofa.

Alex addressed the evening air. 'No, please, do come in.' She closed the door, followed him into the room and sat next to him. Ross immediately stood up and moved over to a chair at right angles to the sofa. 'Ohh-kaaay. This isn't looking good. Just a hunch, are you about to give me some bad news?'

The script he'd rehearsed flew out the window so he asked the blunt question: 'Who are you, Alex?'

She returned his gaze but apart from blinking a couple of times, her expression was totally neutral.

Ross's phone had been in his hand since he'd arrived outside. He tapped it a few times, and passed it to her. 'How about I make things easier for you?' He paused for just longer than a full stop. 'Nina.'

She lifted her glasses from the arm of the sofa. On the phone was a photograph, obviously taken on a bright day. Apart from a sunlit grassy border at the top and on one side, the image was glossy black marble with a gold inscription. It read:

Alexis Mair
1982 to 2000
A wonderful daughter, sister and friend
Taken from us far too young

Her voice cracked. 'Have you been up to the village?'

'As it happens, no. But friends of mine have, and they had an extremely interesting conversation with your friend,

Maree. Or should I say Alexis's friend, Maree? Who's not dead at all, strangely enough.'

Her eyes brimmed, and a soft gasp escaped her throat. 'She was… is, *my* friend.'

Ross shrugged. 'Semantics.' He relaxed back in the chair and crossed his legs, his ankle on his knee. 'So how about you tell me your story again, but this time let's have the true version. And maybe I should remind you we've spoken to Maree, yeah?'

The previous night, Martin had texted Ross on his way home from a boys' weekend away. He asked Ross to come over to his house about six, apparently the twins had some really important information for him. When they told him about their trip to the Highlands, he'd been annoyed at first. Or at least, as annoyed as he could ever be with his goddaughters. But he was truly stunned when they explained his girlfriend couldn't possibly be Alexis, that Maree was very much alive and the amazing tale they'd heard from the woman who had supposedly died all those years ago after experimenting with drugs.

Although Martin could see his friend had had a hell of a shock, he recommended Ross should go into work on the Monday as normal in case his absence set any tongues wagging. That said, they were closeted in Martin's office most of the day while they conducted the research necessary to prove Maree's story was true. Martin called the MD of Esprit IT, whom he'd known for many years, and asked how long Alex had worked there. It transpired she wasn't an employee, she was freelance. Ross had always presumed her to be on staff. The fact she wasn't could never be seen as a show-stopper but, for him, it put a dent in her credibility.

They worked out a plan for Ross to confront *Alexis* and how they would deal with the remaining twenty-four addresses on Leona's list. Ross asked for two weeks' leave to travel down south again. Martin agreed, but it wasn't to commence until Ross had worked his usual three days that week: Monday, Tuesday and Wednesday. This wasn't the boss being unreasonable. It was to head off any staff discontent at the pass. After all, he *had* been out of the office most of the previous fortnight.

So, armed with all the information the twins had extracted from Maree, he was now waiting patiently for Alex to rewrite her history, ready to trip her up should she deviate from the new truth. Once she recovered her composure, she began talking, and Ross let her finish without a single interruption. He also remained silent when she fell apart at certain points. It broke his heart but he was determined to maintain his resolve. He still wasn't sure what, or whom he was dealing with.

'It's true. I *am* Nina, the middle child. The one who screwed up, behaved like a petulant teenage idiot, failed all her exams, was heading nowhere fast. Then Alexis, my darling little sister, who never took a drink and certainly didn't do drugs, came all the way out to the tent that night to watch over me, and Maree, to make sure we were safe. She'd heard those two lads had some crack cocaine, and she was right.

'The older one, I think his name was Bruce, was a sneaky bastard. And somehow, I didn't ever find out how, he convinced her to take an E. She had a bad reaction, one of these one-in-a-million situations. The four of us were all stoned, and we passed out. Somebody woke up at about four in the morning and we discovered we couldn't rouse her. One of the boys ran down to find Dad, but, another shitty coincidence, he wasn't at home. I didn't know, or more likely I was too wrapped up in my selfish little all-about-me world, that he was out on his first date since Mum died. They had dinner at the woman's house out by the station, and he stayed over.

'We were all too scared or too fucking stupid to call the police or an ambulance, and because of the time we wasted, Alexis had fallen into a coma and didn't come out of it. Dad blamed himself for not being there. He was on a real downer, started drinking heavily, and one night he crashed his car. Four times over the limit. He died at the scene. So I lost a sister and my father within three months of each other.'

Just then, her phone rang. She looked at it. 'I need to answer that.'

'Like hell you do.' Ross stuck his hand out and she meekly gave up the phone. He tossed it on the coffee table where it clanked noisily off a black iron candle-holder.

Alexis, or Nina, swallowed once, as if she had just been force-fed a handful of cotton-wool balls. 'My older sister Janis was... *is* still really bitter about everything that happened. We've never been close. Janis was eight when I arrived and apparently I blew her cosy little world apart. She'd had it all her own way up until then. It didn't make any difference that Alexis came along after me. I was still the one she took against. When Alexis died, Janis blamed me and it's hard to argue with that. But when my father died in that accident, somehow that was all my fault too. At his funeral she told me she hated me. She always had and she always would.

'Unfortunately, Janis was the executor of Dad's will because she was so much older than me. I had just turned nineteen at the time. She put the house up for sale and there was nothing I could do about it. She told me I'd get whatever money was due to me but house prices in Lairg weren't brilliant back then, and Dad still had a mortgage and outstanding debt. The only thing Janis ever did for me was to allow me to stay in the house until it was sold. Then she went off to live somewhere in England with her boyfriend, and I haven't seen her since. That was sixteen years ago and I'll be surprised if I ever do.'

Alex stared at a mark on the carpet between her feet. 'And that's more or less the whole story.'

'Oh, I don't think so. You haven't told me the most important part yet.' She looked at him, holding his gaze steady. 'That would be the part where you stole Alexis's identity.'

She exhaled hard, puffing out both cheeks. 'When I was still living there on my own, a letter arrived for Alexis. It was from UHI to say she'd been accepted for a course in Computer Science. They hadn't been notified that poor Alexis had passed away. Must have been some sort of admin glitch. I stared at that letter all night before I decided I would go to uni in her place. We were only thirteen months apart and like two peas in a pod. I'd kept all her documents. Birth certificate, passport, the works. And loads of photos of her. Dad was a bit of a camera nut and some of them had been taken just before she died. I cut my hair, dyed it to match the photos, and that was it.

'So yes, I did steal her identity. I'm not proud of it but it gave me a second chance. *And* I've made the most of it. I knew my sister so I'm totally confident Alexis would have wanted me to. The way I see it, I'm keeping her name and her memory alive. I think about her every day. Every *single* day in life.' She smiled a self-mocking smile. 'But as you'll probably understand now, that's why I can *never* go back to Lairg. Not that there's anything there for me anyway.'

She held out her palms to indicate she was finished talking.

Ross stayed silent for what seemed like a very long time, apparently digesting everything he'd just heard. 'So, do I call you Alex or Nina?'

A broad smile beamed across from the other side of the coffee table. 'Alex, please. That's who I am now.'

'Well, Alex. Thank you very much for telling me the truth…'

'Oh Ross,' she interrupted, jumping to her feet. 'Honestly, you've just no idea…'

He held up two flat palms. 'What I was going to say was I'm glad you've told me the same story as Maree. But you've been deceiving me since the minute we met so how can I possibly trust you ever again? You and that bitch, Carla. You're cut from the same cloth.'

She shook her head, trying to make sense of what she was hearing. 'Ross…'

His hands were still up. 'No, Alex. Enough! I've made up my mind. We're finished.'

And with that, Ross pushed himself up from the chair, negotiated his way past the coffee table, and walked out the door without so much as a glance in her direction.

58

Tuesday

Miles behind with his work, and appreciating Elspeth had been carrying him over the past couple of weeks, Ross was in the office early the following morning. He kept his head down all day, and didn't leave for home till almost nine o'clock in the evening. He ignored a succession of voice messages, texts and emails from Alex, deleting everything without listening, reading or opening. The last one had been mid-afternoon so clearly she had either given up or was readying herself for another salvo later on. He fervently hoped he wouldn't hear from her again but didn't imagine life would be that easy.

Before he settled down for the evening he packed a bag and a small rucksack with enough stuff to last him at least a fortnight including a variety of electronic devices, chargers and his trusty road atlas. He knew he was about to embark on a major undertaking so to reduce the possibility of burnout, he promised himself he would be back in Edinburgh by two weeks on Friday. That would give him a weekend at home to relax, whether or not he'd checked out all the addresses.

Ross and Martin had worked out an itinerary that would take him on a tour round a dozen addresses in the south of England, beginning with Cheltenham in Gloucestershire then following an anticlockwise route through Wiltshire, Dorset, Hampshire, West Sussex and Berkshire. There were two other addresses on the west side of the country: Penzance in Cornwall, and Cardigan on the Welsh coast. Geographically, they were in back-of-beyond territory. Too remote to be tacked on to any others, and last resorts as far as the search was concerned. Martin was tied up with internal audits until the end of the week so it would be Saturday before he could join up with his friend. He planned to fly to somewhere convenient, and they would travel together for as much time as he could spare.

On Wednesday morning, Ross locked up the house, left notes for Joe and Barry saying he'd be away for a fortnight and drove his car to the office. He was taking Martin's car on the trip but the SQ5 wasn't in the car park so he hauled the bags up to his desk. It didn't occur to him to leave them in his car and transfer them later in the day. Elspeth spotted them immediately.

'Off somewhere warm and sunny, Mr McKinlay?' She leaned across the top of her desk, arms folded and nodding at his luggage.

'Ah, em, not exactly.'

Shit. Why did I bring the bloody bags upstairs?

'I'm having a couple of weeks leave, and I'm planning to take off after work and do a tour of friends and relatives, and any other places I fancy. Just to get away for a while.'

'So, are you driving?'

The question seemed to perplex Ross. 'Well, yes. Of course.' Then he caught on. 'But I'm not taking my car, Martin's lending me his. That's why I brought the bags in.'

Elspeth smiled ruefully. She thought that sometimes, Ross wasn't the shiniest star in the sky. 'That's very kind of him.'

For some bizarre reason, he felt the need to explain. 'I quite fancy one, you see. An SQ5. So it's a great opportunity to give it a good try-out. Before I buy one. If you see what I mean.' *For God's sake, man, shut up! Why do you have to prattle on?*

Elspeth's arms were still folded but now she was sitting back. Her smile, if anything, was wider than before. 'I suppose the fortnight you've just spent in the bloody thing wasn't quite enough for you to make your mind up then, eh?'

Back when he was a junior accountant, one of the firm's partners had given Ross an excellent piece of advice. '*When you're already in a hole, stop digging.*'

But he grabbed hold of the spade again. 'Well, lots of the time we weren't really moving.' He closed his eyes.

'I know what you mean. The traffic's murder down there.' He decided he'd dodged the bullet but she followed up with another cracker. 'Is Alex going with you? I expected you two would have been on a holiday together by now.'

He was desperate for his phone to ring, or the ceiling to fall down on their heads. Anything to stop the questions coming. But no such luck. The phone performed a world-class, deaf-mute impression, and the ceiling tiles rivalled the ancient pyramids for stability. *What the hell do I tell her?* Various scenarios skipped through his brain but none of them stood up. Elspeth had to repeat herself a few times before her voice broke through the miasma. 'Ross!' Eventually, he looked up. 'What's wrong, sunshine? Have you two broken up?'

An ostrich egg seemed to have lodged in his throat so all he could do was nod. Until that moment he'd been stoic, hard-hearted even, about the end of his relationship with Alex. Now, surprisingly, his vision blurred. Elspeth scooted over to his side and put her hands on his. A colleague two desks away registered the change in atmosphere and leaned casually back in his chair, wishing like hell he could rotate his ears in their direction.

'Aw, Ross. I'm so sorry. You pair seemed great together.' He could only look down, any other direction was far too difficult. She didn't push it. 'Tell you what, I'll fix us some coffees and then we'd both better crack on. But how about we go out for lunch, and you can tell me all about it. If you like.'

It took a few seconds but the ostrich egg dissolved. 'Thanks, El. I might take you up on that.'

Elspeth's smile was back. Her knees creaked as she stood up, so she bent over to give her right leg a rub. As she did so, her bum caught Ross's road atlas, which was perched on top of his bag. It slapped onto the floor. She picked it up and rebalanced it. 'What's the story with the atlas? Doesn't that posh car of Martin's have satnav, then?'

It did, of course, but Ross had used the atlas to plan out his journey. To visualise his route as a big picture. But he recovered some composure. 'Och. You know me, El. Analogue Man.'

'Too true,' she laughed, turning away. 'I've always wondered where you keep your abacus hidden.'

She wandered off to make the coffees, and Ross called softly after her. 'Thanks, El. You're a wee star.'

'I'm perfectly well aware of that.'

She made a slight curve to her left and cuffed their ear-wigging colleague round the head. 'Nosey git!'

59

'May I offer you some advice, Dani?'

Danijela paused in the doorway to Miroslav's office, not sure what was coming. 'If you must. I can always ignore it.'

'Don't ever play poker for money.'

Uninvited, she sat down in the chair in front of his desk. In itself, that was a signal. 'It's that obvious?'

'It is.' He took off his glasses and placed them neatly on his blotter. 'Come on, then. Tell me.'

'One of our operatives in England was arrested on suspicion of fraud. Annika. I've known about it since yesterday but I didn't bring it to you until I had all the facts.'

Miroslav's brow lowered but he was reacting to the news of Annika's arrest, not to the delay in hearing about it. Danijela had complete autonomy in how she managed the operation, and he trusted her judgement implicitly. She knew their business just as well as he did, and she also knew he had enough on his to-do list without concerning himself with events that *might* happen.

He raised his eyes towards the ceiling. His gaze tracked around the cornice to the intricate section above the window, and back again. 'Annika. Originally from Reykjavik. This is, what, her third assignment?' He drummed his fingers on the arms of his chair. 'Working just outside Manchester, as I recall.'

Danijela didn't bother telling him he was spot on, as always.

He continued. 'How did this arrest come about? Was there any warning?'

'No warning. The police arrived at her house yesterday at lunchtime and took her to the police station. They accused her of operating under a false identity. That her maiden name wasn't really Sylvi Gundersson. Annika told them they must be mistaken. She had all manner of proof: passport, birth certificate, marriage certificate. Everything.'

'So they were fishing?'

'Apparently. Sounds like she remained very cool, very calm. She asked them why they thought these things about her, which is where it began to fall apart for the police. They accused her of defrauding a man she was previously married to. The one who...'

'Had the unfortunate accident with the ladder.'

'Precisely.'

'So, without any corroboration, the police didn't have any proof. Sounds like they expected her to just cave.' Miroslav looked over at Danijela. 'But she didn't?'

'No. It sounds like she stood her ground, stayed calm, and waited to see if they had any evidence. But all they had was supposition and hearsay. I'm very surprised they moved on her with so little to go on.'

'I am too.' Miroslav scratched at his cheek, genuinely mystified. Why, completely out of the blue or so it would seem, would the police bring in Annika for questioning on such a flimsy premise? Who had put them onto her? Unknowingly, they were bang on target but couldn't press the point home. A miss was as good as a mile but if the police had been able to prove their case the potential impact on his network troubled him. 'So let me be clear, their suspicions were based on her previous assignment, not the current one with the man in Cheshire?'

'Correct. Apparently the police explained to him that she was most probably grooming him as her next mark but he didn't believe them.'

Miroslav nodded gently to himself, several times. 'How did you find out about all this, Dani?'

'Annika called the emergency voicemail number, and I picked up the message. I put one of our pet lawyers on standby to represent her but it turned out not to be necessary. They released her without charge but warned her she was still under investigation.'

'Just as a matter of interest, which member of the so-called learned profession did you intend to use?'

'Charles Rutherford.'

He chuckled. 'Does he still have that peculiar, ah, predilection? The one his wife is blissfully unaware of?'

300

Danijela laughed too. 'He does. And he doesn't seem to care that we have him over a barrel because of it.'

'Perhaps, for him, it all adds to the intrigue. But, where is Annika now?'

'As you would expect, her husband was all over her last night but she was able to sneak away from the house, very early this morning. She is now at a safe location, and she will stay there until we are able to corroborate her story.' Danijela paused. 'Just in case.'

Miroslav could see the sense in being pragmatic. Regrettably, there was always the possibility that Annika was spinning them a line. To be fair, it didn't sound like she was but he knew without asking that Danijela would definitely be crossing that particular 't'.

'Assuming it all checks out,' she continued, 'we will wait a week or so before we bring her here. She will stay with us for a while until we decide what she will do next.'

'And how is she?' Miroslav preferred not to immediately think badly of Annika so he was genuinely concerned. He might be running a ruthless and frequently cruel operation but he cared deeply about the welfare of his employees as much as any legitimate business owner. However, he was sufficiently self-aware not to kid himself. He wouldn't be canonised any time soon.

'A little shocked. But smart enough to follow procedures and absent herself from the situation as quickly as she could. There should be no connection to us. She did well.'

He reflected that, over the years, not every operative who had found themselves in the same position had acted with the same propriety as Annika. In all, about a dozen had been uncovered by their partners or by the authorities, either as a result of carelessness or just bad luck. There were only three options available to Miroslav in this event. Rescuing them was his preference, abandoning them to their fate had been forced on him a couple of times, and he had no qualms whatsoever about eliminating them if their disloyalty threatened to place his business in jeopardy. Jarek Zelenka had tied up four such loose ends at his behest.

What was of more concern to him was *how* Annika had been exposed. It would have been easy for him to put it down to bad luck, but no one could ever accuse him of being blasé or naïve. No. If a gap had appeared in his security fencing, he needed it to be located, repaired and any chance of a recurrence eradicated.

His next few sentences concluded the conversation with his partner. 'Contact Jarek. Ask him to come here for a meeting. We need to conduct a security audit. Internal and external.'

60

Ross didn't need to check the car's digital clock to know he'd been driving for far too long, his numb bum spelled that out in shoulder-high capital letters. He was aiming for a budget hotel on the M5, just south of Gloucester. Satnav said it was only six miles away. He really should have stopped at the last service station but he was desperate to complete the 350-mile, seven hour journey. His original plan had been to reconnoitre the target house in Cheltenham but his rapidly waning energy levels and a murderous traffic jam near Preston had consigned that idea to the bin. Since well before Birmingham, the car's computer had been nagging at him to take a rest. Task number one the following morning would be figuring out how the hell to switch the bloody thing off.

Something else he would have to do on Thursday morning was return a call from Oliver. He'd left a voicemail as Ross was negotiating his way past Birmingham and the hell on earth that is the West Midlands' motorway system.

He raked about in the centre console for the last few nuts out of a Healthy Snacks pack. Apart from fuel and toilet stops he hadn't broken the journey. He didn't want to waste time stopping for a meal so he'd been grazing all the way south.

He'd tried to dodge Elspeth's offer but she wasn't having any of it so they'd gone over to the Cramond. When he eventually ran out of small talk, she pounced like a leopard on an antelope that realises just too late it's about to become lunch. 'So, where's your first port of call then, my man?'

He fiddled with the salt cellar. 'Em, Leeds.'

She put her fork down. 'Leeds? Where about in Leeds?'

'Eh? What do you mean?' He realised straight away that had been a stupid question but she'd caught him on the hop, and it was all he could think of to say.

'I *mean*, what part of Leeds, dummy? Elland? Harcroft? Nobody lives in the centre of Leeds, it's a concrete monstrosity. So it must be one of the outlying areas. Bassenthwaite, maybe?'

He dropped the salt cellar, spraying white crystals all over his side of the table. He used one hand to drag them into the opposite palm and flipped them over his shoulder. *Bugger. She knows Leeds. Just bloody typical, that is. Why didn't I say Glasgow?* He hated lying to his friend but he was struggling now. 'It might be the last one. Bassenthwaite. Or near it, anyway.'

Elspeth pushed her chair back. 'You're a piss-poor liar, Ross McKinlay. I've never been there in my life but I do know Leeds United play at Elland Road so I'm guessing there's a place called Elland. I can't even remember the second place I mentioned but I just made it up. And, last time I checked, Bassenthwaite was in the Lake District.' She stood up and began to turn away. 'I'm just off to the loo. When I come back you can either tell me the truth about where you're going or you can tell me to mind my own effin' business. It's no skin off my nose. Just don't lie to me.' And with that, she stomped off.

He stared down at the table, avoiding curious glances from two *ladies who lunch* at the table next to theirs. He'd only known Elspeth since Martin had hired her a few months earlier but he liked her immensely and they worked well together. He was often the butt of her withering sense of humour but at the same time she was a sympathetic and caring person, as she'd clearly demonstrated that morning.

Ross was still dithering on his decision when she returned. But he was in luck. Mine host came over to clear their table. Trev was an odd-looking dude. Totally bald, bushy hipster beard, no moustache and an extravagant taste in lumberjack shirts. The more garish, the better. 'Aye aye,' he said, pointing at Elspeth's side of the table. 'I see we're in beermat destruction mode again. Do you think these things grow on trees?' He stacked their plates in one hand and swiped two jigsaws off the table onto the crockery, where the bits floated on the sweet and sour remains of Elspeth's main course. He put on a mock frown. 'You're cutting right into my profits, you know.'

'Oh sod off, Trev. This place is a goldmine, and well you know it.' Trev left the frown in place and, on his way back to the kitchen, he wiggled a little finger-wave over his shoulder. The couple next to them were just putting their coats on to leave so Elspeth leaned over and filched a couple of mats from their table. She smiled ever so sweetly at them. 'Don't mind me.'

That brief interlude had settled Ross's mind. He decided he would prefer to tell his friend at least some of the truth. She already knew all about Carla from previous conversations, and she'd met Alex in passing a couple of times so he told her about the split.

'But why, Ross? You two seemed to get on so well. And I know there was quite an age difference but, these days, who gives a shit about stuff like that?'

He shrugged. 'I just came to the conclusion that another long-term relationship so soon after Carla wasn't necessarily the best idea. And let's just say there were some trust issues.' He stopped there, not really wanting to tell Elspeth about his suspicions regarding his phone, that Alex may have tampered with it, and the fact she was masquerading as her sister. He supposed those would make him sound either paranoid or deranged, neither of which were desirable characteristics.

And he certainly didn't want to tell her about the missing jewellery. But his resolve flew out the window with her next question.

'What sort of trust issues?'

He closed his eyes and blew a great draught through puffed-out cheeks. *Me and my big mouth.* Elspeth stayed silent while Ross looked around in every direction, bar at her. She could have organised a wedding in the time it took him to speak. 'Long story short, I've discovered Carla stole all my family's jewellery.' Elspeth's mouth opened wide enough to accept a flying doughnut, and the sugar wouldn't have touched the sides. 'And let's just say Alex isn't what she seems to be, so my trust in her has been destroyed.'

The 'O' that was Elspeth's lips was morphing into a question. He held up his hands. 'But if you don't mind, El, let's leave it at that. Huh?'

'Oh, Ross. I don't know what to say.' If he didn't know her better he could have sworn her eyes were moist. 'And this all happened on Monday?'

'I'm afraid so.'

'Have you heard from her since?'

'She tried to call me a few times on Monday night but I didn't answer my phone. Then there were some texts and emails yesterday, but nothing since.'

'So, if she calls again, will you pick up?'

Ross dipped into his cover story. 'Ah well. As luck would have it my phone's gone kaput so I'm picking up a new one this afternoon.'

He and Martin had had several conversations about the possibility of Ross being tracked down while he was on his travels but it was obvious to both of them that he couldn't just keep his phone switched off. While they were as certain as they could be that the device was clean, they decided even a small risk wasn't one worth taking. Then Gail suggested not only should he buy a new phone but he should also change his number. The party line to anyone outside their small circle would be that poor bumbling Ross had struck again. So when she asked what had happened to his phone, he said, 'You'll probably find this funny. I accidentally left it on a radiator, and it fried.'

Elspeth certainly did find it funny. She shrieked like a hyena on laughing gas. 'You're such a *total* plonker, Ross.' She chortled again at the thought, almost setting herself off again.

'I know. But my goddaughter's organised a new one for me. I'm meeting her later on to collect it.' That part was true. He was meeting Gail at The Gyle, a retail park on the west side of the city. It was convenient for jumping onto the M8, before following the motorway network all the way south to Gloucester. Cheltenham lay just a few miles east of the M5 at that point.

'So where *are* you going, then? Assuming it's definitely not Leeds.'

His first reaction was, if I can't trust Elspeth, who can I trust? But he'd made a promise to Martin and the girls so he toed the party line once more. 'Truth is, El, I don't know. I have a fortnight's leave, a loan of Martin's car, and I'm just going to head off and see where I end up. It might be the north of Scotland or the south of England. I don't really mind as long as I can be on my own for a bit. Give me a chance to think about things without anyone else to worry about.'

'Sounds good, Ross. Just the job.' Then she looked at her watch. 'Oops. Better shoot back over the road or we'll be in trouble.' They both stood up and gathered their coats. 'You head back, I'll see to the bill. Your credit card will probably take a bit of a pasting over the next couple of weeks.'

'Thanks, El. My treat next time.'

'Too right, sunshine.' Then a thought occurred and she called after him. 'Ross. Will your new phone have a different number?'

He was almost at the door so he offered an exaggerated shrug of his shoulders.

Elspeth didn't appear to care she had to yell across the room. 'If it does, text it to me, will you?'

He waved back in a *sure will* gesture, while knowing full well he wouldn't be doing that.

61

'He is *where*?' asked Miroslav.

'As I explained,' said Danijela. 'On a cruise. In the Caribbean.'

'Jarek? On a cruise? In the Caribbean?' He was oscillating between stunned and incredulous. 'He never goes *anywhere*. Why the fuck has he gone on a *cruise*?'

'Miro. Be reasonable. The man's entitled to a break.'

The cardboard coffee cup flew from Miroslav's hand. He'd intended it to land in the waste bin but temper threw his aim off. Instead, it bounced off the rim and spiralled into the wall, arcing slivers of black Americano onto the pale green satin emulsion, creating a pattern reminiscent of the double white lines at a junction in the road. Danijela gazed at the stains but she didn't move a muscle in their direction. Instead, she raised an eyebrow at him as if to say: '*Well, that was fairly childish.*'

He whipped two or three tissues from a box on his desk, dipped them in his water glass and dabbed carefully at the rivulets of dark liquid. When he spoke, she detected an undercurrent of weariness in his voice, normally strong and confident. 'I am not disputing he is entitled to a break. But he is not here when I need him. How quickly can we bring him back?'

'Probably late on Saturday, three days at the earliest.' Danijela carried on speaking. She could sense Miroslav's blood pressure was heading for another spike. 'I've tried to make contact but they're at sea for the next thirty-six hours, and I can't raise him. So I called the cruise company's head office, pretending to be his sister. I told them Jarek's father is in hospital after a serious accident, and they've offered to contact the ship.'

'Where is their next port of call?'

'A place called Aruba.'

'Sounds small.'

'It is. And it's a hell of a journey back from there. The routing is Aruba, Atlanta, New York JFK then Heathrow. Takes about a day and a half excluding the hours lost because of the time difference. It's the best option we can find so we're making the arrangements now. And, unfortunately, the flight doesn't land until about nine o'clock in the evening so it'll be the following day, Sunday morning, before he'll reach Cheshire.'

'Is it not possible to fly him direct to Manchester?'

Danijela made a face. 'No. We checked the schedules. But the flight times, Atlanta or New York to Manchester, just don't work in. It'll be quicker if he flies to Heathrow then drives north from there. Plus, there are arrangements to be made vis-à-vis hardware and other items he will need. We have only two or three trustworthy contacts in Manchester but in London, it's not such a problem.' She turned towards the door. 'I must go and check how everything is coming along. I'll keep you posted.'

Miroslav's demeanour had returned to normal. 'Thanks. And Dani...'

Danijela walked over and gently traced a finger along his jawline. 'I know, Miro. But it's better you lose your cool with me than with other people. Don't worry about it.'

She left him studying the coffee stains on the wall and the carpet, which were practically invisible now. But she took a mental note to call their decorator. That had been an expensive cup of coffee.

62

'Oh bugger,' said Ross.

It was seven o'clock in the morning. He was parked across the road from number eight Bellfield Avenue, home of Jeremy and Celia Luckhurst. After the car-disappears-into-the-garage incident back in Durham, he and Martin had tried to plan ahead for every eventuality. But here was something that somehow hadn't occurred to them. *What a pair of dummies.* The properties they'd staked out up until now hadn't been difficult to observe. Houses with open outlooks, railings or low hedging, or with clear lines of sight. Without appreciating it they had been somewhat fortunate. Not this time.

He rechecked Leona's list for the third time, he was definitely at the correct address. The problem: 8 Bellfield Avenue was a block of apartments. Stylish apartments but a block just the same, and no way of telling from the outside which one belonged to the Luckhursts. Most of the houses nearby were large detached Victorian villas on decent-sized plots. He guessed the original house at number eight had been pulled down and replaced by a new build.

After a few minutes puzzling over his predicament, Ross checked up and down the street. There was no one about. He hopped out of the car and dashed across a well-kept frontage of damp grass and low shrubs to the main entrance. On the left-hand wall, he found what he was hoping for. A bank of six letter-boxes with nameplates. Apartment #4: J & C Luckhurst. He smiled, stepped back and glanced up at the building. Including the two apartments at ground level there were three floors, so number four had to be on the first floor. *Okay, but right or left?* He peered through a narrow vertical glass panel set in the door. *The stairs go clockwise. That door on the left is apartment number one, meaning four must be on the right. Gotcha!*

Back in the car, he could see there were three windows on either side of the stairwell. Two small, and one much larger. He imagined that had to be the living room. The light inside was on, even although the morning was now bright enough to do without. As he watched, another light came on in the room closest to the stairwell. Less than a minute later both lights went off and stayed off.

This must be someone getting ready to go out. Seven-twenty-five. Well, unless you're about to walk the dog, it's time for work.

Questions and answers scrabbled for his attention like a class of seven-year-olds who think they know the answer to teacher's question.

Someone's leaving, what do I do now? The next person who comes out the front door just has to be a Luckhurst. Shit! What if there's a back door? Or a side door? I know I was bloody shattered but I should have sussed out the place last night.

Ross could see half a dozen cars parked to the left of the apartments. He thought even if a driver left by a different door, he would be able to spot them. *But what if they're walking? What if there's a back lane?*

What if, what if, what if?

While he was analysing this torrent of imponderables, a rather large, rounded woman emerged from the front entrance. She looked as though she had been middle-aged her whole life. Although her clothing looked expensive, none of it seemed to fit her properly. Her light-coloured raincoat was on the tight side, her navy blue slacks didn't quite reach her shoes, and her Burberry scarf was way too long. As she walked, she tried in vain to disentangle it from a combination of handbag, carrier bag and shoulder bag, all of which were intertwined round her right arm like a nest of hyperactive snakes. She too walked over the grass, crossed the road and marched away from Ross's car. Clearly a lady in a hurry.

The speed at which she moved caught him completely by surprise and, within just a few seconds, she disappeared round a bend in the road. There was no way he could cruise along slowly behind her like some raincoated kerb-crawler, so he had little choice but to leave the car and walk after her. Past the bend, the road straightened out so he was able to keep her in sight quite easily although with only the pair of them in view he felt he stood out like a killer whale in a paddling pool.

He was acutely aware the woman he was following might not even be Celia Luckhurst. The lights being doused in number four and her departure could have been entirely coincidental. Hearing an engine revving behind him, he glanced round just in time to see a car exiting the car park and driving off in the opposite direction. *Shit! Could that have been her instead?* But he was committed now. He decided to keep following this woman but he had no idea how he would find out her name. *Come on, Ross. Think of something.*

The woman reached a T-junction at the end of Bellfield Avenue and turned onto a busier road. He sprinted up to the junction and slowed as he reached it. She was standing at a bus stop just a few metres further on.

Bollocks! What the hell do I do now? As he was walking towards her, she smiled at him and said, 'Morning.' She had given up the battle with her scarf and jammed it into her shoulder bag.

Ross smiled back. 'Morning. Lovely day.' He stood next to her, forming a queue of two, and at a complete loss what to do or say next. *Where the hell's Martin when I need him?*

He knew he had to do something quickly because unless he sat next to her on the bus, there was no way he would be able to engage her in conversation. Apart from that, he imagined The Unwritten Rules of Travel on Public Transport would automatically debar two people, who are waiting at the same bus stop, and who don't know each other, from sitting together on the bus. Most definitely not, unless they were the only two seats left.

Then he realised he had no change for a bus fare so he would have to act immediately. Trying his best to keep his tone light and conversational, he turned to her. 'Excuse me. I'm sorry to bother you. But are you Celia Luckhurst?'

The woman leaned back a little and looked at him more carefully. 'I am. Have we met somewhere?'

'No. But I know your husband, Jeremy, from the golf club, and I've seen you with him in the clubhouse a couple of times.' Even to Ross, this sounded terribly contrived and as weak as a drunkard's resolve. *Okay. I've cracked it. It is her. Now how the fuck do I get out of here?* Then he noticed her eyes had narrowed and she was squinting at him. His pulse missed at least two beats. *Oh no! Her husband doesn't play golf. Or, if he does, she's certainly never been to the clubhouse with him. It's a men-only club or some shit. Fuck!*

She was speaking to him.

'I'm sorry?' he said, blinking.

'I was saying...' Celia paused to make sure he was listening this time. She pointed past him. 'The bus is coming. Are you getting this one?'

Halleh-fucking-luyah. 'No. I'm sorry. I'm not.' He patted pockets for effect. 'I've just realised I've left my glasses at home. I'll have to go back for them.'

Then, Ross being Ross, he added a totally unnecessary complication he could well have done without. 'Tell Jeremy I said hi, will you?' *You complete tool, McKinlay. What the fucking hell possessed you to say that?*

'I will. But you didn't tell me your name.'

'Ah. Yes. It's, eh, Martin. Martin Ross.' *And could you just disappear now. Please?*

'I'll tell him.'

She gave Ross a little wave as she stepped onto the bus, almost tripping over her bags.

As the bus pulled away, he leaned back on the shelter and belted out a sigh that could have been heard clean across the busy road. 'Jesus. That was close.'

Then he remembered he hadn't taken a photo of Celia Luckhurst for the record. *Hey ho. You can't have everything.* Walking back towards the car, he could feel his heartbeat was falling to within normal tolerances, and his hands had almost stopped shaking.

Leona's list was now down to twenty-three addresses.

* * *

The 54 miles from Cheltenham to the next address would only take Ross about an hour and a half even if he used minor roads for part of the journey. Truth was, he was fed up to the back teeth of motorways and dual carriageways. It wasn't yet eight o'clock, but he wouldn't reach Devizes, a small market town perched on the northern edge of the Salisbury Plain, by nine, the latest time he and Martin believed most people

313

would be heading out for the day. So breakfast became his first priority.

On Saturday, two days away, Martin would be flying into Bristol before flying home from Gatwick. All things being equal, Ross hoped he'd tick off three or possibly four addresses before hooking up with his friend but that depended on a host of factors, most of them out of his control.

The most thunderous cloud on his horizon was the possibility he'd actually find Carla. Ross knew that Oliver, his colleagues, Martin and the twins were all working on the assumption he was putting himself through all this because he was determined to run Carla to ground. But, as time passed, as he scored more addresses off, in his heart he was now quite certain that locating his thieving, deceitful wife was the last thing he wanted. On the contrary, if he could have turned back the clock he'd have stuck to his guns and told Oliver where to put his stupid list. Eventually he'd have swallowed the crushing pain of what was surely the last treacherous act of Carla's betrayal.

But he'd acted in haste and was now repenting at leisure. As a result, his overriding aim was to reach the end of the list as quickly as possible, confirm she wasn't any of the women living in these houses and return home to get on with his life. Of course he was still devastated at the loss of his family's jewellery, that wouldn't ever disappear completely. But his anger was gradually diminishing as his quest progressed. He just didn't possess the stamina to maintain it. Or was it the balls? Would even the slightest setback encourage him to take the cowardly option and bail out? He rationalised all these arguments by convincing himself there was no chance of recovering the jewels. They were long gone so why go through the pain?

He would never confess to all this internal agonising, of course. He didn't want to fail or disappoint anyone, especially given how much effort and emotion they'd invested to support him. And he preferred not to think of how much money had been spent. Martin in particular was well out of pocket. Luckily he's not short of a bob or two, Ross reflected, then immediately indulged in a prolonged bout of self-flagellation for allowing that uncharitable thought even to approach the outskirts of his mind.

The morning was becoming increasingly warm and sunny, and the country road taking him south from Cheltenham passed through some gloriously picturesque villages and hamlets, typical of this part of the world. *Whatever anyone says about the English, there's no denying they do villages really well.*

Driving through Colesbourne he spotted an inn with tables outside in full sunlight. A sign in chalk on a blackboard proclaimed:

FULL ENGLISH - £5.99 – INCLUDES TEA / COFFEE AND TOAST

'That'll do just dandy,' he said to his rear-view mirror as he reversed into a space. While he was slogging through a plate piled high with every fried breakfast constituent known to man, he decided he deserved some time out from sitting in that damn car. Just across the road was a green metal heritage signpost that pointed to a two-mile walk along the River Churn. It was still only ten o'clock so he reasoned he could easily justify an hour for a head-clearing walk, especially given the amount of time he had spent in the car the previous day and the rather fraught start he'd had to the morning.

Wandering downstream along the river bank he reflected on the Luckhursts' flat back in Cheltenham, and how he'd been unable to spy on it as easily as the others. He pondered if he might be able to predict the settings of his target houses for the day. Alex had shown him how to use Google Earth but when he checked out his own street, it turned out the area was still a construction site. He looked up a couple of other places like Edinburgh's New Town and the street in Leith where he'd been brought up but the novelty had quickly worn off. He wasn't even sure he could access it from his iPad but thought he would experiment with it later on.

While he was thinking about the iPad he wondered what would come up if he Googled the addresses. If they'd had any building work done recently, perhaps there would be architects' drawings or land registry information.

Then there was satnav. Did it possess any other features that might help? Martin's car was the first time he'd ever been exposed to the navigational aid so, again, he didn't know what it was capable of. *Worth a quick look, I suppose.*

Ross had just reached the halfway point on his walk, and was about to turn and head back to the village, when he met a young woman pushing a buggy in the opposite direction. The screaming child it contained was in stark contrast to the peaceful rural setting. He smiled as he stood aside to let her pass but she ignored his cheerful, 'Good morning.' Leaving them to get well away, he sat down on a tree stump. It was a good opportunity to return Oliver's call.

After the standard opening pleasantries and a quick update on progress since they'd last spoken, Ross told Oliver about Alex. While the other man was sympathetic, he thought Ross was correct to break off the relationship. Oliver agreed there was no proof that Alex was this mythical secondary operative but the fact she'd been caught impersonating her deceased sister certainly placed a decent-sized question mark against her.

But Oliver hadn't called the previous day just for a chat. It was to tell Ross that two days earlier, one of the women he and Martin had photographed in Cheshire a couple of weeks before, had been arrested by the police and charged with *Carrying out a fraudulent activity*. Sadly, the man she had originally defrauded had been the one who died after falling from a ladder the previous year so no one benefitted from her arrest, apart from the poor soul she was setting up this time around. Ross was quietly pleased to have played his part but strangely, it only confirmed that his desire to track Carla down was waning fast.

He ended the call, stood up and stretched. He was enjoying the late summer sunshine and he wouldn't have taken much persuasion to tarry a while longer but it was time he was on the move.

Back in the car he tried Googling the Devizes address but apart from confirming its postcode, no other useful information came up. But, fiddling around with the Audi's multi-media centre, he unearthed a diamond the size of his fist. Martin, bless him, had installed a SIM and enabled Google Street View. Ross thought it was odd his pal hadn't mentioned it but the SQ5 was fitted with so many bells and whistles, he figured Martin couldn't be conversant with them all. He'd only had the car a few months. About a quarter of an hour later, with the help of the vehicle handbook and a YouTube video, the media screen was displaying an image of 38 South Downs Crescent, Devizes. *Just* wait *till I tell him.* Ross could probably have slotted a banana into the grin that decorated his face, he was so chuffed with himself. The screen showed a modern mock-Tudor mini-mansion complete with turret, leaded windows that were unlikely to be genuine, and what he suspected was fake grass. All it was missing was a moat, drawbridge and portcullis, which would have had to be plastic to match the overall effect.

Unfortunately, that turned out to be the highlight of the next twenty-four hours. Parked with an uninterrupted view of the house, Ross's early impression was that no one was home, and nothing around the place gave any indication that was likely to change. Everything was just too neat, too well-ordered. Then he noticed all the blinds had been pulled down to the same level, one-third of the way down each window. *These guys are away, aren't they?* Not long after dusk, lights in two of the downstairs rooms came on, followed a while later by one upstairs. Over the next hour or so, the house did a reasonable job of pretending it contained humans, as different rooms were lit then plunged back into darkness, sometimes within just a few minutes. The only trouble was, even a passing glance would have proved conclusively that the inhabitants were conspicuous by their absence.

While he was sitting there, he thought some more about the woman who'd been arrested in Cheshire. He considered telling Mel about her. Perhaps she would liaise with her colleagues in that jurisdiction to see if they could prove a connection between the two cases.

Gail had shown him how to disguise his number when making calls. One of the potential downsides was the recipient might choose not to pick up. But he was lucky this time.

'Mel Cooper.'

'Oh, hi Mel. It's Ross McKinlay here.'

'Hi, Ross. Sorry, your number wasn't displayed. How are you doing?'

'I'm fine, thanks. Listen, do you have five minutes for a chat?'

'I do. What's up?'

He related his story. According to Oliver, the woman's name was Sylvi Hutchinson but, apart from an address in Wilmslow and the fact she had been arrested on the Tuesday for crimes similar to Carla's, he couldn't give Mel any more information than that. He finished by suggesting she *might* consider it worthwhile comparing notes with her counterparts down south.

'You could be right, Ross. If I'm honest with you, I'll be surprised if anything comes of it. But I'll give them a bell and let you know.'

'Thanks, Mel. Appreciate it.'

'No problem. But before you rush off, may I ask how you found out about this woman? Was it in the papers?'

Ross put his hand on his forehead, he hadn't worked this through. 'I, em, heard about it from a friend. I'm not sure where they got it from but they called me, em, yesterday so I thought I'd let you know.'

'Not particularly convincing, Mr McKinlay, I have to say. But leave it with me and I'll get back to you.'

'I'll need to give you my number.'

'That won't be necessary, Ross.' Mel's words were drenched in sarcasm.

He closed his eyes and had to work hard to keep his tone light and airy. 'Okay, Mel. Thanks. Speak to you later.'

As the evening wore on and boredom settled on him like a shroud sewn from chainmail, he was tempted to pack it in and find a hotel. But he remembered what Oliver had said about this being vital drudge work so he stuck it out. He became rather obsessed with the people who owned this house, and their elaborate attempts to indicate it was occupied. He amused himself by penning an open letter:

Dear housebreakers, cat burglars and miscreants of nefarious intent,

We are uncertain if people in your profession still 'case the joint'. Assuming you do, you could probably drive past our house at twice the speed of light and still have time to figure out we're away on holiday. Truth is, we couldn't make up our minds on the best look to fool you guys. Leave the blinds fully open? Shut them all, or just some of them? Nothing seemed right so we've opted for the part-way-closed disguise. You'll *notice the missus is a bit OCD as they're all closed to <u>exactly</u> the same level. Millimetric precision, don't you think?*

We really hope you like our light show. We gave the kids free rein to set timers all over the house. They really went to town, didn't they? Bless 'em.

Anyway, the house will look exactly like this until next Saturday so, please, come on in.

Signed, the Owners.

PS. We forgot to set the alarm so you don't need to worry about that.

At ten o'clock, Ross gave up, crestfallen as he drove away. Bound to happen eventually, he thought. But it hadn't been a total waste of time. He'd checked out the locale for the next few houses, two of which looked like they would cause him problems. One was behind high walls and solid wooden gates on a twisting country lane, with great clumps of leafy rhododendron bushes obscuring every angle. And he couldn't find the other one on Google Street View. Its address was Melbury Farm, Fontmell Magna, so he guessed that would be the reason why.

* * *

That same evening, Sally and Amanda were in town for dinner and a couple of drinks. It wasn't meant to be a heavy night because they both had work the following day but Amanda suspected her friend already had a head-start on her.

Sally was particularly voluble that evening and Ross was the hot topic. Amanda had been listening to Ross this, Ross that, and Ross the next thing, practically since she'd walked in the door. They had just put their main course cutlery down when Amanda spoke. 'Come on, Sal. I know you've made it clear, crystal clear in fact, that he can have you if he wants. But…'

'But what?'

Amanda being Amanda would normally have given Sally both barrels but deliberately chose to keep her tone gentle and kind. 'Don't you think he's made it just as clear he's not interested in you sexually? I mean…' she hesitated. 'I mean, after the night at his house when you…'

'Took my kit off in his front room?'

Amanda spread her palms wide. 'My point exactly. You served it up on a silver platter, and he still said no thanks. Anyway, what about Rob?'

'Screw Rob. That died a death a long time ago. I've no idea why we're still together. All he's interested in is sodding football and his sodding darts team. The only time I ever get a shag is if I instigate it. In fact, he won't even perform...'

Amanda stuck a flat palm in her friend's face. 'Enough, Sal! I shudder to think what you were about to say there.' Sally opened her mouth to continue her line of conversation but Amanda held up both hands this time, *and* looked away over her shoulder. 'Sal! When I used the words *I shudder to think,* that actually meant *shut the fuck up*. Mental images of you and Rob having it off would give me nightmares, and I'd prefer it if we didn't discuss your sexual preferences. We're not students any more, after all.' She was well aware her friend had been promiscuous at university. Her maiden name was Sally Day, and around campus she been christened *Sally Day, the Easy Lay*. Sally had been well aware of her nickname and did nothing to refute it. Quite the opposite, in fact.

They lapsed into momentary silence as the waiter cleared their table. After he walked away, and both women had stopped checking out his rear-end, Sally leaned forward on both forearms. She spoke at a much lower volume. 'Anyway, you'll never guess what. You know how Ross kept all his mother's jewellery *and* all the expensive stuff belonging to Liz?'

'Yeah. Why?'

'Well, he's just discovered it's all gone.'

'What do you mean, all gone?'

'I *mean.*' Sally paused to enhance the effect. 'It's all been stolen. All Liz's good stuff, his mother's, and his mother-in-law's too, I think. Carla, the thieving cow, must have taken it and he's only just realised it's missing.'

'Shit, no!' Amanda had her hand over her mouth.

'It's true.' Sally looked like she'd just lost a pound and found a tenner. 'And, guess what else.'

Amanda sat back and stared at her friend as if to say, *'Go on then.'*

'He dumped Alex. They're finished.' That tenner had just turned into a twenty.

'Bloody hell! Didn't see that coming.' A thought occurred to Amanda. 'Wait a minute. How on earth did you find all this out? Did Ross tell you?'

'No, he bloody didn't! He's only gone off on holiday somewhere, hasn't he? On his lonesome, too. If only he'd told me, I could have…'

'Yeah, Sal.' Amanda being kind to Sally had quickly worn thin. There's only so much a girl can take. 'So how *did* you find out then?'

'Well, I happened to be talking to one of Martin's twins.'

'You mean, you happened to be pumping the poor girl for info about Ross.'

Sally picked up the dessert menu, and peered down her nose at it. 'You say tomayto…'

Amanda left her menu where it was, coffee would do for her. 'Was it Gail or Beth?'

Sally didn't look up. 'I've absolutely no idea. I've never been able to tell the difference. Can you?'

Amanda sighed. *Twenty-odd years you've known those girls. What planet do you live on, Sal?*

63

The following morning Mock House, as it was now known, looked exactly the same as the previous night. Ross compared it with a photo he'd taken. The blinds had neither been raised nor lowered so clearly, no one had come home. *I'll just have to come back at some point. Damn!* The prospect depressed him. The end of the list, his personal pot of gold, was now further away than it had been yesterday. This definitely felt like two steps back.

From Devizes, he made the relatively short hop across the Salisbury Plain to the village of Codford. The area truly was *Beautiful House Central*. Thatched roofs and leaded windows were ten-a-penny and the honey-coloured stone, local to the area, lent a warm hue to the proceedings on this bright and sunny morning.

By noon he was on his way again. He'd watched as Ivan and Jill Cooke pottered around the front of their cottage. According to a plaque on the wall it had once been an important staging post between Shepton Mallet and Salisbury. Ivan was polishing the resplendent bodywork of a vintage Riley Kestrel that dated back to the forties, but still was younger than its owner. Meanwhile, Jill had several plant pots on a wall by a seriously-crooked porch, and was enthusiastically repotting them with what looked like winter pansies. By Ross's reckoning, neither of the Cookes would ever see eighty again, but he admired their cheerful dispositions and the energy they were putting into their respective tasks. If Jill was in the process of defrauding Ivan of his life savings, as far as Ross was concerned she was leaving it quite late.

He stopped in a layby to review progress. Including Mock House, there were now 22. Had the owners of the Devizes property been home yesterday, he would only have to tick off a couple more and he'd be halfway through his quest to find, or perhaps not to find, his missing wife. He found it strangely unsettling to be annoyed at a vacant pile of bricks and mortar, and a family he'd never clapped eyes on. But that was how Ross was feeling right now.

He briefly considered lunch but, instead, had a bacon roll and a mug of black tea at a roadside café that had been constructed with no small amount of ingenuity from the shells of two single-decker buses welded together, end to end. The seats were bone-hard however, so he didn't linger, deciding to press on to Fontmell Magna, a village just a few miles south of Shaftesbury. No matter how much he dawdled, he would be there in way less than an hour so he pulled out and accelerated south along the A350.

He'd no sooner started moving when his phone rang. He glanced at the display: *Mel Cooper*. There was a parking lay-by fast approaching and he braked to turn in, forgetting to indicate. The angry blast of a horn startled him as a black BMW roared past, straddling the white line.

'Mel? Hi, sorry, just pulling in.' He stopped next to an overflowing waste bin. Thoughtlessly discarded polystyrene containers and cardboard coffee cups littered the ground. 'Okay, that's me stopped.'

'Where are you, Ross? Is it convenient to talk?'

'Oh, yes. I'm just out and about, you know?' He had a mental image of the DS smiling on the other end of the line.

'I've spoken to Cheshire Constabulary this morning about your Mrs Hutchinson. It sounds to me like they weren't sure of their ground. Certainly they didn't have enough evidence to charge her, so she was released. They were acting on a tip-off, apparently. So I was wondering, does this have anything to do with your *friend*?'

'What?' Mel had caught him cold again. 'No, I don't think so. Why would it?'

'No reason. Just asking.' He didn't reply to that, figuring silence was his best option for now. She carried on. 'Anyway, things became a bit more interesting after that. Yesterday morning, Thursday, Mr Hutchinson phoned in to ask if they had his wife in custody again, and when they said no, why do you ask, he told them she'd disappeared. According to him, when he woke up on *Wednesday* morning, she wasn't there and she hasn't come back yet. Interesting, eh?'

'It certainly is.' *Wife suspected of defrauding husband. Disappears. Husband mystified. All too familiar.* 'Had she taken any of his money?'

'It doesn't look like it. Although it sounds very similar to your case we can't see any definite connections just yet. Mrs Hutchinson being guilty of any crime, or suspected crime, is all supposition just now, and from talking to my Cheshire colleagues, a bit more time will need to pass before they treat her disappearance as anything more than a domestic.' She chuckled. 'Apparently because the husband was a total tosser, according to them. Anyway, where did you say you were just now, Ross?'

It was the timing of her question that nearly caught him out this time. 'I'm just away for a few days. But listen, thanks for letting me know. I'll need to go now, I'm badly parked here. Bye.'

Ross could never be rude enough simply to end the call so he waited long enough to hear Mel's responding *'Bye'* coming back. He sat and let things rumble around before texting Oliver.

Hi. Just been told Mrs H released without charge Tues. Disappeared from home early Wed am. Guilty as sin! R.

He might have stopped in the lay-by for a while longer but an articulated lorry pulled in behind him, lurching a couple of times as the driver tried to manoeuvre the elongated vehicle into the tight space Ross had left. The driver gave a polite *toot* which basically meant: *'Oi, you. Shift forward a bit.'* Rather than do that, he set off again, flashing his hazards at the lorry driver, who blipped his headlights in thanks.

As he drove along, he wondered what he would face at this next house. Google Street View couldn't give him an advance preview this time.

Thirty-three minutes later, he had his answer.

'Aw, shit.'

And he really did mean that.

64

'He's up to something,' said Mel.

Andrew swivelled round to face her. 'Who?'

'Ross McKinlay. That was him on the phone.'

'What about?'

'Somehow, he's found out that a woman in Cheshire was taken in by the local plod on suspicion of perpetrating a similar fraud to his missing wife. But they had no evidence so she was released, and now she's disappeared. Done a runner, it looks like.'

'How does he know that?'

'The clue, *Detective Constable Young*, was in my use of the word *somehow*. So I don't fucking know, do I?'

'And will you be trying to find out?'

'I'm not sure.'

Andrew turned back to his PC. 'Well. What an unbelievably interesting conversation. So glad I was here for *that*.'

Her gaze darted quickly over her desk. Both the stapler and the paper-weight were too heavy, the keyboard and the mouse were attached to her PC, and the box of tissues was too light. She settled for a plastic tub of screen wipes but missed him by at least two feet.

'Bugger!'

Andrew was quite relaxed. She'd never hit him yet.

65

Oliver hadn't ever professed his database to be one hundred per cent accurate, and Ross's experiences so far had demonstrated there were a few couples who didn't match Leona's algorithm. According to the list, the next address was home to Roger Perryman and his wife, Pam. Ross hoped he'd be able to prove conclusively, and preferably within minutes, that the pair had been happily married for years, with grandchildren and everything. Alas, when he eventually found Melbury Farm, a few miles northeast of Fontmell Magna on a winding country lane, his hopes suffered an immediate dent.

The traditional stone-built farmhouse was in a total pig of a location, high up on a rise and set back where the terrain levelled off. From the road, he could see only the tops of the ground floor windows, and wasn't able to determine if there were any cars in front of the house. The driveway was no more than a steep, rough track that exited to the road directly at a sharp bend.

He'd already driven past the entrance once. Coming back from the opposite direction he bumped the car up onto the grass verge in an attempt to gain some sort of view, any view really, of the house. But even during the few minutes he sat there, two tractors had squeezed past pulling trailers piled high with bales of plastic-encased hay. The harvest was in full swing, and the second driver's animated gesticulations made it abundantly clear he had to move. He took one last look at the track up to the house. He was confident the Audi would make short work of it.

He drove for well over a mile before he was able to park in the overgrown entrance to a field, next to a heavily rusted metal gate. He took some time out to consider his options.

There's no way to keep watch on this house. Bugger! I'll just have to drive up to the front door and wing it. Thinking about it, maybe this one's too difficult for one person. Should I wait for Martin to arrive? Pause to consider. Then: *Come on, Ross, stop being such a bloody wimp. He won't be here till tomorrow. And after all, this is your problem, not his.*

What if I just log this one as nobody home? Who would ever know?

But Ross rejected the idea immediately because *he* would know, and that was enough for him. Resigned, he drove back to the farm track and eased the car up the slope.

Standing on the weathered sandstone doorstep of the farmhouse, he began to feel faintly ridiculous as, even to him, the market research pretence was wearing thin. He and Martin had run it several times but this would be the first time he would try it on without his friend there for moral support. Or, closer to the truth, to take the lead.

iPad in hand, Ross rang the brass bell-push and heard a traditional *brrrrriiinnnng* from somewhere inside.

The door was opened by an extremely tall, cheerful-looking man. He looked like he was well into his sixties but that could have been down to the way he was dressed. Brown cardigan with leather elbow patches, pale-coloured checked work-shirt that looked as though it had come straight from *Gardeners' Weekly*, ancient baggy corduroy trousers and battered slippers. All that was missing was the pipe and newspaper. He didn't say anything. He just smiled, obviously waiting for his visitor to explain why he'd turned up at their door.

Ross launched straight into his spiel, surprising himself by how smooth he sounded. Clearly some of Martin's confidence had transferred across to him. By osmosis, he supposed. Roger Perryman, still smiling, waited politely for Ross to finish his introduction. 'I'm not really up on that sort of stuff but my wife is. She uses her laptop all the time. Needs to keep in contact with her family back in Thailand, you see. Just hang on there a minute and I'll give her a shout.' He turned away then stopped himself. 'Sorry, forgot my manners. Would you like to come in?'

'Oh, no. Thanks very much.' Ross hadn't expected the invitation.

'Okay. Two seconds.' Roger walked back through the vestibule door, which he'd left half open behind him. 'Pam! Someone at the door for you.' He smiled one more time at Ross then disappeared into a den to the left of the front door.

Ross was left looking down a long, wide hallway. Easily 30 or 40 feet from front to back, and wide enough for a small truck. *Must be some size of a house. It's really deceptive from the front.* The hall appeared quite gloomy, partly because the afternoon sunlight was so bright at the front of the house but also because there was very little natural light from any of the several doors leading onto the hall. Only two of these were open, directly opposite one another, about three-quarters of the way along. As his gaze flitted idly up and down the passage, a female figure appeared from a room on the left. She walked across the hall from one open door to the other. She glanced out at him, turned her head back then stopped abruptly, right in the middle of the hall. Her body appeared to freeze, as if a tremendous amount of willpower was required to prevent her looking back at him again. After a pause of at least a couple of seconds, she continued across the hall. She never stopped looking straight ahead and disappeared into the room opposite. Ross would have heard the door closing had he not gasped audibly.

He felt like a Sumo wrestler had lifted him by his ribcage, and squeezed him like a toothpaste tube down to its last centimetre. His temperature seemed to rocket, bringing perspiration instantly to his forehead, blurring his vision. He stuck a hand in the direction of the doorframe in an attempt to support himself, missed, and only succeeded in scraping his wrist along the sharp edge of the wood. In trying to correct his position, his grip on the iPad relaxed, sending it crashing to the terracotta tile floor.

Roger came rushing back out of the den. 'My goodness! What's happened?' He took one look at Ross's face, and reached out to him. 'Are you okay?' Ross turned, tried to speak but nothing came out. Roger placed a hand underneath Ross's forearm. 'Pam! Quickly!'

A tiny Asian woman appeared in front of Ross as if Scotty had beamed her up. She was incredibly delicate with amazing almond eyes set aside an upturned nose. She looked like a pixie. 'You okay? Sir, you okay?' In a voice belying her stature, she bellowed, 'Rosa, Rosa. Bring drink water! Quick!' The woman who had crossed the hall a few seconds earlier came back out of the room and turned away from them, through a different door. But Ross didn't see her. He was too busy trying to deflect Pam. 'You have water. Feel better.'

'No. No thank you. I need to go now. Sorry to have bothered you.' He plucked the iPad from Roger's grasp, wincing in dismay as several shiny plastic slivers tinkled onto the floor.

'Nonsense!' Roger glared down the hall. 'Rosa! Where's that bloody drink?' At that, the woman came out of the kitchen and walked towards them, a bright shaft of sunlight illuminating her from the rear. Ross's vision hadn't yet cleared and he began to wonder if he was having a heart attack or a stroke. As she reached him, she stretched her arm out and handed him a tall glass of water. For the first time he was able to see her clearly.

Oh, thank the Lord. You're not Carla. Jesus! What a bloody fright. The constriction round his upper body immediately eased off and his temperature retreated to something approaching normal. He accepted the glass in both hands and managed to take a small drink without slurping it down his chin. He sneaked one more look at Rosa to reassure himself she wasn't his missing wife. He offered her a smile as weak as baby tea, and muttered a grateful thank you. He would find out later she was Filipino. With a jerk of her head, Pam dismissed her. She swished quickly away with her head down.

Roger gestured inside with one arm, and extended the other one to shepherd Ross into the den. 'Won't you come in? And please, sit down over here.' It was the only seat. A rattan sofa with floral upholstery that sat about a foot off the floor. Ross had no idea how Roger found it even remotely comfortable but looking around at all the man-things, this was obviously his hideaway. An enormous Samsung television hung on the wall opposite, a stack of hi-fi separates occupied one corner, while dozens if not hundreds of CDs and vinyl albums fought to remain upright in a bookcase several degrees away from perpendicular. Newspapers, motoring magazines and other masculine periodicals littered the floor, and within arm's reach of the sofa a packed beer fridge hummed noisily behind the door. Clearly, the kitchen was way too distant for Roger, especially when, in a reclined position, his bum would be significantly lower than his knees.

Pam returned with a pot of apple tea and a china plate piled high with sugar-frosted discs about the size of a £2 coin. She fussed over him, making sure he drank some tea and consumed at least half a dozen of these tiny home-baked biscuits. She asked him several times, 'You okay now, sir? You recover, yes?'

Ross assured her he was indeed fully recovered and told her the tea and biscuits were absolutely delicious. He wasn't kidding on that score. The intense sugar hit had been just the job. Roger insisted he sit for a while and they chatted sport, music and Brexit for a good part of the afternoon. Ross was thankful for the company, which he enjoyed immensely. He realised he'd been on his own for almost three days since leaving Edinburgh: receptionists, waiters and barmen aside. Not something he was used to or had even considered prior to setting out on his travels without Martin for company.

As the daylight began to fade he stood up to leave, politely declined Pam's offer to stay for dinner and thanked both her and Roger profusely for looking after him so well. He hadn't seen Rosa again. Just before he drove off down their bumpy track he had the presence of mind to take a couple of quick snaps of the friendly, hospitable yet unlikely pairing as they waved goodbye.

The time he'd spent with them had cheered him up but that state didn't last for long. Ross had some hard thinking to do, and some major decisions to make before Martin flew south the following day to join forces with him again.

* * *

Not long after he turned onto the main road heading south, Ross stopped at one of those classic olde-worlde inns that litter the highways and byways of rural England. *The Wheatsheaf* dated back to 1820, if the sign above the door was to be believed. Ducking through the low doorway into a large room with roughcast ceilings and black, burnt-oak beams, he decided the sign probably told the truth. Everything about the pub declared, *'I'm nearly 200 years old, you know.'* He reached up and rapped his knuckles off one of the beams, just to satisfy himself.

He worked his way through the healthily busy lounge bar, past families eating dinner and other customers enjoying drinks and arrived at the bar.

'You've no idea how many people do that,' said the barman. 'And I always ask them if they would be able to tell if the beams were genuine or fake. In fact, there's a pub down the road called *The Plough*, believe it or not. It's only about ten years old but when they built it, they made the first two beams in from the front door from real wood. All the rest are plastic or some other rubbish, and there's not a solid wall in the place. They figured people would only test out the first or second beam, tops, and would be convinced the pub was the real deal. All the tourists, especially the Yanks, fall for it, and it gives the locals a good laugh.' Ross wondered if the barman was winding him up. 'It's true, honest. But never mind all that, what can I get you?'

The drink-driving laws in England were not as severe as in Scotland, where even one pint of beer was liable to put him over the limit. But he'd been badly shaken by his encounter with Rosa and it had brought home to him just how lonely he was, even although it had only been three days since he left Edinburgh. He decided a pint would hit the spot, and decided he would have just one. Then he saw a sign behind the bar that changed his mind.

WE HAVE ROOMS UPSTAIRS. ALL EN SUITE.

The atmosphere in the inn felt cosy, comfortable and welcoming. They served food, decent beer, and he wouldn't need to drive any further today.

'I'll have a pint of Guinness, please. And I'd like to book a room for the night.'

Within minutes he had a room organised, booked in for dinner at seven-thirty and was settled with his beer at a small table by the window. The weather had just broken down and squalls of rain were battering off the small thick panes of leaded glass which, even without the drips running down them, were fairly impenetrable. He could discern blurred headlights in the car park but that was about it. Sitting there with his beer, sheltered from the elements and with the promise of dinner to come, Ross was delighted with his impromptu decision. *Not like me at all.*

It didn't take him long to fully accept the conclusion he'd reached as he drove away from the farmhouse. His motivation for this quest had fallen off a cliff. Ross had never been one to suffer genuine stress but, on reflection, his reaction when he believed he'd seen Carla in Roger and Pam's hallway was far from healthy. Driving away from the foot of that steep rutted track, he had been sorely tempted to point the car north. And to hell with speed cameras.

Right then, he felt as low as he'd felt since Liz had died.

I've just about had enough of this. Maybe it's time to call it quits.

Then he thought perhaps it was just that this last house had been such an awkward one, where a full-frontal assault was the only option. And, he'd been on his own. As he began to rationalise, the pendulum swung the opposite way. *What if I look up the next few addresses on Google Street View, and only do the easy ones myself. I won't go near anything difficult till I see Martin. After all, I can't be stressed out just sitting watching a house. Can I?*

Ross instantly felt more positive now he had found an acceptable compromise. Had he just bailed out completely, he knew he would have been disgusted with himself, especially as Martin in particular was really putting himself out to help. Then there were the twins. Not forgetting Oliver, and all the people working with him. They'd all lost so much.

No, he certainly wouldn't be throwing in the towel. But he *did* intend to be sensible.

In the break between his starter and main course, he picked up the iPad. He'd been avoiding opening it, scared the screen would be shattered after its fall. *Can you replace the screen on an iPad?* He had no idea but he figured even if it were possible, it wouldn't be cheap. He lifted the edge of the cover and was immediately heartened when a coloured light shone out from under. More confident now, he opened it fully but groaned loudly when he saw the lower part of the screen looked more like crazy paving than an expensive electronic accessory. He jabbed tentatively at the surface and was amazed when it responded to his touch. *I'll let Martin see it. It'll give him a giggle anyway. Good old Ross strikes again!*

As he was eating his main course, beef casserole with wild rice and green beans, he studied the list. That first night with Oliver, when they plotted the addresses on the map, he wondered why there was such a concentration in this part of the country. Now he was here he could quite easily see the reason: money. He was sure there was plenty of the stuff in other parts of the UK but no doubt, this was a well-to-do area. Even the people around him seemed to have that intangible affluent look. Well turned-out, as his mother would have said.

As he worked his way through Google, he jotted down some notes. In brackets, he put order he would visit the houses.

- Sherborne, behind high walls, no view. Martin & Ross? (1)
- Cerne Abbas (village), not on Street View. M&R? (2)
- Poole, terraced villa, wide street. Ross. (4)
- Christchurch, semi, good view. Ross (5)
- Brockenhurst (New Forest), new house, well-tended garden, open view. Ross. (6)
- Lyme Regis, apartment in large block (sea view). M&R? (3).
- Littlehampton, bungalow, GSV not clear, too far away? (7)

The waiter asked if he'd enjoyed his food. 'I did, indeed. It was excellent. Really tasty, thanks very much.' But he declined dessert, patting his stomach to suggest he was full. Yet, strangely enough, he had space for another Guinness. The waiter laughed and said he'd put it on the tab. Ross congratulated himself once again for deciding to stay. The difference in his frame of mind in just a couple of hours was night and day.

He thought it was about time he called Martin, to find out when his friend's flight was due into Bristol and also to run his ideas past him. Whatever Martin's faults, and some would say they were plentiful, he had always been a fantastic sounding board. That, and he had a zero tolerance bullshit threshold. A spade was a bloody shovel as far as he was concerned.

Martin answered immediately. 'Hey, sunshine. How goes it?'

Ross had intended to sound all cool and matter-of-fact but he immediately started babbling on about how *everything* had been a disaster, and how he was about to give up on this ridiculous fool's errand. When he eventually registered that Martin hadn't spoken at all, his diatribe spluttered to a halt. 'Are you still there?' he asked, as if he were terrified there would be no response.

'Sorry, Ross. I missed all that. What were you saying?' Ross drew in a breath, about to kick off again but Martin interrupted him before he was out of the blocks. 'Fuck's sake, Ross. I was kidding. Now, tell me exactly, why has your trip been such a disaster? And Ross?'

'What?'

'Slow the fuck down, man.'

So Ross explained about being caught out because the Luckhursts' lived in an apartment block, and about his bizarre conversation with Celia at the bus stop.

'Nice one,' said Martin, thinking it was lucky Ross couldn't see the faces he was pulling.

Then Ross played his trump card. How he'd worked out how to use Google Street View from the car to preview the next few addresses.

The disbelief came pouring down the airwaves. 'Jesus! Ross McKinlay, the IT wizard. Whatever fucking next?'

Ross was chuffed, naturally, but then he explained about Mock House in Devizes, and how the owners were away so it would have to be revisited. 'Hardly a disaster though, eh?' said Martin. 'Especially taken in context with you being a genius on the Street View front.'

Ross conceded that was true then described Ivan and Jill, the sprightly octogenarians in Codford.

'So that's another one ticked off, isn't it?'

Ross said it was. Then he hesitated and Martin broke in smoothly. 'Looking at the timings, it looks like you had time to check out one more house today. So, come on then, what happened?'

When Ross told him about how tricky the Perrymans' house was, and then how badly he was affected by the Rosa encounter, Martin empathised immediately. 'That really *was* tough, and I'm sorry I wasn't there to help, but...'

'But what?' Ross hadn't intended to speak so sharply.

'*But*, leaving aside the Rosa thing, I'd say you've actually had quite a successful few days. You've ticked three more off the list, and you couldn't do anything about the other one. And not to mention, thanks to you, we'll know exactly what we're facing, well before we roll up to a house.' He changed the subject, hoping to prevent any negativity filtering back in. 'So, where are you phoning from?'

'I've booked into a hotel. I've just eaten dinner then I'm having one more drink before I head for the land of nod.'

'Sounds like you're doing exactly the right thing there, my man. Well done you.'

Then Ross explained how he'd researched the next half a dozen addresses. How three of them looked straightforward and three definitely did not. And that he didn't fancy tackling the latter trio on his own.

'I don't blame you. I wouldn't either. But, let's look at this from another angle. Where are we with numbers?'

'Including the one in Devizes that we'll have to go back to, we've checked 16, so 21 left.'

'Well, there you are. If we both check out the three you're not keen to do yourself, we'll be halfway through. And hopefully, if the others are as straightforward as you think, you could do those yourself at the start of the week when I'm back up here.'

Although Ross could see the sense in Martin's line of thinking, it only introduced a greater sense of foreboding. The way he saw it, the more houses they checked, the more chance they had of finding Carla. And that was the last thing he wanted, as he'd already admitted to himself. Several times.

'I know it can't be much fun on your own all this time but I'll see you tomorrow. And I was also thinking, you told me you'll be coming home by next Friday at the latest. Well, it's not mandatory that you stay down there as long as that, is it? If things are beginning to get you down, cut it short. No need to wait till the end of the week, just head back up the road. Stop at a few nice places. You'll deserve a break by then.'

It hadn't ever occurred to Ross that he might call a halt earlier than planned. In his mind, he was away for the duration. Now he immediately felt more upbeat and told his friend that.

'Excellent.' Martin chuckled before carrying on. 'Oh, nearly forgot. Sal phoned me today, she was asking me where you were. Quite insistent, she was. Seemed *ever* so keen to talk to you.' If a smirk could be transmitted by mobile phone, one would have smacked Ross right in the ear at that moment. 'You two aren't… em…'

'You *must* be kidding.' Ross had never confessed the Sally-was-pissed-and-got-her-tits-out story to Martin because he knew the eternal abuse he would suffer. 'Mind you, it's not been for the want of trying on her part.'

'I wouldn't worry about it, pal. You wouldn't exactly be a member of an exclusive club. Right, I'm off now. My flight arrives in Bristol about nine in the morning so to save time, I'll hire a motor and drive down to meet you. I'll ring you once I'm sorted and see where you are. Sound okay?'

Ross agreed it sounded perfect. He finished his beer and was briefly tempted by one-for-the-road. But tiredness had settled on him like heavy snowfall so he called it a night. He was really looking forward to having some company for the weekend.

66

Saturday

Martin pulled his hired car into a lay-by on the A30, two miles west of the historic market town of Sherborne. It was 11:15. The rain of the previous evening had moved on, leaving a warm dry day with the sun trying its best to burn off a thin layer of cloud. He flashed his lights at Ross in the SQ5. The two friends shook hands warmly. It's fair to say they were equally pleased to see each other but not so much that they did the man-hug thing. *'Pretentious pish,'* according to Martin.

After a few minutes' chat, they set off in convoy into Sherborne, from which point they experienced a run of good fortune they could never have anticipated, ticking off three addresses in not much more than six hours, all in the county of Dorset. As Ross would comment later, they spent more time driving between the places than confirming the married couples who lived there.

But the last target for the day left Ross in the doldrums again. It was 30 Hinchcliffe Terrace, home to Tom Allison and his wife, Belle. They found the street easily enough, and numbers 28 and 32 were easily identifiable. But as far as number 30 was concerned, it was just one big hole in the ground. The two men stood on the pavement, gawping. A giant latticework of scaffolding and timbers as thick as railway sleepers prevented the houses on either side from tumbling into the gap. They double-checked the numbers to confirm they weren't hallucinating but there was no mistake, 30 Hinchcliffe Terrace was no more. A gentleman passing by told them: 'Gas explosion, apparently. The building collapsed as if someone had pulled the foundations out from under it. Thank God no one was home at the time.' The man had no idea who had lived there or where they had gone.

Ross was in a funk. For some reason even he couldn't explain, he managed to convince himself that Carla had lived there but now they couldn't prove it. And somehow that really annoyed him. 'I know I'm being irrational. I don't even know if I want to find her. But it's annoying to miss the chance because of some stupid gas explosion.'

Martin didn't even try to understand Ross's logic and was on the point of telling him to *Put a sock in it.* But he recognised his friend was under stress so instead, he cajoled him along. With four in the bag he suggested they call it a day, and a highly successful one at that. They had passed the halfway point having checked 20 out of the original 37 houses. Leona's list was now at 17, including a return trip to Mock House in Devizes.

Ross spotted a small hotel with five stars, overlooking the harbour. They agreed it would make a pleasant change to overnighting in bog-standard chains. They checked into a twin room, had gin-and-tonics in the hotel bar and set off to sample the local hostelries.

After a few beers they landed in an Indian restaurant, and ordered curries with a host of accompaniments and a bottle of red wine. Their table overflowed with dishes to the extent their waiter had to utilise an adjacent one. They'd been blethering on all evening with Martin bringing Ross up to date with all the office goings-on. Eventually he dropped the big news bombshell: a competitor had offered a *pile of cash* to buy him out.

'Wow!' was all Ross could manage past a mouthful of naan bread dripping with tarka dhal. That had always been Martin's endgame so the news itself wasn't unexpected but undoubtedly the timing was.

'El's been helping me put some figures together but she thinks it's more about the company *making* an acquisition, and not the other way round. So keep it to yourself for the moment, yeah?'

'Will do.' Ross reached over to spoon some tandoori chicken onto his plate. He didn't notice his shirt sleeve had trailed through the remaining dhal. 'I'm afraid I pissed her off a bit when we were out for lunch. Told her a wee fib about where I was heading for this week.'

Martin laughed. 'Aye, she mentioned it. Says you're the world's worst liar. Did she give you a bollocking?'

'Elspeth doesn't miss from that range.'

Martin adopted a sly smile. 'I actually think that our Elspeth has a wee soft spot for you. She did ask me where you'd headed off to in the end. Maybe you should have brought her with you.'

'Aye, right. And how would *that* have worked?'

'Fair comment.' Martin put his fork down. His phone was vibrating on the white linen table-cloth. He only just managed to keep a straight face as he held it up for Ross to read.

Sally mobile.

'I'm just off to the loo.' Ross staggered slightly as he stood up.

'Bloody coward.' Martin swiped to reject the call. 'Mind you, I wouldn't either,' he said to himself, raising his index finger at a passing waiter and pointing at the empty bottle of red.

By the end of the evening, takings at the casino in Lyme Regis had been boosted by about £600, while the barman had to replenish his stock of vintage Dom Pérignon as his last two bottles had bitten the dust.

67

Sunday

'There's no way on earth my wife would be involved in something like this,' said Gareth Hutchinson to the policeman, whose ID declared he was from Europol.

Hutchinson hauled the waistband of his unidentifiably stained trousers over a pot-belly that suggested frequent and sustained investment in alcohol and fatty foods. 'I mean, Sylvi's besotted with me. Worships the ground I walk on. There has to be some mistake. She'll be back soon, and I'll be reminding the ungrateful cow how well off she is, now she's married to me.' He nodded to himself. 'She knows which side her bread's buttered on.'

Jarek Zelenka had met Annika, a.k.a. Sylvi, a few times. She was Champions' League to this man's Sunday morning pub team. He was certain the only time she would consider any form of ground worship would be if Gareth Hutchinson was beneath six feet of it. 'I do hope so, sir.' In this guise, he had no need to conceal his accent but he kept his contempt for this disgusting, pompous windbag well in check. 'But in the meantime, I have to do my job so may I ask you some questions, please?'

'If you must. But I don't really see the point. She'll come running back to me soon enough.'

Fool. Jarek pretended to take notes on a pocket-sized spiral-bound pad. 'In the lead-up to the local police detaining your wife did she meet with anyone who perhaps was a stranger to you?'

'I don't think so, but how could I possibly know that? Sylvi wasn't a prisoner. She went out. Into town. Met friends. I wouldn't know, or care, who she met.'

Jarek scribbled a few characters down. 'Did anyone visit here, come to the house?'

'No. Not while I was here. But then again,' he huffed, 'I'm not a prisoner either. I have lots of friends. I'm out all the time.'

Jarek refrained from groaning audibly. 'Perhaps someone just came to the door. Didn't actually come into the house?'

This time, the man seated opposite just shrugged and stared out the window. 'That seems a stupid question to me. I mean, people come to the door all the time. Postmen, couriers, people selling stuff. How would I even notice?'

Jarek sat up a little straighter in an attempt to maintain his rapidly diminishing composure. He thought if he genuinely had been trying to find Sylvi, he would probably gift her his life savings to fund her escape from this loathsome buffoon.

'Because we *are* sure she was in the process of defrauding you, and we think someone came here to warn her she was about to be apprehended.'

'Well that doesn't make any sense either. If someone *did* warn her, why didn't she piss off right away, eh?'

Jarek could almost feel the life being sucked from him but now he was coming to the crux. He lifted an iPad out of his back-pack. 'Bear with me on this, Mr Hutchinson. I'd like you to look at some pictures of men we think are involved in this, ah, deception.' He tapped the screen a few times then spun the tablet round so the other man could operate it. 'Just swipe the screen to the left...'

'I *know* how to work an iPad. I'm not completely thick.'

Jarek move his hands below the table to stop him smacking this imbecile about the head. 'Quite, sir. But if you could just look at them, please?'

Hutchinson was oblivious to his visitor's tone, and began idly swiping through the images. Jarek scrutinised his body language, particularly facial expressions, for any hints of recognition. If anything, the man was too relaxed, as if he were just going through the motions. Naturally, the pictures were not of alleged conmen. In fact, they were snapshots of all the men Annika and her fellow operatives had defrauded in the UK in the past few years. He was just beginning to think this was a complete waste of time when Hutchinson stopped swiping, and stared closely at the screen.

'I hate to say it, but this guy looks familiar.' He pondered for a few seconds. 'I've definitely seen him somewhere before.

Now, let me think.' Jarek forced himself to remain silent and relaxed. Then Hutchinson slapped the table with both palms. 'Got him!' He looked up, almost triumphant despite his earlier negativity. The ersatz Europol officer gave him an *enlighten me* look.

'You asked if any strangers had come to the house. Well, I do remember now. A week or two ago, two blokes came to the door. Something to do with market research. This fella was one of them but he didn't do much talking. I wasn't suspicious at the time but the following day I was talking to my neighbours on either side, and the men hadn't been at their doors. I thought that was a bit funny but then I forgot about it completely.'

Jarek pretended to jot down a note. 'So, he was here a week or two ago. Can you be more specific about the date?'

Hutchinson scratched at his ear. 'Sylvi was making a white sauce, so it would have been for fish. And we always have fish on a Wednesday, so that would have been... the twenty-first. Yes. Definitely the twenty-first.'

'That's great, Mr Hutchinson.' *Fuck, what a life. Everything centres around what you eat on a particular day of the week.* 'Now, do you remember what they were researching?'

'Ah, well, they wouldn't speak to me. Said it had to be the wife. Internet shopping or some such crap. I'm not interested. It's all double-Dutch to me so I shouted for Sylvi to come out.'

'So did you hear what the conversation, this market research, was about?'

'Like I told you, I couldn't have given a shit. I prefer to buy things in a real shop where you can see what you're paying for. Anyway, she was making dinner at the time. Sent me in to watch the sauce while she spoke to them.'

'And she behaved perfectly naturally when she came back in?'

Hutchinson smiled for the first time that morning. Jarek thought it was probably a strain for the man. 'Oh, aye. Gave me a bollocking for not stirring the sauce properly.'

'I see. And you couldn't be mistaken, Mr Hutchinson?' He pointed at the iPad. 'You're absolutely certain this man came to your house.'

'Definitely. I'd stake my life on it.'

The man from Ostrava reached inside his jacket and produced an automatic pistol. Before the fat man even had the chance to register surprise, Jarek put two bullets in the middle of his chest. The impact propelled Hutchinson and his chair backwards, where they both crashed noisily onto the black and white ceramic-tiled floor. Jarek moved smoothly round the table and shot him once more, this time in the forehead. For a moment he considered a fourth shot to the groin but desisted. The action would have been self-satisfying and unprofessional. 'Thank you, Mr Hutchinson. You've been most helpful.'

He picked up the iPad and his backpack, and didn't look at the body when he said, 'Don't get up. I'll let myself out.'

68

Miroslav's mobile rang.

'Yes?' He saw it was Jarek but names were frequently taboo in his line of work.

'The gentleman confirmed he was visited by one of our competitors.' Jarek used similarly oblique language to describe the market research scam Ross and Martin had employed. He finished his brief explanation with, 'The jpeg filename is 45323.'

'One minute.' Miroslav opened an application on his PC, typed the number into a database search field and hit Enter. A small window appeared on the screen. It reported: *Ross McKinlay; Edinburgh; Concluded 19/02/16; Elisabetta Massaro (Carla Marinello).* That gave him the headline information but he clicked on the *More* button and quickly read the supplementary data. He closed the window, he had all the answers he needed. 'And you've met with our colleague from Reykjavik?'

'Her analysis is consistent. There are no issues there.'

'Good. Now, I may need you to attend another meeting on my behalf, perhaps two. One in Scotland, the other in the South of England. But I must consult with my associates here first, and someone will contact you as soon as we are able to confirm the location. Please be ready to leave immediately.'

'Of course.' Jarek wasn't certain Miroslav had stayed on the line long enough to have heard him. He considered his location, currently a few miles east of Wilmslow in Cheshire. He lifted a road atlas from the passenger seat and studied it. It didn't matter whether he would be heading north or south, he was within five minutes of the M6 motorway. And if, for any reason, he was told to drive in a different direction, he had ready access to Manchester's motorway network. He used his phone to search for the nearest filling station in the direction of the M6, and set off to find it. Within twenty minutes he was parked in a run-down industrial estate less than a mile from M6 junction 19, with a full tank and a bag of sandwiches, drinks and snacks. He ripped the wrapper off a BLT on brown, and settled down to wait for instructions.

* * *

Miroslav had called Danijela. She was with him now, pen in hand and a spiral-bound reporter's pad balanced on her knee. Although his voice was calm, she recognised he was in classic *swan* mode, apparently unperturbed above the waterline but webbed feet thrashing nineteen to the dozen beneath the surface. 'I have just spoken to Jarek. I don't know how this has come about, but McKinlay has been to Annika's house. It looks to me that, perhaps, he is trying to track down his missing wife so, somehow, our UK network has been compromised. I will concern myself with identifying the flaw in our security later, but in the meantime, we must locate McKinlay. Make contact with our colleague in Edinburgh. I want to know where he is at this precise moment. If he is at home, we will deal with him there. If not, then I want him found.' He didn't need to state the obvious to Danijela. She knew this was top priority and would act accordingly.

She was back within the hour with the answers to every question she anticipated he would ask. After all these years she knew him inside out. She also knew he would *not* be pleased about what she had discovered so she gave it to him straight. No flowery language or weasel words. 'We have two problems to deal with, McKinlay *and* Elisabetta Massaro.' She had seen the window open on his screen earlier so didn't waste time explaining that Elisabetta and Carla McKinlay were the same person. She also didn't need to be told to keep talking, his expression made that abundantly clear.

'I believe you're right about McKinlay searching for his missing wife. And I think the reason he is looking for her is he has recently discovered she stole jewellery from him as well as the money she acquired. The jewellery belonged to his late wife and his mother, among others.'

'So, that is why after all this time, he is looking for her now. He is angry. But why is Elisabetta a problem for us?'

'I've checked the inventory against McKinlay's records. No jewellery.'

He sighed and looked out the window. *Another Jean-Luc Dornier. Just what I needed.* 'It's clearly of enormous sentimental value to him so I do not imagine it was cheap costume jewellery. Do we know the monetary value?'

'I can't be precise but he is telling people it's close to £200,000.'

Danijela remained silent while Miroslav's cogs rotated at speed. 'When was the last time we spoke to her?'

'The end of last month. She is making progress with her assignment but nowhere near a conclusion.'

'And this is where? Refresh my memory.'

'Hampshire. South coast of England.'

'And she is not acting as if we suspect her of anything?'

'Not as far as I can tell. Of course, I didn't know about this when I spoke to her so I wasn't looking for anything.'

'Understandable. What we need is for Elisabetta to call in without raising her suspicions. To confirm she is still on assignment. Then she can be dealt with.' He looked pointedly at Danijela. 'Conclusively.'

Miroslav's partner knew all the organisation's operatives personally and she was fond of Elisabetta. They were of a similar age, had had a few laughs together and shared a few wild nights in the hot-spots of Prague. But she had absolutely no time for disloyalty. She understood perfectly what he meant by *conclusively,* and she wouldn't lose a minute's sleep over Elisabetta's ultimate, and imminent, demise. *Stupid greedy cow. She could easily have made that sort of money from her next two, possibly three assignments.*

'But enough of Ms Massaro for the moment, Dani. Have we found McKinlay?'

'No. But a little bit of back story, if I may. I'm told he has been travelling a lot during the past few weeks. Business trips with his boss, Martin Redpath.'

'When did these so-called *business trips* begin?'

Danijela checked her notes. 'September thirteenth. And the supposed researchers spoke to Annika after that date.'

'Are they away on another...' he did the quotes thing, '"business trip" at the moment?'

'I can't be certain but it doesn't look like they're together. It transpires McKinlay has taken two weeks' holiday from work.'

'Are we able to track his phone?'

'Not now, no. We did have a tracker app on there but it stopped working a while ago.' Miroslav raised an eyebrow, and Danijela continued. 'That could be quite innocent. As we know, he has been learning more about IT so perhaps he deleted it without knowing exactly what it was.'

Miroslav stood up and stretched. He stifled a yawn with the back of one hand. It had been a long day and it looked as though it had some life left in it yet. 'Ah. Let's not give any credence to the great god coincidence. I've never trusted her, Dani.' He walked over to the wall opposite and leaned back on it. 'What else have you tried?'

'Just on the off-chance, I called his mobile from my desk but it rang out.'

'No voicemail? That is unusual.' He was silent for a minute, drumming his fingers on the wood panelling behind him and staring into middle distance. 'And none of these trips raised any alarm bells with our Edinburgh colleague?' He answered his own question this time. 'No. I don't suppose they would. A perfectly normal thing to do.' He appeared quite dejected he'd arrived at that conclusion so quickly. 'Is McKinlay taking this holiday alone?'

'I was coming to that. I've just discovered he broke off his relationship a couple of days before he left. Now, I *definitely* should have been told about that. It's a major fuck-up and I'll be having words. But there is one thing that is odd about this *solo holiday*, he is travelling in his boss's car.'

'And you think this is odd?'

'For two weeks? Definitely. Or slightly unusual at best.'

'Is it a much higher spec than his Volkswagen Golf?'

Danijela smiled openly. Although she was frequently amazed at his apparently prodigious memory, she also knew he employed a wide assortment of tricks to underpin it. No trick this time, however. He'd read about Ross's car just a few minutes previously. 'Not really. It's only an Audi SQ5.' They both drove high performance BMWs so the Audi was hardly impressive in comparison.

Miroslav raised a finger. 'But, a more suitable vehicle for conducting surveillance.'

He sat down again. 'Right. Let's set a few hares running. One, Elisabetta. Establish her whereabouts. Two, call Jarek.

Send him to Scotland to track McKinlay down. And tell him he'll be going after Elisabetta immediately afterwards. Three, contact Edinburgh again. We need more information on McKinlay *and* Redpath.' He paused until Danijela looked up from her pad then asked, 'Have I missed anything?'

'It's just occurred to me. Redpath's car. I'll find out his registration number. If we can locate the car, we'll find McKinlay.'

He clapped both hands together. 'Oooh, Dani. You are good. I may even go so far as to say you are amazing.'

Danijela could be coquettish when it suited her. 'I *have* been told that before. Several times, in fact.'

Despite himself, Miroslav broke into a smile as wide as the Vltava.

69

'Whose fucking bright idea was the Dom Pérignon?' It was almost noon on a dull and cloudy Sunday but Martin was wearing shades nonetheless.

'Well, it wasn't the tooth fairy.' Ross was still annoyed they hadn't woken in time for breakfast at the hotel.

They were wandering around the marina at Poole harbour, killing time for one specific reason. Neither man was even close to being legally entitled to drive. They'd worked back the number of alcohol units consumed the previous night, and concluded two o'clock was about the earliest possible time they could safely be back behind the wheel.

As Ross had commented earlier when they dropped their bags off at the cars, 'That's our plans for the day shot to buggery, all because we let our collective hair down. Or what we have left anyway.' Martin had neither the inclination nor the energy to disagree with his friend's accurate summation.

When they had first sat down to relax the previous evening, their plan for the day looked like this: up early, breakfast, and away from the hotel by about nine o'clock. Drive the ten miles or so to Christchurch and check out the couple who lived at the next address. If time allowed, they would both move on to the New Forest village of Brockenhurst, a similar distance again and taking them into Hampshire for the first time. However, Martin's flight from Gatwick departed at eight in the evening so he'd need to leave the area by mid-afternoon. The stretch target in their draft plan was the next destination: Littlehampton in Sussex. It was an hour and a half's drive away so Ross would probably go there on Monday.

But that plan was washed away by an alcoholic deluge of biblical proportions, and a pair of stonking hangovers their owners richly deserved.

At two o'clock they set off in separate cars, arriving in Christchurch less than half an hour later. Mike and Emma Robinson owned a semi-detached villa in an estate that dated back to the sixties. Despite that, most of the houses were extremely well maintained. The number of people out working on their properties and gardens was testament to that. Sadly, 86 Beaconsfield Circle was devoid of any visible activity and there were no cars on the short tarmac driveway or in front of the house.

Martin left on schedule at three-thirty and Ross was back to flying solo. Within five minutes he was conducting a full-scale internal argument. Cut and run, find a hotel and crash out for the day. Or tough it out. He chose the latter but placed a six o'clock limit on his stay. The paracetamol he'd taken back in Poole were fighting a failing rear-guard action against the twin assaults of piercing headache and generally feeling crap. Not long before his self-imposed deadline, his suffering was rewarded. An ancient but pristine Rover saloon stopped outside the house, and two elderly couples climbed out. Their impeccable dark clothing strongly suggested they'd been to church and perhaps gone somewhere posh for Sunday lunch. The foursome chatted on the pavement for at least ten minutes before an extended palaver of goodbye hugs, kisses and handshakes ensued. So Ross was taken aback when each couple entered adjoining houses and closed their doors behind them. He texted Martin to say Christchurch was done and dusted.

By seven o'clock he'd found a hotel in the town centre, eaten a light bar-supper and was fast asleep in bed. Brockenhurst would just have to wait until the morning, and Littlehampton an indeterminate period beyond that.

Twenty-one down. Sixteen to go.

70

Jarek performed some stretching routines by the side of the van. Apart from one toilet stop just south of Edinburgh, he'd driven the 230 miles from Cheshire to the city in one hop. Danijela had made it crystal clear he shouldn't hang about, and he'd have reached the capital earlier had it not been for traffic jams around Manchester and interminable delays at several sets of roadworks on the M74, north of the Scottish border. He had stopped in an expensive residential area called Inverleith, about a mile from Ross's house. Looking around, all he could see were large sandstone villas, wide roads, sportsgrounds and recreational parkland. The entrance to Edinburgh's Botanical Gardens was just visible through a row of mature sycamores, elms and horse chestnuts.

He set off on a brisk fifteen minute walk round the park, striding out to elevate his heart rate. The walk was time well spent as far as he was concerned. Better to have some exercise and fresh air now, than turn up at his destination stiff as a board and drowsy through inactivity. He was also aware that if he didn't find his target at home, almost certainly his next move would be to make the exhausting journey post-haste to the south of England. A daunting prospect but one he would worry about later.

By seven-thirty he'd parked just round the corner from Ross's house. It had been a dull day in Edinburgh. Any remaining light was fading fast and streetlights were popping on all over the place. Jarek knew he wouldn't have the luxury of a walk-past to reconnoitre the house but that didn't bother him. The direct approach had always been his favoured option. As any thief or conman will tell you, behave as naturally as possible and people generally won't pay the slightest attention.

Jarek rang the doorbell twice with no response. There were no lights on anywhere inside as far as he could see, and the high wooden gate between the house and the garage was locked from the rear. He stepped into a flower bed to peer in through the front window, the only one easily accessible to him.

'Can I help you with anything, mate?'

He turned to find an elderly man staring intently at him from the pavement, his back as straight as a pool cue, eyes locked on to Jarek and a scruffy-looking dog milling about his ankles. Jarek walked away from the window and directly towards the man. There was no other way. He plastered on his best I'm-all-innocent face, confident he'd be able to bluff his way out of this quite easily. He was now standing face-to-face with Joe. 'Oh, hi. I've just dropped in to visit Ross but he doesn't appear to be at home.'

Joe could do blunt with the best of them. 'That's an unusual accent you have there. Where have you *dropped in* from?'

Spare me, thought Jarek, mildly amused by the old man's front. He ignored Joe's question. Instead he asked one himself. 'Do you know where Ross is?' A low, insistent growling came from the ground by his feet. He looked down to see the dog's hackles up and her lips pulled back from her teeth. The growling continued.

Joe looked down at his dog then back up at the foreigner who was standing *just* too close to him. But he didn't back away. 'Bella's always been an excellent judge of character so, if you don't mind, I'll not be telling you where my neighbour's gone.'

Jarek bent forward from the waist and moved further into Joe's space. 'Listen to me, old man…'

'Joe!' came a shout from further down the street. A woman stood there, waving something in her hand. 'You forgot to take poo-bags, you silly old fool.' They both looked over at her, and Joe took the opportunity to take a step back. He was a brave man, but he wasn't stupid. 'Who's that you're talking to, Joe? Is there something wrong?'

Jarek still believed the situation was retrievable and took another step towards Joe, lifting what was intended to be a conciliatory arm as he did so. And that was too much for Bella who began yapping and snarling furiously at him, straining at her leash with both front paws waving about in front of her.

Joan walked towards them. 'Joe, what's wrong with Bella? It's not like her to bark like that.'

352

A series of small but interlinked events then occurred that convinced Jarek he was mistaken, this wasn't going to work out at all. A door opened across the street and a younger man wearing a white polo shirt and black tracksuit bottoms came out of the house, swinging a black refuse sack. He lifted the lid of a wheelie bin, arced the bag inside, dropped the lid and began pulling the bin towards the pavement. The clattering noise of the wheels on the stone chips of his driveway made a racket that could be heard up and down the street. Barry looked over at the group, eyes a little wide as he noticed Bella still trying to pull Joe off his feet. 'Hi Joe. What's up? Bella okay?' He walked to the kerb, peering over at them, his arms folded against the evening chill.

He was about to cross the road when a small red car puttered into view and slowed as it approached them. It came to rest halfway over Ross's driveway, the front nearside wheel perched precariously on the kerb by about an inch of tread. Before the driver had switched off the engine, Jarek decided enough was enough. He had no choice but to vacate the scene, and quickly. There had been occasions in his past when collateral damage was unavoidable but four civilians plus one yappy hound in a residential street was beyond the pale. Besides, the old man had already told him what he needed to know by the form of words he had used. *'I'll not be telling you where my neighbour's gone.'* That didn't suggest Ross was shopping for groceries or out for dinner with friends. No, the word *gone* intimated he was somewhere away from Edinburgh so Jarek would report that back to Danijela. If necessary, he'd revisit the old couple later and persuade them to tell him more. He knew where they lived.

He muttered something deliberately unintelligible and walked off briskly behind the car, just as the driver stepped out. They exchanged the briefest of glances and, although her expression remained blank a miniscule pulse of recognition registered as a single beat in Jarek's brain. He disappeared from view round the bend in the street. Of the others, only Barry moved, jogging swiftly back to his house and in through the front door.

Alex swung the car door closed with a soft click, the type of sound that indicated the lock hadn't engaged properly. She looked at Joan and Joe, who was ruffling Bella's ears with both hands while telling her what a brave little girl she was. The dog peed in a nearby shrub in celebration of her resounding victory against all the odds.

'Who was that?' Alex looked back down the street, then at each of Ross's neighbours in turn.

'No idea,' said Joe. 'He was looking for Ross. But something tells me he wasn't here to tell him he's won the lottery.' He looked down at his dog, now enthusiastically scratching her ear with her hind paw. 'He was a bad bugger. Wasn't he, Bella?'

At that moment, the *bad bugger* had just made a fast three-point turn in a cul-de-sac he'd turned into by mistake and was accelerating past the foot of the street at a speed way beyond the limit. And, because he was momentarily flustered, he didn't see Barry standing under a tree looking at his phone, which showed an image of Jarek's van with the license plate perfectly in focus.

71

'This is an announcement for passengers travelling to Edinburgh on British Airways flight BA1516. We regret to advise that this flight has been cancelled due to technical difficulties. Would all passengers please make their way to the British Airways Customer Services desk in the main terminal where alternative travel arrangements can be made. Again, British Airways flight BA1516 to Edinburgh has been cancelled. We apologise for any inconvenience caused.'

'Aw, you bastard!' said Martin, with some vehemence. Similar phrases and blasphemies were voiced by other passengers as they stood, grabbed their bags and stormed off towards the desk in question.

'No, sir. We don't have a spare plane available.'

'No, madam. There are no other flights to Edinburgh or Glasgow tonight. Ours was the last flight.'

'No, sir. We couldn't get you to Heathrow in time for a later flight, even if there was one.'

'Yes, sir. There is compensation available but that might not include the cost of an overnight stay in a hotel.'

'Yes, sir. I can reserve a seat for you on our 07:25 flight tomorrow morning.'

'Excuse me, madam. I appreciate you're upset but there's absolutely no need for language like that.'

Martin heard all of these and more as he queued relatively patiently with the other passengers for almost an hour and a half. He knew from past experience there was little point in either arguing or becoming irritated with the BA ground staff. Plus, he was absolutely shattered. So he reserved a seat on the Monday morning flight, booked into yet another hotel and was in bed within minutes of checking in. Before he fell asleep he set his phone to vibrate and laid it on the bedside table. He couldn't imagine anyone would be looking for him urgently, and was confident he would hear the phone if someone called.

Regrettably, he was wrong on both counts.

Perhaps the three double gins he'd consumed while waiting for the aborted flight were a contributory factor but he dropped off immediately. Not quite comatose but not far off. The time was one minute to nine.

His hotel room was decent enough but it catered for business people and travellers. There wasn't a matchbox-worth of genuine wood in the room, all the surfaces were veneered MDF. So when Barry called at nine-thirty-five, his phone vibrated and the lack of friction caused it to skitter across the shiny top of the bedside table and plop softly onto the carpet. As a result, he also missed a series of increasingly frantic calls from his daughters between eleven o'clock that night and one in the morning.

Had Martin taken any of those calls, the sequence of events that were already in motion might have turned out very differently.

72

Joe and Alex perched on stools at the island in Barry's kitchen diner, while he organised coffees. The trio had chatted for a couple of minutes on the pavement but the weather had an edge to it so they moved inside. Bella was having a good sniff around, her claws clacking on the floor tiles. Joan had left them to it. According to Joe, she phoned her sister every Sunday at this time. Armageddon wouldn't interrupt the two-way flow of gossip and tittle-tattle that would last well over an hour.

Jarek, naturally, was the sole topic under discussion. Alex had witnessed only his departure so the others filled her in on what had gone before. They all agreed the visitor's behaviour would probably have been filed under *strange* had Barry not filmed him burning rubber.

'That was quick thinking, Barry,' said Joe. 'Nipping in for your phone and snapping his number plate.'

'Spur of the moment thing, really. But I'm not all that sure what to do with it now.' Barry handed out mugs of hot drinks and offered the other two a biscuit. Alex said no but Joe wasn't a man to pass on anything sweet.

'Well, I don't want to sound like some crazy old man but the only time I've ever seen Bella behaving like that was last year, when those Gyppos came to the door offering to do me a tarmac driveway.'

Barry smiled. Joe hadn't deliberately used a racist term, it was just an indication of his age. When Joe's vocabulary had been formed, political correctness was fifty years off.

Barry picked up his phone. 'I'll give Ross a call.'

'Do you think you should?' asked Alex.

'Why wouldn't I?' He was a little surprised at the question.

Alex took a sip of her coffee. 'I don't know. Isn't it a bit alarmist?'

'I don't see how. I'm only planning to say something like: Hi Ross, some foreign bloke was here looking for you, sounded a bit Eastern-European, drives a white van, bit of an odd-ball. Ring any bells? And if he says, oh aye, that's my mate,

Stefan, or whoever, from Poland, there isn't a problem. On the other hand…'

'I think you *should* ring him, Barry,' said Joe. 'Better safe than sorry.' He looked at Alex. 'Bearing in mind his wife was foreign, and she ran off with all his money.'

Barry tapped Ross's contact. He held the phone to his ear, and waited. The others could hear the calling tone. It burr-burred about ten times before he tapped the screen once more. He looked puzzled. 'I'll try again.' He repeated the process, with the same outcome. 'Funny. No voicemail?'

'Does he *use* voicemail?' asked Joe. 'Not everybody has it switched on.'

'Oh, aye. I'm always leaving messages to arrange games of tennis.'

'And you definitely have the right number?'

'Don't see why I wouldn't have. Alex. What number do you have for him?'

'It'll be the same as yours.'

'Well, let's have a look then.' They both had identical details stored.

'Could he have changed it?' asked Joe.

'Not as far as I know. I'm sure he'd have mentioned it.' He looked over at Alex, who shook her head. He kept his gaze on her a little while longer. 'I meant to ask, Alex. What brings you over here tonight?'

She had no idea if Barry or Joe knew Ross had broken up with her but she wasn't about to enlighten them. 'I just came to see Ross. It was a bit unexpected. I was supposed to be working this evening but I finished early.' *As if it's any of your business.*

'So you didn't know he was away, then?'

'No.' The denial came with a light coating of frost. 'I haven't spoken to him this week and he didn't mention anything about going away. Where's he gone, do you know?'

'If we knew *that*,' Barry retorted, 'we wouldn't be sitting here in the dark. Would we?'

'Excuse me, you two,' Joe butted in. Bella was now making deep breathing noises, curled round his feet. 'But this isn't helping. Is there anyone who would know how to contact him?'

'Just his boss, Martin,' said Barry. 'Or his daughters. They're close with Ross so they might know.' He scratched at his ear. 'But I've no idea how to get in touch with any of them. I've only met Martin a couple of times. I don't even know his surname, and I couldn't tell you the twins' names. Alex?'

She hesitated. 'I don't know his last name either. And I haven't met his daughters. Sorry.'

Barry hadn't missed the hesitation, and his eyes narrowed at the fairly blunt response.

Joe spoke next. 'I guess the key question is, do we think Ross could be in any trouble? Especially,' he jerked his thumb towards the door, 'with our foreign friend.'

'You said it yourself, Joe,' said Barry. 'Carla was foreign. She stole all his money, and more. Unfinished business?' Again, he focussed his attention on Alex.

She shrugged. 'Difficult for me to say. Apart from the guy walking away, I didn't see any of the other stuff.'

'Joe?'

'I must say, Barry, I don't like it. Not one little bit.' He stretched his arms straight out in front of him, fingers intertwined. 'I think we need to try to speak to him tonight. We don't know where he is, but possibly the bloke who was here does. I don't want to sound *alarmist*,' he glanced at Alex, 'but I'd never forgive myself if I did nothing, and Ross was hurt.' More thumb jerking. 'I don't know *him* from Adam, but something tells me he has a dangerous side. Maybe we should even phone the police.'

'Oh, come on,' said Alex. 'Phone them and say what? We think our friend could be in danger because a foreign guy, who we think was a bit *strange*, turned up at his door. For all we know, he was an opportunist burglar, and we scared him off. *That's why* he buggered off in his van at a rate of knots. Phone the police? No, that's a step too far for me.'

The room fell silent. Then a wide grin popped up on Barry's face. He snapped his fingers. 'I know how we can find out Martin's number. Joe, you have a key to Ross's house, yeah?' When Joe replied that he did, Barry said, 'Right. Let's go and fetch it.'

* * *

359

Once Jarek had put a few streets between himself and Ross's interfering neighbours, he pulled over and called Danijela. In coded form, he explained briefly what he'd encountered and told her he strongly suspected Ross was indeed away from home, and Hampshire was his likely destination.

'I agree,' said Danijela. 'Now, we'd like you to go there and formally terminate their contract with us. Unfortunately, there are no suitable flights from Edinburgh or Glasgow tonight so I must ask you to drive.' Jarek didn't react, he was the consummate professional.

Danijela would never say so, but she hoped he would take a break on the journey. She knew she was asking a lot of him, especially given what he'd have to do once he arrived there. 'I'll text you an address and a postcode. Is there anything else you need from me?'

'If I should meet our Edinburgh contact do you wish me to terminate their contract too?'

Danijela had her answer ready. 'Yes. The Managing Director would like all these loose ends tied up. The issues we have been facing must be resolved.'

Jarek said he understood. Danijela had known him for a long time. She wished him a safe and successful journey, and she meant every word.

He then drove straight to Edinburgh airport, the best option locally to hire a decent car quickly and easily. The Mercedes van had been perfectly suitable for his requirements up until now but for this next journey he would need something more powerful and more comfortable. Also, the hardware necessary for the next part of the job would be minimal so a saloon car with an enclosed boot was his preferred option. He parked the van in the basement of the short-stay car park, as close in to a corner as he could find. He was also careful to reverse it tight up against the wall to deter opportunist thieves or inquisitive passers-by. No sense in advertising what the vehicle was carrying.

Inside the airport, he was dismayed to find queues of customers at the two car-hire outlets that remained open. It took the best part of an hour before he walked away with the keys to a Volkswagen Passat with the correct specification: comfortable, a powerful engine with an automatic gear-box, cruise control, and satnav with the latest version uploaded.

The sales agent tried her best to upsell various insurance options, and was rather disappointed when he turned them all down flat.

He drove his new car back to the Mercedes, transferred his luggage and the equipment he'd need, and locked the van. Finally, he tossed the keys down a nearby drain.

He switched on the satnav and input the postcode from Danijela. He refrained from groaning aloud when the system computed his journey at seven hours, and 461 miles.

He filled the tank with fuel and drove out onto the M8, heading west for the M73, M74 then the M6 for all points south. It was the same route Ross had driven four days previously.

The clock on the car's dashboard showed 21:30.

* * *

Minutes later, having sneaked the key out of the house with Joan none the wiser, Barry, Joe and Alex were in Ross's kitchen. Bella had elected to stay home by her favourite radiator. Barry was raking about in drawers. 'Found it!' He brandished a little book with a black hardback cover.

'What is it?' asked Joe.

'Despite his new-found IT skills, Rossie-boy still uses an old-fashioned address book. I remember cracking up when he wrote my number in it. And my address, believe it or not.' He opened the book, flicked forward till he found Martin's contact details. 'No surname. Well, there wouldn't be I don't suppose.'

He keyed in the number and listened as the call rang out. He mouthed, *voicemail*. 'Martin. This is Barry Taylor. I'm Ross's neighbour. I've been trying to call him but his phone's ringing out and I'm not getting voicemail so I can't leave a message. But I really need to speak to him very urgently, so could you get in touch and ask him to call me as soon as possible. Any time. It doesn't matter how late. Thanks, Martin.'

'Right,' said Alex. 'When Ross calls you, ask him to ring me afterwards, will you?'

'Sure.' Barry wasn't certain he meant it.

'Thanks. It's late, and I'm tired. I'm off home. Good night, gents.'

Joe said *Good night* in return but Barry just waved a hand at her retreating back. The front door closed behind her.

Barry pulled his eyes away from the door. 'I'm with you, Joe. I think we should call the cops. But, and I hate to say it, I do agree with Alex, we can't just phone up and say we're worried about our pal. They'd give us short shrift. But if we could contact the two officers who were investigating Carla's disappearance, that would make more sense. It was a woman DS and a younger bloke but I couldn't tell you their names. Not much help if we're speaking to some civilian bod on a central switchboard.'

Joe stood up. 'I've got an idea. Let's lock up here. You go back to your house and I'll be over in a minute.'

Barry was just putting the coffee cups in the dishwasher when Joe rang the bell and came in. The impersonation he performed of Joan was uncannily accurate by virtue of pointing his nose up at an angle, raising his voice an octave or two, and mimicking a posh Scottish accent reminiscent of Maggie Smith playing the title role in *The Prime of Miss Jean Brodie*. 'Detective Sergeant Melissa Cooper and Detective Constable Andrew Young, based at Queen Charlotte Street, in Leith.' Joe handed over Mel's business card. 'Didn't take to her at all. Although, the young man *was* rather dishy.'

Barry couldn't be certain his neighbour hadn't made up the last part. He had to wait till he stopped laughing before picking up his phone again.

* * *

After stomping out of the house, Alex drove her car a couple of streets away and parked by the blank garden wall of a corner house. It was nine-forty, and there was no one about.

She tapped the Google app on her phone and searched for a couple of minutes. A smile flitted briefly across her expression before it vanished like cream on a cat's top lip. She'd found what she was looking for.

The search result showed a mobile number. She tapped it and her phone began dialling. When the call was answered, she introduced herself. Then, 'I'm phoning about Ross McKinlay.'

The conversation didn't last as long as she thought it might. She closed by saying, 'Thank you. About ten minutes, tops.'

Alex put her car into gear and drove off. She wasn't sure how she would feel by the end of the evening but she was about to find out.

73

Miroslav's burner phone rang. An obsolete Nokia that could make phone calls and send texts. Danijela had bought hundreds of them with their now old-fashioned SIM cards from a contact in Shanghai a couple of years back. They were perfect for the job.

'We've found the Audi,' said Danijela. 'Its last recorded position was this afternoon at 14:20, travelling east in the county of Dorset almost at the border with Hampshire.'

He had no need to ask how the car had been located. In the UK, as in other countries, they had a number of key people in their pockets. Police, lawyers and bankers to name a few. They had control of these officials simply because the individuals were weak, and they had no hesitation in ruthlessly exploiting those weaknesses. The levers could be girls, boys, drugs, cash, power. Miroslav didn't care, as long as they produced results. Recently, Danijela had set a honey trap, and a senior officer from the Metropolitan Police had been caught, covered in the sticky stuff: both metaphorically and literally. The carefully edited video footage of her with those two men was damning, conclusive and irrefutable. When it was presented to her, along with a sheaf of high resolution stills that portrayed her in a variety of decidedly hard-core situations, in her panic she didn't notice her eyes were closed or partially closed in all of them. An observer may have mistaken her expressions as lustful or orgasmic. Actually, she'd been drugged till she was practically comatose but left malleable enough to appear a convincing subject. As a result, this highly educated, powerful and extremely attractive woman would do almost anything in order to protect her career and her family. In that order, Miroslav suspected. He wondered briefly if it had been this police officer whom Danijela had leaned on to locate the car. No matter, it had been found.

'So we were correct. He *is* trying to find Elisabetta, whom he knows as Carla, and now he is very close. Have we heard from her since you left the message?'

'No, and I'm failing to understand why not.' It was cast in stone that all operatives must check for voicemails every day at specific times, and respond to any messages as soon as was practical. 'I called her not long after three o'clock UK time and, as her scheduled check-in times are 08:00 and 22:00, she should have been in touch by now. I'm not happy.'

'What does her phone tracker say?'

'That she has been in or around her home most of the day. Like everyone else, she knows the app is there so circumventing it wouldn't be difficult.'

'And the tracer we put on her car?' Miroslav was referring to devices that had been installed on all their operatives' cars, this time without their knowledge.

'Ah well. That one also says her car hasn't moved all day so unless she has somehow found it, or suspects it is there, she is not driving.'

'Okay. Perhaps there's a genuine reason she didn't call. Let's see what tomorrow morning's check-in brings.' Danijela's muffled harrumph indicated clearly she wasn't disposed to being quite so generous.

He changed tack. 'What about our colleague? Where is he now?' This was the second call he'd taken from her that evening so he already knew about Jarek's abortive trip to Edinburgh.

'Driving south as we speak.' She carried on speaking as Miroslav threatened to interrupt. 'I know, I know. But the last flight from Edinburgh to anywhere near London had gone and as we don't have any contacts in Scotland, we had to hire a car. And after all, our friend is not known in the UK so there is no risk attached.'

'It will be a very long drive.'

'True. But he'll actually reach Hampshire more quickly by road than if he had flown. And of course, the equipment he's carrying isn't suitable for air travel.'

Danijela remained silent while Miroslav ruminated. If there were any flaws in her reasoning or planning, he would almost certainly find them. She wouldn't be annoyed or surprised if he did. They'd spent the majority of their adult lives bouncing off each other.

But this time, he was in complete accord apart from one remaining question. 'And our Edinburgh colleague, what has she been doing all this time?'

'Apart from licking her wounds after the bollocking I gave her earlier, she is also trying to confirm where her Scottish friend is at the moment.'

'Okay, Dani. Thanks. We'll speak again soon.'

She knew that was more of a command than a passing comment.

* * *

At ten minutes to ten, Mel Cooper's voicemail recorded a message from Barry. But her phone was turned off and lying in a drawer in her bedside cabinet. She was in bed with her husband. Cuddled into his side, her head nestled in the crook of his shoulder and snoring gently. Today was her first day off in twelve. On top of her normal workload, she had been assisting in a drugs-running case that had come to fruition that day with the arrests of two men from Edinburgh and three from Newcastle-upon-Tyne.

The kids were away. It was the start of the school holidays tomorrow and they always spent the first week of any break with their grandparents. Mel and her partner, Callum, had been out all day enjoying themselves. A long walk, a couple of cheeky wee cocktails, a Thai meal with wine, *and* they stopped off for a nightcap on the way home. It was one of those days when all the planets, the stars, the moon and the sun had lined up perfectly.

Barry would have to wait until the morning to tell the police officer just how concerned he was about his friend and neighbour.

* * *

Elisabetta Massaro sat cross-legged on the heated floor of her en suite bathroom. The time was fast approaching midnight but sleep was as distant as the back-end of Mars for this enormously troubled woman. Her husband had no such concerns. She could hear his muffled, regular breathing through the bathroom door. She looked down at the phone nestling in the vee created by her slippered feet. It was an old-fashioned Nokia yet it looked like it had hardly been used.

Elisabetta had listened to the voicemail several times using the earpiece she kept hidden along with the phone in her spare toilet bag. Her new husband, Dennis, was a stickler for respecting other people's privacy and would never dream of looking in there. She thought about listening to it once more but what was the point? She'd picked up the voicemail at ten o'clock that evening when she checked in at her designated time. The recording was timed about seven hours earlier, at 15:06. She should have responded to the call immediately, that was protocol. But because of what she imagined was the *real* agenda behind Danijela's apparently innocent message, she hadn't. And that had been a mistake. Of that, Elisabetta was in no doubt. None whatsoever.

In her heart, she had been waiting for such a call since that day she read the email depicting the unimaginable suffering of Jean-Luc Dornier. She'd considered running but her nerve failed her, and the moment was lost. Her next check-in time was at 08:00 so she *could* call in then, making up some sort of improbable tale about how or why she hadn't heard or received the voicemail. But she didn't believe she would be able to pull it off. Danijela was smart, she'd spot it in an instant. And when that happened, Elisabetta knew she would be living on borrowed time. If she wasn't already.

So she knelt in front of her bathroom cupboard, lifted out her spare toilet bag, carefully stored the phone and the earpiece in an inside pocket, closed the zip, and the bag, and the cupboard door. Then, quietly and carefully, she crept back into bed beside her still sleeping husband.

And for the next seven hours Elisabetta lay wide awake, wondering how, and when, her end would finally come.

* * *

'Still nothing?' asked Gail. The time was quarter past one on Monday morning.

Beth didn't answer. Her face said it all.

After a few seconds Gail repeated a comment they'd both made several times before. 'It's really strange we can't contact either Dad or Ross.'

In the past two hours they'd left numerous voicemails, and sent texts and emails to both their father and his best friend. At first the girls had been curious about why neither man had responded. As time dragged by, curiosity became concern. Then concern upgraded to anxiety. They were just managing to keep panic at bay.

'There could be lots of reasons, all completely innocent. We're probably just letting our imaginations run riot.' Beth looked up at the clock. 'Anyway, they'll both be in the land of nod by now. May as well leave it till morning and we'll try again.'

By half past one, both had retired to their respective bedrooms.

By ten to two, Gail was tucked up in bed with her sister.

74

Monday

It was just before six, and the sky over the Wiltshire city of Salisbury was an hour away from sunrise. Looking at the low, claustrophobic cloud base that was obscuring all forms of celestial light, Jarek Zelenka thought it unlikely he would be breaking out the sunblock any time soon.

He wondered, and not for the first time, why on earth he was driving all over the UK, most of the time in the hours of darkness. No, he should still be catching Caribbean rays. Solar, rather than aquatic. Although his loyalty to Miroslav was absolute, he was definitely pissed that he'd been dragged back from holiday. He didn't often travel abroad, cultural European city breaks were his preferred destination. So to have his first ever cruise cut short had been annoying, to say the least.

Jarek had been surprised to find the whole cruise experience was enjoyable, not what he expected at all. As the days and the destinations drifted by, he relaxed into it, gradually slowing down to match the ocean-going tempo. He'd seen some amazing islands and wonderful sea-life, eaten delicious food, won enough money at blackjack to make him feel like a low-to-medium roller, surprised himself by purchasing a piece of art from the ship's gallery, and had a one night stand with an American divorcee who'd looked glamorous and sultry with the benefit of the low casino lighting. The sex was enjoyable, not great, but as the night wore on and more of her allure and her clothing was stripped away, he gradually discovered there was hardly a part of her that hadn't been surgically altered.

Jarek smiled wearily at the memory as he paid for fuel and a reheated all-day-breakfast sandwich at a filling station on the dual-carriageway that would take him away from Salisbury to the southeast.

He looked at his watch. *Half an hour till I reach Elisabetta Massaro's house. A couple of hours, tops, to tidy up, and at Heathrow by mid-day latest. With a bit of luck I'll be back in Prague tonight.*

He was dog-tired and desperate for a good night's sleep. Preferably in his own bed.

75

At about the same time Jarek was starting his engine, Martin was gradually surfacing, being dragged towards consciousness by the insistent yet muffled tone of his phone alarm, which sounded like it was buried in a roll of fibreglass insulation. He slapped his hand around on the bedside table but when he couldn't locate the offending device, he raised himself up on an elbow and peered over the edge of the bed. He lifted the fallen phone, swiped off the alarm and flopped back down, hoping to squeeze another few minutes from what had been an excellent sleep in a rather comfortable bed.

But that prospect vanished like the dreams of a jilted bride immediately he spotted the *Missed Call* and *Voicemail* symbols along the top line. He tapped it to reveal the list of callers: a mobile he didn't recognise followed by Beth, Beth, Beth, Gail, Gail, Beth. He didn't stop to listen to his voicemails and, seconds later, he had number one daughter on the line, who immediately tore several strips off her old man.

'I'm sorry, pet. I didn't mean to worry you. My phone was on vibrate so when you rang, it must have fallen off the table and landed on the carpet. I didn't hear any of your calls.

'But I'm okay, honestly. Nothing to worry about. I was just shagged out so I had an early night.

'No, I'm perfectly fine. Just about to head for the half seven flight home so I'll see you tonight. We could all go out for a meal. What do you think, eh?

'Ross didn't answer either? Probably something similar, Beth. I'm afraid we had a bit of a night out on Saturday. We hit the hot-spots of Poole, would you believe.'

Then, a pause.

'You're kidding! What the hell did *she* want?

'She said *what*?

'And when did all this happen?

'Bloody hell, that was late. But no, he hasn't called me so maybe he doesn't know anything about it either.

'Okay. Listen, pet. You hang up now, and I'll give him a call straight away. In fact, I've had another missed call but I didn't recognise the number. I'll check my voicemails and see what's what.

'Yes, I'll keep you posted. I love you both.

'Yes, we'll speak soon. Bye, Beth.'

A minute later he was calling the other number. 'Come on, Barry. Answer your piggin' phone.'

And as soon as he finished speaking to Barry, he called Ross.

The call rang out then diverted to voicemail.

* * *

Ross was in the shower when Martin called. His phone was already tucked in the outside pocket of his bag. Like his friend, he'd muted it the previous evening. A full night's sleep had been top of his agenda too. *After all, who'd be trying to contact* me *during the night? Not Martin. He'll be home already. Lucky git.*

Ross didn't even look at the phone when he woke up so there were several symbols and notifications he didn't see. Missed calls, voicemail, and most importantly: *Your phone battery is very low on charge. Connect to a power supply immediately.*

By half past six he grabbed a bacon butty from the breakfast buffet and walked towards the car park. Next stop: Brockenhurst. Although, the way he was feeling this morning, he could see it far enough.

* * *

Four hundred miles to the north, Mel switched her phone on for the day. She was slicing a banana to put on buttered toast when she heard voicemail chirping. *Jesus. No rest for the wicked.*

There were two messages. From Barry and from Navid Chowdhary, the DC from Cheshire Constabulary she'd spoken to the previous Friday. He'd called less than ten minutes ago. Barry sounded a bit concerned but perhaps not. Voicemail messages rarely sound natural. Mel wondered why he was calling. She would ring him later, once the morning rush had died down.

But then she listened to Navid's message, and that totally altered her mindset. Over the next fifteen minutes or so, Mel had conversations with Navid, with Barry and finally with Andrew, who promised he would, indeed, get his arse into the station: pronto.

Ross, Ross, Ross. What the fuck are you playing at? And more importantly, who the fuck are you playing against?

76

Now only a few miles from his destination, Jarek had made good time driving south, especially on the motorways, where he'd set cruise control at seventy-six. The speed limits were of little concern to him but the last thing he needed was to be stopped by a police patrol for driving ridiculously fast. He had taken a break just south of Manchester. Sleep had become imperative as a couple of times he found himself drifting off, the rumble strips at the outside edge of the overtaking lane jolting him back to life. He grabbed two hours sleep in the passenger seat and combined the rest stop with the other necessities: toilet, refreshments and fuel.

Since Bristol, about 100 miles back, he had been driving on A-roads. He'd been pushing it, as witnessed by the occasional double flash of a speed camera in his nearside door mirror. No matter, he wouldn't be paying any fines.

He passed a sign announcing he had crossed into the New Forest National Park, and drove along an arrow-straight minor road for two or three miles before reaching the village of Lyndhurst. He followed signposts through the village for the A337, the continuation of that road would take him due south to his appointment with Elisabetta Massaro.

One thing that had always amazed him about the British was how early they set off for work. Here he was, just after half past six on a Monday morning, in a tourist village in the middle of a forest, held up by a line of slow-moving traffic. *Where are all these people driving to at this time?* As the narrow one-way village street straightened out, he was able to see ahead. The reason for the delay became apparent.

Parked just in front of a traffic-calming chicane about 50 metres further on, wearing Day-Glo leathers that reflected his blue flashing lights, was a police motorcyclist. The angle of his helmet suggested he was scrutinising every car that passed.

Jarek instinctively looked in his rear-view mirror but found a car drawing up close behind him. A delivery lorry then filled the space at the back.

He had no choice but to keep moving forwards.

* * *

Ross had bought a copy of the *Times* and a large-scale map of the New Forest. He studied the map while munching his bacon roll. He'd be travelling east for a dozen miles before turning north for approximately half that distance again. He circled the street in Brockenhurst where Dennis and Laura Bentley lived. Leona's list just said: *No 2, The Paddocks*. He slung his bag, containing his iPad and his phone, into the boot. The act was symptomatic of his mood that morning. He just couldn't muster any enthusiasm for yet another day prying into other people's lives, on the off-chance of tracking down a woman he had absolutely no desire to find anyway. He couldn't fathom whether this was down to Martin returning home, thereby leaving him on his own again or whether the hangover he'd suffered all through yesterday was still lurking about in his system. He suspected both factors shared the blame equally.

One thing he was certain of. He was totally fed up looking at, using and having his every thought and action dictated by electronic devices. Satnav had undoubtedly proved invaluable but today he was leaving it switched off. A map printed on good old-fashioned paper would do just fine. A day without his iPad wouldn't kill him either. Then there was his phone. He clicked into his seat belt, then thought he probably should have the phone up front with him. But he made the same erroneous assumption as Martin. *Nobody's likely to be calling me anyway*. He reasoned he could always fetch it from the boot if he needed it.

Between the throaty growl of the engine as he accelerated away, plus the layers of leather, foam, plastic and Cordura between him and the phone, he failed to hear it warbling out one final beep before the battery died.

The last time registered on the display had been 06:40.

77

The line of traffic containing Jarek's Volkswagen Passat crept forward. It took a full five minutes for him to draw level with the motorcycle cop. He could now see clearly that the mounted officer wasn't even slightly interested in the oncoming vehicles. He was just bored out his skull. Jarek surmised the policeman's sole responsibility was to deter impatient drivers from performing illegal manoeuvres on the one-way street. A passenger in a car three ahead of Jarek left his vehicle and wandered over to ask a question. The response was a crash helmet shaken briefly from side to side. Light rain began to patter onto the car so Jarek switched his wipers to intermittent wipe.

A good ten minutes later, the traffic began to move a little more quickly and he wondered if the obstruction on the road ahead, whatever it was, had been removed. But no sooner had he cleared Lyndhurst when the traffic ground to a halt once more, and this time he swore aloud. The section of road south of the village was remarkably similar to the northern part, straight as a die under a fairly solid canopy of trees. Clearly the Roman legions had spent some time in the area back in the day. For about a mile he could see a lengthy series of red tail-lights. Tellingly, there were no headlights approaching from the opposite direction.

He was considering looking for an alternative route when a pair of blue-white beams appeared over a rise at the head of the queue and moved gradually closer. Through the rain-spotted windscreen he watched the police car stopping briefly at each of the vehicles in the line, before moving on to the next one. Some of them made three-point turns, and the police driver allowed them to pass and return to Lyndhurst.

Eventually the police car pulled alongside. The driver looked serious but relaxed so Jarek mirrored the policeman's manner as they exchanged a few sentences through their drivers' windows and across a gap that was now a little curtain of light rainfall.

'I'm afraid you won't be able to drive any further south through the park just now, sir. You're likely to be stuck here for a while. Sorry about that.'

'What's the problem, officer?'

'We're dealing with a road traffic collision a few miles south of here, so the road will remain closed until further notice.'

'Do you have any idea how long that will be?'

The policeman's gaze remained blank. 'I'm sorry, sir. I couldn't say.'

The police driver put his car into gear, ready to move on to the next car in line.

'Wait a moment, please,' said Jarek. 'Is there an alternative route to where I'm going?'

'That depends, sir. Where *are* you going?'

Jarek instantly regretted his question, realising too late he could hardly answer the officer without revealing information he would rather keep to himself. But he couldn't dodge it because the policeman was now paying him more attention than was healthy. So he worded his response in such a way as to camouflage his real destination by concealing it behind a different one. Magicians and illusionists use this tactic. It's known as distraction. 'I'm on my way to Bournemouth but I'm picking up a colleague on the way.' He really didn't want to say any more but he was desperate to find out if this *accident* would prevent him reaching Elisabetta Massaro's house. This morning, he was discovering that events were conspiring to deny him choices. This was yet another example.

But what is it they say? In for a penny, in for a pound.

'He lives in Brockenhurst.'

78

While Jarek was speaking to his policeman in the New Forest, Mel was walking towards her desk. She shucked her coat off her shoulders as she made her way past her colleagues, exchanging *Good Mornings* with some of them. Others needed at least two belts of caffeine before they became even remotely communicative. Andrew had arrived just before her and was booting up both their PCs, which would take an age to come to life.

'Right, my boy. Do I have a story for you.' Andrew passed her a coffee he'd picked up from the Italian café across the road and settled back to listen.

'Remember Gareth Hutchinson, the husband of the woman that our Cheshire colleagues took in for questioning last Tuesday? Then they released her and she did a runner?' Andrew nodded over the top of his coffee. 'Well, DC Chowdhary...' She paused momentarily until Andrew had placed the name, 'he called me early this morning to say Mr Hutchinson had been found dead. Yesterday afternoon. Murdered. Actually, assassinated is probably a more accurate term. Two bullets to the chest and one to the forehead.'

Andrew took another mouthful, his eyes were a lot wider now. 'How did they find him?'

'Classic nosey neighbour, as it happens. An old biddy across the road peering through her net curtains spotted some bloke letting himself out of Hutchinson's house about ten o'clock on Sunday morning. He drove off in a white unmarked Mercedes van. She thought it was a bit odd. First of all he let himself out, and second, she didn't think he looked the type to be driving a white van. According to her, he wasn't, quote: "Dressed right." Anyway, she went straight over and rang the bell. When no one answered, she phoned the cops. Her thinking was, if Hutchinson wasn't in, what was this bloke doing in the house? And if he *was* in, why didn't he answer the door?'

'And was she nosey enough to take down the registration?' Andrew smiled and reached for his notebook. He reckoned he already knew the answer, and jotted down the number that Mel read out.

'Now, do you also remember on Friday I said Ross McKinlay was up to something? Well, it looks as though I was right. Last night, Ross's neighbour, Barry Taylor, left me a voicemail. I called him back this morning. About half seven last night, he and another neighbour, the old chap from two doors down...'

'Joe.'

'That's right. There was some sort of stooshie outside Ross's house. Some guy with an Eastern European accent was asking where Ross was. Said he was a friend dropping in for a visit but Joe was suspicious. When he quizzed him, the bloke exited somewhat sharpish.' Her eyes lit up. 'And guess what he was driving?'

Andrew placed the point of his index finger against his bottom lip and pretended to look puzzled. 'So this foreign chap and his van were near Manchester in the late morning, and up here by early evening? Perfectly possible.' He pondered a moment. 'Okay, it's your call. What do you want me to do?'

'You check out the van.' She didn't qualify her request in any way. Andrew knew exactly what she was looking for. 'And while you're doing that, I'll call Ross and find out what the hell he's got himself mixed up in.'

Unlike Barry, Mel did have Ross's new number from their conversations a few days previously. But he wasn't surprised when her call went to voicemail.

'Ross, this is DS Mel Cooper here. It's oh-seven-thirty on Monday morning. I need you to call me back the minute you hear this because I think you could be in real danger. This is very serious, Ross. Call me.'

Then it clicked that Ross had changed his mobile number. *Not particularly unusual, people do that all the time. Two questions, though. Why? And does it have something to do with you having disappeared off somewhere? Now, there's only one person who would know the answers. Your boss and big-time buddy, Martin Redpath.*

Mel tracked back in her notes to find Martin's contact details. She called and waited for him to answer.

* * *

Considering the entire transaction was processed by computer, and he'd not long handed back a hired car to the same company, Martin couldn't believe how long it was taking to organise a new car. At first, he asked for a continuation of the original hire but he was told that wasn't possible. 'It's back in the system now, sir. We'll have to start from scratch, I'm afraid,' said the ten-year-old who was serving him. Martin had never seen anyone who worked quite so slowly and deliberately. *Jesus Christ, laddie. Would you fuckin' hurry up!*

What seemed like hours later but actually was just after seven-thirty, he was hurrying towards the hired car pick-up point when his phone rang. He didn't recognise the number but, given the circumstances, he answered it immediately. 'Martin Redpath.'

'Martin, this is Detective Sergeant Mel Cooper. We met back in February when I was investigating Carla McKinlay's disappearance.'

'Oh. Hi.' She had caught him by surprise. 'Em... can this wait? I'm in a bit of a hurry just now.'

'It can't wait, no. This is extremely important. I'm trying to contact Ross but he's not answering his mobile. Do you know where he is?'

'Hang on a few seconds, it's very busy where I am.' Martin glanced around, and moved over to stand next to a vacant retail unit. He took a breath before speaking. 'A few of us have tried to call him last night and this morning, and we can't raise him either.'

Before Mel could respond, there was a loud *ping* followed by airport announcement. Martin flinched.

'Martin. Where are you just now?'

He didn't see the point in lying. 'Gatwick.'

'Ohh-kaaay. And Ross isn't there with you, I take it.'

'No. He's not.' Martin hesitated. But only momentarily, he had a brain in his head. 'I left him yesterday afternoon in a place called Christchurch. It's in Dorset. But he'll probably have moved on by now.'

'Where to?'

'A village in the New Forest. Brockenhurst.'

Mel had always been good at adding single-digit numbers together. 'Right, Martin. Thanks. But now I want you to listen to me. And listen to me carefully.'

By the end of the call, he'd told her what she needed to know including that Ross was driving Martin's car, not his own. She'd shared some information in return but she didn't say just how seriously she was taking the threat from their suspect. Martin didn't need to know that, and she told him in no uncertain terms to back off. Leave the police to deal with it.

But unfortunately, neither Mel nor Martin were in possession of one key fact. The address in Brockenhurst that Ross was aiming for. Although Martin had looked at Leona's list from time to time, it was his friend who referred to it most. As a result, he'd only registered the name of the village, not the street. This was a problem for him and the police officer, but neither considered it to be insurmountable. Only time would tell if their optimism was misplaced.

But as far as her closing instructions to him were concerned, he ignored those completely.

He carried on towards the hired car pick-up point. He suspected that the policewoman hadn't told him the whole story, and his gut feeling was his friend was possibly in a lot of trouble.

Martin was no hero but, geographically, he was closer to Ross than anyone else. Just like Jarek, he had no choice.

79

Jarek was in a real quandary, no question about that.

Should he wait it out, or try to find an alternative route? A second traffic policeman had estimated the road would likely reopen between eight and eight fifteen. Jarek was forced to gamble between possibly reaching Brockenhurst by eight-thirty if he stayed put, or as much as an hour and a half later if he opted to drive there by an alternative route. The policeman had explained, in a tone as dreary as the weather, that although it was only a journey of about 15 miles, no matter which route he chose, they were all likely to be jam-packed. Including those vehicles who had already abandoned the queue, all traffic coming into the New Forest from the north was being diverted down the same roads. A couple of them were single track in places.

The police had also set up traffic controls on these minor roads to try to avoid log jams at tight bends and at narrow bridges because some of the vehicles involved would be light commercial, coachloads of tourists, and even caravans motoring south to catch the Lymington ferry to the Isle of Wight.

Jarek's initial reaction to all of this had been: 'What a farce!' But, on reflection, he recognised that in mountainous regions in particular, if a road was closed the diversion could be 70, 80 or upwards of 100 miles. Of course, the effect on him was magnified several-fold because of why he needed to reach the next village *on this damn road*. And that was what pushed him into a decision, whether it turned out to be the correct one or not. He wasn't driving to Brockenhurst to visit an elderly relative, or to deliver furniture to newlyweds. If either of those were the purpose of his journey, he could sit where he was all day. Instead, he was going there to execute Elisabetta Massaro and, possibly, Ross McKinlay. So he set a deadline of eight-fifteen and if the traffic hadn't moved by then, he would cut his losses and find a different route.

* * *

Mel called Andrew over to her desk. 'I've just been speaking to Martin Redpath. I don't know the details yet, but apparently some guy called Oliver made contact with Ross and gave him a list of addresses up and down the UK where, *get this*, Carla McKinlay might be living. This Oliver person is apparently the head of some vigilante group who are hunting down women they suspect are defrauding men, in the same way Carla ripped off Ross. These women are supposedly part of an international gang. And it's not just women. The gang has men scamming their partners too. So, believe it or not, for the past few weeks Ross and Martin have been traipsing all over England checking out these addresses. Thirty-seven of them, by all accounts. And although principally, they're looking for Carla, they take photos of the women who live at these addresses, and send them to Oliver.'

Andrew looked like he'd been slapped with a wet haddock but he recovered quickly. 'And what does this guy do with them?'

'If they spot anyone they recognise, he reports it to the police.'

'Ah. The woman in Wilmslow?'

'Precisely. Turns out she was probably guilty after all.'

'And the Cheshire cops released her.'

'Ach, they were flying a kite. They couldn't prove anything so I'm not surprised they let her go. Anyway, here's the thing. Our two bold heroes had been to that woman's address at some point before she was questioned, so they sent pictures to Oliver and he reported her. Now, just in case it changes what I'm thinking, what's the story with that white van?'

'You won't be surprised to hear the Merc and the plate don't match. It's from a Fiat Punto that was scrapped.' Andrew looked down at his notes. 'So… according to ANPR, there were no sightings of the Merc, *anywhere*, until it popped up in a place called Harmondsworth on Saturday night at 20:56.' By ANPR, he was referring to Automatic Number Plate Recognition, a UK-wide camera-based system capable of reading number plates. Without human intervention, it is able to verify the character sequences as being those from a valid vehicle license plate.

Mel wore a blank expression. 'And Harmondsworth is…?'

'About two miles from Heathrow.'

She whistled. 'Go on, then. Where's it been since it left Heathrow?'

'It was driven more or less directly to Hutchinson's house in Wilmslow and reached there Saturday morning at 08:14. Stationary at a service station just north of Birmingham, for three hours between half three and half six. Maybe he stopped for a sleep, I don't know. Left Wilmslow at 11:06, stopped near Ross's house 19:28. Left there 20:01, and its last noted position was on the A8 at Gogarburn at 20:25.'

'What the fuck would he be doing at Gogarburn?'

'The airport?'

It wasn't like Mel to be so dim but she took it on the chin and moved on. 'So it's possible he dumped the van at the airport and took a flight somewhere. Well, maybe I know where.' She told him more about her conversation with Martin, about their trips to various English counties, and ending up with Martin leaving Ross in Christchurch to catch a flight from Gatwick, only to be stuck there overnight.

'So,' said Mel, 'tell me if this stacks up. Our man picks up a van near Heathrow. He has an Eastern European accent so it's reasonable to assume he's flown in from that part of the world. Could be he's part of this gang. He drives to Wilmslow overnight. Question: has he been sent just to assassinate Hutchinson? We know he's not gone there to see the wife because she's done a runner.' She paused while she worked through her hypothesis in her own head. 'No. *We* know Ross and Martin have been there, but the fact that he then drives to Edinburgh tells me *he* knows that too. But how? How does he know?'

'When all Ross's money was taken, we agreed this was obviously an organised criminal network. So it strikes me if they're that organised, they would have files on the people they've scammed.'

'Including photos.'

'Indeed. And if they have photos, it could be our suspect shows a photo of Ross to Hutchinson, who tells him yes, this chap's been here recently.'

Mel tapped a fingernail on her desk. 'So he bumps off Hutchinson to tie off that line, and then drives up here to, what, kill Ross too?'

'Yes. The gang might not know that Ross is working through this list Oliver gave him. They might *even* not know about Oliver. But they do know Ross *somehow* tracked down Mrs Hutchinson, so our suspect comes to Edinburgh. But when he checks out Ross's house, nobody's home.'

'Okay, fair enough. But what sends him off to the airport? Barry said they didn't tell him where Ross was. They couldn't, because they didn't know themselves. But I wonder what form of words they *actually* used. Maybe it was enough to make him realise he *knew* where Ross had gone.' She snapped her fingers, jumped up out of her chair and began pacing the floor. 'Ahah! That's it! Because they know where Carla is. She's still in the UK, still part of the gang, working on another con. And where would that be, Detective Constable Young?'

'Brockenhurst?'

'Gets my vote. Right, I'll phone Barry again. Joe too, I think. Find out exactly what they said to the suspect. Then I'll leave another message for Ross. You check out flights from Edinburgh to the deep south last night, and then let's see if the van's still at the airport.'

80

Ross was parked outside number one, The Paddocks: a beautifully laid out development on the western outskirts of Brockenhurst. There were only five large detached houses, all striking in appearance but completely different in design. They all had extensive grounds, double and even triple garages, and long lines of fencing or hedging to separate them. He'd picked a suitable spot that gave him a clear view of number two. Raindrops notwithstanding.

There were two cars on the driveway, a fairly new powder-blue two-seater Saab convertible and one of those cute retro Fiat 500s.

He'd tuned the car radio into a local station, although he detested these commercial broadcasters with a passion. Half a dozen adverts with cringe-worthy jingles every five minutes, and a DJ who just had to be on class-A drugs given how bloody chirpy he was at that time in the morning. Ross had just heard the eight o'clock news bulletin, where the newscaster informed listeners that a road leading north out of Brockenhurst was closed due to an accident, which had caused all the other roads to be much busier than normal. Although Ross registered some of the details he didn't imagine it would affect him. When he left here, his next destination would be Littlehampton in Sussex. He would be driving south so the traffic issues shouldn't affect him. But his mood this morning hadn't lifted. Littlehampton was a sizeable *if*, rather than a *when*.

Following the news, a weather forecaster warned his audience there would be heavy and sustained rainfall over the region until well into the evening.

'Oh, deep joy.' Ross took another glance at the Bentleys' house, where there was still no sign of life. He licked his thumb, and flicked over to the next page in his newspaper.

81

Andrew was fairly certain their suspect hadn't flown south from Edinburgh for one good reason. The man was carrying a gun. If he *had* come into the country via Heathrow, he'd obviously sourced the weapon from somewhere, so he would probably be able to lay his hands on another one. But that would mean dumping the gun he had, and something told Andrew that would be anathema to your average assassin. Plus, he'd need to source a replacement, which would take up precious time.

But Andrew worked the airline possibility anyway, he had a well-deserved reputation for being thorough. He studied flight timetables from the capital to Heathrow, Gatwick, London City, Bristol and Southampton. He dismissed Stansted and Exeter as being too far from the New Forest. Then he worked out timings based on the suspect being logged near the airport at eight-twenty-five. He allowed fifteen minutes to park and walk into the terminal, a few more to buy a ticket, and the standard thirty minutes for the gate to close in advance of take-off. He calculated their man could only have caught a flight that had left Edinburgh after nine-fifteen at the earliest.

The timetables told him there had only been one flight to any of those airports after that time, the 21:40 to Southampton. But he called the airport to check there had been no late departures. The woman he spoke to sounded rather proud to report that all their flights had left on time.

Next, he called the airline that flew to Southampton and asked for the passenger manifesto. He explained he was looking for male passengers with Eastern European sounding names. It hadn't been a busy flight so the operator read out the full list, including ones that were most definitely Scottish. None of them caused Andrew to perk up.

Andrew told Mel this wasn't conclusive proof but it was enough to discount the possibility for the moment. She agreed, and he moved on to the car rental companies.

* * *

Meanwhile, Mel had spoken to Barry and then to Joe, who was able to recall what he'd said. *'I'll not be telling you where my neighbour's gone.'*

That was enough for Mel. *Gone* definitely inferred *travelled away from this locality*. ANPR had confirmed Martin's car had been south of the New Forest that morning so she was confident she had worked out a logical sequence of events. Ross has gone to Brockenhurst; he hopes to find Carla there; he will move on to the next address if he doesn't; the alleged assassin intends to stop Ross speaking to his missing wife; he knows where she is; and potentially, all three will coincide at the same place. And that may or may not be Brockenhurst.

The issue that concerned Mel the most was not that this killer intended to stop Ross. It was *how*. However, she was absolutely certain it wouldn't involve finger-wagging.

So she called him again. 'Ross. DS Mel Cooper again. Listen, this is now critical. I've spoken to Martin this morning and I know where what you two have been up to over the past few weeks. I also know you're somewhere around Brockenhurst. So please, Ross, stop what you're doing. Get yourself to the nearest police station and call me back. Immediately!'

Andrew had his head down, and Mel could hear he was talking to the rental companies. She popped a Post-it on his screen that said, 'I'll call airport about van.'

She knew the car parks at Edinburgh Airport had installed ANPR systems, just one of the many defences airports had been forced to implement against possible terrorist attacks. So within minutes she had confirmed the van had entered the short-stay car park immediately in front of the terminal at 20:31 the previous evening, and the system showed it was still there. Somewhere. It made perfect sense to her that it would be in that particular car park, it was the closest one to domestic departures.

Her next call was to Border Policing Command at the airport. Could they send an officer to look for the van and report back to her? She explained the urgency, and a rather gruff-sounding officer said he was right on it. It took almost quarter of an hour but the man was true to his word. A white Mercedes van with that registration plate was parked in space B/4/11. Meaning Basement level, section 4, bay 11.

'We're standing right next to the vehicle, DS Cooper. What would you like us to do?'

Mel didn't hesitate although she did wonder momentarily how she would explain her actions at an inquest if her colleagues were blown to smithereens by a booby trap bomb. 'Break in and tell me what you find. I'll hold.'

A couple of minutes later. 'DS Cooper?'

'Yes.'

'Is your suspect the Marquis de Sade? Or that chappie in Fifty Shades?'

She laughed. 'No. But I get your drift. Does it contain any firearms? A handgun, most probably.'

'Not as far as I can see.'

A disappointment, but not entirely unexpected. 'Okay. Thanks for your help. Please make the van secure and have it towed somewhere safe. I'll send someone to look at it later.'

'Will do.' Then, half a second later, 'Jimmy, put that down for fuck's sake! You've nae idea where it's been.'

Mel cracked up and jotted herself a note to send a thank you email to the officer's boss.

She turned round to hear Andrew finishing a call, and tapped him on the shoulder before he started another one. She beamed at him. 'Good news. We've found the van.'

Andrew wasn't beaming, quite the opposite in fact. 'Well done. But I have some news too, and I'm afraid it's not as good as yours. I'm pretty sure our man hired a Volkswagen Passat from Executive Cars at 21:10 last night.'

'Tell me.'

'The customer's ID said he was one Andrzej Wyglenda. I'm not sure if I've pronounced that correctly but it doesn't matter because…'

'It's a false name.'

'I Googled it, just in case. Turns out Mr Wyglenda was quite a famous Polish motorcycle speedway rider in the nineteen-sixties. So, fair to say, it's not him.'

'Do Executive Cars use tracking devices like…' She stopped speaking as she interpreted her colleague's reaction. 'Ah. I guess not.'

'The top-of-the-range models do but the Passat he hired doesn't fall into that category.'

'ANPR?'

'Yes. He's been recorded all the way down the well-worn route between here and points south. M8, M73, blah blah blah.' Andrew already had a map displayed on his screen. He pointed at a blue section of road, a few miles northwest of Southampton.

Mel had been studying a similar map following her conversation with Martin so she knew exactly where it represented. She sighed. 'When?'

'Twelve minutes past six. This morning,' he added, somewhat unnecessarily.

She looked at her watch. 'It's half eight so he's already been in the New Forest for what, two and a quarter hours?'

Andrew figured that fitted neatly into the rhetorical question category but he nodded anyway. It was always a good idea to agree with Mel when she was right.

After a brief silence while they considered the implications for Ross, Mel used a swearword she didn't even like herself.

This morning, however, she felt she was entitled.

82

Jarek decided New Forest time ran more slowly than the rest of the world.

He stared out of the windscreen to prevent himself constantly monitoring the clock, and considered the key factor that had stopped him moving sooner: he was shattered. Since he'd disembarked the cruise ship on Friday morning, he'd been on the move the whole time. Flying the Atlantic is hardly a relaxing experience, especially with two stopovers plus the accompanying jet-lag. Someone had once told him it was worse travelling west to east, and he was beginning to believe it. Since leaving Heathrow, he'd driven the guts of a thousand miles in thirty-six hours, most of it overnight, and with less than five hours' sleep.

Without the option of extended periods of sleep to naturally counteract these negative influences, there was only one answer: drugs. So far he had ingested amphetamines, barbiturates, coffee, Red Bull. And coffee *and* Red Bull together. He detested fizzy energy drinks so he avoided them, and alcohol was a complete no-no, regrettably. But he did use cocaine, and had dipped sparingly into the small supply that Danijela had thoughtfully included as part of the equipment inventory provided with the Mercedes.

There was no doubt about it, he wasn't in the best of condition. But he didn't imagine he would need to be on top of his game to successfully complete his objectives for the day.

As the time dragged closer and closer to the policeman's estimate of eight-fifteen, the number of vehicles abandoning the queue increased. Jarek was mystified. He couldn't understand why they would concede defeat before the first deadline had passed. He wondered if perhaps they were returning home, or back to base because their travel plans had been ruined, or even to declare their day a washout.

He was jolted from his reverie by the steadily increasing rain, which made a drumming sound as its intensity cranked up another notch. It was time to consider his options because the instant the number fourteen on his digital clock upgraded to the next digit, he too was heading back to Lyndhurst. Gridlock or not. He'd been studying his roadmap and had plugged various route permutations into satnav to calculate distances and times. But if the policeman was correct about all the roads being nose-to-tail, it made no difference which route he took. There were no shortcuts, by car at any rate.

As he was mentally testing out a potential viable alternative, a police car appeared over a rise about half a mile ahead. He watched as it stopped briefly at each vehicle in turn, and as soon as it had moved on, that vehicle's tail-lights brightened. He could see the faint mist of hot exhaust fumes rising towards the trees as the drivers began manoeuvring their vehicles to turn around.

Jarek squeezed back towards the car behind to give himself space to do the same, totally ignoring the angry *paaarp* of the driver's horn.

* * *

The man from Eastern Europe wasn't the only person stuck in a traffic jam that morning but at least he wasn't using foul language to vent his frustration at a strip of tarmacadam. Martin had considered three different routes to take him from Gatwick to Brockenhurst, and had chosen the motorway option. His car didn't have satnav but it was a fairly straight run so he wouldn't need it. This route was longer than the others but he reasoned he would be able to drive faster on the motorways. He would reach his destination, and his friend, earlier.

Unfortunately, he miscalculated badly. He totally underestimated how busy the M25 would be at that time on a Monday morning. In Martin's view it was: 'No more than a fucking car park!'

He'd left voicemails for Ross three times in the early stages of his journey but he saw no merit in leaving more. He knew Barry, Gail and Mel had left messages too. They were long past overkill.

He also decided against calling his daughters to explain his change of plan. *'What they don't know, can't hurt them,'* was the excuse he used to justify his action, or inaction. As he saw it, if he had caught his flight as planned, he wouldn't have arrived home until almost ten o'clock so he still had some time to play with.

If the traffic didn't thin out soon, Martin could see it being after ten before he would reach Brockenhurst. Then he would have to track Ross down before the man found himself in trouble, in whatever form that might be. His impression of DS Cooper was that she was a fairly sensible woman, but some of the things she had said to him, or more likely the way she'd said them, suggested there was something serious to worry about. But as he didn't know what that was, he pushed it from his mind.

Of more immediate concern was how he would locate Ross in Brockenhurst without an address. But then he thought, it's only a village. I'll just drive around till I find him.

Soon after, he reached the point where the M25 turned towards the north. Martin followed signs west for the M3, which he could already see was significantly quieter.

Jesus! At last. Now I can pace on a bit.

* * *

'About bloody time!' said Ross, as electric light from inside the house lit up the frosted glass panel in the front door of number two.

People actually live here. And, by the way, who the hell takes until after half eight to come downstairs on a school day? A few seconds later, someone opened the blinds behind an enormous bay window to the left, but due to a combination of the rain outside and the lack of lighting inside the room, he couldn't see who it was.

Yet again, he scanned all the windows for any other signs of life but there were none. He came to the conclusion that this couple spent most of their time in rooms at the back of the house. For the next half an hour the only other indication the house was occupied came in the form of a small tortoiseshell cat that appeared in the bay window. It looked out as if to say, *'No danger I'm heading out in that weather,'* and promptly curled up on the window ledge and fell asleep.

Had it been a dry day, it was inevitable someone would eventually come outside. But in this rain it was entirely possible the inhabitants would stay indoors all day, as their cat clearly intended to. There was nothing else for it. At some point he'd have to seize the initiative and ring the doorbell, for no other reason than he was cold, uncomfortable and utterly cheesed off. In the ongoing battle of his conscience, *'I just want to go home'* was two sets to love up with a break in the third. He was seriously considering calling it quits. Another option was to just march up to the house and ask outright if someone who was once known as Carla McKinlay lived here, prove it one way or the other then bugger off back to Edinburgh. *Whoever answers the door will think I'm a nutcase. But hey ho, I'll never see them again so who gives a shit?*

But Ross hadn't ever possessed that level of bravado so he set himself a deadline of one hour: nine-thirty.

If nothing happened by then, he was going in. Just like the SAS, although they probably wouldn't ring the bell first.

83

On a whim, Mel tried to contact Martin. His phone rang out *then* diverted to voicemail so she knew he wasn't airborne. She checked the Gatwick and Edinburgh websites, and they both confirmed his flight had taken off. In truth, she would have been surprised if he'd simply jumped on the plane and left his best mate in the lurch. *Shit! Now we've got two people to worry about.*

Martin saw her call coming in but left his phone on the centre console. He would call her when he reached Brockenhurst.

He looked at the phone again, wondering if he should switch it off. He was well aware the police would be able to triangulate his position using GPS but he reckoned finding Ross was a far greater priority for them.

Aye, thought Martin. Ross and whatever else Mel isn't telling me about.

* * *

'DS Cooper, this is Sergeant Chris Hollingworth down in Hampshire. I'm returning your call.'

Mel and Andrew had come to the inescapable conclusion that the only way they could affect matters over 400 miles away from their jurisdiction was to liaise with the local force. So, they'd asked their Control Room to make contact with their colleagues in the south, and Chris Hollingworth's call to Mel was the direct result. Unless Ross phoned in, this might be their last throw of the dice.

Mel quickly outlined the sequence of events since her call with Manchester early that morning. She explained they had a truckload of evidence mounting against their suspect but stitching the facts together to substantiate a case against him wouldn't be easy. Unless they could catch him, of course.

They had descriptions and registration numbers both for the Passat and for Martin's Audi, their last reported locations and a sketchy description of the suspect from Barry and

Joe. They had a missing citizen somewhere in or around Brockenhurst, and another one en route, both of whom were observing strict radio silence. Intentionally or otherwise.

Chris Hollingworth wore a perpetually hangdog expression. He also played bass guitar in a local rock band. Those two things complemented each other perfectly. To Mel, he seemed polite and appeared to be listening intently to her tale.

'I'd like to help you, DS Cooper...' and Mel thought, here we go, he's trying to let me down gently. 'But we're dealing with a terribly serious RTC just north of Brockenhurst as we speak. And, unfortunately, it looks like we have two fatalities.'

'I'm really sorry to hear that.'

'It's a bad one, that's for sure. The upshot is, the main road through the New Forest will be closed for several hours, which is forcing all the traffic down the peripheral minor roads. And they're not designed to cope with it, that's for sure. This is not a heavily populated area but we're likely to have our version of gridlock for a while yet.'

Hollingworth paused for a second. 'But, it sounds as though this is a particularly dangerous man. Not the type of character I want running loose on my patch. My problem is, I have all hands on deck trying to deal with the repercussions of the RTC so how do I reallocate some resource to help you? My men can't move around the area much easier than anyone else at the moment, you see. But let me think about this for a few minutes and I promise I'll get back to you.'

Resigned, Mel was just about to end the call when a filament lit up. 'Wait a minute. Before you go, when did the RTC happen?'

'Oh-five-thirty. It was still dark.'

'Can you hang on please, while I look at the map?' She was thinking aloud. 'So, I'm looking at the route we believe our man took to Brockenhurst from the north, down the M27, south through Lyndhurst and then on to Brockenhurst on the A337. Is it the A337 that's closed?'

'It is. About a mile and half south of Lyndhurst. The road's as straight as a die. We've no idea how two vehicles managed to collide head on.' Chris described the alternative routes through the area, explained the locations of the few

ANPR cameras, where traffic controls had been set up and, therefore, where he had officers stationed.

Mel scratched at her forehead. 'So, I'm guessing that for some time after the RTC, vehicles would still have been driving south out of Lyndhurst and joining the line of traffic leading up to where it happened?'

'That's correct. At first, we didn't understand how serious the situation was and, I'm afraid to say, our comms weren't brilliant in the first hour or so.'

She thought it was big of him to admit that. She sensed she was dealing with an extremely tired man but she continued to probe. 'But you would have stopped people joining the queue at some point. Put diversions in place.'

'Yes. At about six-forty-five my officers started advising drivers the road was temporarily closed. At that time, we didn't appreciate the severity of the accident.'

'And what's the status of that line of traffic now?'

'Well, now we know the A337 will be closed for several hours, we're instructing all the drivers to turn round and find alternative routes. We're clearing the road back to the Lyndhurst village boundary.'

Mel paused while she reviewed what Chris had said. She glanced at Andrew, who nodded. He could see where she was going. 'Okay, we know our suspect was still on the M27 heading south at 06:12. Traffic was still moving south on the Brockenhurst road until 06:45, when you stopped any more vehicles from joining the queue. Based on those timings, Chris, and assuming he didn't stop anywhere, could he have made it through Lyndhurst before you set up the diversions?'

'Yes. Only just, but yes.'

Mel clenched her fist in a minor gesture of triumph. 'In that case, there's a good chance he's either *in* the line of traffic, *in* or around Lyndhurst, or driving down one of the minor roads, trying to reach Brockenhurst. In which case he's likely to hit one of your traffic controls, isn't he?' She looked at Andrew again, speaking to both him and Chris. 'Maybe we're in luck?'

'Well, let's not count chickens,' said Chris. 'But the one thing you do have in your favour is how long it will take to drive to Brockenhurst by an alternative route. Because, one thing's for sure, nobody's going anywhere fast in the forest this morning.' Mel detected a renewed level of energy coming down the line. 'Right, you sit tight, and I'll ask my officers in Lyndhurst to check if there's a Passat with that reg in the queue. If there isn't, we'll look at other options. I'll be back to you as soon as I have anything to report. Bye now.'

He must be there, she thought. He just *must* be.

She checked the time. 08:45.

84

Although it was impossible to tell, Jarek was absolutely raging. Almost half an hour after the police had explained to all the drivers the road would now be closed indefinitely, he was only just approaching the southern perimeter of Lyndhurst.

Jarek was seriously pissed off at the astonishingly anal approach the police had taken to reverse the flow of traffic. He could have turned his car round in seconds, and been ahead of several other vehicles before their drivers had smelled the coffee. But instead, the local plod had insisted the car at the head of the queue, almost a mile down the road, should be first back into Lyndhurst. Followed by the second vehicle and so on, like church pews emptying after an especially well-attended funeral. Any drivers who attempted to short-circuit this ridiculous parade-in-reverse found themselves in receipt of a serious bollocking from Hampshire's finest.

This additional enforced delay had helped him to crystallise an idea. Lyndhurst to Brockenhurst was less than four miles so he could easily walk the distance far more quickly than by following any of the diversions. But there was one problem. The rain wasn't letting up, and he was wearing summer clothes. He had a lightweight jacket in his bag but it would give him no protection against this weather. He'd be certain to arouse suspicion and that was the last thing he needed, especially as he would be carrying a loaded semi-automatic pistol.

The time was now fast approaching nine o'clock when, he assumed, the shops in Lyndhurst would open. He hoped one of those would be an outdoor clothing outlet or something similar.

He glanced up at the sky, hoping for a break in the weather. But, if anything, the rain was even heavier now.

* * *

It had just turned nine when Martin passed a junction for Basingstoke, which by his reckoning meant about 40 miles to Brockenhurst. He'd be there in an hour, more or less. He was pushing it as fast as he dared but didn't want to be pulled over. Stick or twist? Collect or gamble? The tortoise or the hare? Arrive late or not at all? He couldn't imagine a few here or there would prove costly but with every mile, negative thoughts were elbowing their way in.

He shook his head as if to chase them away but that didn't work so he turned the radio on. It was a local commercial station so he left it playing but he smiled as he recalled the various debates he'd had with Ross concerning the merits and demerits of local radio.

Unfortunately for Martin, even thinking about his friend allowed the stream of negativities back in again.

* * *

Sergeant Chris Hollingworth was back on the phone to Mel. 'My colleagues have cleared the traffic from the A337 so we've missed the chance to pick him up there. But the good news is one of our uniforms remembers him and the Passat from your description. Definite accent, Polish or Czech, somewhere from that area. Anyway, the even better news is, he stayed in the queue until we told everyone to turn round. Given what you've told me about him, I'm surprised about that, but I can only imagine he gambled on the road opening versus the extra hour and a bit along B-roads. It's lashing with rain down here, and it didn't look like he was dressed for the weather so he'll stand out a bit if he goes anywhere on foot. They're looking for him in Lyndhurst as we speak, and we're in contact with all our officers on the ground, especially at the traffic controls. So he can't go anywhere. As soon as we find him I'll be back in touch.'

85

On the stroke of nine, Jarek entered a camping and outdoor shop. He left ten minutes later fully kitted out with waterproof trousers and a cagoule, a medium-sized day-sack and a tourist map of the forest he'd picked up from a stack on the counter.

He stood in a bus shelter and studied the map. A green dotted line ran more or less parallel to the A337 all the way from Lyndhurst to Brockenhurst. According to the legend it was a cycle and walking path. According to the legend, green routes were classified as *Easy*, which made him certain he could cover the ground on foot in a good deal less than an hour. But then an enhancement to his original plan began to form in his mind, and he smiled as he saw exactly what he was thinking about, not 30 yards from where he was standing.

Five minutes later, a fitness instructor who lived two miles from the village came out of the Tesco Express across the road from the bus shelter. He was rearranging the items in his backpack so they would be comfortable against his body on the cycle run home. Later on that morning, while he was filling out an insurance claim form, he was trying to figure out how to answer question 4a. *Was the bicycle secured or left in a secure location e.g., garage or outbuilding?*

* * *

A few miles away from the New Forest, Martin's radio signal faded, crackled and hissed seconds then switched automatically to a different programme. He'd obviously just crossed a transmission boundary between two local stations. The cheery DJ he'd been listening to was replaced by a gentleman with an accent more akin to the West Country, was far more subdued, and who played much better music, closer to Martin's taste than the poppy crap favoured by his predecessor. Following a timeless rendition of 'Nobody Knows You When You're Down And Out' by Eric Clapton, the DJ faded out the music and brought in Penny with a traffic update.

'Welcome back, Penny. Sounds like you've something important to tell us.'

'Indeed I have, Jacob. The police have just advised the A337 south of Lyndhurst is likely to be closed until late in the afternoon to allow investigators to analyse the scene of the accident we reported earlier. So, the advice for people travelling through the New Forest is...' And Penny explained the various permutations for people trying to reach Brockenhurst and the south coast.

'Thanks Penny. We'll hear from you again just after the ten o'clock news. And now, here's one from the late, lamented David Bowie. It's 'Oh! You Pretty Things' from his critically acclaimed album *Hunky Dory*, released in 1971 and featuring classics like 'Life on Mars' and 'Changes'. And not forgetting the inimitable 'Kooks'.'

'Martin sang along at the top of his voice, trying to dispel the tension mounting in his gut. He looked for a place to pull over, wondering what effect this would have on his ETA. Five minutes later, he had worked out the best way to reach Brockenhurst and was still reasonably sure he would be there just before ten o'clock.

* * *

'DS Cooper, it's Chris Hollingworth again. I have some news for you but it's not particularly good.'

Not the opening line Mel had been hoping for. 'Go on, then.'

'I'm not sure why, but it looks like your man's ditched his car. We found it in Lyndhurst at about nine-forty. So, if he's heading for Brockenhurst, it could be he's hitched a ride, jumped on a bus, stolen a car. I don't know.'

'Fuck!'

'Quite.' Industrial language was commonplace in Hollingworth's profession but he'd never sworn in his life. He considered those who did to be somewhat lacking in vocabulary. But he didn't act all high and mighty about it. He understood perfectly that Mel must be highly frustrated, given how little influence she could have on events so far away from her own patch. 'And you still don't know where he's aiming for. Is that correct?'

'Yes. I know it's somewhere with a Brockenhurst address but not exactly where.' She gave him the last recorded location of the SQ5.

'Okay, we'll keep looking. I've managed to relocate two units back to the village. I'll keep in touch but if you hear any more information about where this guy or your missing citizens are, give me a shout.'

* * *

Even during the worst weather the UK slings at its inhabitants, people leave the warmth and shelter of their homes eventually. And so it proved with the house Ross was watching. A middle-aged woman wearing a long dark waxed raincoat opened the front door, peered out in disgust at the rain teeming down, and promptly turned away again. A man of similar vintage then appeared, took an equally dim view of the conditions then reached behind the door and produced a black and red golf umbrella. He shepherded the woman past the Saab to the little Fiat. Clearly she was grateful because she gave him a tight hug and a kiss on the cheek before squeezing into the car. He waited while she sorted herself out and as soon as she moved off, before she was even out of the driveway, he jogged back to the house, shook the umbrella on the steps and closed the door behind him.

To Ross, it had been a touching little cameo. Gallant husband saves wife's hair from being ruined by dreadful rain.

So that was that for Brockenhurst and the New Forest. Address number 22 ticked off, and Littlehampton next on the list. Yet he didn't move for several minutes, staring past the windscreen but not as far as the horizon. He was cold and his backside ached. He was desperate for exercise but bereft of energy. He was jaded, exhausted, drained. There was no spark, no desire to continue with this nonsense of a quest. Overall, he was just totally hacked off with the whole thing.

This bore no resemblance to how he had felt when they started searching, three weeks ago, up in the northeast of England. *Where was that again? Oh yes, Durham. The couple who drove their car straight into the garage and disappeared, leaving us outside like a right pair of lemons.* He started humming the Pink Panther tune. An old joke that normally would bring a smile to his face. But not today.

Ross had had enough. He checked the notes he'd made on the map, just to make sure. Littlehampton was *too* far away and, more importantly, too far away in the wrong direction. Driving there would take him another 80 miles away from home. What had Martin said? *'If things are beginning to get you down, cut it short. No need to wait till the end of the week, just head back up the road. Stop at a few nice places. You'll deserve a break by then.'*

For once, Ross didn't hesitate. *Martin's absolutely spot on. I do deserve a break. Littlehampton can wait for another day. Assuming there is another day. Probably not, given how I feel this morning.* He wondered if the traffic problems he'd heard about on the news were still ongoing. *I'll drive into the village and find out. Take it from there. Have a coffee and something hot to eat. Jeez, I'm bloody freezing!*

Before he set off, he thought he should fetch his phone from the back of the car. He'd intended to do that three or four times already that morning but the rain had never relented.

He pressed a button low down on the door and waited until the motorised tailgate was fully open. He was just about to nip out when a movement at the house caught his attention. He glanced over, curious. *Is the husband coming out again?*

Then he looked more carefully. There was a woman. A different woman, a younger woman, bending down at the open door. She laid something down on the step. *Rubbish? Recycling?* When she stood up, he stared. He stared at her so hard, with so much concentration, the back of his head tightened with the strain. A nerve above his right eyelid caused it to flicker erratically.

'I don't *fucking* believe it.'

86

Martin had just picked up a map of the village from the tourist information point. He spread it across the steering wheel.

The layout of the village resembled an oddly proportioned number seven, with a fat horizontal head running east to west, and a straggly tail more or less north to south. He was parked at the top of the tail near a railway line that ran north and south. He noticed most of the streets in this area were dead ends, terminating at the railway. Looking at the map, it seemed logical to search the area around the tail first, then zigzag east to west along the head, and finally work his way round the remaining little streets that stuck out at odd angles around the perimeter of the village.

He dropped the map on the passenger seat and took the next right turn. As he drove along the side of a park, he slowed down to let a cyclist cross the street ahead of him. *Daft bugger. Cycling in this weather.*

* * *

Ross was so stunned, that, for an instant, it seemed as if he were only able to move his eyes. His entire focus was concentrated on the doorway because, framed against the pale wood, was Carla.

She had changed her hair. It was shorter, lighter, almost blonde. But the woman was most definitely his missing wife. She squinted briefly at the SQ5 then turned, walked through the open door and pulled it shut behind her.

Ross hardly seemed to move a muscle but in a moment he was at the front door, his right hand leaning on the doorjamb and his left index finger hammering at the little white button of the doorbell.

The door opened. Carla smiled at him but only with her mouth. Her other facial muscles didn't so much as twitch.

'Hello Ross. I've been expecting you. Come in.'

And with that, the woman who was known by several names: Carla Marinello, Carla McKinlay, Laura Bentley and Elisabetta Massaro stood aside while the man she had met, seduced, married, defrauded and deserted, all in less than two short years, walked past her and into the house.

* * *

It wasn't much after ten o'clock when Jarek bumped the bike off the end of the trail and rolled across a kids' play park into the village of Brockenhurst. He stopped and used Google Maps to locate The Paddocks. He was gratified to see it would be easy to find. It was less than half a mile away.

Setting off again, he glanced left before joining the road. Perhaps mindful of the teeming rain, a motorist slowed to let him cross in front. Jarek waved his thanks. Possibly a trifle incongruous given the circumstances, but it had been a natural reaction.

* * *

Ross didn't think he'd been inside a more striking house. The front door opened onto a large semi-circular foyer with a wide spiral staircase constructed from pale timber, glass and brushed steel. The floor was dark grey granite tiling with a striking black gloss bead. To the left was a double-width doorway. The right half of the pair of doors was only open about a foot but its partner had been pushed back far enough for him to see out the bay window and onto the driveway.

He walked through the space and found himself in a cavernous living room that stretched through to the back of the house. The tortoiseshell cat ghosted past his ankles and made itself scarce.

The centrepiece of the room was a white marble fireplace that looked as though it could comfortably accommodate the Fiat 500 that had been outside earlier. Three full-sized leather couches in acres of floor space brooded silently over a black stone hearth, and the walls displayed several pieces of highly dramatic art that looked original and expensive.

Ross turned to face Carla, who stood about one step further away than was normal for a social conversation. She kept her gaze below his eye level and picked at her nails. Had her knees been knocking, she couldn't have looked more uncomfortable.

Even in this enormous space, the tension was gut-twisting. Ross was trying to formulate a cohesive sentence that wasn't peppered with swear words, and he was struggling to find a civilised way to break the silence. He was saved the trouble by a voice that came from behind him. 'Who's this, Laura?'

Ross turned to find a man standing in a doorway that presumably led to the kitchen. His right hand rested on the door handle, and he held a yellow and white checked dish-towel in his left. It was the same man who had shielded the woman from the rain. Ross wondered now who that woman had been. He had made the assumption she was the wife of the house but if that were true, where did Carla fit into the threesome?

'Laura?'

Ross was surprised. The man had pronounced the first three letters of her name, L-a-u, with the same sound as L-o-u in the word *loud*, as opposed to the normal English sounding name, L-a-w. When Ross had seen the names Dennis and Laura Bentley he'd immediately assumed the couple were British. He wondered now if Carla had deliberately chosen an Italian name that read as if it were English.

Although Dennis was probably in his sixties, he was undoubtedly fit. His cream-coloured t-shirt showed a tight, muscled body in clear definition. Even at rest, his arms displayed tendons corded like climbing ropes. A flattened area across the bridge of his nose suggested he'd spent more than a few hours in a boxing ring at one time in his past.

Laura was still studying the floor so Ross spoke for her. 'Will you tell him, *Carla*, or will I?'

'Carla?' said Dennis. 'Who's Carla?' He walked over and stood in between them. Despite the height difference, he had no problems whatsoever in making direct eye contact with Ross. 'And more to the point, who the fuck are *you*, pal?' Ross could not have misinterpreted the threatening tone that underpinned the question.

But Carla was either unwilling or unable to talk so Ross spoke again, holding Dennis's stare as he explained: 'My name's Ross McKinlay. When I first met *your* wife, Laura,

just less than two years ago, her name was Carla Marinello.'
Surprised his statement didn't elicit a reaction, he ploughed
on. 'When she married *me* in July last year, she became Carla
McKinlay. But I haven't seen her since February, when she
disappeared ripping me off to the tune of £600,000.'

He stopped speaking for a moment to let the impact of
his words sink in. 'And, unless I'm very much mistaken, it's
likely she intends doing something similar to you.' He swung
an arm round, indicating his surroundings. 'Possibly more.
Who knows?'

Dennis looked like his heart had stopped. He kept his eyes
locked on Ross but he addressed his wife. 'I could be wrong,
but there's something about this guy that says he's telling the
truth, Laura.' He paused to look at her. 'Is he?'

Had this been a film or a TV drama, it's likely Carla would
have spoken imploringly and come out with something
beginning, 'Dennis, please, I can explain.' But to her credit
she just said, 'Now that you've found me, Ross, will you be
calling the police? Have me arrested?'

Now both men were looking at her, and her second
husband was aghast. 'Yes, Carla. Of course I will. But, just
in case you're wondering why I've turned up after all this
time…'

'Your family's jewellery,' she interrupted.

Ross was terrified to ask but Carla saved him the trouble. 'I
have it upstairs in the safe. I will bring it to you.'

She turned away and he moved to follow her but Dennis
stretched out his arm and grasped him by the wrist. His hold
appeared effortless but Ross feared bruising, at least. 'Just stay
there, pal. Trust me, she's going *nowhere*.' No one thought it
absurd he was still holding the dish-towel in his other hand.

Ross nodded, and the two men stood still like a surreal
depiction of a judo hold frozen in time. Then Dennis, clearly
certain Ross was staying put, released the taller man's arm.
After a few minutes they heard Carla's feet tapping lightly
down the staircase. She walked back into the room carrying
a small royal blue cloth bag, fastened by a cream-coloured
drawstring. She sat down on one of the couches, slipped the
knot and let the glittering contents slide gently out onto a
solid wooden coffee table.

'Jesus, Laura!' said Dennis. 'You stole those?'

She blinked up at him, sending a silent message of confirmation, acceptance and apology.

But Dennis was in no mood for handing out absolution. He leaned forward till he was right in her face. She flinched.

'Who the fuck *are* you, Laura. I mean, who are you *really*?' The raw menace in his voice was unmistakable.

But, despite how close Dennis was to her she wasn't looking at him, nor at Ross. Instead, her attention was concentrated past them, towards the back of the room. To the same doorway her husband had walked through a few minutes earlier.

Standing in that doorway was a man. He was dressed in mud-spattered waterproofs, and he had a small backpack slung over his left shoulder. Rainwater dripped silently from his clothing onto the carpet. His canvas shoes were sodden and filthy. In his right hand, he was carrying a handgun that Ross and Dennis noticed long before they registered the state of his attire.

The gun was pointing unwaveringly at their little group.

'Actually,' said the man, 'her real name is Elisabetta Massaro.'

Jarek Zelenka pointed at the little pile of jewellery. 'And I'll take those. If you don't mind.' He smiled benignly, but none of the other three did the same.

87

Martin would never have described himself as logical. That was Ross's domain. But his decision to pick the lower hanging fruit paid off: big time. While two patrols dispatched by Chris Hollingworth were painstakingly checking out every nook and cranny in the main body of the village, he found his car in the fourth cul-de-sac he tried.

As he drove up behind it he muttered out loud, 'Ross, you muppet, you've left the boot open. *And* it's pissing down.' But there was no sign of his friend, so Martin supposed he was inside one of the houses. The car was parked directly outside number one, and they wouldn't normally observe a house from that close. Number two was just ahead but all the others were too far round a curve in the street to be the obvious target. It had to be the second house.

Martin lifted a pale blue windcheater from the back seat. He shrugged it on as he trotted over to his car and pressed the button to close the tailgate. As he walked along the passenger side he noticed three things in quick succession that stopped him in his tracks. First, he could see the ignition key was lying on the centre console. Why would Ross do that *and* leave the boot open? Second, there was a mud-caked mountain bike lying on the driveway. The crazy angle of the handlebars and the front wheel suggested it had been dumped. So who goes out on a bike in this weather then abandons it outside? And third, a gate that led round the side of the house was swinging in the wind. Now, that on its own wouldn't have caused a casual observer any concern but Martin's warning systems were flashing red. 'Something funny going on here,' he said out loud as he walked past the bike. Then, silently, *I think I'll call Mel.* But he was stopped short even before he could reach for his phone.

He had some experience so he recognised the sound of gunfire. So when he heard a woman's scream, followed by two flat cracks of a firearm being discharged and finally a third shot, he had conclusive proof his friend was inside.

He dropped to one knee and put the flat of his hand on the ground for balance. Martin wasn't a coward but his sense of self-preservation meant he resisted the temptation to charge straight in. He took a few seconds to think then staying low, he crabbed over to the front door, which had been left slightly ajar. Had this been television, the hero would have pushed it open and walked in without the slightest hesitation. Martin stopped to listen but there were no further sounds to give him any clue what was happening inside.

The door opened on the side away from the bay window, which he presumed was the living room. *Will it squeak when I open it?* The door looked heavy, the house was fairly new and clearly expensive, so he guessed it wouldn't. He steeled himself, took a breath, and gently nudged the door. It swung open silently so he continued pushing. There was no reaction from inside.

On hands and knees, Martin had no alternative but to risk a look. He willed himself on, reasoning that if something bad was about to happen to him it would happen instantly and he would know precious little about it. He stretched forward to peer round the edge of the door, using one eye, his nose practically touching the cool, smooth wood.

Ross was sitting on the floor of the living room, his back against a wall between a gigantic television and a fireplace, and directly in Martin's line of sight. His legs were sticking straight out in front of him, heels on the floor a couple of feet apart. His left trouser leg, furthest away from Martin, was soaked in blood at the knee.

Martin looked further into the room. On the carpet, partly obscured by a leather couch, lay a woman. She had short blonde hair and was lying on her side, one arm flung out at an unnatural angle. She wasn't moving a muscle. Although she was facing away from the door he had no doubt it was Carla.

He moved a little further into the space then froze when his friend spoke. Ross said two words to Martin, but without looking in his direction. 'Carrot cock!' He had spoken quickly and quietly, but in a commanding tone. Ross had never called his friend by that nickname. That had been Liz's personal piss-take. Martin stayed frozen, his eyes glued on Ross.

Then a voice came from behind the right hand door. 'What? What did you say?' The man spoke with a Slovakian accent. Ross shook his head two or three times as if he were trying to avoid listening to the question. The action produced a few more tears. His right hand was tucked down by the side of his thigh, flat on the floor and tight against his trouser leg. He tapped his index finger on the carpet, twice in rapid succession to attract Martin's attention. He followed that up with his palm directed at Martin, his fingers tightly together. A definite *don't move* gesture.

Martin nodded and stayed precisely where he was. He heard a groan from the man behind the door. Ross changed the angle of his hand into the *stay down* signal, then pointed behind the door and simulated the shape of a gun. He rolled his head lazily in Martin's direction and breathed in sharply through his teeth as if the movement had caused him great pain. He caught his friend's eye, locked on for just enough time for Martin to nod straight back at him then continued with the head roll until he was looking behind the door again. It was obvious to Martin *who* this man was, but he didn't understand *why* he seemed to be stuck in one place, especially as he was in possession of a gun.

Now Ross had his hand curved, making tiny waves from right to left, to indicate Martin was free to cross to the other side of the foyer. Martin crawled gingerly across the tiled floor till he was kneeling by the wall to the right of the door. Jarek was on the other side of that wall, no more than a couple of feet away. Martin was now able to squint through the gap at the hinges, and could make out a pair of muddy waterproof trousers. He thought it curious that the gunman's seated position was identical to Ross's. The change of angle meant Martin could now see Carla's face. Her eyes were closed, she still hadn't moved and she appeared not to be breathing. He knew she was dead.

But the change in angle also meant Ross's thigh was blocking Martin's view of his signalling hand. Martin wasn't sure what he should do next but if he was going to rush the aggressor, he had to ready himself. He was rising to a standing position when Ross barked out the single syllable word: 'Hud.' He used precisely the same tone as a few moments earlier.

Through the door Martin heard the man asking, 'What did you say? What is hud?' Martin immediately settled back down, adopting a position similar to a sprinter on the starting blocks.

'What?' said Ross, 'I don't fucking know, do I? I don't know anything I'm saying right now. You killed two people right in front of me and you shot me in the kneecap, you bastard!'

But Ross knew exactly what he'd said. *Hud* is a Scottish slang word. It means *hold*. In the context of Martin beginning to move, it was short for *hold on* or *wait there*, and his compatriot understood perfectly. Martin waited for the next instruction.

After what seemed like several minutes' silence, Jarek spoke. 'We need each other, you and I.'

Ross's face was soaked with perspiration, but the bloodstain around his left knee didn't appear to be spreading. 'How do you figure that?'

'Because, if I do not survive this then neither will you.' Martin didn't understand, but he was about to be enlightened. Jarek jabbed a finger at the prostrate figure of a man slumped against the legs of the coffee table. Martin risked peering further round the door, and it was all he could do not to gasp. The bullet that had killed Dennis at point-blank range had entered through his right eye and blasted away a piece of his skull the size of an apple.

'He did this.' Jarek pointed at his stomach. The handle of a medium-sized chef's knife jutted out of his abdomen, just below his waistline. Only an inch of blade was still visible but, strangely, there wasn't as much blood as one might have imagined. The yellow and white checked dishtowel lay on the floor a few feet away. A small wooden spoon nestled within its folds. 'I assume he missed my vital organs and so, I have been fortunate. But that may not last. It is probably safer to leave the knife where it is than to remove it.' He paused while he gathered himself. 'You must take me to your car and drive me to people who can help me. I would be surprised if the police do not arrive soon, and I do not want to be here when they do.'

'And what if I refuse?'

'Then as soon as I hear a police car or any other person approaching the house, I will shoot you. Or if I think I will lose consciousness, or if you try to escape. For you, there is only one outcome. Unless you help me.'

413

'And what if I do help you away from here, where would we go?'

'To London. I have friends there, and once we are on our way I will make a call.'

'Why don't you just call now?'

Jarek smiled at Ross, but he didn't put much enthusiasm into it. 'My employer can be a ruthless man. So, although I am reasonably sure he will help, if he thinks I will not survive or he cannot provide assistance in time, it is possible he will abandon me to my fate. Or worse.'

'How can you be sure of that?'

'Trust me. I am sure.'

Martin was still on high alert but having listened to the exchange, he felt much more confident in his own position. He was fit, healthy and awash with adrenalin. Plus, he had the advantage of total surprise. He could only foresee one reason why he wouldn't be able to take out the other man, who after all was badly wounded, and that was the fact he had the gun. That balanced things out. However, if he were to be believed, he didn't intend to use it unless he absolutely had to. So they had a temporary stalemate, which would give Ross time to think and Martin time to act. But Ross was speaking again, and his voice was shaking.

'This… this arrangement of yours. There's just one problem as far as I can see.'

'And what is that?'

'You've explained very clearly how dispensable I am to you. So what's to stop you killing me once I take you to your friends?'

Jarek shrugged. 'Absolutely nothing. But despite what you have seen today, and what you probably imagine, I *am* an honourable man. If you help me to reach a place of safety, then I guarantee no harm will come to you.'

Ross seemed to be weighing things up. 'Unfortunately, I think you're forgetting something.' Jarek inclined his head. 'My knee. I think it's shattered. I'm not sure I can move, far less walk.'

'The bleeding has stopped. You are not in any danger. Your injury may be very painful but you will survive. But this is not a subject for discussion. You do not have options.'

He paused to point out of the window. 'Your car is an automatic?'

'Yes.'

'In which case you only need one leg to drive it, and your right leg is unharmed. But you are running out of time, Ross McKinlay. If you do not help me, my situation will become hopeless, quite soon I expect. And then...'

Ross held up his hand in an *okay, I get it*, gesture, but he aimed it directly at Martin. Then, just before he dropped his hand away, he changed the signal to a single finger. His index finger, and only for an instant. Martin nodded and returned the same signal. He was to prepare to make his move.

Ross looked around, pulled a carved wooden box over from the fireside and, keeping his wounded leg straight, he levered himself up to sit on the box. He paused there for a break. The exertion had caused another rush of perspiration to his forehead. He swept the back of his wrist across his face. A decorative upright chair with a high back stood next to the fireplace. He dragged it until it was in front of him, spun it round and, using it like a Zimmer, he hauled himself up onto his right leg. By leaning over to that side, he was able to keep his left leg from touching the ground. He paused for longer this time until Jarek barked at him. 'Stop wasting time!'

As he hopped and dragged himself towards Jarek he began to move out of Martin's eye line. Just before the right hand door came between them Ross jerked his head in one last signal: *Get up, now!*

Hidden behind the door, Martin rose into a near vertical stance primed to move at minimum notice. Martin squinted through the gap and saw Jarek use the gun to wave Ross away from the chair.

His friend had no choice but to put some weight on his injured leg. Ross cried out and staggered badly before regaining his balance. Slowly, carefully, Jarek used the seat of the chair then the back to drag himself upright. Although he was virtually incapacitated and unstable on his feet his right arm was rock solid, and he kept the gun pointing directly at the side of Ross's head.

'And now,' said Jarek. 'We go.' He left Ross to support himself using the back of the nearest couch.

Martin watched as the two men crossed the room like walking wounded from a hard-fought medieval battle, shuffling towards the open door with Ross on the far side of Jarek. When Martin judged Jarek was directly behind the door, he launched his attack. He smashed the door open, barrelled in behind it and braced himself to follow through with all his weight, anticipating the heavy impact of him and the solid wooden door crashing into the gunman.

But the sequence of events Martin had foreseen didn't materialise. The door swung wide open, encountering no resistance until it bounced crazily back off its hinges, before coming to a shuddering halt a short distance from the wall.

Leaving Martin off balance and staring at the business end of a semi-automatic pistol. It was pointing directly and unwaveringly at his forehead.

88

'DS Cooper? Chris Hollingworth. I have some news for you.'

Mel's pulse quickened immediately as a bucketful of adrenalin hit her gut. 'What's happened?'

'We received a call from a gentleman in Brockenhurst about twenty minutes ago, saying he'd heard what sounded like gunshots coming from a nearby house.'

'Just a single call?'

'Yes. But he knows guns so we're concerned enough that my Inspector has two ARVs on their way to the location as we speak.' By ARV, he meant Armed Response Vehicle. 'I don't know for sure yet, of course, but it seems likely the people you're looking for are involved...' Mel was itching to ask why, but she remained the patron saint of the bitten tongue. 'Because the caller told us there's a grey Audi SQ5 parked just down the street. The registration matches the number you gave me earlier.'

'How soon before your ARVs reach the house?'

'ETA eight minutes. I'll keep you posted.'

* * *

'I don't know who you are,' said Jarek, jabbing his gun at Martin's face. 'But step back.'

Martin was petrified. The concept of not complying didn't enter his head. As he tottered back a couple of short paces, he glanced over to where Ross was lying in a crumpled heap on the floor. Jarek had crashed the butt of the gun into the side of Ross's face a split second before Martin launched his abortive attack.

Jarek jabbed the gun again, and Martin moved further back till he was standing on the tiled floor of the foyer. His full attention was back on the gunman. Jarek still had one hand on the back of the chair as he stood, not quite so steady as before and bending forward slightly to avoid straining his wounded stomach. He had no colour in his face.

'But how…?' said Martin, too confused to finish his question.

'Next time you attempt an ambush, I suggest you wear darker clothing. I saw you through the gap, just before you tried to hit me with the door.'

Martin gasped. He believed he'd been invisible. The solid wooden door had given him what now transpired to be a false sense of security.

Jarek moved on. 'Now, who are you?'

'Martin. I'm… em… Ross's friend.'

'I see. Well, Martin…' Jarek winced as a series of pain tremors coursed through his lower abdomen. After a lengthy pause he was able to continue, albeit more shakily. 'He was just about to drive me to London but you are clearly a more suitable option.'

Martin was still unbearably tense but less frightened. Jarek had promised earlier that no harm would come to Ross if he drove him to safety. So Martin decided that taking take this exceptionally dangerous man away from here could only be a good thing.

'Okay. What do you want me to do?' He made to move forward but stopped abruptly when Jarek jerked the gun at him again. Martin raised his hands. 'I thought you wanted me to help you.'

'I do. But there is one item that I must take care of before we leave.' He offered Martin a bleak smile. 'Unfortunately, I cannot leave your friend free to contact the authorities.' And without stopping to elaborate, he swung the pistol round to aim at Ross.

'Nnohhhh!' Martin screamed, horror-struck.

The noise he was making almost masked an accompanying yell from behind Jarek as Ross charged across the room, swinging his right arm round in a wild haymaker. The gun looped out of Jarek's grip as Ross slammed bodily into him and the chair, which was ripped from Jarek's grasp and crashed to the floor beneath his falling body and the onslaught of Ross piling in with all his weight.

Martin threw himself at the floor after the gun, which had skittered across the tiled surface.

Ross rose to his knees and hooked his arm back to drive his fist at the fallen man's head. But he stopped mid-strike, and let his arm sink gradually to his side, relaxing his fist at the same time.

'Fuck's sake, Ross!' bellowed Martin. He was scrabbling to gain a solid grip on the gun against the granite floor. 'Fuckin' smack him!'

Ross sat back on his heels. He didn't speak. He just pointed at the fallen man's body. The knife embedded in Jarek's stomach was caught between the spindles of the chair back. The fall had ripped the blade halfway out of his body and twisted it at the same time. Blood was gushing out of the wound but, as the two men watched, horrified, it slowed to a gentle glug as Jarek's major arteries emptied and his heart fluttered to a stop.

The man from Ostrava gave out one final soft sigh then lay perfectly still.

Martin climbed slowly to his feet and walked over to his friend, giving the dead man a wide berth as if he still had the ability to do them some harm. Ross stayed where he was until Martin stretched out an arm and helped him up. Together, they stared at the body, the knife and the blood-sodden carpet.

Eventually, Martin looked down at Ross's trouser leg. 'Your kneecap. You said it was shattered.'

Ross shrugged. 'I lied. I think the bullet passed straight through my leg without hitting anything.' He looked down at his knee. 'Well, anything major at any rate. I think you'd call it a flesh wound.'

Martin took half a step to the side and gaped at him.

Ross screwed up his face. 'But it's still bloody sore.'

The two men laughed and, *pretentious pish* or not, they hugged like reunited twins who'd been separated at birth.

EPILOGUE

EPILOGUE

Edinburgh: Three Weeks Later

'Buon appetito.' Martin laid a bowl of macaroni soup at his place at the table. Three replies came back as he sat down and flipped his napkin onto his lap.

Ross took a tentative sip of the rich red liquid. 'Mmmm. Not bad, Martin.'

Gail laughed. 'Dad makes a mean pot of macaroni soup. But not much else.'

Ross carefully spooned two or three different types of pasta and a lump of potato from the bowl. As he made to eat it, a strand of spaghetti plopped back into the soup. He stared in dismay at several splashes of tomato sauce that decorated the front of his shirt.

'I knew I should have put the blue one on.' He dabbed at the marks with his napkin. 'Macaroni soup, eh? That's a new one on me.'

'It's an old family recipe,' said Martin. 'My Nana taught me how to make it. She was Italian.'

'Pity that's where the cooking lessons stopped,' said Beth. 'Are M&S providing the main course, Dad?'

'Naturally. And the dessert.'

When the fourth spoon had clinked onto its empty bowl, he stood up. 'Anyone for seconds?'

* * *

Two hours later, the table resembled the aftermath of a Viking banquet, minus the pillaging.

The conversation had been sailing along, as it usually did when the four of them got together. But now there was an awkward silence of ear-splitting proportions. Ross knew precisely what was coming and wondered who would blink first. The opening salvo came from an unlikely source.

'Uncle Ross?' Gail had been quiet for longer than the others.

Ross looked sideways at her. *Here we go.* He imagined the twins rehearsing their script.

'Have the Hampshire police found out who the dead man is yet?'

'Don't think so, pet. He was using false ID. Polish, I think.'

'And was he the guy at your house the night before?' asked Beth, right on cue.

'Can't have been anyone else, I don't imagine. Joe and Barry had a good look at him, so did the police in the New Forest. According to Mel the weight of forensic evidence against him is practically overwhelming. They're almost certain he shot this chap in Wilmslow a few weeks ago, so I suppose if it was the same gun they'd match the bullets or something. It looks like he was part of this criminal gang and poor Dennis was, or would have been, their latest victim.'

'Dad says you've been speaking to them about Carla's... em... remains.'

'I have, yes. At first, I thought about just walking away and leaving her to the authorities. But with Dennis gone, she doesn't have anyone else.' He paused for a second. 'The police have told me they'll keep in touch but nothing's likely to happen for a while because of her involvement with the gang.'

Martin was next. 'Speaking about Dennis, did you ever find out who that other woman was? The one who left the house earlier that morning?'

'Her name's Janet. She was his cleaner. Been with him for years and years. I've heard the poor woman is absolutely distraught.' They all fell silent till Ross spoke again. 'She told the police that Dennis was beginning to suspect there was something not quite right about Carla. Or Laura, as he knew her.'

'Really?'

'Apparently, yes. He confided in Janet but he said there was nothing concrete, just certain things didn't hang together. It doesn't sound like he was on the point of confronting her, or anything like that. But now I think about it, when I walked in the door and told my little tale he seemed to take my side straight away.'

'On that note, you've never said much about what happened in the house before I arrived.'

Ross regarded his friend with an expression that transmitted loud and clear: *And that's how I'd like it to stay, thank you very much.*

But Martin wouldn't be dissuaded. 'Did Dennis save your life, do you think?'

Ross was reluctant but he replied, 'Yes, he definitely did.' He tried to leave it there but was hit by three expectant looks. Spaniel puppies couldn't have done a better job. He sat up a little straighter, drank some water and retold the same story he'd given the police just over three weeks earlier.

When Jarek told Carla to hand over the jewellery, she walked towards him with a look of relief on her face, saying, 'I'm so glad you're here. I need to get away from these men.' But he hadn't been fooled and when she flung the jewels in his face, screamed and threw herself at him, he shot her. At a range of a few feet he couldn't miss. She died instantly. At the same moment, Dennis charged across the room in an attempt to bring Jarek down. He nearly succeeded. Jarek pulled the trigger once, failed to hit his target but didn't miss with his next shot. The impact of the bullet almost stopped Dennis in his tracks, but not quite. His momentum carried him into Jarek and he had enough left to jam the kitchen knife into the other man's abdomen. Dennis died a few seconds later, not knowing he'd inflicted grievous damage to his killer.

'Did you know Dennis had that knife?' asked Martin.

'I didn't, no. I can only think he'd been drying it and was just holding it in the folds of the towel, never imagining he would need to use it as a weapon.'

Gail's bottom lip was beginning to tremble so Ross reached out and gave her a cuddle. He spoke to Beth over her sister's head. 'Your dad and I are travelling down south to Dennis's funeral next week.'

'But how did *you* end up being shot?'

'I was just unlucky. The bullet that missed Dennis hit me.' He paused to look over at Martin. 'And who knows what would have happened if Batman here hadn't turned up in the nick of time.'

'Aye,' said Martin. 'To bail Robin out of trouble. Yet again.'

Prague: A Few Months Later

The little group of three were just finishing their second drink, nearly time for Miroslav to head for home. His female companions were going out on the town so he wanted to make absolutely sure business was all tied up before they went their separate ways.

Danijela excused herself, leaving the other two to talk alone.

'So,' said Miroslav. 'Ross McKinlay. You think you can become closer to him? Closer than before?'

'Absolutely. And, after everything that's happened, his guard will be down. So, yes, I've been working on him.' She puffed her chest out a little. 'I'm sure I can move our relationship on to the next level.'

'And his wife's money. It is accessible?'

'I've seen the paperwork. I know where he has it invested.'

Miroslav nodded, satisfied with her answers. All she had to do was return to Edinburgh and make it happen. It would take time but that extra million and a half was certainly worth targeting. And if she did a good job, in the future there would be other opportunities for her.

'Where does he think you are just now?'

'A girls' weekend at a spa hotel in Oxfordshire. And, we're taking in a show in London. *Wicked*.'

He smiled. 'Ironic. Will you enjoy it?'

'No. I saw it last year. I hated it.'

At that point, Danijela came back. She was happy the vibes were good. A few minutes later, the women left. They were heading back to Danijela's place to change and, Miroslav suspected, have a few more aperitifs before hitting the bars and clubs.

He sat for a moment, savouring the last mouthfuls of his beer. Tonight, he thought, I'll shave off this beard. See if anyone in the office spots the difference.

Before he left, he arranged the three empty glasses into a neat triangle in the centre of the table. He tutted as he saw the debris the woman had left. He leaned over, cupped his right

426

hand and swept the torn pieces of beermat into a tidy little pile next to the glasses.

What a strange habit, he mused, before making his own way to the door.

Edinburgh: A Few
Days Later

'Congratulations, Ross,' said Martin. 'That all went very smoothly, don't you think?'

'Yes. It's been a great day.'

The two men were sitting at a table towards the rear of the function suite. The main business of the day was over, and people were milling about. Talking, shaking hands, exchanging hugs and air-kisses. Ross was happy to be where he was, out of the limelight for a while.

He picked Alex out in the crowd. She was working her way towards him but was only making a few steps before being stopped by yet another well-wisher, anxious to congratulate her on her new status.

She was one big beaming smile, and Ross thought she looked radiant. She *brushes up rather well,* to use her own words.

Martin followed his line of sight, and gave Ross a nudge. 'You're sure about her now?'

Ross nodded. 'I wasn't absolutely certain till I heard she'd visited the girls at their flat, the night she was with Barry and Joe. Then we spoke to the owners of that house she was looking after, and they totally convinced me she was genuine.' He paused for a second. 'But it was when Alex came to see me that clinched it. She had this box with her, one of those flowery cardboard things you put together yourself. It was full of keepsakes. Mementoes, personal stuff, photos of her younger sister. I don't know *why* she didn't show me it before. A bit of insecurity, I guess.'

'So this secondary operative that Oliver talked about. A myth?'

Ross shrugged. 'Who knows? Oh, and by the way, he called me yesterday. The police arrested another woman from Leona's list, and this time they're confident they'll be able to charge this one.'

'Who was she?'

'Her name's Pam, down on that farm near Fontmell Magna. From Thailand originally, apparently.'

'Ah. The house where you almost chickened out?'

'Hmmm. Anyway, I'm glad they caught her. Her husband, Roger, he was really kind to me when I had my little meltdown at his front door.' He had paused to reflect on the incident when something else occurred to him. 'I've just remembered. Turned out the hired help, Rosa, was working here illegally. She admitted afterwards she was terrified I was the police or a Customs officer come to arrest her.'

Both men fell silent for a moment. Alex wasn't far away now. Just a couple of people to negotiate and she would be home free.

Martin gave Ross another nudge. 'Any chance of you two becoming an item again?'

'No chance at all. And actually, it's better that way, especially now we're on a business footing.' He stood up and gave Alex a hug. She pretended to mop her brow as she collapsed into the seat beside Martin.

The idea had been born one day he and Alex were out walking on Arthur's Seat, Edinburgh's extinct volcano. Ross was fretting about the money he still had from Liz's business so Alex said, 'Why don't you do something good with it?' A couple of hours later they had a concept sketched out, and today was the culmination of their ideas and efforts: The Liz McKinlay Trust.

There were two strands. Support and education for disadvantaged Scottish teenagers to help them to make a career or start a business centred around Information Technology. Secondly, advice and guidance to the vulnerable, including senior citizens and carers, to give them the knowledge and the confidence to detect and prevent identity theft and financial fraud. Ross had spoken to businesses, banks, mortgage lenders, financial advisers and government officials, and had pledged an initial sum of £1,000,000 if those bodies committed to match it. Two weeks previously, they had passed the incredible milestone of £3,000,000. They'd blitzed their original target and today's press conference was the official launch.

Martin was lead adviser for the Trust, a social enterprise company with charitable status. He had lots of time on his hands now he'd sold his company. And, he had made a significant contribution to the fund. Beth and Gail would act as trustees. Ross, as MD, would front the company, while Alex had been appointed Operations Director. She was delighted to be given the opportunity to help others follow the route she had eventually taken, albeit without some of the unfortunate side streets she'd ventured down in her teenage years. She had already recruited a small team, and presented an operations plan and budget to Ross and the others. It had been signed off that morning.

Alex slung both arms around Ross, placing his ribcage in serious jeopardy. 'This is all just absolutely amazing, Ross. I'm so proud of you. And I'm sure Liz would have been too.'

He didn't trust himself to answer her. Instead, he swallowed and blinked his eyes furiously.

Martin saved the day by changing the subject. 'And you're moving back into your old Viewforth flat, are you? That's all confirmed?'

'I am. When my solicitor approached the young couple who own it now, they thought it was a wind-up as you would expect. But it turns out the girl's pregnant, and they were wondering how they would manage, being three floors up. Obviously the solicitor explained why I was offering to swap properties and they're completely over the moon at moving to a three-bedroomed house, with a garden for the kiddie.'

'Yes, and at zero cost to them.' Alex looked at Martin. 'He's paying all their conveyancing and removal fees. Did you know that?'

'Ach. He's a good lad, is Ross.' He winked at her. 'Well, so people tell me anyway.'

He turned back to Ross again. 'I'm guessing that between your investment in the Trust plus what you're shelling out to move back into the flat, you must be just about broke?'

Ross smiled. 'Not quite. But there was no point in me having all that spare cash. I'd never have done anything with it.'

'Fair point. When will everything be signed and sealed with the flat?'

'All being well, in the next week or so. But I can't imagine anything going wrong, it's a definite win–win for both parties.' Alex beamed at him. She thought it was a terrific idea, and Ross was delighted to be returning to what he felt was his spiritual home.

Martin clapped his hands together. 'Well, I think it's a brilliant plan. I'm looking forward to seeing the old place again. Jeez, Alex, you'll never believe some of the crazy stuff we got up to in that flat. I remember when...'

'Excuse me, Alex. Got a minute?' It was one of the audio-visual techs asking for advice. Ross was more than a little relieved when Alex wandered off towards the sound desk. He had no idea what Martin had been about to say but there was an excellent chance it would have been highly embarrassing.

Martin turned to his friend. 'How about we all go out for a drink to celebrate?'

'I'd love to, mate. But I'm already going out tonight so a few pints in the afternoon is probably not a good idea. Thanks anyway.'

'Who *are* you out with tonight?' said Martin, as Gail and Beth came over to join them. 'As if I didn't know.' He winked at his daughters.

'Oooh. Do tell, Uncle Ross,' said Beth. 'Who's the lucky lady?'

Ross was delighted his friends were in such high spirits. It was just unfortunate their mirth was at his expense. 'I'm going out for a meal with Elspeth.'

'Again?' said Martin. 'That's three or four times you've been *out* with Elspeth in the past week.'

Gail waved her arm around the room. 'Does she know about all this?'

'No,' said Ross. 'She doesn't. She's just back from a spa weekend away, somewhere in Oxfordshire. I'll tell her all about it over dinner. Hopefully she'll be really chuffed for me.'

'I'm sure she will, my boy,' said Martin. 'I'm sure she will.'

The End

Acknowledgements

To everyone who has encouraged and supported me throughout what has been an incredibly enjoyable, occasionally tortuous, yet ultimately rewarding writing experience – you have my deepest gratitude.

Specific thanks go to (and if I've missed anyone I really do apologise):

My niece Dr Anna Wight, and Dr Linda Gerrie for expert assistance on all matters medical; Debs Warner for invaluable guidance during my early scribblings; Derek Bain for detailed advice on police procedures; Drew Dick for information about GP processes and systems; Fiona, Linda and Shona Niddrie for their insight to the behaviour, and misbehaviour, of twins; Jennifer Johnstone for a very handy map of the trees in Inverleith park; Joanna Fraser for help with newsroom procedures and reporters' activities; Kareen Jolly for explaining how supermarkets operate behind the scenes.

My tennis chums Nathan Lamb and Stuart Murray for sharing your time and in-depth knowledge concerning banking systems and practices, and the investigation of complex financial crimes respectively. Mike Cunningham for a spot of advice on falsifying a mortgage application, and Debbie Mitchell for guidance on the security of online investment portfolios. If I'm ever looking to defraud someone, folks, I know where to come.

My early readers - Alison Cusiter, Julie McDonald and Chris Livingston. I *knew* you would be totally honest and forthright with your analysis, opinions and insights. Just as well, really.

Leila Green and the team at I AM SELF-PUBLISHING. You provide an amazing service that I can wholeheartedly recommend.

Pete Salmon for an incredibly detailed and razor sharp critique that helped me enormously with the final full revision - which you then had to edit. Well, somebody had to and I'm delighted it was you.

My cousin Joyce Nisbet, for reading draft #4 in record time and making dozens of brilliant suggestions for improvement. Also for continuing to provide sound and sensible advice on many different aspects of crime fiction writing.

Graham Smith, t-crosser and i-dotter extraordinaire, for the final final proofread. Any errors that remain in the narrative are entirely down to me.

And, finally, to my amazing wife, Shiona. Thank you … for being a beta reader; for working through the novel, word by word, page by page – aloud – and twice; for helping me to sculpt this work by chipping away at the many hundreds (if not thousands) of tiny imperfections that improved each revision by a magnitude; for not once saying, 'Alan, would you take your nose out of that book,' - although I do realise you were *that* close on many occasions; and for shelling out your pocket money towards publishing costs. And, finally again – just THANK YOU. I love you. HTM.

Letter from the author

Dear Reader

Thank you so much for buying and reading my debut crime thriller Way Beyond A Lie.

Honest reviews are worth their weight in gold to any published author so I'd be delighted to hear what you thought of my work. If you loved it or if you didn't love it quite so much, all constructive feedback is welcome and will help me continue to improve my writing.

And if you did enjoy it, please pass the word along.

The easiest way to keep up to date with the latest Harry Fisher scribblings is by visiting my website at: www.harryfisherwriter.com where you can register to receive news updates and free content.

Follow me at: facebook.com/harryfisherwriter/ or contact me direct at: harryfisherwriter@gmail.com

I promise I will never ever share your contact details with anyone. They can go find their own.

All the best,
Harry